A YEAR AND A DAY

ALSO BY LESLIE PIETRZYK

Pears on a Willow Tree

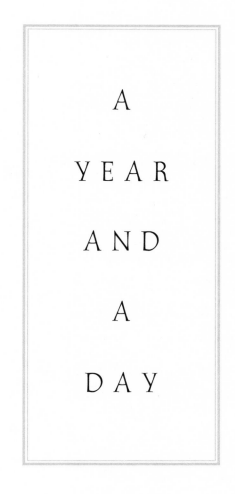

A

YEAR

AND

A

DAY

LESLIE PIETRZYK

wm

WILLIAM MORROW

An Imprint of HarperCollins*Publishers*

The author gratefully acknowledges *TriQuarterly,* where
"Slumber Party" first appeared as "Slumber Party, 1975,"
in slightly different form.

Grateful acknowledgment is made for permission
to reprint the following excerpt from "Lament," from
All My Pretty Ones by Anne Sexton.
Copyright © 1962 by Anne Sexton, renewed
1990 by Linda G. Sexton. Reprinted by permission of
Houghton Mifflin Company. All rights reserved.

HarperCollins books may be purchased for educational, business,
or sales promotional use. For information please write:
Special Markets Department, HarperCollins Publishers Inc.,
10 East 53rd Street, New York, NY 10022.

FIRST EDITION

Designed by Jo Anne Metsch

Printed on acid-free paper

Library of Congress Cataloging-in-Publication Data

Pietrzyk, Leslie, 1961–
    A year and a day : a novel / Leslie Pietrzyk.—1st ed.
      p. cm.
    ISBN 0-06-055465-7 (acid-free paper)
    1. Teenage girls—Fiction. 2. Spiritualism—Fiction. 3. Mothers—Death—Fiction.
  4. Maternal deprivation—Fiction. 5. Grief—Fiction. I. Title.

PS3566.I428Y43   2003
813'.54—dc21   2003044218

04 05 06 07 08 WBC/QW 10 9 8 7 6 5 4 3 2 1

for Steve

The supper dishes are over and the sun
unaccustomed to anything else
goes all the way down.

—ANNE SEXTON, "Lament"

CONTENTS

A YEAR AND A DAY

BIRD

MAMA came back three days after her funeral. That was my mother, as symbolic as they got. Three days, like she was Jesus Christ himself. "Alice," she whispered as I was frying up pancakes, willing the bubbles to pop so I could flip them, "it's Mama. I'm back."

I reached for the spatula, oddly calm. I'd read the paragraphs in Dr. Spock's baby book about the ways children cope with death. Okay, I was fifteen, not a child, but information was information. He didn't talk about hearing voices. So was this real?

She said, "You've got that syrup turned way too high."

Sure enough, a brown scorchy smell was edging into the kitchen, and the syrup's surface looked sticky and pocked. I turned the gas burner down to that barely steady level where you don't want to breathe because you're afraid you'll blow it out, then I flipped the pancakes. Maybe I should have started to panic. Instead, I stared down at the half-done pancakes, touched one with the tips of my fingers. It was warm, springy, real; I loved the shade of brown pancakes when they were done just right. There was nothing else like that color. That was something Mama had always said: What she liked best was anything there was nothing else like.

Again: "I want you to know I'm right here." Her words floated like dandelion seeds, breathy, shadowy whispers—nothing like the way she had talked when she was alive, loud and too fast, so I always felt a sentence behind, my ears straining to catch up, not wanting to miss a word she said.

This was crazy. I yanked my germy hand off the pancake, cleared my throat. "Okay." My voice felt too big in the kitchen. Maybe this was a dream, though the smell of pancakes, the rising steam, the flour splotches on the counter all seemed real enough. I poked the spatula under the edge of one pancake—done—then carefully stacked the pancakes on a plate, draped them with a tea towel, popped the plate into the barely warm oven.

"Aunt Aggy likes bacon at breakfast," she said.

"I know," I snapped. But I'd forgotten about the bacon. Wasn't it enough that I was making pancakes the first Sunday after my mother died? She had always made pancakes on Sunday morning, so here I was. I banged shut the oven door with one foot, then started to cry. My eyes were puffy and sore from nearly a week's worth of crying, and my nose was rubbed raw, so I tried to stop, lifting my elbow to my face so I could muffle the sobs and blow my nose into the sleeve of my brother's old Vikings sweatshirt. I had no pride about that sort of thing anymore. Last night at supper, I'd used the corner of our red-checked kitchen tablecloth after my paper napkin had gotten soaked through into damp shreds.

"Oh, dear." And then she was gone. But how could she be gone if she wasn't really there? It made no sense, like that question about the tree falling in the forest making no sound.

I smeared more tears on my sleeve, ladled batter onto the skillet, waited for the bubbles to pop, a trick Mama had told me. She knew a ton of secrets so her cookies came out perfect and the hash browns never burned, and she was such a good cook she sold wedding cakes to practically every bride in town. None of us needed to learn a thing about cooking because Mama did it all. But now and then I'd help with pancakes. She hardly slept, not like a normal person anyway, and on Sunday mornings she was slow, sleepy, overflowing with yawns and murmurs. I could ask questions that sounded desperate any other time, like, *Am I pretty?*

Who do you love best? Do blondes really have more fun like the TV commercial says? She'd ask me questions, too, not what other mothers asked, like why was I flunking chemistry, and not what adults asked each other, dull questions about Nixon and Watergate, but what did I think was really at the center of the earth and why couldn't it be a gigantic diamond instead of boring molten lava; or how come no one made movies about people living in Iowa like us, and wouldn't a movie about us be interesting, and who would I want to play her and who me and who my brother and who Aunt Aggy? Sunday morning was my favorite time with Mama, the slow swirl of her questions coaxing out my own, worth getting up early for.

Plus now I could make pancakes that even my brother, Will, couldn't tell from hers.

The kitchen door swung open, and Aunt Aggy walked in. She was my mother's aunt, and though technically Mama had inherited this house from my grandmother, Aunt Aggy came along with it, like the brown plaid couch, the dinged-up kitchen table, and the rest of the furniture. She'd lived here when Mama was growing up and had never left. She was tall and thin and when she walked or sat, she leaned forward so much you could almost hold a protractor to her and say, "Eighty degrees." Will and I thought it was strange that Aunt Aggy had never been married even though she was already fifty-two, but Mama had said, "Not everyone fits into a happily-ever-after life." Aunt Aggy claimed she'd broken off six engagements "with the rings to prove it," not that I'd ever seen them.

"Alice," she said, surprised. She tightened the belt of her robe. "What are you doing?"

"Making pancakes for breakfast," I said.

"It's Sunday?" She looked at her wrist, as if she'd find a calendar there though she didn't even wear a watch. She stared for as long as it took me to flip the pancakes. Then she glanced at the clock on the wall. "Seven-ten," she said.

"Did you get any sleep?" I asked.

"No, thanks," she said. "Orange juice for me."

"I said, did you get any sleep?"

But she walked across the room and poked her head out the side screen door. A spring breeze whisked in, tickled my ankles. A cardinal trilled, the only birdcall I knew. "Beautiful day," she said. "There should be lightning and thunder. Tornadoes, floods, blizzards. A plague of locusts."

April in Iowa. It could happen. Anything could happen. Your mother could die just like that in April in Iowa.

Still looking outside, Aunt Aggy shouted, "How dare you mock me?," and strode out to the backyard, letting the screen door bang behind her. How secretly satisfying it must be to yell at the weather. But I'd never been dramatic like Aunt Aggy.

I added this batch of pancakes to the stack in the oven and ladled more batter. Through the window above the sink, I watched Aunt Aggy stalk to the apple tree, then back to the house, walking carefully, as if she were counting her steps. Back and forth between the apple tree and the house she went, as I made pancakes, mixing up another bowl of batter, cramming three or four plates in the oven, each with a tower of pancakes so high they started to lean and tumble off. I liked watching those bubbles; I liked that there was one thing I knew how to do perfectly.

The bubbles had popped on my last batch when Aunt Aggy shrieked, "Come quick!," and I ran outside barefoot, spatula in my hand. She was crouched under the apple tree, staring at the ground.

"What?" The grass was damp, and last fall's dry twigs cracked and broke as I tried to hurry in spite of my tender bare feet.

"Baby bird," she said.

I immediately slowed. How many baby birds had fallen out of how many nests and how many times had I tried to keep them alive in a shoe box under a lightbulb? How many of those birds had been buried in a corner of the yard, their graves marked with tiny stick crosses that got run over by the lawn mower? How many had been dropped in garbage cans with a sad thought? And, finally, how many had been left to die under whatever tree they'd fallen from? "Survival of the fittest," Will always said. Even Mama had told me not to feel bad that I couldn't do anything, though she came to every bird funeral I had.

"I need a shoe box." Aunt Aggy started yanking thin blades of grass by the roots, making a little pile, then raked up dry leaves with her fingers. "We'll make a nest and dig worms."

I reached where she knelt in the grass. The bird had no feathers: blotch-gray and quivering, its lungs pulsing impossibly fast, bulging eyes fused shut. "That bird's going to die," I said.

"A robin," she said. "Or a sparrow. Let's name her Clementine. Clem if she's a he."

Tears pushed behind my eyes. "Please don't do this."

"Nothing should die nameless." Aunt Aggy picked up the bird in one hand. It let out a thin squeak. She flicked off a couple of ants with her pinkie.

What would Dr. Spock say about this? He wasn't an authority on adults, but right now his book was all I had. Aunt Aggy had always been threatening to fall apart, constantly promising, "This time I mean it, I'm really going to fall apart." So we stayed ready, expecting a big bang—a noisy, messy, interesting thing with yelling and hyperventilating and maybe even fainting. I never thought falling apart would be like this, that she'd simply dissolve.

"That bird is going to die," I said, sharpening my voice. But what was the point? Aunt Aggy was Aunt Aggy, as Mama would say when I complained about how strange she was.

She hurried past me, into the house. I stood under the apple tree, staring up at the blue sky. This day couldn't be prettier; there couldn't be more birds twittering; the fresh, new grass couldn't feel fresher or tickle my bare feet more. It was easy to hate a day like this.

I went back into the kitchen, but Aunt Aggy wasn't there. I couldn't believe how many pancakes I had made, several stacks keeping warm in the oven and three plates on the counter, each piled with a leaning pancake tower on the verge of toppling over. No one could eat this many pancakes, not even my brother who'd once eaten seven hamburgers at a cookout. I reached for the flour bin, but it was empty, so I stared at all those pancakes. Thinking about eating them made my stomach go queasy.

"Freeze some," my mother's voice said, still breathless, but as distinct as if she were standing next to me. "Slip wax paper between so they don't stick."

It was what Mama did, freeze up leftovers and forget about them because she'd gone on to new recipes. Every three months or so, when the freezer got too packed to fit even an ice cube, I'd throw out the petrified remains of meals gone by. It was like a scrapbook—"Remember when Mama was into potato soup?" I'd say to Will. "Remember Mama's experiments with fresh dill?" Why not toss the pancakes in there—months from now it would be: Remember when our mother killed herself, leaving us all alone in the world, and how I thought everything would be fine if only I made enough pancakes?

I pulled plates out of the oven, lined them up with the others on the counter, forming a little wall. Oh, brother. I yanked the tea towel off one plate, started wrapping pancakes in wax paper. Maybe I was the one going crazy—I mean, it was one thing to try to save a baby bird or to throw a baseball at a pitching net the way Will did all day yesterday. But this? Hearing your dead mother's voice seemed to me a whole different kind of crazy.

My mother laughed, and it was her laugh, all right, sort of silvery, like ice clinking in a cold glass. "Don't worry," she said. "You're not crazy."

Like hearing her say that would make me feel less worried or less crazy.

Aunt Aggy's footsteps thumped down the stairs. "Found a shoe box!" She dashed past me, pushing the door open with her hip, ran to the tree, box in one hand, bird in the other. I watched her pile grass and dead leaves into the shoe box. Could a day already feel too long this early in the morning?

Will came into the kitchen half asleep and rumpled. He was a year older than me, and four inches taller, though I was pretty tall compared to my friends. They all thought he was cute, and probably he was: light brown hair, eyes that looked green or blue depending on what he was wearing, skin that never got zits. And a tiny gap between his two front teeth that kept him from looking too perfect. I used to like watching him spit watermelon seeds through the gap. He was a good brother, nice to me even in front of his friends at school, and when I talked, he listened to what I was saying along with what I didn't say. I pointed out the window. "Aunt Aggy found a baby bird."

Will tugged at the neck of his Fran Tarkenton football jersey; Mama had given it to him last Christmas, and he'd worn it all day yesterday and the day before. Then he walked to the counter, pushed aside one of the plates. "Look at all those pancakes."

"We eat pancakes every Sunday."

He blinked several times. "How many do you think we eat?"

"I like watching the bubbles pop." He should understand that.

We both looked out the window. Aunt Aggy was coming toward the house, walking carefully, as if she thought she might trip, her arms stiff like a cartoon sleepwalker's, the shoe box straight in front of her. "That bird's going to die," I said to Will.

"Maybe not." He sounded tired—not sleepy, but worn away, like paint fading off a barn. Then he set his hand on my shoulder in a comforting way that made me feel like frying so many pancakes was perfectly normal, and I could've stood there forever, the two of us, but he crossed his arms against his chest and asked, "Think we'll ever feel better?"

"No," I had time to say before Aunt Aggy came through the door. She thrust the shoe box under Will's nose.

"Meet Clementine," she said.

Will peered into the box, stuck a finger in and rustled something. "You know that—" He didn't finish, just swallowed hard, pulled at his shirt, then said, "Want me to dig some worms for her?" And that was exactly why everyone liked Will so much, because he could see what you wanted to hear, whereas I was the one saying things like, "The bird's going to die." Will was going with Kathy Clark, and last week in the cafeteria line I had heard her tell Ann Trinder that Will was the sweetest boy in town. I'd meant to tell him; it was cute how his ears turned red whenever anyone talked about Kathy.

"Maybe it's stupid trying to save a bird," Aunt Aggy said. "Not like there aren't thousands of others."

I nodded—not enough that they noticed—but Will said, "I think it's noble."

"Rescuing a bird won't change a single thing," I said. "Mama's dead."

Will and Aunt Aggy stared at me, their eyes wide and horrified. Aunt Aggy blinked quickly, but that trick to keep from crying never worked: Tears spilled down her cheeks. Will's body sagged so he suddenly looked a foot shorter. He said, "We'll set the box near a lightbulb to keep Clementine warm." He draped his arm around Aunt Aggy's shoulder, like now they shared something special, then they carried the box upstairs. According to everything I'd learned in English class about symbolism, they were probably taking that bird straight to my mother's room and plopping it in her bed by the night table with the red-lightbulb lamp ("for atmosphere"), magazines, and a pack of Virginia Slims at its side.

I felt totally alone standing there in the kitchen, surrounded by pancakes.

A moment later, I whispered, "Mama," my voice an embarrassed croak. Why was I talking to her? She was dead. Passed away, deceased, dearly departed, in a better place—dead. The only sounds were outside: birds calling to each other. I slammed the door shut so I wouldn't have to hear them, then stomped to the refrigerator for orange juice.

I peeked inside the red pitcher and shook it gently, watching the juice swirl. There was only a glassful left. Mama bought Hy-Vee frozen juice, but she added a secret ingredient that made hers better than the juice I drank at my friends' houses after slumber parties. I had begged Mama to tell me her secret, but she had refused, saying, "Who would I be if I didn't have a few secrets? A magician without any magic." When I'd whined that it was just juice, she'd shaken her head. "Even juice is never 'just juice,' Alice."

I stuck the pitcher back in the refrigerator. All the stuff neighbors had brought over crowded the shelves: Pyrex bowls and molds of Jell-O in a rainbow of colors with every type of canned fruit suspended in them, pot roast, potato salads, coleslaw, six packages of hot dogs from Mrs. Lisk (half-price at Hy-Vee, she told us), three-bean salad, Mrs. Van Hamme's spaghetti made with cream of tomato soup, chocolate pudding, Tupperware we hadn't popped open. Lots more. No one would have to cook for weeks, not that we were hungry.

Mrs. Felper (green Jell-O with canned pear halves, pineapple chunks, and marshmallows) had been the first person to come by. I'd opened the front door, and there was Mrs. Felper (who we usually saw only when she was complaining about our grass being too long). She held out a bowl of Jell-O: "Lucky I had this ready for tonight's card game with the girls. What happened to your poor, sweet mother was awful, simply awful, though I don't understand how—"

"Thanks." I grabbed the Jell-O, but she pushed her way in.

"Aren't you the picture of your poor dead mother? Same hair— you'll be happy enough for that natural wave one day." She plopped on the couch, patted the cushion next to her. "Go ahead and cry, honey. Let it out." The Jell-O I held quivered as my hands shook. We liked red Jell-O, Mama's favorite color, not green. "She's in heaven, dear," Mrs. Felper said. "That's a comfort." Then she launched into long, rambling stories about other dead people and how they had died.

I walked away in the middle of a sentence, taking the Jell-O into the kitchen, where Aunt Aggy was on the phone. When she saw me, she put one hand over the receiver, pointed at the Jell-O. "Now it's official. We have a death in the family."

"I don't want it," I said.

She waved toward the refrigerator. "This is all they know to do," and she resumed her conversation with Mr. Moore, the funeral director, murmuring words ("next of kin," "legal guardian") that almost made her sound like a regular adult.

I went back to the living room, sat next to Mrs. Felper, listened to her, listened to them all as they came and went, singly, in groups, end-lessly ("a tragedy—can't understand—such a terrible thing"). I took their Jell-O and Tupperware into the kitchen, crammed it into the refrigerator, certain I couldn't fit one more thing in there but I always found room.

Now, footsteps clumped upstairs; I heard the linen closet door creak open, Aunt Aggy shouting that a hand towel was big enough, more foot-steps. How could they have left me all alone down here in the kitchen? How could Mama be dead?

I grabbed the Pyrex bowl of Mrs. Felper's Jell-O and heaved it to the middle of the kitchen. The bowl flew in a beautiful arc, then landed in a sunny patch of the floor, where it smashed into jagged pieces of glass and Jell-O that glowed greenly on the linoleum.

Everyone knew you were supposed to wash and return those dishes.

I reached into the refrigerator and grabbed Mrs. Yoder's plate of red Jell-O (a mold like a fish with fruit cocktail and little holes where Will had gouged out the grapes) and sent it across the kitchen. The plate broke in half and the Jell-O fish splatted into pieces.

Next was Mrs. Reinecke's orange Jell-O with mandarin oranges, then Mrs. Wilson's yellow Jell-O with pineapple and walnuts, and Mrs. Drake's red Jell-O mixed with Cool Whip, and then potato salad and coleslaw and three-bean salad. Macaroni salad, someone's home-canned pickles, fudge. A hacked-up ham. Stroganoff polka-dotted with white mold spots. It all hit the kitchen floor, even Mrs. Lisk's six packages of half-price hot dogs that I ripped open and squirted out of their shiny plastic casing one by one.

Finally, there was nothing left in the fridge except the bottles of olives and ketchup and stuff in the side shelves and the pitcher of Mama's orange juice. I closed the door and leaned against it.

The floor looked like the barrel in our school cafeteria where you dumped your tray. The kitchen filled with a sweetly overripe smell. I'd never done anything like this; I was cracking up for real.

"Good for you to do things you've never done before," my mother's voice murmured.

Easy for her to say. She wasn't the one who'd be spending the day cleaning up glass and melting Jell-O. I bent and picked up a hot dog, chucked it at the garbage, but it hit the wall and fell into a splotch of green Jell-O. This wouldn't have happened if Mama were still alive.

Will's footsteps hammered the stairs as he called, "What was all that noise?" Then he was in the kitchen, looking at the floor and at me squatting in the middle of it. I hoped he was going to laugh because I was about to cry. "Wow. Did you drop something, Baby Sister?"

I stood up. "Don't call me that," I said, though I secretly liked it when he did.

"What happened?" He shook his head, his mouth partway open.

"I don't know," I said. "One minute I'm looking at Jell-O and the next I'm throwing it on the floor."

"That doesn't sound like you." He still hadn't laughed, and I couldn't tell what he was thinking. He should be calling me an idiot, or putting his hand on my shoulder, or promising that everything would be all right. He should say, *Mama's dead, and I know exactly how you feel.*

There was too much silence. I asked, "Where's Aunt Aggy?"

"Upstairs singing 'Born Free' to that bird."

"See? Everyone's cracking up," I said, faking cheerfulness.

"I'm not," he said, "nobody is," an edge on his voice. He crossed his arms against his chest. We assumed he looked like our father because Mama and I had dark wavy hair, but Will's was stick straight and lighter. We were all tall, but where Mama and I were skinny, Will had muscles. We'd never known our father. The story—Aunt Aggy's story, since Mama never talked about it—was that Mama had moved away when she was seventeen and came back four years later with Will wrapped in a red, hand-knitted blanket and a stomach out to there, pregnant with me. She never told anyone where she'd been or what she'd done, except to say that with her, secrets went to the grave. As for our father—no pictures, no letters, no phone calls. We wanted to know, but asking made Mama turn silent and sad and empty, like a lamp that's been clicked off. And she never answered anyway, not even a tiny hint. Will and I used to imagine who our father might be—cowboy, policeman, movie star, circus ring-master—until a few years ago when Will's face started looking like Mama's any time I talked about our father. So I stopped.

When I was younger, I thought one summer day he'd knock on our door, and he'd drive us out to Dane's Dairy for double-dip ice-cream cones that we'd sit and eat at the far table under the big pine tree. He'd be the kind of father who grabbed handfuls of extra napkins, who wouldn't yell if you dropped your cone but would right away give you a dollar to buy another. We'd talk—he'd ask lots of questions, though that part was fuzzier to me than the double dips. It was silly, but still, I couldn't go to Dane's Dairy without wondering about him, whoever he was.

Will snapped his fingers in front of my face. "What are you thinking about?" He sounded annoyed, and I shrugged. He went on: "Anyway, you should be nicer about that bird."

"I hate that it's going to die."

"And I hate that you wasted all this food." He waved one bare foot at the mess. "I thought we'd be eating Jell-O for weeks," he said, and almost smiled.

I didn't think he was angry for real, but I said, "Please don't be mad."

He shook his head, sighed. "Baby Sister, I could never stay mad at you."

I loved that he was so perfect. "So you'll help me clean up?"

"Didn't say that," and he abruptly left the kitchen, going through the living room and out the front door, probably to pitch into his baseball net. I waited for a minute, hoping he'd come back, but he didn't. He was going to be the Strong One, he always was. And no one could compete with Aunt Aggy on being the Crazy One—if I said I was hearing voices, she'd hear more voices, louder voices, voices offering stock-market tips, whatever it took. So who was I supposed to be?

I tiptoed to the broom closet, taking big, odd-sized steps to avoid the broken glass, got out the mop so I could push the mess toward one corner. I flipped on Mama's radio by the sink and was about to switch to my station—where you could win ninety-nine dollars by being the ninety-ninth caller—but then realized the radio was still tuned to Mama's station, the one from Iowa City, where people talked all day long. What was the point of a radio station that didn't play music? I wondered, but Mama said she liked hearing those words floating in the air. Sometimes I would catch her sitting at the table, mesmerized, a pile of beans to be snapped and an empty bowl on her lap, the water in the pot on the stove already boiling.

A woman spoke: "Let me tell you why this is." Her voice was very smooth, the kind of voice that doesn't know people yell at each other, that doesn't wobble when it's sad. "When you set out dried eggshells around your garden, slugs and snails crawl over them and their bodies are sliced to ribbons." She chuckled, but not meanly. "Maybe you're thinking how terrible for the poor creatures. Fine, be sympathetic to slugs, but you won't get much salad with the lettuce they leave behind. That food's for your family, not the creepy-crawlies. You may not care to know this, but there are at least a million species of insects in the world, and scientists haven't even discovered them all. That's a fine job, crawling around looking for new bugs! But back to slugs—which may not officially be bugs now that I'm thinking on it—your other choice is to set out a plate of beer at night. Might as well plug in a neon sign that blinks 'Bar'!" She chuckled again.

I stopped to listen, leaning the mop up against the counter.

She continued: "We're nearly out of time, but I have a letter from Mrs. Henry Wilbur from Tiffin, asking if anyone has a recipe for beef stew made with Coca-Cola. She thinks she saw it in *Family Circle* a couple months back. That's the kind of recipe you wonder, Should I clip this? and you don't because no one's complained about your beef stew yet. But you catch yourself thinking how Coke might soften a tough cut of beef and how the kids would get a kick out of eating pop for supper, and soon enough you can't get it out of your mind, so you're putting pen to paper like Mrs. Wilbur. Frankly, I wouldn't mind trying out beef stew with Coke myself: 'It's the real thing!' Mrs. Wilbur, we'll get that recipe. These are the best listeners in the world, and they haven't failed me yet. Time to wind up *Dotty King's Neighborly Visit*. This is yours truly, Dotty King, coming at you live on KXIC-800, thanking you for listening, thanking you for being you. Bye-bye!"

I pictured her waving at the microphone, the kind of "bye-bye" that was accompanied by a little wave where you hold your hand still and flap your fingers down. I waited through a fertilizer commercial and a commercial for loans, but then a religious program started, and I knew Mama never listened to anything like that; she was born and raised Catholic but we hardly ever went to church. Even though Mama had made me and Will take CCD classes until our confirmation, Mama said church was for people who were too afraid to go out and look for God themselves.

I turned off the radio and started shoving the gloppy mess toward the sink—broken dish fragments, hot dogs, a rainbow of Jell-O, smelly chunks of potato salad. Clearly I'd have to give up on this mop and pick up things with my bare hands. Ugh. I pushed the mop harder. I liked

Dotty King. Her voice was sweet but in charge, as if she really knew what she was talking about.

My mother's voice was scornful: "Anyone can look up in a book facts about slugs. But a bunch of facts won't tell you anything worth knowing."

"A fact is a fact," I muttered. "Something true."

"So it's a fact that we're having this conversation?" she asked.

I shook my head, but when she didn't respond I wondered if she could see me or just hear me. What were the rules to all this?

"Rules?" She laughed, and I remembered playing Candy Land with her, when she would clap her hands and shout, "You didn't close your eyes when you landed on Lollipop Woods, so go get an ice-cream bar for everyone!" When we finally found out that wasn't a real, written-out rule, she had said, "It should be."

I heard Aunt Aggy's footsteps on the stairs, and I started pushing the glop faster. It would be a heck of a lot easier if I had just broken plates, like a normal person. "Clementine won't eat," she called out, and then she was in the doorway, hands on her hips. "Well," she said, stretching the word into two long syllables.

I stared at the melting blobs of red and green and orange interspersed with Stroganoff and coleslaw, waiting for her to offer to help, to tell me she would finish cleaning up the awful mess; I was waiting for her to wrap me in her arms and hug me, squeeze me so tight I couldn't breathe for a minute, the way someone else's aunt would.

Instead she said, "Next time let me help you smash up stuff."

Of course there wasn't going to be a next time. I kept pushing and sliding, letting glass scrape the linoleum. A couple of tears splatted onto the clean part of the floor—hers, not mine. When I looked up at her, she stretched out a smile, like quickly pulling on a pair of gloves. "Well, the good thing is . . ." She didn't finish. I didn't ask her to.

LATE THAT night when Aunt Aggy and Will were asleep, I tiptoed into the kitchen. Aunt Aggy and I had cleaned it, deciding that if a neighbor asked for her dish back, we'd say the dog accidentally ate from it, and cross our fingers that no one would remember about our dog running away last month. We had even cleaned the inside of the refrigerator, since it was empty, sponging the built-up gunk off the shelves, alphabetizing the condiments—Aunt Aggy's idea for keeping busy.

The light over the garage was still on, and the kitchen was filled with bluish, shadowy shapes. I stood in the middle of the room, listening, as my eyes adjusted; all I heard was the refrigerator's quiet hum, the drippy faucet no one could fix, and then, the longer I stood, my own breath in and out like a faint whisper, and then my heart beating. I waited for ten minutes, fifteen. Nothing.

So. The voice wasn't real. Maybe I wasn't cracking up after all.

There was nothing to do but trudge upstairs. But I noticed a shoe box balanced on top of the garbage can. I shook it slightly, listened to the dry rustle of Clementine's body sliding back and forth inside. Aunt Aggy hadn't said anything over supper (leftover pancakes), and neither had Will. I set the box back onto the pile of garbage, but it was off balance and slid to the floor, popping open so that grass and Clementine herself spilled out. Quickly I bent to scoop everything up but stopped, staring at the bird instead, mesmerized, its tiny body nothing but angles. Impossible to imagine that this empty thing once had the potential to fly.

I reached to pick her up, like grabbing a used, crumpled tissue. She was light and stiff in my hand.

Were you supposed to leave a bird with a name in the garbage? I went outside in my slippers and nightgown and walked to the apple tree. One of those sliver moons hung in the sky, sort of smiling and tantalizing, annoyingly jolly. No wind, no noise. No cars passing. No train whistle in the distance. Nobody screaming at their kids through an open window. No barking dogs. When did the world become so quiet? I switched Clementine to my left hand, squatted, and started pawing at the loose dirt under the tree with my right hand. It got easier as I started really digging in, dirt caking under my fingernails as they bent backward and broke, something in me not minding the pain.

I dug until I had a hole just big enough for Clementine. In all that time I didn't hear one single thing, just the scrape of my hand, my breath moving fast. When I finished, I wiped the loose dirt off my hand and onto my nightgown.

I shivered, looked at Clementine. "Poor little bird," I said. I did the sign of the cross, whispered the Lord's Prayer, tried to remember if there was a specific saint for birds and came up with Saint Francis of Assisi, who liked animals. "Saint Francis of Assisi, I think you're the animal saint, and if you are, please guide the soul of this bird Clementine into the Kingdom of Heaven, amen." Then I tacked on a Hail Mary. I couldn't remember any words from Mama's funeral mass except "the Lord is my shepherd," which didn't sound appropriate for a bird, so I tried again with Saint Francis: "I'm pretty sure you're the one who takes care of animals, so please help this bird find eternal happiness, amen." I got halfway through one more Hail Mary, then stopped, listening to the overwhelming silence.

I couldn't put the bird in the hole.

I couldn't hold the bird in my hand forever.

Tears rolled down my face, one after the other, like an assembly line. I let them go for a while before wiping my face with the back of my dirty hand, tilting my head to blow my nose hard into the shoulder of my nightgown. The noise was awkward, an embarrassment in the empty darkness of the backyard.

Where was my mother's voice? Where was a message from God or Saint Francis? Even a car driving by our house would be something, or the leaves rustling. Nothing, nothing, nothing.

I threw the bird's body as hard and as far as I could. I didn't hear it hit the ground.

NO ONE woke me up the next day, so it was eleven-thirty before I got out of bed. There was school, but was I supposed to go back now? If not now, when? Who was going to tell me when I was ready? Would I ever be ready?

Some of my friends had come to the funeral at St. Mary's: Becky Mann, my best friend, and Linda Johnson, my second-best friend. They sat in the back with their mothers, and I hated how I was in the front, my mother in a box. After the funeral, when everyone was eating lunch in the church basement, they hugged me the same as everyone else, and out of the corner of my eye, I saw Becky's mom heading over with two paper cups of lemonade, one for herself, one for Becky; and Linda's mom was hanging up Linda's coat on the coatrack, and I hated them even harder.

Aunt Aggy had persuaded Father Carroll to let Mama be buried a Catholic, probably by threatening to fall apart, or maybe even by falling apart, I don't know. Considering Mama didn't belong to any bridge groups or the Craft Guild Club or the Holy Name Society or the League of Women Voters, or have a husband who was an Elk, Moose, Eagle, or Knight of Columbus, there were still lots of people at the wake and then at the funeral the next day: People from the Shelby *Beacon* where she had worked part-time in classifieds. People who remembered her growing up in Shelby. Neighbors. PTA members. Women whose wedding cakes she had baked. Some ladies she'd sold Avon to when she was doing that. Teachers who knew me and Will. Parents I baby-sat for. The fathers who had coached Will's baseball teams from Little League on up. Parents of kids we went to school with, parents of kids who'd been in 4-H with us. Will's girlfriend, Kathy Clark, with her mom. The old ladies who went to every funeral. And plenty of people who were simply nosy. The women told me I was a brave young lady, and the men mumbled as they stared at their shuffling feet. "It would be easier being the body in the box," I whispered to Will, and he laughed so loud that everyone stared at us, and hearing Will laugh was the only half-nice moment in the whole horrible day.

Now, the house was quiet, abandoned feeling. Suddenly I hated living here, and I looked at the globe on my bookcase (one of my few educational presents from Mama, off the list they handed out at parent-teacher conferences). I spun it around so all the pink and blue and green and yellow countries blurred together into one big place where I wasn't. As an official orphan, I could live anywhere—Chad, Turkey, Paraguay, Antarctica.

The phone rang. I placed one finger lightly on the spinning globe; it slowed and my fingernail made a soft, scraping sound as continents passed under it. The phone rang again. When the globe stopped, my finger was smack in the middle of the Atlantic Ocean.

No one was getting the phone, so I hurried downstairs to answer it, glad to have something to do.

"Alice, it's Mr. Rhinehart." Our embarrassing high school principal with the huge Adam's apple. He cleared his throat, and I imagined that big lump in his neck shifting. "This must be difficult for you and your brother, having a mother who, uh, died so unfortunately." His voice squeezed out like toothpaste from a tube, thin strips of words. "Your teachers have been informed, and we made an announcement to homerooms. We plan to—"

"I'm fine," I interrupted. As if things weren't awful enough, now I was the topic of a homeroom announcement, my name floating all staticky out of the box on the wall, everyone looking at each other, knowing why I was part of an announcement.

"The guidance counselor showed me in a book that after someone dies, you go through stages: denial, anger, depression, acceptance." Papers rustled on his end of the phone. "But once you get through this first year, you're fine. Mrs. Flesner photocopied the chapter."

A year felt too long and too short. Would I really be fine, like the book said?

"Of course when someone died in my day, we cried for a week, then life went on," he said. "People didn't talk about their feelings. But we can talk, Alice. Let me be your friend." He gave a stupid, hollow laugh that he turned into a cough when I didn't laugh with him. I imagined him flipping through my student-profile folder, the photocopied pages from the guidance counselor's book. Maybe he was rolling a pencil on his desk, wishing he didn't have students whose mother parked on railroad tracks, waiting for a train to plow into the car.

In a very calm voice, the kind of voice adults use when they're trying not to yell or cry, I said, "Actually I'm fine right now. No one woke me up today, but tomorrow I'll set my alarm clock so I can be at school on time." I hung up before I started crying, because Mama used to wake us up, belting out songs like "There's No Business Like Show Business" as she walked into our rooms, tickling us if we looked grumpy, making us silly with laughter, happy to be awake.

I turned on the kitchen radio to push Mr. Rhinehart's thin, squeaky voice out of my head. "This is Dotty King, live. Isn't technology wonderful that I can be here and in your house at exactly the same time? A miracle. Speaking of miracles, how about this sunny day? Take a look out your window right now. Go on."

I glanced out the window. It was a beautiful sunny day—pure blue sky that felt wider and taller than usual, as if someone had stretched it out to fill up all the empty spaces in the world. It even looked like there were more leaves on the trees today than yesterday.

Dotty King continued: "Could we ever hope to do any better, sunny day-wise? Still, you're not listening to me for weather reports, so let's get down to kitchen business. Today we've got a foolproof way to make cookies from a box cake mix. You'll be amazed!"

Aunt Aggy burst through the side door, two Hy-Vee paper sacks in her arms. "Not that chatterbox again," she said, plopping the groceries on the counter. She reached over and twirled the dial; the hog report came on. Aunt Aggy cracked her knuckles. "Who can be cheerful in a world where babies are bloated and starving in countries we never heard of and someone's sweet, beautiful mother could die?"

"Mama listened to her show," I said.

Aunt Aggy didn't seem to hear me. She started emptying the grocery bags, setting things on the counter: chocolate chip ice cream, Neapolitan ice cream, butter brickle, vanilla, chocolate, orange sherbet. She lined them all up evenly, pretending not to notice me staring. Finally she said, "Which is more soothing, Neapolitan or chocolate chip?"

I walked over and put my arms around her. She was thinner than Mama; bones stuck out in different places, wrong angles. She never said, the way Mama had, "Boy, I needed that," after you hugged her.

Aunt Aggy sighed, half-hugged back, distracted. "I couldn't decide. Which?"

"Chocolate chip."

"You've always been the decisive one," she said. "Decisiveness is a special gene, and I don't have it." She squinted at me, as if peering into my DNA, noting exactly where the decisiveness was located, next to the brown hair, across from the hazel eyes.

I said, "Mama liked Neapolitan because it has some of everything."

She nodded. "I'm going to leave this Neapolitan ice cream in the sink and watch it melt. What do you think?" She started moving the rest of the ice cream to the freezer, jostling for space, shoving aside frozen pancakes and tilting ice trays.

What did I think? That we were all crazy.

The Neapolitan ice cream remained on the counter. She closed the freezer door, then pulled the paper strip along the carton, popped open the lid. Brown, white, pink—always the same order. Aunt Aggy lightly tapped one finger on the strawberry stripe, then the chocolate. "Thanks for burying Clementine. That was sweet."

I looked away from her, toward the beautiful day happening through the window. "Do you know where Will is?" I asked.

"Do I know anything anymore?" she said. "Did I ever know anything in the first place?" I was about to make a quick remark, thinking she was just being her usual dramatic self, but when I looked at how she kept touching that ice cream with her finger, pink and brown, pink and brown, I kept quiet. "Your mother didn't even leave me a note." She carried the box of ice cream to the sink, tipped it upside down, pressed the bottom with both thumbs and then the palm of her hand, until with a sucking sound, the rectangle of ice cream dropped down.

What was I supposed to say? None of us got a note. Nothing. Just emptiness and whatever's emptier than that and emptier even than that. Why couldn't Aunt Aggy just hug me and tell me everything would be fine?

Instead we watched the ice cream melt, the colors blending into an indistinct sludge. It was surprisingly soothing until Aunt Aggy sighed sharply and turned on the hot water full blast, hurrying the ice cream along. When it had disappeared, she said, "I'm off for a drive," which meant she was going to Mr. Cooper's house, the man she had been in love with since I was in sixth grade. He lived with his old, crotchety father in one of those houses kids always picked to TP because no one ever bothered pulling the toilet paper down out of the trees—it would stay for weeks until it disintegrated in the rain. Mr. Cooper and Aunt

Aggy didn't exactly go out on dates or anything romantic, but she organized his life for him, setting up doctor appointments and making sure the bills got paid on time, supervising roofers and writing out his grocery list. He was boring. The only things he liked talking about were how Nixon should have finished the job in Vietnam and his beer can collection. He and his dad had more than four hundred different beer cans all lined up in a room, displayed on special shelves they had built. Sometimes I asked Aunt Aggy if she was ever going to marry Mr. Cooper, and she'd laugh and say, "That old buzzard. Like I couldn't do better. I broke off six engagements, you know!" But once I overheard her tell Mama, "Oh, I'll outwait him all right. He's my only chance."

As soon as Aunt Aggy was gone, I put the radio back on Dotty King's station, but it was too late in the day, and a different woman was interviewing a dentist about flossing techniques. I sat at the kitchen table and listened anyway, and the more I thought about Dotty King, the more I was sure she would never melt perfectly good ice cream or smash plates of Jell-O or let a baby bird die or hear voices in the kitchen or kill herself or do anything that wasn't exactly right, done in the shortest, most efficient, cleverest way.

Aunt Aggy had left a tablet of paper and a pencil on the table with half a list written on the top sheet: "groceries, lawyer, bank, insurance, iron blue skirt, thank-you notes, new dog—??" (which wouldn't happen; Aunt Aggy hadn't liked how the old dog kept chewing up her shoes, and only hers, like they had the best flavor).

I ripped out a blank piece of paper from underneath and started writing:

Dear Dotty King: My mother is dead. There was something special she did to frozen orange juice that made it taste like not-frozen orange juice. What was it? Please help me.

I underlined *"Please"* twice, then added, *She loved your radio show very much. Me too. We listened together.*

I stared at that, then turned the period after "together" into a dash and added "all the time," which I also underlined. My words looked like a scribbled-up coloring book that you give to the youngest kid, who can't color right. I shouldn't have lied about listening together all the time.

Will came in from outside, clumping heavily, tugging off his jacket. "Where were you?" I asked.

"Walked to school." He sat across the table from me. "Couldn't go in, so I sat in the bleachers."

"Mr. Rhinehart called." I said that hoping Will would say something funny about his giant Adam's apple.

"Maybe I'll never go back." He turned away to look out the window.

I nodded. But he would go back just as I would go back and everything would be awful for a long time, for a year. After that, we'd be fine. I thought about explaining this to Will, but something stopped me, maybe because I couldn't see his face; anyway, he probably already knew.

THE NEXT day I finished breakfast as Will waited in the car for me, constantly pressing the gas with his foot so the engine zoomed and paused. He continued to play with the gas while I found an envelope and a stamp for my letter to Dotty King, wrote out her name and the radio station, feeling as if I were sending a list to Santa at the North Pole. I made Will stop at the end of the driveway so I could stick the letter in our mailbox, raising the red flag for the mailman. Will didn't ask.

The drive to school felt shorter than usual, and we sat in the parking lot all of first period, not saying much. I stared out the windshield at a big willow tree where the smokers hung out at lunch. The grass had worn away underneath the tree, and cigarette butts were scattered like confetti. The limp, leafless tree looked the way I felt.

Will picked at a hangnail, gnawed it. I was about to ask what he thought it would be like living with Aunt Aggy when he said, "Kathy told me I should grow my hair longer."

"And look like a hippie? How long?"

"Mama said she liked ponytails on men." He touched the back of his neck, grabbed what little bit of hair hung down and gathered it into a microscopic ponytail.

"And you always laughed when she said that." I almost wanted to laugh, it was so absurd to think of clean-cut Will with a ponytail down his back.

He let go of his hair, raked his fingers through it to fluff it up. "Right, it's not me."

I didn't mean to make fun of him, it was just that I would never expect him of all people to want long hair. Only this past year Coach Thorbeck had quit making guys on the team keep their hair above their collars. The silence between us felt heavy and awkward now, not comfortable like before. Why was he thinking about his hair now anyway? I didn't mean to sound angry: "Will, our mother is dead."

He pushed open his door, banging into the car next to ours, Joe Fry's old blue Mustang.

"Are you leaving?" I touched his sleeve. It was the red jacket Mama had given him one birthday so he would look like James Dean. "Who's he?" he asked after he read the card, which surprised me; Mama talked to me about James Dean all the time, and when his movies were on TV, she and I stayed up no matter how late to watch them, sharing a big bowl of too-salty popcorn. Even after Mama had explained, "The prince of fast living," Will still didn't get it, so I added, "Mama's favorite movie star," and Will put on the jacket and decided he looked cool.

"Don't say that." With his thumb and forefinger, he flicked the keys dangling out of the ignition so they jingled.

"She's dead; it's a fact," I said.

He sat half in the car, half out, one leg on the parking lot pavement. A bell rang—first period was over. History class was next. We were doing the Civil War: five thousand dead men at Bull Run. The air seeping in through the open car door smelled new, like it was from somewhere else and hadn't been breathed before. "Well, just stop saying it," he said. His voice cracked apart the word "stop." He got out of the car, slammed the door shut.

I watched him walk through the parking lot, weaving through the rows of parked cars. When he got to the door of the school, he yanked it open but then turned and waved. He probably couldn't see me, but I waved back.

The bell rang again; second period had officially started.

Sunlight was burrowing into my side of the car, so I rolled down the window to keep from getting too hot. Two girls came out the same door Will had just gone in—Ann Trinder and Lynn Mason. They hurried to a car parked six or seven away from where I was, and they both stared at me before driving off, going the long way through the lot so they wouldn't actually have to come near me.

Aunt Aggy and Mama were good at being dramatic; they liked scenes and attention and people scurrying around to make things better for them. Not me. I just wanted to go to school like a regular person who has a regular mother and, since this was all just daydreaming, a regular father and a dog. Everything the way it was for everyone else.

"So how come you're sitting out here if you want to be a regular person?" She was back, reminding me that I was not at all regular, because regular people didn't hear voices in their head.

"You should be talking to Aunt Aggy," I said. "She'd appreciate this sort of thing."

"Aunt Aggy can manage," she said, as matter-of-factly as if we were sitting at the kitchen table, working out my geometry proofs homework.

"Buying ten cartons of ice cream is not managing."

"I'm talking to you."

Who said I had to listen? I leaned over, twisted the key, turned on the radio, and twirled the dial to Dotty King's station. A man was giving the weather report. His voice was calm, like the weather he was forecasting. Everyone on this radio station was soothing. I imagined quiet offices, gray furniture, a soft hum from heating or air-conditioning always in the background, hushed footsteps along carpeted halls.

"You can't ignore me," Mama said.

I turned the radio louder. The man was talking about regional weather, about the calm, smooth spring and summer the state could expect. "Rainfall predicted to be at normal levels," he intoned. "Temperatures generally in the normal range."

"I'm still here," Mama said, but impatience edged her voice.

I thought about the normal spring and summer Iowa would be having. Last spring a tornado hit Washington, half an hour north. Tornado sirens went off, and Will, Aunt Aggy, and I had raced to the basement, terrified, but Mama stayed up in the kitchen. We were all begging her to come downstairs, and Will even went back to try to drag her down—she fought him off. When the sirens stopped, we took the stairs two at a time, shrieking questions, anger overflowing. Mama didn't say anything, just let us rant and yell and sputter until we were hoarse, recycling the same old words. Then Mama quietly said, "I'm still here, aren't I?" Aunt Aggy was breathing hard—she'd been doing most of the heavy-duty fussing— and she held up one finger, waggled it a bit, then shook her head. "Why'd you go and scare us like that?" Will and I looked at each other; his face was pale and tight, and I wondered if I looked that fearful too. After a long pause, Mama mumbled that she was sorry, but she kept standing at the kitchen sink, staring out the window into the dark. I think maybe we all noticed how tightly her hands clutched the edge of the kitchen sink, the knuckles bulged up like grapes, but no one said anything about that or about what she had said or about what if the tornado had hit. We all went back to bed, and in the morning everything felt like a weird dream. In fact, I'd forgotten about that night until now, until the calm man got me thinking about the calm weather we were supposed to have through- out this calm spring and calm summer. I turned the volume of the radio louder. He was more loudly calm, but still calm.

There were a million things to ask my mother.

I turned up the radio again, as far as it would go, making the man's words garble and gnarl. If she didn't need us, then I didn't need her. There were plenty of other ways to get my questions answered, like ask- ing Dotty King for the orange juice secret. I would be fine without my mother. "You're not supposed to do this." My voice rose into a whine, a wail, and I snapped off the radio. "Don't you know that? You're dead."

"Yet here I am," she whispered.

Only Mama would be bold enough to refuse to believe she was dead—after killing herself! That was crazy; hearing voices and believing them was also crazy. What were you supposed to ask a dead person any- ways? "I suppose you're in heaven and all that, with angels and harps?" I asked, though I couldn't imagine it. "You and James Dean?"

"Absolutely," she said. "We play checkers every day. He's not very good."

I couldn't believe she was teasing me! Not that I cared much about heaven: The CCD teachers had told us heaven would be perfect and we should trust God, but right now, my mother was dead, gone, and heaven was an insignificant, uninteresting detail compared to that. "So, what do you want from me?" I asked.

She whispered, "The same thing you want from me," and then she wasn't there.

"What kind of answer is that?" I shouted in the empty car. What did I want from her? For one thing, to be alive. For another, to be like everyone else, starting with, if you're dead, stay dead. If she would leave me alone, I could just sit here and be sad like I was supposed to be—crying and remembering how wonderful Mama was—not yelling at her, not getting worked up and angry. Thinking about that made me more furious.

The school bell jangled into my thoughts. Third period would start in four minutes. There couldn't be a better entrance than my psychology class, listening to Miss Wenzel talk about wackos like me. Suddenly I wasn't mad anymore, just lonely and sad all the way down to my bones.

I pulled the keys out of the ignition, slipped them in my pocket, got out of the car, and slammed the door. The sound seemed to echo across the parking lot, though I knew that was impossible.

THE BEST thing that could be said about those next few weeks was that they blurred into a big glob of Getting Through Things, as in, one of us was always saying, "Well, we got through that," whether it was dealing with the bank or the sheriff doing his death investigation or the lawyers or a neighbor's nosy questions.

Nobody at school knew what to say to me. Groups turned silent and stared at the floor when I approached. The biology teacher, Mrs. Lane, was one of the few people besides Becky and Mr. Rhinehart who would say hi first in the hall, but she wasn't even my teacher, so she probably thought I was someone else. My own teachers would say things like, "Reports on *The Red Badge of Courage* are due Friday. Except Alice, of course. Alice, whenever you're ready, whatever you want. Are you okay, dear?" Mr. Rhinehart must have warned them that according to his photocopied chapter, I might fall apart in some uncomfortable, Aunt Aggyish way. Instead of taking advantage, I worked harder, handing in reports a day early and studying all night for tests I wouldn't have cared about before. I finally—almost too late to do any good—understood the concept of moles in chemistry class, and I passed a weekly quiz for the first time since February. (Not that any teacher would have the guts to fail me.)

Mama's voice came mostly at night now, when I was studying at the kitchen table. She'd slowly whisper, "Here I am," and I'd keep reading through the facts about Antietam in the book in front of me, staring at the words that made the sentences that explained what I needed to know to pass the test. I'd stare so long and hard that the words would begin to seem foreign, like a language spoken in a country I'd never heard of, a language I didn't know existed. "Here I am." What was I supposed to do? I started my paper on *The Red Badge of Courage*: "How Henry Becomes a Man." I copied out the characteristics of autistic children. I read the chapter about Appomattox.

A couple of Sundays later, I was in front of the open fridge, staring at the shelves of food, looking for breakfast. We had voted on no more pancakes until further notice. Aunt Aggy also decided to stop restricting foods to certain meals, which meant she was fixing up hot dogs and potato salad for our breakfast, which was strange but fun. The condiments retained their alphabetical order, though Will kept switching ketchup to the *c*s, claiming it was spelled "catsup." So I moved the bottle away from the capers and squeezed it in next to the maple syrup.

I heard Aunt Aggy's footsteps on the stairs, all thumpy and quick, the way she walked in high heels. She came into the kitchen, filling it with the scent of Charlie, which she wore because Mr. Cooper gave her a bottle every Christmas. "I'll fry you a hot dog," she said.

I shook my head. "How old is this leftover tuna salad?"

"Either two days or more than a week. Plastic bowl or metal?"

"Plastic."

"More than a week." She crowded me aside and reached for the bowl. "Pee-yew," she said as she let the contents slide into the trash. "What else have we got in there?" She reached inside and started shuffling things around, reaching toward the back.

I knew what she'd find. "I'll do this," I said, wishing I could push her away and shut the door. "You look like you're going to Mr. Cooper's. I don't want to keep you."

But she was already muttering to herself. "Here's the good tuna, but let's move that to the front so we remember to eat it. What's in this foil? When did we have pork chops? Better pitch this." She was leaning way into the refrigerator and one arm suddenly extended behind her, a foil-wrapped package in her hand. I took it from her, deposited it in the garbage. Will's attempt at making pork chops, dry and stiff, like the single shoe you see along the side of the road now and then. Then she emerged from the refrigerator holding the red pitcher of Mama's orange juice. "This is old," she said, sniffing it through the spout.

It was stupid to keep old orange juice. I mean, how long could it stay in there? "Mama's special recipe," I mumbled. Something shifted in the garbage can, making a slight rustle. The open refrigerator cast a glow across Aunt Aggy as she stood in front of me, pitcher in her hand. It was easy to return the juice to the refrigerator and close the door.

She said, "I'm no fancy psychiatrist, so I don't know what to say, but I can make the same juice for you."

"There's a secret." I crossed my arms and stared out the window, but couldn't describe what was out there because I didn't see it. I didn't see anything.

After a moment, she spoke softly: "Orange Kool-Aid. Sweetened. Two spoonfuls."

I let out my breath all at once—I hadn't thought I'd been holding it in. "Really?"

"Really." She moved over to the sink, tilted the pitcher, let it hover above the drain. "Keep or dump? Whatever you want."

"How come Mama wouldn't tell me?"

"Your mother was up to there with secrets," Aunt Aggy said. "It's unnatural. What kind of person needs all those secrets?" For a quick second as our eyes met, I thought I should tell her about hearing Mama's voice. But then she coughed; her arm joggled, and a tiny stream of juice dribbled out of the pitcher, splashing into the sink. She coughed again, theatrically, and more juice spilled out. She'd pour away that juice even if it meant faking tuberculosis.

I reached over and pushed the pitcher so the juice poured out in a thin orange stream, straight down the drain. We both watched until there were only a few drips. She set the pitcher in the sink.

"We heal, Alice," she said. "Whether we want to or not." She pulled a can of concentrate from the freezer and plunked it on the counter, then continued: "Like yanking a Band-Aid. I say all at once." She ran water in the pitcher, swirled it around, dumped the water. It made a tiny gurgle, the soft sound of a bird. She handed me the pitcher. Water dripped off it onto the floor. "Well, we got through that anyway."

I didn't feel like I'd gotten through anything, actually. Instead, I felt as if I had reached the beginning and was finally starting whatever it was that I was starting. I stared at the wet pitcher in my hand. I could have Mama's juice. It was just a matter of orange Kool-Aid.

Dotty King would get to my letter eventually and read it on the air— no radio host would ignore a letter from a girl with a dead mother—and her answer would be smooth, efficient, cheerful, and calm: two spoon-fuls of orange Kool-Aid. And that's all I wanted now, answers to questions. Not voices in my head. Not more secrets. Just facts and the truth. Maybe everything would end up being as simple as orange Kool-Aid.

ELEMENTS

SPILLING out the juice was just the beginning for Aunt Aggy. "What we need is an old-fashioned spring cleaning," she kept saying. "When was our last spring cleaning?" Not that she really wanted an answer, but clearly none of us had much interest in cleaning beyond keeping the clutter in stacks and the visible-crumb level low.

Since Aunt Aggy was always pronouncing this or that, I assumed her interest in spring cleaning would pass, so for the next couple of weeks, I agreed, "You're absolutely right," and did nothing.

She didn't mean "spring" cleaning. She meant "go through stuff" cleaning—and it wasn't her stuff, my stuff, or Will's stuff she wanted to go through.

We hadn't done anything with Mama's room, hadn't made up her bed or emptied the ashtrays or put the lids back on the tubes of lipstick on her dressing table. There was an empty coffee cup on the nightstand that no one took down to the kitchen to wash. The African violets on the windowsill dried up. No one closed the half-read magazines with the folded-back covers. Her dirty clothes stayed in the hamper. Tempting, but neither Will nor I took the folded dollar bills and change on the bookcase. Dust clumped under the bed, rolled along the walls. I stood at the doorway and looked in, but it was like peering into a museum room, as if a waist-level velvet rope was keeping me out.

Will turned his head when he passed by. More and more he was driving around with Joe Fry, who everyone said was wild; or hanging out with the guys from the farms who knew about hunting and fixing cars and which places sell beer if you're underage. His girlfriend, Kathy Clark, would call looking for him on Fridays or Saturdays, but barely seemed surprised when I told her he wasn't home. "Just please tell him I called," she'd say in her sweet voice, and I'd slide the scrap of paper with the message under his closed bedroom door. Will stayed out late, and Aunt Aggy fussed, but he didn't come home any earlier the next night. It was like she hadn't said a word, like that paper with Kathy's name was blank. Even I wasn't seeing him much, though he still called me Baby Sister and I still pretended to get mad when he did. But we never talked about things like not going into Mama's room. Or even talked about how we weren't talking. In a way, it was easier to say nothing. I was afraid that if we started talking, I'd tell him about Mama's voice, and he'd say it was impossible to hear her talk when she was a dead body in the ground. I couldn't argue against that.

Anyway, what was there to say? *What's going to happen to us? Are you afraid that one day you'll start crying and never stop? Why did our mother die?* Will didn't want to hear that stuff; no one did. He would just get mad and stay out even later at night. It was like the baby bird—better to pretend building a nest in an old shoe box and digging up worms could save its life.

Maybe Mama's stuff could stay where it was forever, as if everything would be fine. That was probably what Will was thinking, and for a while I tried to be like him, walking past Mama's room without looking in, but something always stopped me. The overdue library books: *Fear of Flying*, *Once Is Not Enough*, Barbara Cartland romances. The postcard, leaning on the windowsill, of Iowa City's Old Capitol dome. The sewing machine in its white plastic case. How could Will not see Mama's left-behind things when they were there in front of us?

IT WAS a rainy Saturday afternoon, and because like usual since Mama died, none of my friends had invited me to do one single thing the whole weekend, I was in the kitchen reading my chemistry book.

"Those scientists think they can explain everything with their precious facts," Mama's voice murmured.

Aunt Aggy's footsteps came down the stairs, not the usual trippety-trip, but more clumpety, which meant something. Everything always meant something with her—there were many levels of symbolism, and if she were a character in *The Red Badge of Courage*, I could've easily written a ten-page paper about her. "Alice!" She stood in the doorway, waiting for me to look up from my book, to give her my full attention. She always wanted full attention, even just to announce that supper was ready or that she was going upstairs to take a nap. So I looked up, gave her my fullest attention. "Time for an old-fashioned spring cleaning," she said.

That. I glanced down at a series of impenetrable chemical equations. Even the words in English looked like one long equation. But my chemistry teacher, Mr. Miller, got all soft voiced and dreamy eyed when he discussed kinetic theory or isotopes; he wrote on the board with flowing strokes, like he thought he was conducting an orchestra or painting a mural. My friend Becky thought he looked like Robert Redford in *Butch Cassidy and the Sundance Kid*; she had a crush on him, and she showed me how if you wrote out her name and his name and crossed out the letters that were the same and counted, "love, marriage, friendship, hatred," with the remaining letters, you'd get "love" if you used his middle name and her middle name, and you'd get "marriage" with his middle name and her middle initial.

No matter how many times I talked to Mr. Miller after school (Becky jealously waiting in the hallway, peering in at us through the small glass pane in the door), I couldn't understand even the simplest, easiest principle of chemistry. Because of my dead mother, he wouldn't flunk me, but it felt important to do well on my own, like that would prove I was fine. So I asked Mr. Miller for extra credit if I memorized the periodic table of the elements: names, symbols, atomic masses, and atomic numbers. His voice slipped into dreaminess: "Learning the elements, the building blocks of life. The essence of it all, the source. Your thirst for knowledge is to be commended." I nodded, tried to look thirsty for knowledge and not just for a good grade.

So far I could recite the first ten elements, hydrogen through neon.

Suddenly Aunt Aggy slammed shut my book. "Right now."

It took a moment to remember she was talking about cleaning. "I'm studying."

She stared, as if she didn't quite get the concept. "Studying?"

"Chemistry," I said. "For school. Where I am Monday through Friday."

"I know about school," she said. "There are all kinds of educations, and school is the least likely place to learn anything worthwhile. I've got thoughts on the subject. I should run for school board: I'm a solid citizen. I vote every November and in the primaries—"

I cut off her rant: "It's just chemistry. I'm memorizing the periodic table of the elements for extra credit."

"Table?" She made a disparaging hiss with her tongue. "Sounds like shop class."

"Everything in the whole world is made from these elements," I said. "They're the most basic substances. Mr. Miller says you can't understand the world until you understand the elements; his favorite is phosphorus." Aunt Aggy shook her head, so I kept explaining: "For example, water is made up of two elements, and its formula is H_2O—two atoms of hydrogen and one of oxygen."

"Lovely concept for something so scientific." Aunt Aggy's mouth twisted to the side, her forehead furrowed. Then she asked, "What's hydrogen made of?"

"It's made of hydrogen," I said. "It's an element."

"There must be billions of elements," she said.

"Actually, there are ninety-two naturally occurring elements."

"Is dog hair made of elements?"

"Everything in the world is made of elements." I was sounding dreamy, like Mr. Miller, same phrasing, same emphasis on "world."

"Dust?"

"Absolutely," I said.

"Milk?"

"For sure." I'd have to tell Mr. Miller I was talking about chemistry on a Saturday. Maybe he'd pile on extra-extra credit.

"The human soul?" she said. "God? Love? Death?"

I stared up at the ceiling.

She walked to the window. I looked at her back, at the rain through the glass. It was about as hard a rain as they come. Why couldn't she just say, "Good luck"? She and Mama could be so difficult. I said, "I meant everything in the physical world."

"Who needs that explained?" Mama asked.

I looked at the cover of my chemistry book, black with three white starbursts that looked like explosions. According to the photo credit, it was the formation of a polyester. Mean-looking red letters blared across the top; they spelled "chemistry," but they meant "You won't get this." I said, "All I want is to pass chemistry." Passing chemistry like a regular student was a big goal. Memorizing the periodic table of the elements was impressive.

Aunt Aggy turned away from the window. There was a wet line down her cheek, the trail of a tear. Outside, the rain beat down. She murmured, "She called me Annaggy, one word, like we were sisters." A tear slid down her other cheek. Sodium chloride (NaCl) was salt, and H_2O was water. Is that what tears were? Aunt Aggy continued: "Annaggy, Annette. She liked how the names sounded together. 'I wish you were my big sister,' she'd say. Or, 'I wish we lived by the ocean. I wish I could fly to the stars.' Your grandmother didn't like that kind of talk—'Going to the stars when you can't even get to school on time,' she'd say. Telling me not to encourage her, like that made a difference. When you add up all those tiny things about Annette. . . ." She looked at me like I was supposed to pick up my pencil and calculate, adding it all up to find the sum of my mother. I did pick up my pencil, chewed the eraser. "Anyway, I can't stand looking at that room one more day," she said. "Closing the door won't do it." She went to the cabinet under the sink and pulled out a box of trash bags that she dropped on top of my chemistry book. "It's what she would want."

The pencil eraser snapped off in my mouth. Did Aunt Aggy really know what Mama would want? Sure, she was the one who knew Mama all the way from when she was born, and yes, she knew the secret about the orange juice, but almost any time you saw Aunt Aggy and Mama sitting together at the kitchen table, it was Aunt Aggy doing the talking,

Mama just nodding. What if Mama wanted everything left exactly the way it was? I spit the eraser into my hand, rolled it between my thumb and finger until it popped out and hit the floor, skidding under the stove.

Aunt Aggy nudged the box of garbage bags until it was perfectly centered on my book. She mumbled, "We'll turn the room into an art studio," and I assumed I didn't hear right, but then she spoke more boldly: "I'm taking up painting. I've decided to become an artist."

"An artist!" Wait till Will heard about this.

She lifted her chin. "People have to do something, Alice; people have to find ways to express themselves, especially people as wracked with grief as we are. Your mother would understand if . . . if she were here." She sniffled, pulled a tissue out of her pocket, delicately dabbed her nose. "That room is a boulder strapped to us." She rested her hand on the back of my neck, tightened her grip slightly, then loosened it. "We'll all end up underwater. Or, as your scientists would say, under H_2O." She leaned in, whispered, "Like a Band-Aid. Rip it off." She leaned away, picked up the box of garbage bags. "I ordered a set of oils from the Sears catalog today and checked out a learn-to-paint book from the library." She started to leave the kitchen but paused at the door. "I can't do this alone. I'll fall apart, I really will."

How was I supposed to know what to do? Rain ran through the gutters, beat at the windows. Dotty King's listeners asked how to get jelly stains out of their grandmother's lace tablecloths or whether dry yeast was as good as cake yeast. Questions with answers.

Mama was silent. So I stood up. My chair scraped the floor. Aunt Aggy didn't say thank you, just went up the stairs one by one as I followed.

There was a certain smell to my mother's room, perfume and ground-out cigarettes and dust and candle wax all mixed together. I breathed it in. This was something Will wouldn't notice as he hurried by Mama's room.

Aunt Aggy leaned against the doorway. "Can't believe one person has so much stuff."

I sat on the unmade bed, bounced a little to make it squeak. If I'd been the one who died, would Mama and Aunt Aggy be in my room, cramming my stuff in garbage bags? Dirty underwear, old yearbooks, the wooden box with the secret compartment Becky had given me for my birthday, the hand-me-down Trixie Belden books that Mama had read, my collection of Agatha Christie paperbacks. I leaned back on the bed, looked up at the ceiling. It was just stuff. It wasn't actually her. Water was water when you drank it, you didn't think of hydrogen and oxygen.

"I'm going to fall apart." Aunt Aggy twisted the doorknob back and forth.

I stood up, yanked open the closet door, grabbed a handful of hanging clothes and plopped them on the bed. I held up the top dress, a red sundress with white trim. It was like something from the fifties, a big poufy skirt, a little waist, zipper up the back. Something Marilyn Monroe would have worn in late-night movies. I'd never seen it on Mama.

Mama said, "That's the dress I wore on the train to Chicago."

I had never been to Chicago. None of us had. I held the dress against my body; it looked like it would fit me, maybe be cute in an old-fashioned way.

"Ask her." Mama's voice was breathy but urgent.

Aunt Aggy said, "What do I know about being an artist? About paint?"

"Ask about Chicago," Mama insisted.

I glanced at the underside of the hem. A store dress. "Have you ever been to Chicago?" I asked.

She stopped fiddling with the doorknob. "Why do you say that?"

"I don't know." I picked up the next dress, one Mama had sewn, white polyester with blue seagull-like designs scattered across it. Mama called this her "adult" dress; she wore it to PTA meetings. I reached for the red dress again, draped it across one arm. I lifted the skirt, stretched it, let it drop, watching the fabric swish into place. Then I pressed the dress to my nose and sniffed. Nothing. "I've never been to Chicago," I said.

Aunt Aggy crossed her arms tight across her chest. "Capital of Illinois."

"Actually, Springfield is the capital of Illinois."

"Oh, Alice," she said. "Everything with you is about facts." She came into the room and sat on the bed, pushing aside the dresses so the wire hangers tangled. "I suppose it wouldn't hurt to tell you that your mother and I took the train to Chicago once, and this is the dress she wore."

Mama in Chicago. I instantly wanted to know every tiny detail, but Aunt Aggy always had to tell things her way—which meant slowly—so all I said was, "Pretty dress."

"She was gorgeous," Aunt Aggy said. "The conductor kept coming round to check if we needed anything, but it was Annie he stared at the whole time. She was just seventeen and had never been out of Iowa, and there we were heading to Chicago. I'd never been either, and I was old enough to know better, but I was as giddy as she was. Oh, the two of us! We were going to stay with Mavis Felper's cousin and eat at a white-tablecloth restaurant and ride escalators in the Marshall Field's department store. Look at paintings in the art museum, see Buckingham Fountain lit up at night, sit in the Palmer House lobby to watch the fancy people pass by. In Chicago all the women were beautiful and all the men handsome and everyone so rich that when quarters fell out of their pockets, they didn't bother picking them up. 'The capital of Illinois,' Annie kept saying, though your grandmother corrected her every time." Aunt Aggy stopped speaking.

I shifted the red dress to the other arm. "Why were you going to Chicago?"

She took a long time to answer: "Your grandmother thought it was a good idea to show Annie there was more to the world than what was in Shelby."

I said the first thing I thought of: "Was Mama pregnant?"

"Good Lord, no!" Aunt Aggy's voice shot up a notch. "Don't talk that way about your mother. That's not the only reason to leave town, Alice. Look, we were just going on a fun little trip, okay? See some sights. Have fun." She picked up the seagull dress. "Hated this one," and she slid it off the hanger, dropped it on the floor. Then she shoved the whole stack from the bed to the floor, kicked at the crumpled heap with one foot.

I clutched the red dress harder. She wasn't telling me everything. "Mama never talked about going to Chicago."

Aunt Aggy jumped up and went to the closet, where she started yanking things off hangers, tossing them onto the pile on the floor. "She never actually went to Chicago." There was an angry space between each word of her sentence.

"Did she get sick?" I asked.

She kept throwing clothes on the floor; empty hangers rattled in the closet.

"Did the train wreck?"

Aunt Aggy reached way back, slid forward an armful of clothes on the rod, making a screechy noise. "She met your father on the train and instead of getting off with me at Chicago like she was supposed to, she went on to New York with him."

I laughed nervously. "No, really."

Aunt Aggy looked at the clothes on the floor, then started picking things up, putting them on hangers and returning them to the closet. "Really."

I sat on the bed, spread the dress on my lap, then was suddenly afraid to touch it. "Try it on," Mama urged. I shook my head, but she kept talking: "In the mirror your waist shrinks and your legs get long. You'll find curves you didn't know were there, swish when you walk. Every woman needs a dress like this." I pushed the dress onto the bed, stood up.

Aunt Aggy said, "Couldn't take his eyes off her." Her voice slowed, sounded far away. "He was something to look at, not tall-dark-and-handsome, but a face you watch, someone who's been plenty of places but who looks at you like for all that, you're by far the best thing he's seen." Aunt Aggy stared at the clothes she had just hung up, smoothed out a plaid skirt. "Only saw him that one time," she said, and scooped up an armload of clothes, handed them to me. I held them as she ripped a garbage bag off the roll and fingered the slippery edges, trying to find the opening. "They don't make this easy," she snapped, but finally she separated the two sides from each other and poked both arms down to the bottom, shaking and rustling the bag all the way open. "Here." She held the bag toward me.

The clothes were heavy in my arms. They were just clothes, just pieces of colored fabric stitched into the shape of my mother. I shoved them in; we both looked at the saggy, half-full bag. Rain pounded the roof.

Aunt Aggy said, "Pants would be better for traveling, I said. But she knew she was gorgeous. She looked like someone else, a movie star." She gave the bag a little shake, letting the clothes settle deeper. "Keep going?"

I thought she meant about the train, so I nodded, but she set the bag down, reached into the closet. "We should check these pockets," but she didn't before stuffing another armload of clothes—hangers and all—into the bag.

I sat on the bed and watched. She didn't ask for help, and I didn't want to help—I didn't want to watch, but also I didn't want to leave the room. This was the last time I'd see Mama's things: the red blouse she wore to my birthday picnic last year when it was so unseasonably hot that the frosting melted off the cake; the silky black slip she slept in on summer nights when waves of sweet honeysuckle scent drifted through our open windows; the corduroy jumpsuit she'd made off the cover of the *Vogue* pattern book; the man's ski sweater she'd bought at Mrs. Jurgens's garage sale for a quarter; the old blue bathrobe with the cigarette-ash holes that she wore when she was sad. Who knew what stories were behind the clothes I didn't recognize, like that red dress or the fluffy pink sweater with the trail of brownish stains along the left sleeve? Something as simple as a pair of black high heels could hold the secret to everything, and we were shoving it all into garbage bags.

Aunt Aggy stopped suddenly. "You're so quiet."

"So are you," I said. "I'm fine."

She sat next to me on the bed, a couple of sweaters in her lap that she shook out and refolded. "He asked her once—one time!—to go to New York, to stay on the train, and just like that she said yes. She left us like it was so easy."

"Who was he?" I asked casually, to make her think the answer didn't matter.

Aunt Aggy said, "He gave up his seat so she could sit by the window. We'd found two seats together, but she wanted to sit by the window and so did I. Who could blame us—our first train trip? He was at a window across the aisle, catty-corner, listening to our squabble. 'Please, one of you sit here,' and he slid over. Annie smoothed the skirt of her dress, looked out the window we were fighting over, then looked out his,

comparing the view. Outside, the farms were passing like channels flicking on a TV. 'Well, one of you,' he said, voice all honey, and he didn't care
who. He was only doing a favor. It could've been me. I was more his age
maybe. But Miss Red Dress Annie stuck out her tongue at me and
pushed past his knees, plopped in the seat next to him. I sat alone in my
own window seat, pressed my nose against the glass. It was just more
farms out there, same as the farms near Shelby." She paused, lifted one of
the sweaters up to her nose, inhaled. "White Shoulders perfume. I
smelled this on someone else the other day, and . . . well."

She set the sweater back in her lap; I reached over and took it,
inhaled. Mama. Right then I decided to wear White Shoulders for the rest
of my life. Mama had told me it was too sophisticated for a girl, and she
took the bottle out of my hand, setting it back on her dressing table. "You
earn a perfume like this." I would say having a dead mother qualified.

I tossed the sweater into a bag of clothes. It seemed like more than a
month ago that I was worrying about secret ingredients in orange juice.
That was nothing. "She never told us about any train ride," I said. *Or my
father.*

"One minute we're going to Chicago," Aunt Aggy said. "The next
she's staying on the train all the way to New York. No time to talk, hardly
a chance to say good-bye, what with this man—I didn't even know his
name—pulling twenties off his money clip, telling the conductor that
he'll be buying a one-way ticket to New York for the young lady. Of
course I butt in, informing the conductor that I'm the one responsible
for my niece, but he's already got those twenties in his hand. So I turned
to Annette, looking out the window like she was already somewhere else.
'Are you sure?' I asked her, begged, and I threatened to run for a policeman, but she said, 'There are other ways to leave,' and that awful way she
said 'other'—oh, I had to let her go, had to. God himself couldn't have
stopped her. I always wondered, what if I'd taken the window seat next to
him? What then?"

She looked at me as if I should speak up with the answer.

Hydrogen popped into my head, helium, lithium, beryllium,
boron.

"I always thought . . ." She reached to the red dress draped across the pillows at the head of the bed, stroked her hand along the smooth, shiny fabric.

I guessed what she thought: If she had convinced my mother to wear pants or if she'd taken the window seat by the man, then my mother would've gone to Chicago and seen Buckingham Fountain and the people in the Palmer House lobby. They would've taken the train back home and Mama would have married some nice Iowa boy and be alive right now.

Aunt Aggy kept rubbing the red fabric as if a genie might pop out and grant wishes.

"I want the dress," I said, surprising myself.

She snatched her hand away. "I assumed I'd keep it."

I looked straight ahead, not at her, not at anything in particular. The room suddenly didn't feel like Mama had ever been here. I crossed my arms; Aunt Aggy pulled the dress into her lap, folded it once, twice. It was just a stupid dress.

"If I'd been wearing it that day," Aunt Aggy said.

"Maybe it all would've happened no matter what."

"It was my dress," she said. "I'd bought it up in Iowa City at Siefert's, special for the trip to Chicago. But Annette tried it on, and we both saw it was hers."

There was silence except for the rain pelting the roof and windows. I should let Aunt Aggy keep the red dress—Mama had probably forgotten it was in her closet. Let Aunt Aggy be the one going around saving baby birds and dresses. But when I opened my mouth to tell her, I coughed instead.

Finally, Aunt Aggy said, "She disappeared, never wrote for her things. Everyone blamed me of course, but what else was there to do? Someone wants to go so bad, you got to let them. Your grandmother threw away everything of your mama's—high school yearbooks, clothes, stuffed animals from when she was a baby. Everything, just needing to do something. Like us now, I guess," and she gave a dry laugh before finishing: "Never the same after, and next thing you know, she passed on."

I caught myself staring into the empty hallway. "Then Mama came back." My voice sounded harsh and sudden.

"And so sorry about everything," Aunt Aggy said. "Pregnant, a baby, and nothing but a suitcase she could barely lift. 'Here I am,' she said, like all I'd been doing was holding Sunday dinner for her. What was I supposed to do—slam the door in her face? I guess some people would—you made your bed and all—but I figured if there was any other place to go, that's where she'd be. And believe me, there wasn't a question that didn't get asked—not that she answered a single one. Claimed not to notice everyone in town gawking and gossiping."

"What happened when she was away?" I asked.

Aunt Aggy stroked the red dress like it was a cat. "She wouldn't answer my questions, never said a word. Almost as if it never happened. I started wondering if it was real. Had she really gone?" Without looking at me, she walked out of the room with the dress entwined in her arms. Her bedroom door clicked shut.

I glanced at the garbage bags, at the things we hadn't gone through. It all was just a bunch of stupid things to throw away or take to the church rummage sale, things that meant nothing—like that story. It was incredible, sure, but what happened in the end: Mama came back, as if she'd never left.

I stood up and pulled the top dresser drawer all the way out: a tangle of silk scarves, sunglasses with a scratch across one lens, a Timex wristwatch, a barrette missing one of the glued-on stones. No letters, no notes, no diary. No piece of paper that started out, "Here's why I killed myself." Nothing that was the thing we were looking for—without any of us actually saying we were looking for it, without us knowing exactly what it was.

The next drawer was filled with underwear.

The drawer below that was crammed with socks and panty hose.

Nightgowns, slips, and bras exploded from the bottom drawer.

If I had been Aunt Aggy, I would have found a way to make Mama tell me what had happened. I shook my head, then dumped everything from these drawers into a single garbage bag, double-knotted it. Amazing how quickly I could make things disappear. I thought about how Mama didn't have any baby stuff or yearbooks—"I have no past," she would joke when I used to ask to see old pictures. Hearing her say that had bothered me, though I never understood why.

I sat on the tufted stool at Mama's dressing table. It had belonged to her mother: kidney shaped, shiny, dark wood with a round mirror attached to the back. The wood was nicked up where Mama said I had bitten when I was teething. I had watched Mama in this mirror plenty of times while she put on makeup: holding her breath as she stroked mascara upward on the lashes of one eye, then the other, her mouth partially open; I'd hand her the big blush brush with the pale bristles; the sudden quiet as she did her lipstick, blotting her lips with Kleenex. There was always a tube of lipstick in my Christmas stocking, but I didn't wear makeup; "Nature doesn't mind enhancement," Mama had said to me. "Look how much prettier a pine tree is with some tinsel."

Most girls at school wore makeup, at least some eye shadow and blush, a little lip gloss. Girls who wore real lipstick—not just a clear slick of shiny pink—were the girls who climbed into guys' cars after school, got driven off with a big rush and roar, their hands limply trailing out open windows as the rest of us pretended we weren't watching, wondering which empty park they were headed to, wondering were they really going to do that? You'd hear those girls—Paula Elam, Donna Slade, the others—in the second-floor bathroom, puffing on cigarettes as they stared closely at themselves in the mirror, saying things like, "Lemme try your new lipstick." Becky and Linda were afraid of the second-floor bathroom, but I secretly liked the way Paula and the others talked, how they always knew what they were doing—"Dump him, he's an asshole," one would advise another, and a week later she'd be in some other boy's front seat after school. Or one would ask, "Should I go blond?" and the others would walk around her, looking, then they'd all nod; on Monday her hair would be bleached. Last week when I was washing my hands, Paula Elam told me she liked my clogs. Becky was combing her hair next to me, so I pretended I hadn't heard. Then Paula laughed and blew smoke at us, dropping her cigarette onto the floor, crushing it with one of her own clogs, which I actually thought were cuter than mine. Becky dragged me out to the hall even though I hadn't dried my hands. But usually when I was in the bathroom, those girls didn't see me; if I said, "Excuse me," to get to the sink, they'd shuffle aside without taking their eyes off themselves in the mirror.

Mama's mirror looked empty with only my face in it. I stared so long that suddenly it wasn't me anymore; it was just a face, not a very pretty one, not like what you see in magazines or the movies. The shape was narrow and my teeth were too big for my mouth. Sometimes people said I looked like Mama—in a less beautiful way, I assumed. Now she was dead, so people would forget that about us.

I picked up an open tube of lipstick—Crushed Cherry—and slowly unrolled it under my nose. It smelled like the basket of wax fruit on the coffee table; I had bitten off a chunk of the apple once when I was little, surprised it didn't taste as good as it looked. There was a groove in the lipstick where Mama's lips fit, a deep J shape worn down that way by Mama's own lips, the tip wafer thin and fragile, as if one more application might snap it off.

I closed up the tube, dropped it on the dressing table. It rolled along the wood surface for a moment, stopped when it knocked up against a bottle of White Shoulders. It was silly to think that lipstick made those girls the way they were, and it was silly to think that my mother's life had changed because of one red dress on one afternoon. Still, what if I wore lipstick? Who would I be?

"Start with the eyes," Mama's voice murmured. "Pretty eyes make you feel beautiful right away."

"I'm not beautiful," I said, blushing briefly.

"Always the same with you," Mama said. "Only seeing what you're looking at. Being beautiful and feeling beautiful are two different things. Anyone can feel beautiful."

I looked in the mirror. I didn't look beautiful and I didn't feel beautiful. In fact, the harder I stared, the worse I felt and looked.

"You're not trying," she said softly. "What makes you feel beautiful?"

I picked up the bottle of White Shoulders and spritzed some on my neck, then rubbed one wrist after the other across the wet patch on my throat in the exact way Mama did. Then I sneezed as the perfume tickled my nose.

She laughed in a nice way. "Let's do your eyes. First you want to curl your eyelashes with that metal thing. It will be cold, so put your fingers through the loops—right—and hold the other end in front of your mouth and breathe."

I blew onto the metal eyelash curler. It looked like a tiny vise.

"No," she said, "how you breathe into your hand to check your breath. And prop your elbow on something. I ripped out my eyelashes once when my arm jiggled, and for something so tiny, you miss them when they're not there. Squeeze gently—listen to your heartbeat five times, relax, then five more. Start conditioning your eyelashes at night with Vaseline."

I listened carefully, counted off five heartbeats, relaxed the pressure on my eyelashes, counted five more, then did the same on my left eye. I examined my eyelashes in the mirror. They were definitely bent, but did having bent-up eyelashes mean I was beautiful?

"Olive-brown eyeliner," she said. "That silver pencil. When it needs sharpening, pop it in the freezer for a half hour so it doesn't crumble in the sharpener."

I held it in my hand like it was a regular pencil, fighting a sudden urge to write my name across my forehead.

Now Mama was talking faster, as if words were backing up and she had to get them all out: "Quick, solid line on your lid, then underneath, along the lashes. It's the most important part of eye makeup. If I could have only one thing, it would be eyeliner."

Maybe she was right, because as soon as I finished, my eyes seemed to jump forward and sparkle in a way they never had before. I couldn't stop looking at them.

"Eye shadow is easy," she said. "I haven't used anything but Gold Dust for years. Inside to outside. Even strokes. Always use earth tones. Brown, beige, gold, dark yellow."

"Becky's mom wears blue," I said.

She snorted. "Blue is not a color that should be found on the face. Mascara's tricky. Magazines say don't wear black unless you're a dark brunette—ignore that. Always wear black. And spend money for the good brand. Use that silver tube, and pull the wand out slowly—that's how to keep from clumping. I've worn a lot of mascara, and this is one thing I know. Stroke upward; take your time. Lower lashes are harder. Gently draw the brush across them like you're holding a feather. For special occasions, you'd dust baby powder on your upper lashes right now, then do another coat. False eyelashes look fake. Never underestimate eyelashes. Women who take care of their eyelashes are noticed."

My eyelashes looked darker and thicker, for whatever that was worth. Mama never told me any of this when she was alive. This was the way I imagined Becky and her mom, Linda and her mom—how it was supposed to be.

"Sweetheart Pink blush," Mama said. "First blow on the brush to clear out old color. Stroke across the blush, left to right. Think of the most handsome man you know. When you smile, that's where you put the blush. Think, Alice."

I didn't know any handsome men personally, so I thought about James Dean, who Mama liked so much, and I did smile, so I stroked on the blush in upward-V motions.

Mama said, "Now across your forehead at the hairline, your nose, your chin. Quick and light," and I felt as if I was doing the sign of the cross at church.

"Now for lipstick," Mama said, then paused.

My heart beat fast. "Maybe just lip gloss." I sounded uncertain, like an echo.

"A woman's not finished without lipstick."

I thought of those girls in the second-floor bathroom, stroking on their lipstick as the bell rang, not caring if they were late—if they went to class at all. My mother wasn't secretly one of those girls, was she? I unrolled the tube of Crushed Cherry lipstick, looked at that odd-shaped space her lips had worn away. My hand trembled as I fit my upper lip into the groove; Mama's lips were supposed to be there, not mine. But I curved the lipstick downward to the right, then went back to the top and curved down on the left. I filled my bottom lip in one stroke all the way across. My lips felt slick and heavy, as if they'd been coated with mud, and I rubbed them together, thinking lipstick should taste like something. My hands were still shaky, so I set them against the edge of the dressing table.

"Always check your teeth," she said. "Nothing ruins a good impression faster than lipstick smears on your teeth."

I smiled into the mirror. My teeth were lipstick free.

"You need a Kleenex," she said, and I reached for one, slipped it between my lips and kissed. "Think of that handsome man," she said. "Never waste a kiss," but again, who was there for me to think about? James Dean was dead. I wadded up the tissue with my wasted kiss and dropped it in the trash, along with the crumpled-up tissues that held her lip marks and shavings from sharpening the eye pencil and the cotton balls she had dabbed with perfume, then tucked into her bra.

It was late afternoon, and the rain had stopped; the light was coming up soft and gray. I pushed my face close to the mirror; everything blurred and I drew back. I couldn't say I looked beautiful. But maybe I felt a tiny bit beautiful.

"This is you all along," Mama said. "We only needed to put it all together."

I watched myself smile in the mirror. How could Mama have found this in me? It was like the way Dotty King could tell you to perk up a bitter cucumber by sprinkling it with cider vinegar and pinches of salt and sugar, then rinsing it half an hour later.

Without thinking, I asked, "Why did you go with the man on the train?" I couldn't say "father." I pulled my hair back, held it with one hand. Maybe that looked better. I let go. She wasn't answering my question. "Do you like my hair up?" I asked.

"Lucky you with your oval face," she said. "About any hairstyle will work."

I pulled my hair back again, thought about how more people at school would tell me they liked my new hairstyle than would tell me they were sorry about my mother dying. Changing your looks was easy and meant nothing. But everyone would know exactly what they were supposed to say for a haircut: *So cute! Looks great!* I stared up at the ceiling, noticed some cobwebs in the corner, blew my breath out hard at them so they'd sway. I wasn't asking such a hard question, and I asked again, "What about the man on the train?"

Mama spoke briskly: "Replace mascara every six months even if it's not gone. And don't pay real money for clear lip gloss because Vaseline works fine."

"Mama, why won't you answer my question?" I grabbed hold of the edges of the dressing table, squeezed hard until my arms turned sore and stiff. This wasn't like wanting to know what was in the orange juice. Couldn't she see? If I just had the answer to one thing. I spoke very quietly, on the verge of crying: "One simple question. Why don't you answer it?"

"Nail polish." But she didn't go on.

There was a silence. A sudden beam of sunlight cut diagonally through the window behind me; in the mirror I watched dust float through the light.

"Please." I dragged out the word long and slow, like a ribbon of syrup.

"Chicago wasn't far enough," she said.

"Far enough for what?" I asked, insisted.

"Alice, honey, please." Her voice sounded tired, far away, dead.

"One simple question," I said, releasing my grip on the table, shaking the achy feeling out of my hands. A cloud passed, and the sunlight behind me disappeared. How strange to think that the dust was still there though I couldn't see it now. I was tired of my face, so I closed my eyes.

Finally she said, "Are the questions that make up a life ever simple?"

I hated questions being answered with questions; it felt like cheating. So I said, "Yes. Why'd you leave me? Don't you love me? Don't you miss me?" How hard was it to answer those questions?

After a moment, I opened my eyes, and with one hand pulled my hair back from my face. It looked good that way. And my face was shaped like an oval—I'd never noticed.

"Look at you," she said. "You're going to be, you are, a beautiful woman."

I pictured Mama, how beautiful she was, the way she smiled sideways and how that little round bone stuck up at the top of each shoulder and the tiny mole under her chin that you could see only if she were looking straight up into the sky or if you were little and sitting on her lap. Aunt Aggy could throw away every piece of clothing and shut down the White Shoulders factory; I could wear my hair in a new style every single day for ten years in a row—and still this would be the way it was: My mother left me. It was so hard to ask again: "Don't you miss me?" A simple question with only one answer.

A floorboard creaked, and I opened my eyes, turned quickly. Aunt Aggy stood in the doorway, the red dress draped over one arm. "Try it on." Her eyes were puffy from crying. She walked over, held the dress up to my body, her hands pinning it against my shoulders.

I looked down at how the dress hung—a couple of inches above my knees, the waist tucking in where my own waist tucked in a bit, the straight-across neckline that you didn't see often except maybe on Audrey Hepburn in the late-night movies. "It's Mama's dress."

Aunt Aggy said, "At least try it on once." She took her hands off my shoulders, so I had to catch the dress as it slipped.

I pulled my T-shirt over my head, dropped it on the floor. It was May, but the damp day had made the room chilly, and my skin prickled. I'd never worn any of Mama's clothes before—they weren't what you'd ever wear to high school. Mama's clothes looked like they came from the movies, even when they were things she'd sewn herself or picked up at a garage sale. It was the way she wore them, tying scarves in fancy knots, belting a man's shirt a certain way, tucking pants into dress boots. Not like Becky's mother, who wore regular clothes Becky borrowed all the time. I secretly liked that Mama looked more glamorous than other mothers, but we got into arguments anyway, because she couldn't understand why jeans and sweaters were fine with me. "At least some fun, hot-pink socks," she'd suggest, "or how about this chunky bracelet?" No, no, no—and then she'd accuse me of wanting to look like everyone else, as if that was something awful.

I pulled down the zipper; it was longer than they made zippers on dresses anymore, and it sounded loud and scratchy in the quiet room. I stepped into the dress, pulling it up over my jeans. Then I reached under the skirt and unbuttoned my jeans, pulled them down and off, kicked them away. I turned, so Aunt Aggy could do up the zipper, which she did slowly, not making a quick zip sound, but a ratcheting up, as if the dress were being closed tooth by tooth. She took a step back and put one hand on my shoulder, turned me all around, stared at me for a moment. "You're her," she said. "You're Annie, Annette."

I shook my head quickly, terrified to hear the words.

She pushed me over to the mirror. "Look."

It wasn't really my mother in the mirror. It was me, same old me, but that dress turned my neck long and elegant, the way Mama's had been, and my eyes looked more green than brown, and cheekbones cut across my face. I tilted my head to the left the way Mama did, smiled one of her slow, crooked smiles.

Aunt Aggy's face was right behind mine in the mirror, her mouth partially open, her eyes studying my face that was also Mama's face.

What would it be like to think your life turned upside down because you wore this red dress on the train to Chicago? I said, "She must have been something."

"Like someone else, like a movie star," Aunt Aggy said. "Knowing exactly what line comes next."

"Movie stars don't really. They're just reading lines writers give them." I lifted my hair on top of my head. I looked like her, I was in her room, wearing her makeup, her dress. I should know what Mama was thinking; I should at least have an idea. I let my hair loose, shook my head. "Did she, um,"—it was a stupid, obvious question—"fall in love? I mean, on the train? Right then?"

Aunt Aggy's eyes met mine in the mirror. "Why else would she have left?" Neither of us blinked, and I didn't know if I should believe her, if she believed herself.

"She never talked about him," I said.

In the mirror, Aunt Aggy and I kept looking at each other, like those staring contests kids have. I was never good at them, and finally I dropped my eyes. "Not even one word," I murmured. I picked up the tube of Crushed Cherry lipstick and set it upright, next to the perfume bottle.

Aunt Aggy said, "People make certain choices in life and that's that." It sounded like an unfinished sentence, but she didn't go on.

The dress was stiff and scratchy and the waist was too snug, so I couldn't take a full, deep breath, and suddenly I wanted out. I was about to ask Aunt Aggy to unzip me when she spoke loudly: "The one thing I know is that she loved you and Will very much."

Then why did she leave me? But I couldn't say those words out loud.

Downstairs the door slammed, and footsteps pounded the kitchen floor, more than just Will's. He'd been out all day, neither of us knew where, and he called, "I'm home," said something we couldn't hear, called again, "Where is everybody?" There was some loud laughter I didn't recognize.

Aunt Aggy leaned her head out into the hall, and shouted, "Up here."

"Tell him not to track mud," I said. Like she'd care, since I was the only one who mopped, but it sounded better coming from her instead of me.

Instead she yelled, "Come see your sister."

"No!" I reached behind my neck to get at the zipper, but Aunt Aggy grabbed my arm.

"You look gorgeous," she said.

And exactly like our dead mother, I wanted to say, but there were footsteps already coming up the stairs, matching the thump-thump of my heart. What if he freaked out? I was almost used to Aunt Aggy half-falling apart a couple of times a week, almost used to my own never-ending tears, but Will never cried or panicked. I would feel terrible if me looking like Mama was the thing that made him fall apart.

Will got to the doorway, and I saw his eyes go straight to the garbage bags, the upside-down drawers on the floor, the piles of hangers, the pushed-aside chairs. And then me, standing at the dressing table, Aunt Aggy behind me, her arm around my shoulder. "Look at your sister in your mother's dress," she said.

He stared hard at me. Maybe his jaw clenched a bit, and he lightly kicked one wet adidas against the bottom of the door a couple of times. I felt oddly disappointed; didn't he notice that I looked exactly like Mama?

Then Joe Fry came up, peered around him, and our eyes locked as he saw me, saw only me in that red dress, and no one spoke until finally Will laughed, an abrupt, hoarse snort, and Aunt Aggy said, "Like a Band-Aid, Will. I thought this would be best," and Will tromped downstairs. I held Joe Fry's gaze for another long minute, which, when you thought about it, didn't mean much other than two people staring at each other, and then he thumped downstairs after Will, and I felt like I could breathe again, though I hadn't noticed I wasn't.

Aunt Aggy's eyes glistened with tears. "I can't get over it," she said.

"You keep the dress," I said.

She shook her head, leaned over and picked up my T-shirt and Levi's, draped them over one arm. "Like Annie. It's yours." She tossed my clothes on Mama's bed. "We'll finish up tomorrow. Or the day after. Or never."

I nodded, still looking at myself in the mirror. I thought about Joe Fry, and when I smiled, I saw exactly where Mama had told me to stroke blush.

JOE FRY stayed for supper, but he hardly talked, except in a low voice to Will, mostly about baseball. Aunt Aggy told a long, meandering story about a dream she'd had last night where she was standing at an easel on the top of a mountain, looking out over the whole world . . . but the world was in black and white, "just like an old movie," and as soon as she touched her paintbrush to the canvas, color sprang forth, "and that's when I knew I had to dedicate my life to being an *artiste*." I was embarrassed by how Aunt Aggy rambled, but Will seemed to be listening intently, and Joe Fry even asked a question.

I couldn't catch Joe looking at me, but I felt he was, the way a cat watches one person in a crowded room. I wasn't wearing the red dress, and I had cleaned off the makeup with Mama's Noxzema, but still Aunt Aggy stared nonstop, and Joe Fry had never stayed to supper before. I was surprised by how polite he was, actually draping his napkin across one knee, which prompted Will to do the same.

Anyone but Will would be mad at me or ask about that dress or want to know what was going to happen to Mama's room now. But he sat across from me, cutting his minute steak into neat little squares, eating them one by one. He always completely finished something before going on to the next thing. I waited for him to speak, but Joe was talking about the Boston Red Sox, catching my eye midsentence. My stomach flopped, and I pushed away my plate, letting Aunt Aggy scold about wasting food, and Will couldn't say anything even if he had wanted to.

Finally, dessert. Will stuck a cookie in his mouth, grabbed three more. Joe thanked Aunt Aggy for supper, and he and Will banged through the screen door. I started to carry my plate to the sink but paused to watch Will and Joe standing next to Joe's car. Joe slouched against the hood, both hands in his pockets. Will was eating a cookie. They were looking up at the sky, and Will pointed at something I couldn't see. I couldn't imagine what it was.

Aunt Aggy set dirty dishes on the counter. "I don't know. Will and that boy. You and that boy."

I watched Joe Fry laugh at something Will had said or done. He threw his head all the way back when he laughed. I'd never noticed that before. A thin line of dark hair edged the neckline of his Led Zeppelin T-shirt.

"You're not listening; you're Annie all over again." She started crying.

I put my arms around her. "I'm listening." I heard a car door slam and then the roar of Joe Fry's Mustang pulling out of our driveway fast and hard. I held Aunt Aggy and thought about flying down the dark highway in that car with Joe Fry. Thought about how I'd tilt the rearview mirror my way, slowly sliding Crushed Cherry lipstick across my mouth, pulling a tissue from my purse to blot my lips with a kiss, thinking of Joe, the used-up tissue fluttering out the open window like a white flag.

AFTER I did the dishes, I dragged out my chemistry book and turned to the inside cover where the periodic table of the elements was printed. It was so tidy. The lines were very straight and orderly. Every number meant something. Atomic mass. Atomic number. Groups. Periods. Some kid in Mexico could be looking at the periodic table this very minute and he'd see the same numbers. Maybe there was a different way to say "carbon" in Spanish, but it was still the same thing: one of the building blocks for the whole world.

Will came inside, carrying both his new baseball glove and his old one. "Let's play catch, Baby Sister."

Being alone with my brother. Not like we would talk about chemistry. I closed my book, though up until then, I had been concentrating pretty well. "I thought you guys left."

"He did, not me," Will said.

"So where were you?"

"Just sitting outside." His voice was quiet; I had to lean forward to hear him.

"It's funny how you and Joe are suddenly friends," I said, my face blushing to hear myself say "Joe."

He shrugged. "Want to play catch or not?" He tossed the old glove on the table, and it landed on my chemistry book. His name was written in faded Magic Marker across the thumb. This was the glove Mama and I had picked out for his tenth birthday six years ago, and his handwriting still looked the same.

I put my hand in the glove, not sure why I was hesitating. "Isn't it getting dark?"

"Scared of the dark?" he asked. "Afraid of ghosts?"

So I followed him outside to the backyard. The grass was heavy with the day's rain and needed to be cut, Will's job that he wasn't doing anymore. The sky was gray-blue, and already several early stars were out, so I couldn't make a wish on the first star of the night, but I did anyway, just in case. A cardinal in the apple tree hurried his last song of the day.

Will started, throwing the ball to me nice and easy. When I went to his baseball games, I'd hear people saying things like, "That boy might have what it takes." Will was good at football and basketball and pretty much any athletic thing, but he loved baseball best. "The rhythm of it," he had said when I'd asked why.

He'd taught me how to throw ("No sister of mine is going to throw like a girl"), and we used to play catch all the time. He could play for hours. Sometimes Mama would sit on the picnic table and count how many throws it took to make Will get tired. The record was 3,437 one August afternoon. She brought out cherry Popsicles afterward, the kind with double sticks that you were supposed to break in half, though she always let us eat the whole thing.

Will didn't say anything for a while, but finally, when it was so dark that the ball startled me every time it came hurtling at me, he said, "All that stuff of hers. You just shoved it in bags."

It was too dark to see his face across the yard, so I couldn't tell if he was angry. His voice didn't exactly sound mad. I held on to the ball, rubbed my finger over the seams. "Aunt Aggy says that's better for us."

"It's all we have left of her," he said.

"Those things aren't Mama," I said. "They're just things."

"Throw the ball," he said, and I did. Then he didn't say anything as we tossed the ball back and forth in the dark, remarkably accurately considering, and I thought about what I had said. Were they just things? Or did putting them all together like that add up to Mama? I'd worn her clothes and makeup, but I wasn't her.

I was waiting for the ball. "Hey." I slapped my fist in my glove.

He shouted, "Nothing will ever be the same again."

The ball came at me, way over my head, and crashed deep into the raspberry bushes along the fence behind me. I was pretty sure he'd thrown high on purpose. "No way I'll find the ball," I said, unwilling to shout back and start a fight.

"I don't want to do this anymore." I heard him walking through the grass, saw him, a dark, blurry shadow.

A breeze drifted across my face, making the sweat there suddenly cool. I had never kept secrets from Will before. Now I had two: Mama's voice, the train. "What about this?" I called. "What we're doing, playing catch. The two of us. This is almost the same."

The screen door creaked open. "Almost isn't 'the same,' " he said, and the door banged shut.

The ball, the gloves, the sound of the ball hitting the gloves; the yard we'd grown up in, with the apple tree in the back Mama had taught us to climb, the high wooden fence, the trellis where Aunt Aggy planted beans every year, and the clothesline behind the garage; the squares of light shining from the windows of the house, our house; Iowa, bland small-town Iowa with the neighbors who knew us or knew of us or knew our mother or great aunt or our long-dead grandparents; the stars sprinkled across the sky above our small town; me and Will and Aunt Aggy and Mama—only one thing had changed and suddenly everything there was and everything I could imagine was different. The school principal had said I would be fine in a year. Was that possible?

I pressed the glove against my face, inhaled its leathery mustiness, closed my eyes, breathed slowly and deliberately. Hydrogen, helium, lithium, beryllium, boron, carbon, nitrogen, oxygen, fluorine, neon. There was a beauty, a poetry, a deep, scary thing I'd never seen, never felt, and all I could do was keep breathing, and speak out loud: "Hydrogen, helium, lithium, beryllium, boron, carbon, nitrogen, oxygen, fluorine, neon," over and over, and Mama's voice joined me; how long did I stand there? It would've been all night—no one thought to call me inside—but the rain started up again, soft and slow like warm breath, then harder, then pouring down buckets. "H_2O," Mama whispered as I ran into the dark kitchen, locking the door behind me. And, yes, it was H_2O, but truly what it was was rain.

A WEEK later, Mama's room was all the way cleared out and cleaned up. We didn't throw away anything or donate it to the church rummage sale; instead we piled those garbage bags and cardboard boxes and the furniture in the basement, filling up the corner room we ran to during tornado warnings. Will didn't help.

I dragged Mama's dressing table and all her makeup into my room before Aunt Aggy could announce she planned to store paints there. I looked at Mama's lipsticks and sometimes put one on when I was by myself; my favorite part was kissing the tissue and crumpling it up. I decided that what lipstick tasted like was Mama, the way you felt when Mama kissed you in the dark when she thought you were asleep.

Also, a week later, I could recite the periodic table by heart. (Mr. Miller had said I could ignore those new elements at the end since they weren't naturally occurring: "Those are for nuclear scientists," he had said, scornful.) When I got to uranium, Mr. Miller pressed his palms together, chest level, as if he were praying, and seemed about to cry. Then he sprang wide his arms, like opening up into a hug, but he didn't hug me. "Now you know something truly remarkable, Alice," Mr. Miller said.

Did I?

It was at least another two weeks before I stopped sneaking into the basement at night, poking through the bags and boxes of Mama's things a second, third, and fourth time, fluttering open the pages of the books and magazines, sticking my hand in every pocket, looking for whatever it was that each of us secretly knew had to, simply HAD to be somewhere in Mama's things—but wasn't.

SLUMBER PARTY

ON the last day of school, Mr. Rhinehart called me into his office to tell me how I'd gotten a tough break but that I was one of the lucky few who made lemonade from lemons. It might have been a nice speech except that he read it straight out of a book. And every teacher pulled me aside to whisper that they had given me an A, murmuring something like, "You have enough to worry about." Summer vacation was going to be a relief: I could stop pretending I didn't notice how people stared at the floor when I passed them in the hallway, that they hunched over their lunch trays and silently examined their sloppy joes when I walked down the cafeteria aisle, that no one except Becky invited me to the movies or shopping. Now and then, Paula Elam might say hi in the second-floor bathroom, but only if she needed me to move away from the mirror so she could brush her hair. Mostly people were afraid, like they thought their mother might die, too, if they talked to me.

The first week of summer was easy enough: I weeded the garden, gave the house a real spring cleaning, baked five dozen brownies for the bake sale to raise money for Will's baseball team (all sold in a snap, thanks to Dotty King's secret recipe that called for Hershey's syrup), played an all-day game of war by myself with four decks of cards, and bought new spices after Dotty King explained that spices lost their zip after a year. "I replace my whole spice rack on my birthday, which is June ninth," she said. "I'd be sadder than sad if my rhubarb pies weren't their absolute rhubarbiest with pinches of allspice and cloves from spanking-fresh bottles."

But the second week dragged out dull and sad. I used to love summers because I'd help Mama take on projects, like making strawberry jam, molding sand candles, writing a murder mystery set in Shelby, learning how to fox-trot, and reading all the books in the library about a particular subject like coral reefs or Joan of Arc or Alaska. We'd already discussed projects for this summer; it was something she liked talking about on those long, dark, snowy days when she said simply getting out of bed each morning was an act of courage: learning to play croquet like experts and looking up all the *National Geographics* at the library as far back as they went and sewing new curtains for the bedrooms and making curry. She was always saying that each summer was probably going to be the last, but I couldn't imagine a summer without Mama and her projects. "You'll be busy chasing boys and sneaking cigarettes and I'll be here all alone," she had said.

Aunt Aggy was way too busy to spend time with me (not that we had spent much time together in the past). Mr. Cooper's crotchety old father had finally died after ten years of telling everyone it would be a miracle if he lasted the week, and she was supervising the rehaul of the house—new furniture, wallpaper, carpet, appliances—"adding that special feminine touch" (except to the room with the beer can collection). I worried about what would happen to me and Will if Aunt Aggy married Mr. Cooper, but Will scoffed, saying, "They're too strange to get married." Maybe he was right—Aunt Aggy was serious about being an artist. She constantly wore a moth-eaten beret and refused to wash paint splatters off her hands because she said true artists had a rainbow of colors under their fingernails. It was hard to believe that if Leonardo da Vinci's hands were clean, no one would've known he was an artist, but Aunt Aggy was so certain. Along with her how-to-paint books, she read books about artists' lives, sharing tidbits like, "When Chagall first got to art school, he was the only one to paint in purple."

I went to Will's baseball games. He was batting .456 and people predicted that couldn't last the season . . . but what if it did? Every time Will was up to bat, he seemed to become a bigger, taller, stronger version of himself, a stranger. I sat behind home plate, so I saw the opposing pitchers realizing the same thing: My brother wasn't going to stay a boy forever; maybe he wasn't even a boy anymore. Baseball games and practices were about the only times I saw Will because he'd gotten a job as usher at the movie theater. Joe Fry was doing summer maintenance at the school, making double minimum wage because he had an in with Mr. Liebbe, the janitor; "That's the job to have," Will said, "not this glamour job: tearing tickets and mopping kids' barf." But working at the theater seemed glamorous to me: He was the first to scope who was dating, broken up, or cheating. He wore a necktie and ate popcorn for free. He called previews "trailers," and he even got to stand on a big ladder to put the letters on the marquee on Thursdays, when the movie changed. Kathy Clark still called, but now I could tell her where he was: "Baseball tonight," or "movie theater." Sometimes I saw her at the games; she sat along first base and kept score in the program. Usually she was with a group of other seniors, cheerleaders or the girls who ran the pep club. I wished Will was nicer to her, but I was afraid to say anything. Lately he was always snapping at me to mind my own business. I was glad I hadn't told him about Mama's voice or Chicago.

I was terrified I'd spend the whole summer by myself, so what a relief when Linda Johnson called to invite me last minute to a surprise slumber party for Becky. Even though Linda had been my second-best friend since fifth grade, she was one of the worst about head ducking and lunch-tray hunching. Whenever I talked to her, she'd mumble, "Oh, um, hi," like she'd forgotten my name, or she'd give me a wide, fake smile that looked carved across her face like a jack-o'-lantern's. Her family was perfect—father, mother, two boys, two girls, dog, cat, and four fish. Linda was the oldest, sure to end up homecoming queen when we were seniors. Her father was mayor, and her mother was president of the PTA, and when she was our age, she had been the pork queen for the state, not just Henry County. One brother played the violin like someone in a real orchestra, and her sister had won the Iowa spelling bee and a free trip to Washington, D.C.

I was happy to hear about the slumber party even though it was the next night. "It's not a surprise anymore," Linda said. "Becky found out and asked if you were invited. I told her we didn't know if you were still in mourning, or what."

"I was never in mourning," I said.

"You know, because your mother . . ." Long pause.

Killed herself. Like I'd forgotten. Still, I really wanted to go to the party, so I smiled, which turned my voice smiley: "I can go."

"In *Gone With the Wind*, Scarlett wasn't supposed to go to the ball because she was in mourning."

"I'm not in mourning," I snapped. It was impossible to shake an idea out of Linda's head.

"So you're all better now?" she asked.

"I'm fine."

"And how's Will?" She loved talking about how cute he was; she'd already picked out names for their four children.

"Fine."

"I saw him with Joe Fry the other night. Since when do they hang out?"

My heart pumped a little extra whenever I heard his name. Becky said he'd call eventually, that boys did things their way, on their own schedule, as annoying as that was. She said I should stop wearing sweatpants around the house, I shouldn't answer the phone on the first ring or it would seem like I was waiting for his call, and I should have three topics of conversation ready so I could chat easily. Becky knew these things because she had an older sister who also gave advice about Mr. Miller.

I twisted the phone cord in my hand. Why was Will hanging out with Joe all of a sudden? I had never actually asked him. Looking at Joe, with all that long hair, you'd think he was nothing but trouble, always in the principal's office. And he was. But also he was one of the best catchers the baseball team had ever had. Joe barely went to class, but Will said he was really smart. He had never been a bully, but everyone was a little afraid of him. I was, a little. Joe wouldn't worry about people in the cafeteria not saying hi to him.

"Hello?" Linda sounded impatient. "Anyone there?"

I said, "They're both playing senior Babe Ruth baseball."

"Everyone knows what Joe's like," Linda said. "Will should be careful."

"What do you mean, everyone knows what Joe's like?" I could guess what she'd say.

"You know," she said. "Wild. Crazy. The kind of guy who gets girls pregnant."

I twisted the phone cord harder, let it snap free. "Who did he get pregnant?"

There was a silence, then Linda said, "No one. Yet. But people say it's only a matter of time. And they'll start thinking Will's like that too."

I listened to myself breathe, in, out, then slowed it down, innnnn, ooooout.

Linda said, "I'm just trying to help. You don't want people gossiping about your family more than they already do."

I wanted to be mad, but Linda was right. People did gossip about us; maybe I would, too, if I were someone else. I thought about going to a Saturday-night movie with Joe and everyone watching me follow him to seats in the dark, back corner, and what people would say: "Ever since that crazy mother killed herself, those kids have run wild."

Mama's voice startled me: "Gossip is empty air blowing through empty people."

Easy for her to say; she didn't know what it was like to walk into the grocery store and see people point and whisper behind cupped hands. I said, "Joe's not that bad."

"If that's the kind of girl you are." I could just about hear Linda tossing her head, flipping all that blond hair and it falling back into perfect place. "Anyway, come over at seven-thirty," and though she was a gossip who didn't know much about me or what it was like to have a not-perfect family, I was happy she'd invited me to her party: It meant I could be part of the real world again and that my summer was going to turn out fine.

THERE WERE six girls at the slumber party: me, Linda, Becky, Pam Kessler (whose father owned Kessler's Restaurant downtown; people said he'd stolen his pork tenderloin recipe from the White Front Café, which his brother-in-law owned); Denise Hendershot (the shortest girl in our class; her mother was taller than her father, and everyone said that's how come he was always roaring way too fast down Broad Street on that ridiculous motorcycle), and Lily Pfister (whose mother took in every stray cat in town).

Linda's mother had made snacks that looked straight out of a *Family Circle* article about "teen parties"—hot-dog chunks wrapped in refrigerator crescent-roll dough, polka-dotted with circles of green olives; cottontail bunny canned pears (dyed pink with food color), with cottage cheese tails, slivered almond ears, cinnamon red-hot candy eyes, nestled on individual lettuce leaves; ants-on-a-log (peanut butter–filled celery with raisins on top); a watermelon that had been hollowed out and carved in the shape of a whale filled with little balls of watermelon, honeydew, and cantaloupe.

Everything was perfectly perfect. Paper plates matched the paper cups that matched the napkins and the paper tablecloth, the fanned-out tissue-paper watermelon centerpiece, and the pink-and-green twisted streamers Scotch-taped from the corners of the basement ceiling and strung throughout the room. Mrs. Johnson took several pictures of the whole setup before she let us pick up a paper plate, making Linda shift the candlesticks to several different locations as she snapped photos, finally deciding to leave them where they had started, in the middle of the table. "Mom, will you scram already?" Linda said, but Mrs. Johnson smiled and took close-ups of the food.

Linda's basement wasn't like my basement, crammed with old boxes, an ice-cold floor, spiders, and that corner room filled with plastic garbage bags of Mama's clothes. Mr. Johnson had finished this basement himself, putting up wood paneling over the cement-brick walls, laying down floor tiles that matched up evenly, moving down the old living room set, placing ceiling tiles that were soundproof (except for the footsteps of people upstairs in the kitchen), arranging carpet remnants they'd gotten a good deal on from the biggest furniture store in Cedar Rapids when they'd bought the brand-new living room set. It was the perfect place to have a slumber party. There was even an extension phone so we could make crank hang-up calls in private.

Mrs. Johnson looked at the back of the camera to see how much film was left. "How about one of you girls?" She lined us up behind the card table of food. "Say cheese," she said, smiling brightly.

"Chee-eese," we droned. The flashcube went off, and I blinked away purple dots.

"These are the best days of your lives," Mrs. Johnson said, tucking a piece of frosted blond hair back where it was supposed to go, behind her ear. Linda opened her mouth, but before she could say anything, Mrs. Johnson spoke again, her usual bright chirp: "Yes, Linda, I'm going," and she smiled in the forced way we'd smiled for the photo, then headed upstairs.

Linda flipped back her hair, shook her head. "Let's eat," she said, taking the top paper plate off the stack. "She'll be back for cake, but then she'll be gone for good." A sudden silence wedged into the room; everyone stared at me. Linda said, "Oh, sorry, Alice. I didn't mean it like that."

My face was as pink as the bunny rabbit pears. I slid a bunny rabbit off the tray and set it on a paper plate though I didn't like canned pears.

Becky breathed on her glasses, wiped them clean with her patchwork blouse. "Maybe these are the best days of our lives. I've heard people say that."

Linda said, "She's just crabby because she's got her period."

So we ate and talked, which eventually led into who we wanted to marry. Linda instantly said Will and just flipped her hair when Pam reminded her that Will was already dating the nicest girl in school. Becky said Mr. Miller. Denise said Mark Lunde (the boy she'd dated forever; they couldn't stand side by side without their arms wrapped around each other's waist). Lily said Doug Foltz (who'd dumped her last month). Pam said Lee Majors, which got us arguing about whether that counted, since obviously a TV star like the Six-Million-Dollar Man wasn't ever coming to Shelby to meet her, let alone marry her.

Then it was my turn. Becky knew about Joe Fry, but that didn't mean I wanted the whole world to know—which was what happened when you told anything to Linda. Since Mama was always talking about James Dean, I said, "James Dean."

"A dead movie star?" Pam said.

Everyone stared at me. Again.

"He doesn't count," Linda said. "He's dead."

There was a moment of silence. All I could think about was not crying. Then Becky said, "My mother said she used to be wild about James
Dean. All the girls were."

"I think she's holding out," Pam said. "Who does Alice really like?"

Linda flipped her hair. "I know how to get the truth." She started
stacking everyone's dirty plates and cups as she lowered her voice into a
spooky whisper: "Better than truth or dare." She shoved the stack of used
paper plates into a wastebasket with a decoupage rose on the side (made
by Mrs. Johnson) and flipped off the overhead lights. Shadows appeared
on the wall, cast by the lamp in the far corner and the candles on the card
table. It felt like the moment in a scary movie where the ax murderer tiptoes in, so when the upstairs door opened and Mrs. Johnson's voice
called out, "Ready for cake?," we all jumped. Linda sighed and turned the
lights on, murmured, "She's a pain," then shouted, "Okay, Mom!"

A flurry of footsteps tapped across the kitchen floor; the refrigerator
door whooshed open, silverware clinked.

"My mom won't let me have parties because the noise makes her
head pound for a week," Pam said.

Denise said, "My mother would shove fish sticks and Tater Tots in
the oven and complain that—"

"Stop it," Becky interrupted. Everyone stared, like I was a poor little
kitten in a cage.

I quickly said, "My mother was a pain too."

Becky patted my shoulder. "Of course she wasn't."

She was! I wanted to cry. Letting dirty dishes stack up when she
didn't feel like washing them; having Will call her boss at the *Beacon* to
tell him she was too sick to go in when really she just wanted to stay
home and read magazines; constantly losing library books. Now that
voice and her secrets. Not that I could say any of this.

"Cake!" Mrs. Johnson called, and her footsteps thumped the uncar-
peted stairs. She carried a large silver tray with an angel food cake coated
in creamy pink peaks of Cool Whip, sprinkled with slivered almonds.
Sixteen burning candles flickered as Mrs. Johnson walked toward us, that

bright smile on her face. A camera dangled from a strap off her wrist. "I took pictures of the cake upstairs, so we can start singing!" She led us in "Happy Birthday," then said, "Make a wish!," and the flashcube went off several times as Becky blew out every last candle with one long breath. She had that dreamy, Mr. Miller look on her face, so we all knew what she wished for.

Mrs. Johnson cut big pieces of cake, sliding them onto matching dessert paper plates. Finally she sliced a sliver for herself and sat on the sofa, crossing her legs neatly at the ankles. Her back was straight. Mrs. Johnson said, "So, what are you talking about? Boys?"

"Nothing." Linda sighed so heavily that her bangs flew up off her face.

Mrs. Johnson said, "You don't have to tell me; I know all about slumber parties. I'm not some old granny." She finished her cake and scraped the side of her fork along the plate to get the rest of the Cool Whip smears.

"What do you talk about at bridge parties?" Pam asked.

Mrs. Johnson laughed. "I suppose we still talk about boys—but now they're our husbands."

"You gossip." Becky licked Cool Whip off the bottom of a candle.

"Perhaps a tiny bit of gossip sneaks in, try as we do to stay away from that sort of thing," Mrs. Johnson said.

Mama said, "That bunch of cackling hens." Mama didn't go to bridge parties; sometimes ladies invited her, but she made excuses. I had told her both Mrs. Johnson and Mrs. Mann thought it was strange that she wouldn't go—I'd overheard them talking at Becky's house, saying Mama was stuck-up and thought she was too good to play cards—and Mama had only said, "Not every woman is the bridge-party type." Then she peered closely at my face and said, "Are you, Alice?" I was only twelve, so what was I supposed to think? My friends' mothers loved their bridge parties; Mrs. Mann was teaching Becky how to play bridge, and Becky tried to teach me, but she wasn't that good herself so I couldn't get the hang of it, though Becky and I both really liked the word "trump." Why couldn't Mama just play cards with them once in a while?

Linda grabbed her mother's empty plate, stuffed it in the wastebasket, stood for a moment with her hands on her hips. "Aren't you going upstairs?"

"Yes, Linda." Mrs. Johnson stood up, and I had a feeling she didn't want to go, that if Linda wasn't rushing around, stacking serving trays and grabbing everyone's paper plates, Mrs. Johnson would sit on that couch for a good long while and maybe never go back to her upstairs that was as perfect as her downstairs.

Mrs. Johnson smiled so broadly it must have hurt her face. "Alice, dear, would you help me carry a few things?" and she said it so smoothly that I was picking up the cake tray and following her up the stairs before I realized why she had picked me.

"So, Alice," Mrs. Johnson said in that terribly sympathetic voice I had come to hate, with its pity and nosiness. "How are you doing?"—that you-can-tell-me pause—"Really?"

"Fine," I said, and she didn't say anything except, "That's good," as we got to the top of the stairs, went on into the kitchen. Maybe that would be all. I set the cake tray on the counter and turned to head back downstairs, but she handed me the stack of serving trays and bowls she'd been carrying. I glanced around, but there was no more room on the counter.

She started jabbing toothpicks in the top of the leftover cake. It was one of Dotty King's tricks, so you could drape Saran Wrap over your cake without wrecking the frosting. Did Mrs. Johnson listen to Dotty King?

She put the cake in the refrigerator, then took the stack of trays out of my hands and set them in the sink, ran water over everything. "I love my new garbage disposal," she said. "Mr. Johnson put it in for my birthday." She flipped a switch on the wall, and a grinding noise filled the silence. When she turned off the disposal, she asked, "How are things at home?"

"Fine."

"Tell me if that great-aunt of yours isn't taking good care of you. I've seen her wearing that ridiculous beret around Hy-Vee. Mr. Johnson can speak to some people and find a more satisfactory arrangement if need be." She tipped the dirty water out of the top bowl, then flipped the disposal switch, let it grind. "Washing dishes is sure easy with this lovely disposal."

I spoke over the noise: "Everything's fine. Aunt Aggy is fine."

"This thing could take a hand off." Then she flipped off the switch and the water. "We were so shocked," she said. "We couldn't stop talking about it, wondering why, if—" She touched my arm. Her fingers were surprisingly cold. "Your mother wasn't much like the rest of us, was she?"

Mama cut in: "That's what they like to think."

Mrs. Johnson went on: "Fitting in is so important. Everything is simpler that way." She reached under the sink and pulled out a pair of yellow rubber gloves. "I tried with her, I really did. Invited her to bridge parties, begged her to chair the PTA bake sale committee. I told her no one gave it a second thought that she was the only one with no husband. But it was like she deliberately didn't want to belong. Walking around that old graveyard at night, the clothes she wore, that fire-engine-red lipstick to go grocery shopping. Well, what can you do with someone like that? Someone who doesn't care if they fit in or not." She grabbed a dry sponge from the counter, ran water over it, wrung it, soaked it, wrung it. "Not giving one thought to appearances. How is someone like that?" She paused like it was a real question I should answer, stared down at the pink sponge in her hand.

I shook my head, shrugged one shoulder. It felt disloyal listening to Mrs. Johnson say those things about my mother, but pretending Mama had been perfect the way Becky wanted to wasn't right either. Anyway, it was true: Mama never cared about those kinds of appearances. That's why our front-yard bushes were tangly and overgrown, and the Johnsons' were trimmed so flat on top they looked like a table. Not one thing was out of place over here. Sure, the kitchen was filled with messy, dirty dishes now, but within the hour, they'd all be washed, dried, and returned to the cupboards, ready for breakfast the next morning, then lunch, supper, and so on, every day tidy and organized and perfect.

Mrs. Johnson rubbed the sponge too hard along the surface of a serving tray, back and forth. "I remember your mother always talking about running away from Shelby, but I never thought she'd be brave enough to go and do it. What surprised me was that she came back. She always seemed to want something more back then, something different. I remember once I found her notebook she'd left in the cafeteria, filled with page after page of tiny doodled stars, like her thoughts were that far from here. I was just amazed—pages and pages, all in red ink." Suddenly Mrs. Johnson drew in a deep breath, spoke firmly: "If there's one thing I've learned in this life, Alice, it's that the way to get through is to fit in. Simple as that." She tilted the other tray and let the leftover bunny rabbit pears slide off, shoving them down the drain with a fork. Then she flipped the disposal switch and ground them up, though she should know they'd keep fine overnight in the fridge. Mrs. Johnson continued, "People who don't fit in end up with secrets. That's what happened to your mother. And look what—" There was a pause, and she quickly added, "Of course, your mother wasn't like the rest of us. She was—not like the rest of us."

"She wants to say crazy," Mama said. "But she knows that's not true."

Mrs. Johnson seemed so certain. All those stars. Of course it wasn't her mother we were talking about. I said, "She wasn't crazy."

"Of course not, dear!" Mrs. Johnson spoke in that fast, stricken way adults did when they were embarrassed you had figured them out. But then she wrapped me up in a tight hug, careful not to touch me with the rubber gloves. Up close she smelled like a mixture of skin lotion and hair spray. "You know how to fit in, don't you, Alice? You're lucky that way," and it seemed strange to hear myself called "lucky" by someone like her.

Mama rudely butted in: "You have a secret, Alice."

"Come on!" Linda called from the basement.

Mrs. Johnson stepped away, though I could've hugged her longer, forever. Was it awful to wish she were my mother? Maybe that's what she meant when she said Mr. Johnson could speak to people; she could adopt me into her perfect family.

"Remember what I said about fitting in." She smiled, not the say-cheese smile, but a tiny smile that made her look wise or sad or both.

I wanted to ask why Mama came back to Shelby if she was so brave, but Mrs. Johnson flipped on the garbage disposal, and Linda called again, so I headed down the stairs. The overhead lights were off again, and my eyes had to adjust to the shadowed dimness after the bright kitchen.

Becky sounded nervous: "Linda has a Ouija board."

"That she secretly ordered from the Sears catalog," Denise added.

"My mom would kill me," Linda said. "She thinks it's bad luck to mess with ghosts."

"Maybe it is," I said.

Linda yanked me to where the others sat cross-legged in a circle on the carpet. The Ouija board was in the middle, printed with all the letters of the alphabet and the numbers from zero to nine, the words YES and NO in opposite corners, and centered across the bottom, GOOD-BYE. Lily was sliding the spade-shaped plastic pointer back and forth to the letters of her name, her thumb smack in the middle of the round glassy "eye." It was hard to believe that spirits would come from wherever spirits were to spell out our future with this crummy piece of plastic.

Becky said, "I heard about girls who did Ouija at a slumber party and they accidentally called up evil spirits instead of good ones. The pointer zigzagged all over the board, spelling dirty words. Then my cousin's friend's sister started screaming, trying to strangle one of the other girls. The dad had to pull her off. She's still in the hospital, and they tie her arms to her bed with rope every night. People say she's possessed by the devil."

There was a brief silence. Lily snatched her hand off the pointer. It sat there, unmoving, on the letter E until Linda pushed it over to G for "good."

Pam snorted. "Sears wouldn't sell Ouija boards if girls were strangling each other."

Linda picked at a tiny scab on her knee. "Alice can call to the spirit world since her mom's dead."

Becky said, "Linda!" She sounded like a mother who's had just about enough.

Everyone stared at me for what seemed like the millionth time. I looked down at the Ouija board, at the tiny reflection of the candles on the card table in the pointer's round eye. Could you really get your questions answered? Could I reach my mother? Dinky print on the box said, "For amusement purposes only."

"Alice doesn't want to," Becky said.

"Yes, I do," I said, before realizing that I did.

Nobody said anything, not even Linda, who looked down at the floor. She abruptly flicked a crumb across the room with her thumb and forefinger. Then she folded her arms across her chest. It was so quiet I heard Becky's watch. There were a couple of footsteps in the kitchen, then nothing but that quick tick-tick.

Linda unfolded her arms and stretched out her hands to each side like a priest doing "Our Father." She didn't sound very sure of herself as she said, "Everyone hold hands or it won't work." I was sitting between Linda and Becky, and I grabbed their hands; Becky's was sweaty and Linda's was as cool as her mother's had been. When we were all holding hands, Linda whispered, "Go ahead, Alice."

"What am I supposed to say?"

She spoke in her normal, bossy voice. "Say we want the guidance of good spirits to help us understand the secrets of life and the human heart."

"Close your eyes," Denise said, and everyone did. I looked around the circle. Why was it okay to call forth my mother with a piece of plastic on a Ouija board but not okay to tell people I was hearing her voice? The whole thing was ridiculous—like Mama would play Ouija by the rules. She hated rules.

I spoke slowly: "Good spirits, we beseech you, come to us here in Linda's basement. We look for you to reveal the mysterious secrets of the world. Good spirits, answer our questions—show us the truth—of the mind, the heart." I paused and listened to everyone breathing. Then I let my voice drop into a whisper—"We humbly seek a sign of your presence"—as I inched one leg sideways, toward a card table chair I planned to kick over. But right then the door at the top of the stairs slammed shut, and everyone shrieked and opened their eyes. No one let go of anyone's hand; Becky clutched mine even tighter.

A moment later, Linda said, "Probably my mother."

"I didn't hear footsteps in the kitchen," Lily said.

Becky said, "We shouldn't be doing this."

"Go on, Alice," Linda whispered.

I let go of Linda's and Becky's hands and balanced my forefingers on the plastic pointer, one on each side of the eye. "Is there a spirit in the room?" I asked in a hushed voice.

Everyone stared but nothing happened. Then the pointer slowly slid to the word YES. I pulled the pointer back to the center of the board. "Are you a good spirit?"

Lily held her breath, and Becky bit her lip. The pointer inched to YES, and everyone started shouting questions: "Ask if Doug Foltz still likes me"; "Does Mr. Miller think I'm cute?" Linda's voice rose above the rest: "Start with Alice. Who's she going to marry?"

"I'm not asking that," I said.

"Then I will," and she nudged my fingers off the pointer, and put on her own. "Who is Alice going to marry?" I crossed my arms. Didn't they know I had been guiding the pointer? It was a game, something "for amusement purposes only." Like Mama was going to perform tricks at a slumber party.

"Look," Becky said. "J."

Sure enough, the pointer had moved to the letter J—a coincidence, of course—but then it went to O and E. "Stop it," I said, and I pushed Linda's fingers off the pointer.

Linda said, "Joe Fry," like she was accusing me of something.

"I think he's cute," Becky said.

Lily grimaced. "He's scary."

"He's not scary," I said.

Linda shook back her hair and leaned in as she spoke: "I heard Joe Fry got a girl kicked out of her sorority up in Iowa City because he stayed overnight in her room."

"Don't be such a gossip, Linda." Becky spoke in that disgusted-mom voice again.

But Linda continued: "He grows his own pot that he sells in the school parking lot. Everyone knows his brother's a draft dodger. Plus he was in a porno movie—"

"That's not true!" I cried.

Linda grabbed the Ouija pointer. "Was Joe Fry in a porno movie?" and the pointer immediately slid to YES.

"You pushed it," I said.

"My turn," Becky said, and pulled the pointer away from Linda.

"Will I marry Mr. Miller?" What a surprise that the pointer zipped to YES before she got all the words out.

Denise said, "It doesn't count if you ask the question and work the spirit guide." She pushed the pointer back to me. "Alice should do it."

"Why me?" No one looked at me—they stared at the floor, the ceiling, the walls. "Because my mother is dead?" No one spoke. "Do you actually believe my dead mother is here in this room? That she's a spirit you can call up, like we've got her phone number?" Still, no one spoke.

The bulb in the lamp flashed and fizzled out, leaving only the flickering light of the candles on the card table. Linda whispered, "Let's ask something serious."

"No!" Becky said sharply.

"Ask," I said, placing my fingers on the pointer.

Linda smiled, the candlelight turning it into the smile I'd seen on her mother, the sad, wise smile I couldn't figure out. Her voice started normal but was a ragged whisper by the last word. "Is my mother happy?"

I should have been the one asking that. We watched the pointer slide partway to YES, then partway to NO, then stop on the letter R.

"What does that mean?" Linda asked, in the same uncertain whisper.

"Means this is stupid." Pam cracked her knuckles. "Let's make crank calls."

"Why'd you ask that?" Becky said to Linda.

Linda shrugged and flipped her hair. "Why not?" Her voice was back to clear and smooth, like cold water washing up over sand. "Alice, you go."

"I don't have any questions." My head was spinning with questions, but none were ones you say out loud in front of other people.

"You guys are getting creepy." Lily flopped backward on the floor, reached for a pillow off the couch and put it over her head.

"It's just a stupid game," Pam said.

"It's not like Alice's mother is actually in the room," Denise said. "I mean, actually with us." She looked around; everyone looked around. The corners of the room felt awfully dark, like anything could be hiding there.

Linda said, "Oh, please. Alice is moving the pointer herself."

"Am not," I protested.

"Hey, wait." Pam was looking at the picture on the cover of the box. "We're all supposed to have our fingers on the pointer, not just Alice." She set one finger on the pointer. Her nail was bitten way down.

Lily whispered, "Is your mother here, Alice?"

I closed my eyes. Where was Mama? She should be at home reading a magazine or cooking up a big pot of something strange like goulash, listening to Dotty King. If Mrs. Johnson were dead, she'd stay dead and not end up as some annoying voice.

"Come on, you guys," Linda said. "Fingers on the pointer. We'll ask the same question to prove Alice was pushing it."

Everyone leaned in and squeezed a finger on the pointer. Linda started to speak, but I interrupted: "Is Linda's mother happy?"

"Not that!" Linda cried. The pointer started sliding, and even after Linda snatched her finger away, it went partway to YES, then partway to NO, then settled on the letter R, the same as before.

"Oh my God," Lily said under her breath.

"Alice pushed it," Linda said, staring at the ceiling, blinking hard, about to cry.

"Alls we're doing is fighting," Becky said.

It was a ridiculous question; Linda's mother was perfectly happy. But Linda was so upset that I said, "You're right, I pushed it."

"You think this proves your dead mother is right here in the room, don't you?" Linda made each word jab faster and louder. "Well, she isn't—she's dead. And that's too bad for you, but she's never coming back, never."

My mouth dropped open, and air suddenly sucked up backward from my stomach, out of my lungs or something twisted like that, but I managed to say, "I know that," as if Linda had said something simple like *It's raining*. I had never wanted to slap someone as much as I wanted to slap Linda right that second. But I just repeated: "I know that." What was I supposed to do? If I ran up the stairs and made Mrs. Johnson drive me home, I'd never be invited to another slumber party for the rest of my life. No one would sit by me in the cafeteria, no one would say hi to me in the hall.

Denise spoke suddenly. "Ask a question only your mother could answer."

There was a silence. Then we'd know for sure. I'd finally know something.

Denise said, "Keep your finger off. We can see if she's really here."

"She's dead." My voice was so calm I didn't recognize it. "How could she be here?"

"No one thinks she's here except you," Linda said. Her voice was as calm as mine, but each word was like a separate slice of a knife. I heard Becky's watch ticking again. Someone's stomach gurgled. Linda said, "Ask."

I took a deep breath, then pushed the heels of my hands against my eyes, desperate not to cry.

"Okay, I'll ask," Linda said. "Why'd you park that car on the train tracks? Why'd you kill yourself?"

Everyone gasped, and Linda looked surprised, as if those weren't the words she'd wanted to say. But she couldn't unsay them, and without realizing it, Linda had asked the only question there was, the only question that mattered. I closed my eyes, so I didn't see everything that happened next, only heard it: Becky yelled, "That's enough," as she stomped over to the light switch, flipping on the overhead lights, making the inside of my eyelids go from black to orange. Someone threw a pillow at her that knocked into the card table. Linda shrieked, "The candles!"; someone hurried to the bathroom and ran the faucet, and I felt splashes of water on my back. Quick footsteps tapped the floor above us. The door opened, and Mrs. Johnson asked, "What's going on down there?"; Linda called, "We're fine!" More footsteps, Pam saying, "Sorry," Becky saying, "Told you this was a bad idea."

I opened my eyes and didn't look at the mess around me but at the Ouija board; I put one finger on the pointer and waited for it to move, while behind me everyone fussed and called each other stupid and discussed how long it would take Linda's mother to find the wax spots on the carpet and sofa and if there was a way to remove wax stains. Dotty King had said something about pouring hot water over tablecloths with wax drips, but I didn't tell them that. I just let them talk away, their voices filling the empty silence, waiting, still waiting for the pointer to slide, to tell me anything, even if it was only something as simple as the word GOOD-BYE.

AN HOUR later, with the mess cleaned up, the Ouija board back in the box, the box stuffed at the bottom of a garbage bag in the garage, the furniture and pillows rearranged slightly to cover up the wax stains, and Mrs. Johnson safely out of the kitchen, we finished our list of people to crank call.

"Who's going to talk?" Linda said. "Alice is best."

"She never cracks up," Lily said.

"Remember that time we called Mr. Rhinehart, and Alice sounded like an old lady and accused him of running over her poodle?" Denise said.

We ran through great moments in crank calling: the fake order of two dozen pork tenderloins from the White Front Café, telling Mrs. Lane to hold for President Ford, who had selected her as Iowa teacher of the year (she immediately hung up). We were laughing hysterically, and finally, Lily pushed me over to the phone to call her ex, Doug Foltz. As I picked up the receiver, I said, "Give me a minute to stop laughing," which we also thought was hilarious, and I stood with the phone against my ear, watching everyone laugh, feeling very normal and like I fit in just fine in spite of my dead mother. Then I heard whispering on the phone: "Did you hear something? Never mind. I missed your voice," and a man spoke, "Me too." All I heard was breathing, which made me wonder if this was real, but the man said, "She and the kids are at her sister's for the weekend. Come over," and the whisper said, "No, I can't," dragging out the word "can't" into a word of immense longing and desire, and the man said, "Meet me. Just for a minute," and the whisper said, "I can't," and the man said, "One minute," and it was really very lovers-in-movies romantic except that the next whisper was, "My daughter's slumber party. . . ," and I banged down the phone.

Becky noticed I had hung up and said, "What's wrong, Alice?"

I fake-coughed. "Throat tickle," and Denise got me a cup of water. After a few lingering coughs, I took in a deep breath and lifted the phone again. Dial tone. My breath whooshed out in relief. "What's the number again?" I asked, and this time the call went off perfectly. The other calls went well too: Mr. Rhinehart, Mr. Miller, a couple of boys from school. I thought (hoped?) someone would suggest calling Joe Fry, but no one did. Every time I picked up the phone or sat near anyone who did, I heard that whisper in my mind, felt that longing, that desire, saw that secret life I had glimpsed.

At four in the morning—after finishing the six-pack of Pabst Pam had smuggled in and watching Linda teach Denise how to blow perfect cigarette smoke rings and dancing the bump and the hustle until we were sweaty—we finally spread out our sleeping bags. As usual, Becky was the first to fall asleep, and Pam snuck upstairs and hid her bra in the freezer. Then Denise dropped off, and Pam hid her bra in the freezer. Then Pam fell asleep, but we were too lazy to take her bra upstairs, so instead Lily stretched it across a lamp shade and stuffed it into big boobs with wadded-up socks. Then Lily fell asleep—wearing her bra.

"Are you awake, Alice?" Linda said for the sixth time. Linda's voice sounded different in the dark, deeper, more like an adult voice.

I was on my back, staring up at the ceiling, but for the sixth time, I said, "Yes," and then she didn't say anything more. She hadn't exactly apologized for what had happened with the Ouija board and neither had I, but I wasn't mad anymore. I kept thinking about her mother whispering on the phone to a strange man, her mother driving her powder-blue station wagon to meet the man, like Paula Elam and the girls at school who wore lipstick and smoked in the bathroom, who did things good girls like us weren't supposed to do, didn't do.

A moment later, Linda said, "Alice, are you awake?"

I rolled over, propped up on one elbow so I'd actually look awake. "What?"

Linda said, "Do you believe what the Ouija board said about my mother?"

There were ways to explain that whisper. Wrong number. Crossed connection. A joke.

Linda went on: "I'm afraid something . . . You saw the Ouija board. I know you didn't push it that second time."

"You have the most perfect family in town." Everyone knew that.

A moment later, she said, "Yeah, I know," but she didn't sound happy.

Then she didn't say anything else, so finally I whispered, "Are you awake?," and she wasn't. So I rolled onto my back and stared at the dark ceiling tiles. How could you possibly find answers in a Ouija board, something you bought from the Sears catalog?

Mama said, "Some questions don't have answers."

There it was again. That annoying way she had of saying things that made no sense. I whispered, "Most questions do. Like, what is two plus two? It's four. Not five sometimes, not three on every other Sunday. Just plain four."

"You're not asking what is two plus two." Either I was getting more accustomed to Mama's voice or it sounded more natural in Linda's shadowy basement.

"Why did you kill yourself?" I asked. "Why did you leave me? What about the man on the train?"

Becky mumbled and rolled over. She often talked in her sleep, strange sentences like, "Are dinosaurs white meat like chicken or red meat like beef?" She never believed us when we told her what she had said.

I sighed and flipped onto my stomach. Like usual, Mama wasn't going to answer.

Mama said, "Everyone lives their real life in secret. You'll see."

"No," I murmured, thinking of Will, Aunt Aggy, me. But what about Mama's voice? And the story I now knew about Mama and Chicago, that I hadn't told Will. That Mama had never told us. "That's not true," I said, forgetting to whisper.

Becky suddenly sat up. "What's wrong? What's wrong?"

"Nothing." I couldn't tell if she was awake. In the past, she had had whole conversations she claimed not to remember. "I just can't sleep. By the way, Pam put your bra in the freezer."

Becky said, "Your mother didn't mean to."

"Yes, she did, Becky." I spit the words out. I was tired of her being so nice and understanding, always trying to protect me. In a way, that was as bad as how Linda acted around me. I just wanted to be a normal person.

"How can you not mean to park a car on train tracks when there's a train coming? How is that not meaning to?"

Becky said, "Leaving you. She forgot that part." She flopped back down, rolled over, and her breathing slowed until I knew she was asleep.

What was easier to think about: Mama leaving me on purpose? Or Mama forgetting me?

A short time later, I heard footsteps through the ceiling, the kind of tiptoes you make when you don't want anyone to hear you. It was a long night for someone else too. I thought about Mrs. Johnson pouring a cup of coffee, sitting alone in the dark, maybe looking down at the floor, as if by staring hard enough and long enough, she could see through it, down to where all of us girls lay, with our uncomplicated lives, dreaming our untroubled dreams.

Just as I lay staring up at the ceiling, unable to see through those perfect ceiling tiles that Mr. Johnson had placed himself.

I fell asleep at dawn, still waiting to hear those footsteps tiptoe out of the kitchen. I dreamed of nothing.

BEFORE LEAVING the next morning, I thanked Mrs. Johnson for the lovely party. There were dark purple circles under her eyes (fifteen minutes with cucumber slices on her eyelids would fix her up, according to Dotty King). Mrs. Johnson said, "Everything will be fine." She smiled, then added, "Don't forget what I said—fitting in." She didn't look like someone who had ever stayed up all night, who whispered desire and longing into a telephone. "That's the secret to having a happy life," she said, nodding.

We stood in the perfect living room, looking out the window. Will was late to pick me up. Everyone else's mother had already come. I poked at my rolled-up sleeping bag with one foot. "My brother will be here soon," I said.

"I don't know where Linda went," Mrs. Johnson said.

Outside, big fluffy clouds filled patches of the blue sky. I couldn't remember what they were called, though we'd memorized types of clouds in grade school. "Will's always late."

"It's okay." She set her hand on my shoulder. "Everything will be fine."

What would she do if I blurted out what I'd heard her say on the phone? The muscles in her face would tighten, grow hard like cold, gray stone, and she'd yank her hand off my shoulder, maybe even slap me, call me a liar. She would forbid me to talk to her daughter. No more slumber parties.

Will pulled into the driveway, honked the horn like I was the one keeping him waiting. "There he is," I said.

Mrs. Johnson nodded, but neither of us moved. Then she took her hand off my shoulder, tucked her arms across her chest. I picked up my sleeping bag and the grocery sack with my clothes and walked to the front door. Will honked again. Mrs. Johnson followed, held the door for me as I went outside, down the porch stairs to the front walk.

"Alice." I stopped, turned back to look at her. She stood in the doorway; I had to squint into the sun to see her. She said, "I don't think you understand what it's like, how it is." In the harsh light, her skin looked stretched too tight across her face, as if it might tear.

I dropped my sleeping bag on the ground, put one hand above my eyes to shield them.

Linda came up behind her, leaned her head out the door, gave Will a flirty wave. Mrs. Johnson set one hand on Linda's shoulder. Linda flipped her hair and shrugged her shoulder, shaking off her mother's hand. Such a quick, simple move, one I'd probably done a million times myself: *You're embarrassing me.* Mrs. Johnson folded her arms across her chest, called out something cheerful to Will. And either the light had shifted or I had been wrong before, because now Mrs. Johnson looked as happy and pretty as she always had.

SIGNS

JOE FRY was over all the time, his blue Mustang parked crooked in the driveway so Aunt Aggy had to drive two wheels on the grass to squeeze her car into the garage. She fussed to me but wouldn't complain directly to Joe or Will. At night, after Will's shift at the movie theater, he and Joe played catch in the backyard, or they sat outside staring up at the stars; every night ended with them driving off, not getting home until four in the morning, five, six. I'd hear the car door slam through my open window, the engine rumble; they weren't even trying to be quiet. Aunt Aggy complained to me about that too: "He shouldn't be out all hours of the night." But Will just laughed if I told him Aunt Aggy was threatening to ground him. "She's not my mother," he'd say, then glare at me as if I might disagree. The way he was acting now, if Aunt Aggy found a baby bird in the backyard, Will would laugh and walk away. What had happened to him? I was lonely for how he used to be. But how could you tell someone that? Especially since we were all lonely for the way lots of things used to be. Aunt Aggy tried to explain: "He's . . . well, he's sad." But he didn't seem sad to me: He never cried or looked at Mama's picture, or did anything similar to the things I did when I was sad, like fit my lips into the worn-out groove in Mama's Crushed Cherry lipstick. He just went out with Joe Fry and had fun like everything was fine, like everything was still the same, and I kept thinking about what if it were me in Joe Fry's car, me out with Joe Fry until four, five, six o'clock, me having fun.

I was doing everything Becky—actually, her sister—advised: no sweatpants, conversational topics and a joke ready, baking cookies, studying the baseball standings and box scores in the Des Moines *Register*'s Big Peach sports section. Will explained to me how a team that was half a game back hadn't actually played only half a game and what abbreviations like ERA, RBI, LOB, and DL meant. But he didn't ask why I cared about baseball standings, why I was baking all those cookies. Will didn't ask me questions anymore, which made me feel more alone than ever.

Mama was no help when it came to Joe Fry. I asked things like, "Does it mean Joe likes me if he eats a handful of my peanut butter and jelly cookies?" She gave makeup tips—"Flip your head and spray hairspray underneath so your hair looks fuller"—not a real answer.

I'd been to the movies with guys, and I'd gone with Brad Claussen for seven weeks last year that included my birthday when he'd given me a fourteen-karat-gold necklace that was expensive enough to keep me dating him an extra two weeks out of guilt. But Brad Claussen was nothing like Joe.

Joe's dark hair skimmed his shoulders, so long, adults shook their heads and frowned when he sauntered by, but he didn't seem to care or notice; scattered on the floor of his car along with the usual guy stuff (empty pop cans, wadded napkins, baseball-card wrappers with the gum turning sticky in the sun) were battered paperbacks marked with dog ears and tiny scraps of colored paper; even when he said something simple like, "Hey, Alice," his voice was black water with no bottom, as if nothing about him was on the surface. When someone said his name, my body tingled, and my face felt hot and red.

Mama wouldn't admit that that was the same way she had felt about the man on the train, but wouldn't that explain exactly why she'd stayed on past Chicago? Why she left Shelby?

Only Becky understood. We'd talk on the phone late at night, whispering to make everything more important. I'd start easy, like, "Think Joe's a good kisser?" and she'd say, "Definitely," and I'd ask, "How can you tell?"

Becky knew these things because she had an older sister who'd been engaged twice already, breezily breaking both engagements after a month of showing off her ring. Her sister had been a cheerleader, pep club vice-president, and represented France at the model UN in Des Moines; she charted horoscopes and could find your love match; now she swept hair and gave manicures at the Clip & Curl, where she listened to everyone's man problems; and she passed on five years' worth of *Seventeen* magazines to Becky. Becky's sister was happy to explain everything there was to know about boys.

So late at night Becky whispered answers to my questions: "Loose, soft lips mean he's a good kisser," and we'd talk about how Mr. Miller would kiss, and what did it mean that when he called on Becky he licked his lips? And Joe told me I looked good the time I wore my hair back in a barrette—what did that mean? Around and around, we asked the same questions, gave the same assured answers; that was the rhythm of the summer, wondering about Joe and Mr. Miller, talking about kissing, thinking up questions for Becky's sister, repeating the answers she gave us like a magic spell.

One night Becky set down the phone to go pee, and I started thinking about Mama on the train and that single moment when she knew she was going to leave Iowa and her family for that man: tingles, love at first sight, discovering your two lives were destined to be intertwined forever. Mama's voice startled me: "Quite a romantic picture."

"Love at first sight is the most romantic love there is." I was quoting Becky, who had been quoting her sister.

"Pictures only show the surface," Mama said.

Becky said, "I'm back." She was out of breath, but she launched into whispering about when Mr. Miller's birthday was, saying he seemed like a Pisces, a water sign anyway, wondering if it might be worth it to be a student helper in the office next year and peek into his file to find out for sure.

Being a dorky office helper just to find out a birthday? "Or you could ask him."

She was scornful: "That's not very romantic."

"But then you'd know." How come Becky and her sister were such experts on love and I wasn't? How come Mama wouldn't give me advice about what I really needed to know—Joe Fry? How come nothing was how it was supposed to be? Shouldn't this all be easier, like love at first sight? Boom—you're in love; boom—you know. I made my next question casual: "How can you tell if you're ready to have sex?" We didn't say the word "sex," not even when we talked about the girls in the second-floor bathroom. Instead it was, "Think Paula Elam is doing it?" Or, "Has Donna Slade gone all the way?"

"Alice!" Becky was out of breath again.

"Sex!" So Mama really was paying attention to me.

The kitchen phone cord stretched clear to the edge of the dining room, where I sat on the floor in the dark, sliding one hand back and forth along the wood, accumulating grit. Aunt Aggy was using the broom as part of a still-life composition that couldn't be moved, so no one had swept for ages.

Mama's words were fast and angry: "You're fifteen, babbling about love at first sight; you're a girl, a fifteen-year-old girl."

You were seventeen, I thought, picturing Mama in a red dress, staring out the train window while Aunt Aggy pleaded. Mama, knowing exactly what she was doing. Being brave, like Mrs. Johnson had said.

Mama was surprisingly angry: "That boy is nothing but a small-town hood. What is he offering you besides sex in the backseat of a car? Nothing. He's a big nothing going nowhere fast. Nowhere, Alice."

Mama had to understand she wasn't the only person in the world who could fall in love at first sight. Anyway, she wasn't here, and she couldn't stop me. Let her fuss as much as she wanted. I remembered Will saying, "She's not my mother," about Aunt Aggy. Well, our mother was dead and gone.

"I'm right here," Mama said. "Telling you this is a huge mistake."

Dead and gone. I was free to do it with anyone I wanted.

Becky spoke slowly, the quietest whisper possible: "My sister says you can do everything but, but you can't do 'it' or else." We both knew "or else" what. The rules were simple: Nice girls didn't do it until they were married, or at least engaged, or at the very least away at college. When nice girls didn't follow the rules, people gossiped and suddenly

they weren't nice girls anymore, they were hippies or sluts. Becky went
on, "She said don't go all the way unless it means something."

Her tone assumed I knew what "something" was and exactly what it
would "mean": You were in love, you would be together forever. I
doubted that's what it meant to those girls in the second-floor bathroom.
My whisper was almost a breath: "What do you think it's like?"

"Alice!" Becky hissed. "You can't ask that."

Silence stretched long and thin on the phone. I pushed my hand
through the pile of dirt on the floor and scattered it. It would be easy to
go back to asking the same old questions about Joe and Mr. Miller.

Becky sighed. "My mother would kill me if she heard me talking
like this. She'd ground me until I was a hundred."

"No," Mama said. "You're not having sex. I forbid it"—the sort of
thing Becky's mom would say to Becky.

I asked, "What about Joe? Has he done it?"

Becky sighed again, this time with relief because this was easy, a
question we could ponder all night. Her whisper became less strained:
"Oh, definitely."

"How can you tell?" I asked.

"Anyone can tell." After a moment she added, "Watch the way he
looks at girls, like he knows secrets."

"Done it with who?"

She paused, thinking.

Mama had stopped with the makeup tips. Instead she was talking to
me for real, fussing like everyone's regular mother. *I forbid it.*

"Carol Swink," Becky said. "Maybe Dara DeWitt."

Of course a regular mother wouldn't sit in Aunt Aggy's car and wait
for the train to run her down. A regular mother wouldn't be dead.

"Donna Slade for absolute sure," Becky whispered.

I could do it and Mama would be mad but all she could do was talk.

"Paula Elam," Becky said. "She's done it with everyone."

A car rumbled in the driveway, then snapped silent. Two car doors
slammed, one after the other; footsteps crunched on the gravel, headed
to the backyard. Through the window I heard Will and Joe laugh. "How
do you know if a boy wants to do it?" I asked.

Becky was firm: "We're supposed to say no."

Will and Joe laughed again. A shiver of something coiled along my body, tightened.

Becky said, "You know that, right? You say no."

"I've got to go." I hung up the phone, scrunched my hands through my hair to fluff it, tucked my tank top into my shorts.

"Why are you doing this?" Mama said.

"Why did you?" Silence. So I went outside. Will and Joe were sprawled on the splintery old picnic table that no one used anymore because Mama was the one who liked picnics.

"Isn't it past your bedtime, Baby Sister?" Will swung his legs around so he was facing me. His voice was slurry, so I figured he and Joe had been drinking beer after the game.

I said, "Isn't it past yours?"

"The night is young," Will said.

"And so are we," Joe finished. They laughed as if there were an old joke between them no one else could possibly understand.

I stood about ten yards away, on the doorstep, under the yellow bug light someone had left on, probably for a couple of weeks. No one was caring about doing things like turning on or off outside lights anymore. I flipped back my hair the way Linda did. Mama said feeling beautiful meant you'd be beautiful, so I tried hard to feel beautiful. Then I asked, "Who won the game?"

Will crossed his arms against his chest. "We did, six to three."

Joe whacked Will's back. "Your brother, this fucking hero, won it on one grand-slam swing in the eighth inning." He hit Will's back again. "Guy's on fire, he's so hot. Pitcher, slugger—Mr. All-Fucking-American."

I didn't use words like "fucking," but it seemed like such a good word, exactly perfect in its own way, that I suddenly wondered why I didn't. "Congratulations." I flipped my hair again, shifted my weight so one hip jutted out a bit, set my hand on the other hip, pretended to smack a mosquito on my shoulder.

"How come you weren't at the game?" Joe asked.

What would happen if I said, *Fucking busy?* Instead I said, "Busy."

"What's keeping you so busy?" Will asked.

Joe and I stared at each other as if Will hadn't spoken. Then Joe clasped his hands behind his back, straightened his elbows, pulled his arms upward to stretch out his back as his dark blue T-shirt tightened across his chest. He slowly rolled his head from side to side. A bone popped. "Play-offs start Thursday," Joe said.

"Play-offs already?"

"It's July," Will said loudly. "Maybe you didn't notice because you're so 'busy.'"

Joe said, "Come to the game."

My heart beat faster, but I thought about Becky's sister, who had told Becky, "Boys want to feel like they've won something. Make them fight a little." So I said, "Maybe," my voice hard, pure ice though I felt like Jell-O.

"Seven o'clock," Joe said.

I pointed at the sky as if I hadn't heard him. "Shooting star." Mama used to make wishes on shooting stars; "save those wishes for the thing you want most of all," she had said. I suppose Will remembered that, though he didn't say anything about shooting stars or wishes or Mama. No one said anything.

Joe spoke first, all casual. "So, see you at the game?"

I thought of Becky's sister and her two engagements, said, "Maybe."

Will suddenly yawned, one of those squawky, attention-getting yawns that involve lifting your arms up and throwing your head way back. Then he said, "It's an easy question, Alice." No slurred words now, and he added, "A simple yes or no will work fine."

Simple to him. But one wrong move and you're back at square one. Becky's sister's exact words. I flipped my hair, said, "Ha, ha."

Will leaned over and picked up one of the green apples that had fallen from the tree and rolled onto the patio. He tossed it into the air and caught it with the same hand, again and again, each toss flying higher into the dark sky. Joe watched, his head bobbing as the apple rose and fell. It was all so repetitive and boring that I wanted to scream, but both of them seemed to find the whole thing fascinating.

"Nineteen," Will said as the apple landed in his hand. A second later he threw it into the air again and caught it. "Twenty."

"Five bucks says you can't do fifty without dropping the apple," Joe said.

Will held on to the apple, laughed. "Five bucks says you can't go an hour without saying, 'Five bucks says.' " He bit into the apple, then spit the bitten-off chunk onto the patio and side-armed the apple across the yard.

"Five bucks says Alice will be at the game Thursday," Joe said.

Both of them watched me.

My face tingled, and I didn't know whether to look at them or ignore them. So I stared at nothing, thought about how I didn't know what I was supposed to say, thought about Mama on the train, Mama falling in love and riding off with a man, Mama who killed herself.

Joe dug into the front pocket of his jeans and pulled out a crumpled bill that he smoothed in an exaggerated way before slapping it on the picnic table. "Ante up, hero," he said to Will, not lifting his hand off the five-dollar bill.

Will said, "Looks like I owe you another five bucks."

"Hey!" I said. "I'm not at that game yet!"

"So, will you be?" Joe asked.

My whispered conversations with Becky seemed a million years ago. Surely Becky's sister would say I should be insulted, and Becky would tell me *Seventeen* didn't write articles about boys who said "fucking" and bet money on you, and Linda would march into the house with an angry flip of her hair. I licked my lips and meant to say yes, but that very simple word didn't come out, so I nodded slowly, thinking of Mama on that train, sitting there as scenery passed.

Joe smiled and scrunched his hand around the five-dollar bill, wadding it into a tight ball. Will turned away, so I couldn't see his face.

It was just a baseball game.

IN ANOTHER whispered phone call, Becky informed me that I'd look desperate going to the game alone so she was coming with me. Her sister had said she should. We decided to wear T-shirts, Dr. Scholl's sandals, and the shorts we had made that afternoon when we cut the legs off old Levi's, pulling away threads to get fringe until the edge of the pockets peeked out along the bottom, a look Mama had always called "tacky."

We were playing the Mustangs from Mount Union who weren't very good; we had beaten them twice already, but now their best pitcher was back from being a camp counselor, and people around us were worrying out loud about that. Not me and Becky. We bought our hot dogs and Tabs at the boosters booth, then found seats behind home plate for the best view of Will pitching and Joe catching. Becky didn't know much about baseball, so it was easier to talk than watch. It wasn't until the second-to-last inning that we noticed how the crowd didn't fidget when Will pitched the ball and gave bigger-than-usual cheers when, say, our shortstop threw someone out at first on a routine ground ball.

The woman next to me—center fielder Matt Baum's mother—had crossed all her fingers on both hands. "Come on," she muttered every two seconds.

"What's going on?" I asked. She lifted one hand as Will wound up, threw the ball. Strike three, two outs.

As people cheered, Mrs. Baum said, "Can't say," but she looked like she desperately wanted to tell me something.

I tugged at the fringe of my cutoffs, looked at Becky and shrugged, rolled my eyes. Will had told me Matt Baum was weird, that for a dollar he'd eat grasshoppers in the dugout. No doubt that weirdness came from his mother. Then I looked at the scoreboard, longer than the casual glance I'd been giving it. The tie score of zero-zero was interesting—but more than that, the Mustangs had no hits. I nudged Becky. "Will's pitching a no-hitter!"

"Shh!" Mrs. Baum jabbed me with her elbow, and someone behind me said, "Saying it's a jinx."

"What's a no-hitter?" Becky asked, making more people hiss, "Shh!"

"The pitcher doesn't give up any hits," I said.

Becky sipped her last bit of Tab through a straw, then asked, "That's a big deal?"

"It happens like never."

"Four outs away," Mrs. Baum said, dipping her head, maybe in prayer.

The next batter swung at air one last time before stepping to the plate. Squint lines dug around Will's eyes as he stared at the batter, then at Joe, the catcher, who gave him the sign. But Will scowled and gave two quick shakes of his head, saying he didn't agree with the pitch Joe was calling. Again, two shakes. Again.

A Mustang dad yelled, "Pitch the ball!"

Becky said, "What's going on?"

The same dad yelled, "He's been pulling this all night, ump!"

"He doesn't like the sign," I said.

The batter called for time and stepped out of the box.

"What sign?"

I'd already explained it to her a hundred times, but she didn't have a brother to teach her this stuff, only sisters. "The catcher tells the pitcher what pitch to throw. Like, one finger for fastball, two for curveball. Tight inside. High. Low." I demonstrated some signals Will had taught me when I'd catch for him in the backyard. "People think the pitcher's in charge, but really it's the catcher."

"Pitch it," a Mustang mom yelled. "This ain't the World Series."

Mrs. Baum shouted, "Let him pitch how he wants!"

The batter got back in the box, and finally Will threw the ball. The batter fanned—strike one.

Becky kicked her empty cup down to the grass under the bleachers. "So much to remember for a stupid game."

I looked up at the moths swirling in front of the stadium lights. Okay, maybe it was just a game. But when you were sitting in the stands, wasn't it better to think getting a no-hitter meant something? To think that Will batting in the four hundreds was important? To believe crossing all your fingers on both hands might help? The sky beyond the lights was big and empty. People clapped, and I looked at the field. "What happened?" I asked Becky.

"Swung and missed," she said.

Again, Will shook off Joe twice before pitching the ball. The batter whacked a high fly out to center. Matt Baum took big loping steps to the right, then backward, lifting his mitt so it blocked his face from view.

"Don't drop it!" his mother shrieked. Talk about jinxing someone. The ball smacked into the top of the glove's webbing, balanced there like a too-big scoop of ice cream on a cone as Matt Baum tightened the glove and miraculously caught the ball.

The teams changed sides, and Becky said, "I can tell Joe likes you."

She wanted me to ask how she knew—like our phone conversations—but I looked up at the sky instead, bending my head so far back that my neck ached and my mouth stretched open. Sometimes I couldn't believe my mother was really dead, even after four whole months. She used to sit behind home plate when Will pitched, wearing her lucky red sun visor, even on cloudy days or at night, biting the white part off the tops of each fingernail by the end of the game. She closed her eyes when he was up, not opening them until she heard the bat crack, because she said the harder she closed her eyes, the harder he'd hit the ball. When she found out it was bad luck to step on the chalk baseline, she nagged Will until he promised to jump over it. She was convinced those oddball superstitions mattered.

Will was the first batter. He scuffled the dust around home plate, then tapped the bat against one foot, the other, and waggled the bat behind his head; he looked coiled and ready, tensed for the pitch. His mother was dead, but who would know by looking at him? Not like me; I practically had a tattoo on my forehead: "Dead Mother." Mama was haunting me, not All-American Boy, normal Will, who was always so perfect and responsible. No falling apart, no crying. Will picked flowers for Mama's grave once a week, and I hadn't been there since we'd buried her. He was the big baseball star, and I played with Ouija boards. He dated the nicest girl in school, and I . . . I kept thinking about Joe Fry.

He swung hard and missed. Good. For a minute I hated him, hated that his mother had died, too, but that I was the one cracking up, I was the one hearing her voice in my head. How could Will be fine?

Mama murmured, "So much assuming. That you're cracking up. That Will doesn't want to hear from me."

There was a laugh, Will wanting a voice in his head giving makeup tips.

"Assuming facts can answer every question," Mama said.

Will whacked the ball backward, above the backstop, beyond the stands. A pack of little kids, elbowing and shoving, ran after it.

I shifted in my seat, tugged at my cutoffs, which suddenly felt too short. For someone who hated facts so much, Mama sure liked to spout them. Though actually the makeup tips had been useful. My eyelashes were definitely feeling thicker since I had started putting Vaseline on them at night. Or was that my imagination?

The umpire tossed a new ball to the pitcher. He rolled it in his hand a couple of times.

Will stepped out of the box, scrunched his shoulders up and down, then got back into his batting stance. For a moment, he looked like someone I didn't know.

The pitcher wound up, sent the ball over the plate. Will slammed it, *thwaack*—home run, the only run of the game. We all jumped to our feet and cheered; he stood for a moment at the plate, as if charting the path the ball had cut across the darkening sky; then he jogged around the bases as we clapped and whooped and whistled. Behind me, someone said, "Boy's going places," and someone else answered, "Thanks to one heck of a guardian angel." Will stepped on home plate and headed back to the dugout and a line of high-fives from the team.

Old Mr. Summerwill—who went to every game and scored them all in a special notebook—said, "None of our boys ever pitched a no-hitter."

The stands still buzzed about his home run; it had cleared the fence high and clean, the ball traveling far, even beyond the reach of the roving pack of kids. Becky asked me, "Will he play baseball for real?"

"He wants to," I said, but we hadn't talked about things like that for a long time, not since Mama died. Would he do that to me, leave? Turn into a tiny guy in a uniform on a TV screen? I couldn't stand it if Will was gone too; my hands clenched into tight fists. He would tell me if he was planning to go—but suddenly I wasn't so sure he would, and my hands were so tight I had to let them relax.

Becky said, "Bet Joe gives you a ride after the game."

I stared at the outfield lights reflected in her glasses, then asked, "How do you know?"

She sighed in exasperation. "You just can tell."

We watched the game: a base hit, a walk, a double play with a call the umpire blew since the guy was safe by a mile, then Matt Baum getting up to a three-two count on foul balls.

Becky pursed her lips, then said, "Don't blow it with him. It's what you want."

Matt Baum struck out, whacked the bat once against the plate, and stalked back to the dugout to get his glove. Will's last inning to pitch. I crossed my fingers. "What if I don't know what I want?" I said to Becky.

She rolled her eyes and sighed again, annoyed. "Here's what you want," she said. "You want Joe to like you." She leaned her head close to mine and let her voice drop to a whisper. "You want him to kiss you."

Will was taking his practice pitches with Joe. He looked sharp, unbothered, and even paused to crack his knuckles. Maybe he would stop shaking off Joe's signals.

Becky whispered, "Don't you want him to kiss you?"

Will threw the first pitch, a perfect strike that caught the batter looking. Joe tossed back the ball. I noticed two round smudges of dirt on his elbows. I did want Joe to kiss me. My heart got going really fast every time I thought of it. Isn't that what that meant?

Will had the batter totally intimidated; he whiffed at the next two pitches. The following batter hit a pop-up that the shortstop caught, no problem.

"Last batter." My palms felt sweaty as I rubbed them against my thighs.

Joe walked to the mound, raising high one hand with the index finger and pinkie extended, reminding the fielders there were two outs. People in the stands were quiet; even the little kids hanging on the fence along the baselines watched silently.

Joe returned to his position behind the plate, crouched, slapped the back of his hand in his glove once, twice, then dropped his hand between his legs to give the signal. Will shook his head. Again. Again. Again. Joe shoved his mask off his face and strode out to the mound.

You just didn't shake off the catcher so much unless something was wrong: He was the catcher, the one who was supposed to know which pitches when. I started chewing my thumbnail with tiny, precise bites.

Joe draped an arm over Will's shoulder and bent his head down. Will shook his head again, pushed his cap back with one hand, then pulled it forward. This went on until the umpire hollered and started for the mound. So Joe strode back to the plate, crouched, held out his mitt.

Will cradled the ball in his glove, his face shiny with sweat. He looked at Joe, then up into the stands, right at me. I held up my hands with their crossed fingers, but he didn't react, so maybe he wasn't really looking at me. Then he focused on Joe.

"The sign," Becky said, barely a sound.

It felt like everyone in the park had sucked in all the air, holding it, as Will wound up and pitched the ball. I closed my eyes, squished them so hard I saw tight flashes of starry light. The game disappeared, and it was only me and Will and the ball landing plop in Joe's mitt. Except that's not what happened; the bat smacked the ball. Everyone gasped, and I opened my eyes. The ball was zooming high and straight, like an up elevator. I lost it in the lights, but Joe had shoved off his mask as he ran partway toward the mound, his head all the way back, one arm flung straight up as if tracking the ball. Everyone in the stands was on their feet, screaming—"Don't drop it!"; "Get it, get it!"—the coach was out of the dugout hollering, "Back him up"; and it should've been Joe's ball—anyone could see he had it; he even shouted, "Mine!" and waved his arm—but Will was also running straight for it, his glove out, head tilted to watch the ball, a classic Little League error. We saw what was coming—they'd crash into each other, no one would catch the ball. Will knocked hard into Joe, and they both rolled and sprawled on the ground as everyone groaned, but Joe scrambled to his knees, reached out his glove and managed to barely catch the ball, like the catcher he was, like it was all very simple.

Everyone cheered and stamped their feet on the bleachers, and the whole team burst out of the dugout and piled on top of Joe and Will. Mrs. Baum wiped tears from her eyes and Mr. Summerwill kept shouting, "Our first no-hitter!" Becky and I clutched each other as we jumped up and down. Someone from the *Beacon* arranged the team into a photograph for the newspaper, as everyone crowded onto the field; Becky pulled me into the swarm of bodies until I lost her; someone stepped on my toe and a hard elbow smacked the side of my head. Doug Foltz was grabbing girls and kissing them, so I ducked away, bumping into Paula Elam and Donna Slade, both in skimpy halter tops and cutoffs. "Sorry." Paula's lipstick was nearly as red as Mama's, and I nodded, looked away, watched Kathy Clark in the crush pushing toward the locker room. I hung back, standing at home plate, one foot on the base, the other on the dirt, and I heard Joe's voice above the rest, "Hey, Alice." The ball came right at me, and I held up both hands and caught it as everyone headed off the field. I stayed where I was, at home plate, staring at the ball, and when Will passed me, I grabbed his shirt, stopping him. "You were great," and I gave him a hug even though he was sweaty and dusty.

He shrugged. I thought he'd be smiling, but he was scowling, rubbing hard at his jaw with his thumb.

"Here's the ball." I held it out to him on my open palm.

He didn't pick it up, just kept rubbing his face until I pulled his hand away to make him stop. There was a splotchy mosquito bite that he had scratched until now it was bleeding. He said, "It's just a ball, Alice," then swiped away a tiny drop of blood.

That didn't seem like what he should say. I curled my fingers around the ball, felt the rough seams and scuff marks. "A no-hitter," I said. "That's amazing."

"Yeah," he said, but he didn't sound amazed or even happy. He bent over and scooped up a handful of dirt from the batter's box and held it in his cupped hand.

"Glad I was here to see it." We both knew what I wasn't saying: that the person who should have been here was Mama, with her eyes closed and all her fingers crossed, hissing at the umpire, leaning her head back to blow swift columns of cigarette smoke straight into the air. I tightened my grip on the ball. "And Kathy was here," I added. Nothing was coming out right.

Will abruptly spread his fingers so the dirt trickled to the ground, then he kicked it with one cleat.

People passed by, most slapping Will on the back or yanking him into quick, hard hugs. He smiled as he was congratulated, but eventually it was just the two of us, and I still didn't know what to say, but I tried again: "You were great."

Will stared up at the black sky. I followed his gaze. "What are you looking for?"

He shook his head. "I don't know." His voice was tiny, a needle hole jabbed into darkness.

In the long silence, I listened to crickets chirping, the drone of cicadas.

Then he said, "I'm looking for shooting stars. I'm counting how many I see this summer."

"Why?" I asked.

He shrugged. "I don't know."

"So how many are you up to?"

"Thirty-six."

We kept looking at the sky. Then I said, "That's how old Mama was when she died."

"Oh, right." He pulled in a deep breath, held it, then let go of it all at once. "That number's a coincidence."

"We're totally alone now, aren't we?" The words were minuscule for what I felt, with the sky darkening above us, the useless dust under our feet, the ball in my hand that Will didn't want, our mother gone, my brother maybe going, and no words beyond "sad" or "lonely" to express what I was thinking—and no one to say them to anyway.

Will stared down at the dust, so I couldn't see his face, only the top of his hat, the brim. I had seen him writing Mama's name on the inside this morning. Then he said, "She didn't even know a fastball from a curveball." His voice was hard, as if covered by a shell.

I wasn't expecting him to talk about baseball, which in the end was actually nothing but a game. I spoke sharply: "What's that supposed to mean?"

"Forget it." He shook his head and started walking toward the locker room.

I still held the ball. Of course he'd want it. He could look at that ball every day for the rest of his life and know exactly what it meant: no-hitter. According to Mr. Summerwill, no one in the history of Jefferson High baseball had ever had a no-hitter, not Len Davitt, who went on to play for the Detroit Tigers in the 1940s, and not Billy Garrett, the big jock when Mama was at Jefferson, who then played college football at Iowa and later ran for state senator. This ball meant something; Will should know that.

Becky was over by the visiting-team dugout; she pointed to the parking lot.

"Meet you where?" I called.

"Not me," she called back. "Him."

"Don't go!" I shouted.

But she just waved her arm backward over her head as she walked away. I sucked in my breath. I'm sure Mama never felt like this, as though there were two ropes in her stomach tying themselves in big knots. What was I supposed to do? Meet Joe? Try again to talk to Will? Run after Becky and go home? I whispered, "You're always saying you're right here, Mama, but how come I can't hug you?" Tears warmed my eyes, and I blinked, sending them down my cheeks. "Answer me," I said. A moment later, "Answer me." I could guess what was going to happen next, but I said it anyway: "I'm listening," and finally, "I'm fucking listening! Say something! Say fucking anything!" and I was right about two things—that she would stay silent and that "fucking" really was a pretty fucking good word. She wasn't going to help me; she was dead and I was alone.

I looked at the ball in my hand, brushed my thumb over the red stitches, thought about how red was her favorite color. Red dress, red lipstick.

The overhead lights suddenly flicked off, leaving only the glow of the parking lot lights, a few fireflies rising out of the long grass beyond the outfield. I tightened my grip on the ball. Behind me, the backstop fence rattled lightly and I looked up. Joe smiled half a smile at me, as if he wasn't sure what I was going to say or do.

"Great game." My voice was barely above a whisper. I cleared my throat, coughed—sounding exactly like I had TB. Talk about embarrassing.

"It was your brother's game," he said, like it was a fact, no hint of envy.

"You called it," I said. "You were the catcher."

I looked at his fingers curled through the mesh of the backstop, his nails were broad and clipped straight, very short. Several cuts crisscrossed the knuckle of his index finger, and the pinkie looked swollen. He saw me looking, said, "Catcher's hands," pulled them away, shoved them in his jeans pockets, rocked on his heels. According to Becky's sister, you could tell a lot by a man's hands, though she hadn't ever said what.

I stepped closer: If I reached out, I could wrap my fingers through the backstop. He had showered and his hair was wet; he smelled like Johnson's baby shampoo. I tugged at my cutoffs with one hand, pulling them lower on my leg.

"There's a party at Garfield Park," he said.

I thought of the team hooting, hollering, shaking beer cans and popping them open on each other; someone would have the genius idea to bust open the lock on the merry-go-round and get it going. I'd been to those parties, everyone would be there.

Joe shook back his hair; water droplets pelted the dusty ground. "Or," he said, drawing the word out long and slow and heavy.

I tightened my grip on the baseball. "Or what?"

"I like to drive after a game," he said.

"Drive where?" I asked, almost a whisper.

"Anywhere."

Cicadas buzzed; car doors slammed in the parking lot; voices called out various things about the game, let loose with wordless whoops. I listened for Will's voice to rise above the rest. He would go with Kathy to the party at Garfield Park, be the hero.

Finally Joe said, "Well?" But he wasn't impatient; he spoke as if there was all the time in the world to make up my mind.

Mama wasn't saying no. She had stayed on that train.

I walked around the backstop, started toward the parking lot, taking long, purposeful strides, swallowing up lots of ground with each step, as if I had to outrun her voice. But Mama still didn't say anything to me.

"Hey!" Joe called. "Where're you going?" He grabbed his gym bag, jogged to catch up, to keep up.

I spotted his car straight ahead. Didn't matter who saw me: I was going to get into Joe Fry's car and let my fingers trail out the window as we drove into the dark, through the night, and whatever happened after that wouldn't be like throwing a no-hitter—a magical, unpredictable thing—but it would be destiny, meant to be. I climbed into the passenger door and leaned into the warm vinyl, thinking, *This is where Will usually sits*, as if that were important. No. Whatever Becky's sister would say or whatever Becky would tell me to do and whatever Mama's words might mean blurred into something distant like the baseball crowd noise. Matt Baum stared and Ann Trinder's eyebrows shot up as Joe climbed in next to me, started the car, pressed the accelerator to make it roar, and that was all I heard as we pulled out of the gravel parking lot, driving too fast.

JOE'S CAR smelled like a mix of chewing tobacco, Fritos, and beer. We rolled down all the windows, front and back, and let the wind spin through as we drove along old General Dodge Highway, out past the county airstrip and the silos that stuck up like thumbs; the silent, dark fields, here and there a shadowy tree rising from the flatness; the moon glowing big and bright over it all.

I didn't have to resort to my joke or my conversational topics. First, we talked about baseball, and he was impressed I knew that the Red Sox led the division, and that I'd heard of his favorite player, catcher Carlton Fisk, and how everyone called him Pudge; I even remembered that a couple of weeks ago Rick Wise came within one out of throwing a no-hitter. We talked about the designated hitter and I surprised myself by having an opinion that I expressed before hearing his, which, according to Becky's sister, was a definite no-no ("Let him say what he thinks, then agree"), and my opinion coincided exactly with his opinion—"Fucking with the game like that, what's next, ten guys on the field?" He told me real baseball fans understood it was the catcher in charge, not the pitcher, and when I said I already knew that, he believed me.

Then we talked about why the moon looks silver and how could it be true that the starlight we were seeing was actually light-years old, and wasn't it incredible to think of light traveling all that time and space in one year and wouldn't it be amazing to be the one who discovered light-years and why didn't they talk about stuff like that in school instead of making us do equations and formulas that turned everything into dry numbers adding up to nothing? After that, we talked about what would be the greatest thing to have invented, and I said, "Cars," and he said, "A spiderweb"; then we both agreed that bananas were the best all-around fruit because they were self-contained, but that a raspberry would beat any fruit hands down on a good day. We both hated coconut, and his favorite food was bacon and mine was macaroni and cheese, and we spec-ulated that combining those two things into "bac-aroni" and cheese would be delicious. He was an Aries and I was a Libra on the cusp, which seemed like an interesting combination though we agreed that zodiac signs were probably worthless. He described the paperbacks he read about people hitchhiking across the country, people with no plans or des-tination—"It's the journey that matters," which sounded important and true—and he got indignant, saying how in school all we read were books by dead writers, like *The Red Badge of Courage* and *Jane Eyre* and *A Separate Peace*, whose author might as well be dead, naming some poor guy Phineas.

I thought about driving like this with Joe all night, every night, all the way through summer and on into fall, winter, spring, the words around us accumulating like leaves in a forest. I had put Will's ball on the floor, and every so often it rolled up against my foot when Joe slowed for a stop sign or took a curve. It all seemed to mean something—what we had in common, what we said at exactly the same time and then laughed at, the sideways glances we gave each other that stretched longer and longer, my eyes feeling enormous, as if I were trying to take in too much with them, as if I needed to grab things with my arms, and rub them up and down my whole body, inhale them.

We laughed when dead-skunk smell came through the open windows; we counted the number of moths that fluttered across the head-lights; we fell silent when we heard the long, low whistle of a train pass-ing on the tracks alongside us; I pointed to a shooting star and made a wish, and maybe he did, and maybe they were for the same thing.

He turned around outside Cedar Rapids, said, "We should get back."

"Back-back?" I asked. He and Will had stayed out plenty later plenty of times. (Becky's sister told us a guy brings a nice girl home by eleven, possibly eleven-thirty, on the first date: "to show he respects you.")

"Just back," he said. "Drink a beer. Watch the stars and decide which one's best."

I could guess what he was talking about. "Beer's good," I said, though it tasted to me like sour spit.

"I knew you'd be the kind of girl who likes beer."

What did it mean, being the kind of girl who liked beer (or said she did)? "How could you tell?"

He shrugged. A moment later he said, "I know things about you."

I felt my face get warm, so I turned to look out the window though there was nothing to see, just the same old stuff there was everywhere. Farms. Fields. Barns. "Like what?" The words felt like glass.

"Like, your nose crinkles when you laugh," he said too quickly, too easily.

We rode for several miles in silence until I said, "I know things about you too." It was practically a script from *Seventeen*: "How to Flirt So He Doesn't Know You're Flirting," something like that. He was sup-posed to laugh.

Instead he said, "This isn't like everyone else. This is different."

I watched the dark barn that loomed ahead, how it got bigger, big-ger, bigger, then was somewhere behind us. He was doing seventy-five or eighty.

A moment later, he said, "I can't explain it. I just know."

I kept looking out the window, but I wasn't seeing what was there. Boys had said things like I was too skinny or asked where my boobs were or had snapped my bra enough times to give me bruises on my back, and Brad Claussen had said I had a cute walk, and Linda told me Steve Barry told her he thought I was nice, and boys had asked to copy old papers or geometry homework, and once someone yelled, "Nice legs!" from a truck parked across the street, but no one had ever said anything the way Joe Fry just had. It seemed exactly what was supposed to happen when he took his right hand off the steering wheel and set it along the seat back. I leaned into it, letting the hairs on his arm tickle my neck.

We just drove. There was no more talking.

ACCORDING TO Becky's sister, there were four okay places to go parking and two great ones. Her worst-to-best ranking was: the lot by the new tennis courts, Gilbert Pond, Pleasant Valley Nursery (romantic, because you could smell the flowers for sale), the parking lot at the burned-down Stop-Inn motel on old General Dodge Highway, the airstrip, and the county fairgrounds. At the fairgrounds you could find an open barn or walk around the grandstand ring and up into the bleachers. "They never latch the window in the bathroom near the cow-cleaning area," she told Becky, who told me. "So you can crawl through. Never pee outside when you're with a boy."

So I was surprised when Joe passed the airstrip; a couple minutes later we blew by the turnoff to the fairgrounds. If Becky's sister knew these things, so would Joe Fry. Maybe he had changed his mind. But there was his arm on the seat back, still tickling my neck. My breathing deepened, as if it was coming from some new place.

He didn't look at me when he said, "Sure it's not too late for you to be out?"

Aunt Aggy would notice I was gone, but what could she do? Like Will said, she wasn't our mother. "The night is young . . . ," I said, but I sounded stupid and he didn't finish the sentence the way he had when Will said it. The clock on Farmers & Merchants Bank flashed 1:21 and 79 degrees as we sped down West Street. "It's hardly late," I said.

He went right through the stop sign by the movie theater.

I asked, "What do you and Will talk about?"

"Mostly we talk about baseball, drink beer, or shoot pool." He shook his head. "You know the people around here don't go deeper than that."

It seemed like something Mama might say—not that I was thinking about her.

Joe continued: "But you're not like them," and my heart beat harder and faster because he meant that as a good thing.

We were at a traffic light, and though it was green, he stopped the car and pushed the gearshift into park. He leaned over: His lips were warm and soft and our noses didn't bump and our teeth didn't click, and the light turned red then green then red again before he pulled away from me. "I knew you'd be a good kisser," he said.

"How could you tell?"

He ran two fingers along my cheekbone and down to my lips, let them rest there for a second. "Anyone could tell," he whispered, and he pulled away his fingers, shifted out of park, put both hands on the steering wheel, and accelerated forward with a squeal of tires.

"I know a place no one goes to," he said. "The old cemetery on Prairie du Chien Road."

I closed my eyes. A long time ago I had thought doing that made me invisible.

"You should see it in the moonlight," he said. "Old headstones. Overgrown weeds and wildflowers. People who died a hundred years ago. It's like a place that isn't in this world. When you're there, you're not anywhere." He looked at me. "You're not saying anything."

"It's just that I do know that cemetery." I wanted to say, *That's where my mother is.* But we hadn't spoken of her, and it seemed wrong to bring her up. Of course he knew she was dead, but something about saying her name would change everything.

He laughed, said, "You're not afraid of ghosts, are you?"

"I'm not afraid of anything." I put my hand on his thigh, on the stiff fabric of his jeans. His leg was tight muscle. I was lying. There was a lot that I was afraid of. Snakes. Heights. Ghosts. I said, "Especially not ghosts—white sheets and chains dragging."

"There are other kinds," Joe said.

"I'm not afraid of those either." I wanted to sound bold and daring and carefree, like the kind of person who would hitchhike rides across the country. I ran my fingers through my hair to fluff it, licked my lips. I wished there was someone out on the street who knew me, someone to see me drive by in Joe Fry's blue Mustang.

But the streets were empty, and my wild mood lasted only until we pulled into the cemetery entrance.

I hadn't been here since the funeral, since we had dropped her cold, boxed-up body in the ground, covered it with dirt, and walked away. It had been a sunny day and there was a wind, so I had to keep pushing my hair out of my face. Mama used to drive out to this cemetery in any weather, night and day; she said it was the most authentic place she knew, which I decided actually was her way of saying "the saddest." It wasn't like her parents were buried here, and she didn't pull out weeds or try to make the old graves prettier. She just walked around touching the stones, reading the names. In the end, Aunt Aggy picked the spot, said it was what Mama would want.

That day, the wind blew hair in my mouth and face, making it stick to the tears on my cheeks, and the sun was so bright we had to squint. They told me to throw a handful of dirt on top of her. Will picked up a shovel leaning against a tree and started slowly shoveling dirt on her, clods and tiny stones thumping and pinging. I walked away and stood in the dry weeds pressed up against the wire fence at the edge of the cemetery and squinted out at the field before me—too early to be a field of anything in particular, though I knew it was going to be a field of corn because it was always a field of corn; probably it had been a field of corn for the past hundred years and would be for the next. I stood at the wire fence and smeared the crumbs of dirt off my hand and onto my navy blue skirt while the wind wrapped my hair around my face. I knew there was something I should be thinking, but there was nothing to think. No one came over to talk to me for a long time. Or maybe it was just a minute.

I closed my eyes again, opened them before Joe would notice.

The cemetery—which didn't have a name—was small, the size of half a dozen yards pushed together; overgrown, gnarly trees flanked the entrance, stood in the center and along the fence on the far side; a short gravel drive drifted into tall weeds; a hodgepodge of headstones seemed to lean one way, as if pushed by the same wind.

Even with the moon, it felt dark after Joe flipped off the headlights. The windows were down, and the sound of buzzing bugs filled the car. Better that than my breathing and my heartbeat, which, I was sure, were just as loud.

We both stared out the front windshield. "Radio's busted," he said, reaching over to twirl the knob. I hadn't noticed there had been no music all night.

This is how it worked: First, he'd lean over and kiss me. After enough of that, he'd slide his hand on my breast—over my shirt, then under my shirt, and finally under my bra. Then it would be my shorts— over, in, under. Then we'd be doing it. Then we would have done it. Would Paula Elam and the girls in the second-floor bathroom make room at the sinks for me so I could share the mirror? Would boys call late at night and tell me to wait at the end of the driveway, that they'd be by in five minutes? Would Linda whisper nasty gossip about me? Maybe none of that would happen. I didn't look different because my mother was dead, did I?

I crossed my arms in front of my chest, uncrossed them because I didn't look kissable sitting like that. But I crossed them back when there seemed to be nowhere else to put them. I thought about telling the joke Becky's sister had said to have ready, but I couldn't remember the punch line. I shouldn't be here. Becky wouldn't be here, and neither would her sister.

"Want a beer?" Joe reached to the floor of the backseat and pulled up four cans of a six-pack of Pabst, looped together with plastic rings. "Sorry it's warm," and he opened two cans. We drank in silence.

I leaned over and picked up Will's baseball off the floor. "I can't believe Will pitched a no-hitter."

"Did he tell you about the scout from the Cubs?"

I nodded, though Will hadn't said anything about the Cubs or a scout. Lucky Will to be so good at baseball; everything always worked out for him, like the no-hitter tonight. "Maybe he'll be a big star." I thought about Will in a Cubs hat, in faraway Chicago. Was that what he wanted, to leave me behind too? I swallowed hard, looked at Joe and his tangly black hair.

"The ace." Joe put his hand on my knee. My breathing quickened. He had to hear it.

The ball was still in my hand. "Why did Will shake you off?"

"He never pulls that," Joe said. "But I guess he knew what he was doing, since he got the no-hitter." He squeezed my knee, slid his hand higher up my thigh. I had shaved my legs with a fresh razor—Becky's sister said your legs should feel like silk the night of a date.

I said, "Will always knows what he's doing." A moment later, I said, "I never know what I'm doing." And a moment after that, I said, "Except for now." I pushed my lips together, nodded. "I know exactly what I'm doing now."

He spoke quietly: "Do you?"

I nodded again.

"Because just talking is fine," he said.

But I felt like I'd already spent forever talking and all you got with that was a bunch of words that didn't really mean anything, voices endlessly yammering in my head—do this, don't do that, tell him a joke, fit in, liven up canned soup with a squeeze of lemon. I was about to do it with Joe Fry in the cemetery where my mother was buried, and if something was ever going to mean anything, that would.

"Let's talk later." I closed my eyes and tilted my face backward so he'd lean in and kiss me, which he did. His breath was warm and smelled like beer, like darkness, like someplace far away that you think about on long nights when you feel alone. His hands curved my face; his rough calluses rubbed my cheeks, and I let go of the baseball. It dropped back onto the floor, and I latched my fingers into his long, dark hair that was softer than it looked. I let his hair run through my fingers like handfuls of sand on a beach, like there was so much that it didn't matter if you wasted some.

This was easy. All it was was getting into the backseat of the car.

"You're so sexy," he murmured into my ear, his breath damp, his tongue slick and wet.

And maybe this is who I really was: a sexy girl whose mother had killed herself, and if a boy wanted to take me far away in his car, there was no one to stop me from going.

"You're so beautiful," he murmured into my other ear.

What did it mean to feel beautiful? This? A boy's arms wrapped tight around you, a hand pushing up along the bottom of your shirt? People said this was supposed to mean something, but what if it didn't? What if it simply was what it was? Maybe the secret was that I could do this in a car in the cemetery where my dead mother was buried—by a grave I was afraid to see in the daylight—and it would all mean nothing.

"God," Joe murmured. His hand was warm sliding up my stomach. It was as if I'd forgotten how to breathe, what breathing was, that lungs needed air.

I kissed him, kissed his face and his fingers and his neck and his ear and his hair and the top of his head. I wanted to think only about that, about him, but there were a million things in my head, like Mama's grave being right over there, underneath the big maple tree, and how if it wasn't there, I wouldn't be doing this; I'd be at home whispering on the phone with Becky, wondering about doing it instead of actually doing it here in the car with Joe Fry who'd done it with so many girls you couldn't count them on both hands. And what Becky would say if she knew; what her sister would say ("I could tell she was that kind of girl!"). Mama not getting off that train in Chicago. Mrs. Johnson doing it in a car somewhere with that man she whispered to on the phone, and, later, with Mr. Johnson in their bed with the chintz bedspread that matched the chintz drapes. Perfect Linda waiting until she was married. Dotty King always knowing the best way to do anything. And Mama, her grave right there.

"You're soooo . . . sexy," Joe mumbled, like he'd never said it to anyone else quite like that. When he said those things, when his voice moaned all throaty, as if it was caught somewhere deep inside, when his hand slid under my bra, up my cutoffs, into my underwear, when Joe Fry whispered in my ear, that's what meant something. Maybe I wasn't alone, maybe there was someone to tell me to my face I was beautiful, and I wasn't always going to be the one left behind. He promised that he loved me, he promised I was as beautiful as he said, and he told me he'd love me forever and that all I had to do was look into his eyes and I would know it was true. So I looked into his eyes and nodded as though I saw everything, as though everything was there, as if I truly believed that in one night we had both found the thing we were looking for.

AFTERWARD, WE sat on the car hood, leaning back against the windshield, looking out over the cemetery. We held hands, drank warm Pabst. It wasn't that bad once you got used to it. According to Joe that was the way they drank it in England, which was the place he said he'd pick if someone gave him a free trip anywhere. "Or Canada to visit my brother."

"I'd go to Egypt," I said. "To see if the Sphinx holds the answers to the world."

Joe said, "You find answers in the sky, in the stars. Not something man-made like the Sphinx. A star explodes and here we are. That's what it's all about, Alice. One star exploding." He squeezed my hand, then brought it up to his lips, turned it over and kissed my palm. "You're pretty." It sounded different when he said it like this instead of whispering in my ear. Like I should say, *No, I'm not*, or, *You're just saying that*. He said, "When I saw you that time at your house in that dress. God."

Without thinking, I said, "That was my mother's dress." I pulled my hand away, crossed my arms. I might as well have told him Mama was talking to me and let him call me crazy. Or would someone who thought about spiderwebs and stars understand about Mama?

He set his hand in the crook of my elbow. "I'm sorry about your mother and everything."

I nodded, stared straight ahead, blinked hard so I wouldn't cry.

He said, "Must be tough with her gone."

"She's here." I pointed toward the maple tree with the hand that held the beer can. He looked at the far corner of the cemetery. I noticed that my hand shook.

"Fuck," he said softly.

"There's no stone yet," I said. "It's on order."

He put his arms around me and took a breath like he wanted to say something, but he just pulled me close. Actually, his arms around me were better than anything that had happened so far. A moment later, he said, "You should've said something. We could've gone somewhere else."

"It's fine," I said. "I never come here anyway. My mother's here, but she isn't really. I mean, this isn't her. I mean, it's her but it isn't."

"I'm sorry," he said. "Everything." The words sounded very short, cut off. Like the wrong ones to say. The same thing everybody else said.

"I'm fine." I shifted his arms away from me, twisted back to look hard at him.

"I, we shouldn't've . . ." His voice trailed off, and he bit his lip. He looked away with just his eyes. He reached for his beer, drank until there was none left, then he dented the side of the can with his fingers and thumb. The noise was oddly sudden.

He had been here before and said those same things to plenty of girls, and plenty of girls had sipped warm beer with him and tossed their cans out into the cemetery and driven along the roads we had and through the same traffic lights. All of it, every single thing that had happened tonight, meant nothing. He wasn't going to call me tomorrow. He wasn't going to talk to me again. I'd be lucky if everyone didn't find out what we had done; I remembered Matt Baum staring at me, Ann Trinder. I'd be lucky if I wasn't the one he got pregnant. It was one night, it was now, it was nothing.

But I said, "Don't be sorry. I wouldn't change anything, not one thing."

He said, "I actually do like you."

But that didn't much matter. His eyes were still looking somewhere else. He was still biting his lip, and my mother was still dead.

He kissed my hand again. But not my lips. We talked some more, mostly baseball, and he laughed at my joke.

THE SKY was that gray before sunrise when Joe finally took me home. We didn't talk much on the drive, and this time he didn't speed, didn't blow through stop signs. Some farmers were out working; lights shone through windows in farmhouses, making them look cozy and important, like a place you'd want to be going to at the end of a long night.

We got to our driveway and he pulled in crooked, the way Aunt Aggy hated. She was going to be furious I had been out all night. I thought maybe Joe would kiss me, but he looked straight ahead through the front windshield, said, "Guess I'll see you around."

How many times had he said those exact words, not meaning them then either? I picked up Will's baseball, said, "Thanks so much for the lovely evening," exactly as Becky's sister had recommended for the end of the date as you're quickly pushing open the car door so you don't have to kiss him. She told us not to kiss anyone until the third date, maybe the second if he was super cute and he had spent enough money (she didn't define "enough"). I opened the car door, slammed it shut in the middle of whatever he was saying next.

I stood in the kitchen and watched the wall clock; the hands didn't seem to move, but three minutes went by, four, five, and then I heard his car drive away. The kitchen was stuffy and too quiet and smelled like sauerkraut.

Mama's voice was stern and abrupt, a jangling thing you want to knock away with the back of your hand. "You've done something you can't ever undo. Did you think of that?"

Anyone would have to admit that was pretty fucking funny coming from her. But I thought I might cry.

She went on: "Why didn't you listen to me?"

Also very funny.

Then she spoke softly: "Do you know how I know this?," and suddenly, in that second, I knew. There was no love at first sight. The articles in *Seventeen* were only filler between ads. A no-hitter ball was the ball the umpire happened to pull out of his pouch. You could do it and maybe it would mean something but maybe it wouldn't.

I closed my eyes. So she hadn't loved my father. So what.

Mama sighed. "It's complicated."

Or, it's simple. She hadn't loved him. What was the big deal? I mean, Joe didn't love me. Was there more to say?

Again, all Mama said was, "It's complicated."

Like that explained even one single thing when the fact was, you could wake up one day and that might be the day your mother killed herself. I shook my head. I should have known, done something. I should've seen. I should have KNOWN.

"It's all so complicated," Mama said again, even softer than before.

"Shut up already!" I didn't want to cry. Everyone knew what it meant if you cried after you did it the first time. It meant you had done something stupid. The train, my father: was that nothing to her? Did anything mean anything?

I opened my eyes and hurried outside. Will was lying flat on the picnic table. I thought he was asleep, but then he said, "You're back."

"Here's your ball." I set it on the table, next to his hand. Then I sat on one of the benches.

"I don't care about that stupid ball," he said.

I looked at the scuff marks, the official black writing curving across it. I didn't care much about it either. But I said, "You threw a no-hitter."

"You were with Joe," he said, neither a question nor an accusation.

"Just a drive." Couldn't he tell I was lying? Wasn't he going to say something? After a moment, I asked, "How was the party at the park? Did you find Kathy?"

"She went home."

I thought of everyone slapping Will on the back, telling him how special he was, the scout from the Cubs writing Will's name in a little notebook and putting a checkmark by it.

Will folded his arms behind his head. "You have no idea what it's like, feeling this no-hitter happening, and everyone thinking you're in total control, that you know exactly what you're doing. But you don't know anything. All I wanted was one sign—just one sign that meant everything would be all right." His voice started out hollow and empty, and by the end he sounded angry.

"The no-hitter," I said.

"That's not what I wanted."

I thought about it for a moment, then asked, "So what did you want?"

He sat up and stared at me, then knocked the ball off the table. It rolled across the patio and stopped when it bumped against the grass. "You know she went to every home game, every one, Alice. I'd look up and there she was. No one else's mother did that." He closed his eyes, but just a bit too late. One tear trickled down his cheek. I wiped it away with my pinkie. "I just wanted to somehow know she was there." I watched him struggle not to cry and thought about my brother leaving me to play baseball, my brother turning into one of those guys you read about in the sports section, me searching the box scores of the newspaper for news of my brother: Had he been traded, did he get a hit, is he on the DL, was he sent back to the minors? Finally I set my hand on his shoulder. I was afraid he'd push it away, but he didn't. His body rose and fell as he breathed, and I longed to hold on to this moment forever as the sky turned pink and orange around us.

THE NEXT day, Will drove me to the cemetery. For the first time since the funeral, I looked at Mama's grave, at the dried-up flowers that Will had picked from the yard and put there. I looked at the place where the stone would go, at the way light quivered through the leaves in the tree above. I looked at bugs crawling on the dry grass, the dandelions about to go to seed, all the clover with the purple flowers. I pulled one of the clover flowers and took it apart petal by petal, touching my tongue to the sweet, honeyed ends.

I saw all that, all the things that were there.

I had brought the ball, thinking I'd leave it behind on her grave. Instead I went to that place at the fence and stared out over the now-green cornfield, vast as an ocean. Will came up behind me, and I put the ball in his hand and he heaved it out as hard and far as he could, out into that cornfield, a beautiful arc through the blue, blue sky, sailing out to the absolute middle of nowhere.

CORNFIELDS

I TOLD Becky that Joe Fry wasn't my type after all. We kept whispering on the phone most nights, Becky saying the same old things about Mr. Miller, but all that talk about kissing felt distant now, like a fairy tale you believed as a kid.

Mama lectured me about types of birth control, like I didn't already know that from eighth-grade health class and like it wasn't too late anyway. And I'd gotten my period several days after, thank God. What I wanted to know was what to say to Joe if I saw him: Bring up that he'd never called? Pretend nothing happened? Or maybe she could tell me if my life was wrecked forever. But Mama just went on about rubbers, diaphragms, and the pill. It was like the makeup tips she had given me but much more embarrassing.

I apologized to Aunt Aggy for staying out all night, admitted I should've called from Becky's house, where we had lost track of the time, and promised I'd never do it again. Then I complimented her new painting of chickens in front of a barn. After telling me it was actually a still life of an apple and popcorn, she grounded me for a week.

I didn't know what to say to Will, so I said nothing. A man named Lefty Wilkes called the house a few times, and though Will never told me why, I knew he was the baseball scout. We both had our secrets.

Now Joe honked the horn for Will instead of coming inside. And of course it had to be Joe who ended up the hero by winning the baseball championship game with a come-from-behind grand slam on a three-two pitch.

So it was actually a relief when detasseling season started, because working out in the cornfields would keep me too tired to think.

Everyone hated detasseling corn, but everyone did it. It was how to make real money if you weren't sixteen (you only had to be fourteen), and we got minimum wage, time and a half after forty hours, and double time on Sundays, which beat baby-sitting or cutting grass. Didn't matter if it was your first year or second detasseling because you had heard all about it from friends, sisters, brothers. Even parents had detasseled way back when, even Mama, Aunt Aggy, even—hard to believe!—Mr. Cooper. Nothing about the three-week season had changed since then.

We met at the high school parking lot at six in the morning to board a claptrappy school bus that looked like it had been plucked out of a junkyard. The bus wheezed, snorted, clattered, and squeaked, and though the windows were always open, the hot, swirling air never cooled us.

Weather didn't matter to the seed-corn company; we were walking through the cornfields yanking tassels off the tip tops of stalks no matter if it was ninety-five degrees or dumping buckets of rain. Add in bugs, snakes, spiders, and mice; sunburn (your nose peeled and re-burned at least five times); and "corn poisoning," an itchy rash from the razor-edged corn leaves scraping bare skin.

Worst of all were the perky people the seed company hired to "supervise" us, students at the liberal arts college in the town where the seed company was based. They singsonged, "We're all one happy team," like they meant it. They had never had jobs where they were the "boss," though they were carefully trained to say "supervisor," so they lorded it over us. They didn't have to walk the rows, and when it was pouring rain, we were in the fields, mud sloshing in our shoes, but they stayed in the bus, napping.

None of that mattered ultimately: In Shelby, when you were fourteen and fifteen, you detasseled. We always had.

. . .

DAY ONE. After a jiggly, forty-five-minute bus ride out to the first field, Becky, Linda, and I huddled at the back of the group as Cindi, the supervisor, explained the principles of detasseling. "There's six rows of female corn," Cindi said in a chipmunky voice. "And two rows of male corn. Six female, two male." She emphasized every other word. "And what we're doing is"—the boys snickered and elbowed each other, knowing something was about to sound sexy—"making sure only the pollen from the male rows is out there, reaching down to the silks on the female rows and, um, pollinating them." She blushed. I rolled my eyes at Linda, who curled her lip. Cindi continued, her round face all pink: "So we're pulling the tassels in the female rows, and we're not touching the male rows. That's how we grow perfect hybrid seed corn for farmers to plant next year."

"Same speech as last year," Becky whispered. Sunlight glinted off her glasses.

Cindi said, "Male rows are marked with silver paint at each end of the field. What do we do with the male rows?" She waved her arm forward, encouraging our answer but couldn't wait: "We don't touch them! That's key!"

Rod, the other supervisor, rustled papers on his clipboard, uninterested in what Cindi was saying. He wore mirror sunglasses, as did the bus driver, who was leaning his forehead against the steering wheel, asleep. Linda had already pronounced Rod "super cute," and any time he looked up from his clipboard, she flipped her hair—not that he seemed to notice.

Drone, drone: Pull the tassel up because yanking down damaged the leaves; we'd be divided into teams of six to walk the female rows; she and Rod would check that we weren't missing too many tassels. If you had detasseled one cornstalk in your life, you had learned everything there was to know about detasseling.

Mama and Aunt Aggy owned farmland they rented out, somewhere in the opposite direction from here, where Mama had lived until she was ten. Mama had taken me there once a couple of years ago, after I'd

nagged enough about it. The house and barn had been burned down—
Mama said probably kids who knew no one lived there—and all that was
left were cornfields that looked like every other cornfield I had ever seen.
Mama didn't even want to get out of the car; I had to beg her for that, too,
and we stood side by side in the gravel road, looking out at that endless
stretch of green. Finally, I asked what she remembered from living on the
farm. She didn't answer, just kept staring at the field, so intensely I asked
what she saw. Then she laughed and told me funny stories about the cats
that lived in the barn, how she named the kittens after movie stars.

Now, crows squawked and swooped overhead. A light breeze picked
up, and the yellow tassels topping the cornstalks swished and swayed,
rolling with the wind. Even from where I stood, I heard a slight rustle, like
a whisper, then silence. This was a good year for farmers because the corn
was taller than I was. I couldn't see to the other end of the field.

"Kind of like the ocean, isn't it?" Mama sounded as if she was sharing a secret.

I squinted, and though I had never seen the ocean, looking at that
field made me think I might know something about its foreverness and
constant motion. For a minute that cornfield looked beautiful. I opened
my mouth, then closed it. I couldn't say that to Becky and Linda. The
only person who might understand was Joe Fry. How could he be so
hateful but also the kind of guy who could see how a cornfield was like
the ocean?

"Remember that dream where I was lost in a field?" Mama said. "I
called, but no one heard."

Linda whispered, "This is boring." Becky and I nodded. I shifted
my weight onto my other leg. Becky and Linda shifted too. I crossed my
arms, uncrossed them.

Mama said, "You know that dream."

She was always dreaming something—cold snow drifting in silence,
being lost in cornfields, running for a train leaving the station, hurtling
into pure black space on a rocket ship. Mama hardly ever slept through
the night, and when she woke with a scream, so did we. Or it was the
sound of her tiptoes on the creaky stairs, heading to the kitchen to bake
bread or cookies. "No nightmares in the kitchen," she said. It was noth-

ing for us to squeeze our breakfast around six dozen cupcakes cooling on the table. I learned to sleep with the pillow smushed over my head.

"Those cornstalks," Mama said. "Beautiful from far away, but up close, in that dream, like bars on a prison."

Linda muttered, "Come on already," and shifted her weight again, sighed.

The ocean, a prison. Didn't Mama know which?

"Both." Mama's single word was sad.

Cindi was talking about the importance of "hydration" instead of saying, "Drink water," like a normal person. "When I detasseled, I froze cans of pop the night before so they'd stay cold till lunch."

"Works with beer," called one of the boys in the back, maybe Doug Foltz, Lily's ex. Everyone laughed.

"Absolutely no alcohol!" Cindi said, as Rod glanced up: "Very funny, wise guy."

Cindi fumbled the pages on her clipboard. "Rod and I have divided you into teams, so listen up for—"

"We always make our own teams," one of the boys said, and there was a murmur of agreement. Detasseling would be hopeless if you couldn't walk the rows with your friends, gossiping about who was cute, who was going out, who was annoying.

"Not this year." Apparently Rod was not trying the friendly approach.

Cindi raised her chipmunk voice above our groans: "Listen up while I call your names." She screwed up everyone's last names, saying "Noop" instead of "Ka-noop" for Andy Knoop and his brother, or "Denny" like the first name instead of "Den-en-ey" for Theresa Denneny. These were the names I had been hearing all my life. I knew these people: who always forgot their lunch, who tried to sneak in beer, who sucked up to the supervisors, who quit after two days. And they knew me—that I'd stand with Becky and Linda, that I was responsible, that I'd hold it forever before peeing outside. These names were a rhythm, a chant, that Cindi, who wasn't from Shelby, would never know.

I was on the green team, stuck with two loser boys who were only fourteen, Linda, Paula Elam, and Doug Foltz, who whipped a comb out of his back pocket when he heard Linda's name called, making it easy to guess where that was heading.

Rod and Cindi lined us up along the edge of the field, one person per female row; "We'll be checking," Rod hollered. Actually, they'd walk a couple steps in, then hop back on the bus to be driven around to the other end, where they'd wait for us.

Linda and I got into side-by-side rows, and she launched into how cute Rod was and how old was he and didn't I agree she and Rod would have super-cute children because they were both blue-eyed blondes and did I think his real name was Rod or was that short for Rodney, because she liked Rod, but not Rodney, and she wouldn't want to name one of their sons Rodney, but men always wanted a boy named after them, look at her dad and Jimmy Jr.

Two seconds in, sweat dripped into my eyes, and my arm muscles ached from reaching up, grabbing hold, pulling, dropping the tassel; reaching, grabbing, pulling, dropping; reach, grab, pull, drop. I felt like a speck in a plague of locusts, chewing my way through this field. And on the other side, we'd simply turn around and chew back through new rows. Repeat a million times on a blistering-hot day and that was detasseling. Linda's yammering voice was going to get pretty old pretty quick.

We worked significantly faster than the green team boys, who were busy whacking each other with corn tassels and rolling in the dirt, wrestling, trying to pull each other's shirts over their heads.

Paula Elam kept pace with us but didn't talk. She was wearing bright red lipstick, and her jeans were really tight, with a peace sign Magic-Markered on her butt. Her hair was so long and straight that to keep it off her face she tied it in a loose knot without using a rubber band. I let Linda talk while I watched Paula Elam's hands and her bright red nails pulling tassels. She was the one who'd done it with everyone, with Joe Fry. Her father, probably the richest man in town, was the president of Shelby Farmers & Merchants Bank, and no one talked about her two sisters the way they talked about her. I'd said a grand total of ten words to her since grade school, most of them "Excuse me" in the second-floor bathroom. The corn was dense enough that she couldn't see me staring at her hands. I mean, they were just hands.

Linda was still going on, so I tried concentrating on the pop-pop-pop of tassels being yanked, tried to listen to the crows overhead; they seemed to be having a Linda-like conversation with each other. A tiny bug buzzed my ear, sounding enormous. Linda's babble. Crows. Boys yelling far away. Loose dirt crunching under my feet, under Paula's feet. My fingers clutching the tassel. The tassel squeaking and popping. My heartbeat. My breath scraping my throat. All of that repeating itself over and over, one big rhythm of detasseling.

"This cornfield will outlast us all." Mama said it as if she was standing next to me, not like she was dead and the field had already outlasted her. As if this field were somehow more important than a mother.

I stepped on my shoelace, so I bent to tie my shoe. It was cooler down there, shaded by the cornstalks, the blue sky and hot sun suddenly more distant, the dirt warm and soft underneath me, the air much closer. I thought about Mama underground. Maybe it was like this. The rustle of the corn leaves was louder, closer, like a hot, wet whisper in your ear, like . . . I shook my head hard to stop thinking about Joe and closed my eyes. I could sit here forever, as Linda and her voice moved beyond me. How long before she'd notice I wasn't there? Doug Foltz thrashed through his row, called, "Hey, Linda! Wait up!," barely pausing to pull any tassels. Rod and Cindi wouldn't fire him because Doug Foltz was not the kind of boy who was fired from jobs or got caught when he cheated on tests. I imagined Doug and Linda ending up together, their two boys and two girls growing up and marrying Becky's two boys and two girls or Pam's or Lily's. No man on a train for Linda. No Joe Fry and his secret whispers in the backseat of a Mustang. Nothing that wasn't exactly the way she had planned.

I clutched a fistful of dirt, brought it to my nose and sniffed. This had been here since the beginning of time, or at least since the glaciers retreated from Iowa. That unit on Iowa history in sixth grade, something about glaciers, seemed far away. Right now everything in the world seemed far away, especially Mama. It was forever ago that I had painted the fingernails on her right hand so she wouldn't smudge doing it herself or watched her take groceries out of paper bags. Forever ago that she helped me bake oatmeal cookies to enter in the county fair or brought home from the newspaper office those big pieces of layout paper with the blue lines that I used to like to draw on or read one of my book reports and added commas in all the right places. I sniffed the dirt again, then sneezed.

"Bless you," Paula said.

I opened my eyes. How long had she been standing there, peering at me through the cornstalks, her lipsticked lips a smear of red? Who wore lipstick when they detasseled? "Thanks." I stood up, dropping the dirt, brushing my hands against my Levi's. We were the same height. Her lips were so red I couldn't stop looking at them.

"Are you all right?" She tilted her head, squinted.

"I'm fine." I yanked a tassel, dropped it on the ground. But I didn't keep going.

"Don't get all snippy," she said. "You were just sitting there in the dirt." She stood with her hands on her rear jeans pockets, leaning back a bit so her big boobs jutted out like glasses on a table. For half a second, I pictured Joe Fry's hands cupped around them.

I yanked another tassel. It would be easy to keep going, catch up with Linda. I could help the green team be first out of the field and win points toward our team total in Cindi's "motivational" contest. I was always doing that sort of thing because that was the kind of person I was. I chucked a tassel, like a spear, down my row. We watched it soar, heard it knock some cornstalks, then hit the ground.

Paula reached down the front of her shirt and pulled out a tube of lipstick, slicked some on her lips, held it out to me. "Want some?"

I shook my head.

"It's melting," she said. "But, God, I can't not wear lipstick. Might as well show up naked." She reached back down the front of her shirt and poked the tube into her bra. If I did that, everyone would see the lipstick outline on my tiny chest. "Aren't you the one whose mother killed herself?"

It was strange to hear Paula say, *Aren't you the one*, as if she knew certain things about me. I noticed how she had said "killed herself" instead of "passed away," the way the neighbor ladies or teachers did. I nodded.

"That sucks," she said. "I remember your mom—she was pretty. I have a baby sister who died. We put her in the crib, and she was dead the next time we looked."

I nodded again, not sure what to say. I couldn't think of anyone besides me and Will with a dead person in their family except for normal dead people like grandparents.

"God, I need a cigarette," she said. "Got one?"

"Sorry, I don't smoke."

"You should. It's relaxing."

Mama loved to smoke. "I look good doing it," she always said. I told her smoking was bad for her; "I'm not going to die from a little cigarette smoke," she had scoffed.

Paula touched a corn leaf, ran her thumb across the leaf's veins. "We don't talk about Debbie—my sister—except to say she's an angel in heaven." She let go of the leaf, crossed her arms against her chest, bumping up her boobs. "That's a load of crap. It all is. Like not talking about her makes her go away."

I kicked at the dirt with one foot, then the other. I'd never be brave enough to call heaven a "load of crap," but hearing people tell me Mama was an angel in heaven didn't make me feel better either. She wasn't even religious. And nothing about being an angel was as good as Mama actually being here.

Paula uncrossed her arms, went on: "People don't know shit. That guy Rod your friend was going on about? He's an asshole."

I liked how she'd say anything. *Asshole.* "How do you know him?" Maybe she had done it with him.

"I don't have to know him to know he's an asshole." She looked straight at me as she added, "Because they all are. Believe me." My face reddened, as if she knew I was thinking about Joe. She stared up at the sky, squinting into the sun. The underneath part of her neck was very pale. It seemed our peculiar conversation was over, so I picked another tassel—it would take some hustling to catch up to everyone else—when she suddenly said, "Shit," and leaned over and threw up onto the ground, her shoulders shaking, the choking coming from down deep, little hacking gasps that lasted long after everything had come up.

I hadn't watched anyone throw up since the time Becky ate fourteen s'mores at a 4-H cookout. This was just as awful, and I wanted to walk away and pull tassels and catch up with Linda and win points for the green team. But I said, "Are you all right?"

She coughed, straightened up, didn't look at me. "Oh, yeah, I'm fine. Just peachy."

"I mean, can I do something?" I shoved through the cornstalks and into her row, avoiding the barf on the ground, thinking I would hug her, but once I was next to her, I was afraid to. Her arms were crossed again, tight against her chest, and unfallen tears glittered in her eyes. I reached in my pocket. "Want a Kleenex?" Girls always had Kleenex for peeing in the fields.

Paula looked away and spat, then took the Kleenex and wiped her face with it, smearing her lipstick. "My mouth tastes like a toilet," she said, and she spat again. Then she wiped her mouth with the back of her hand, looked at the lipstick on her skin, and wiped with the tissue until there was no lipstick left.

"I bet Linda has a Tic Tac," I said. Linda was into fresh breath.

"I don't want one of Linda's stupid Tic Tacs," she said. "Don't tell anyone you saw me puke. Especially not big mouth Linda."

"I could get a Tic Tac without saying you threw up."

"Just forget the whole thing." She grabbed a tassel in each hand, yanked hard so they popped out. Then she grabbed some more, yanked. I watched for a moment, then stepped back in my row, started pulling tassels, keeping behind her so we wouldn't have to talk.

When we reached the other end, I got a couple of Tic Tacs from Linda and took them over to Paula, who was standing with the smokers. They stopped talking as I approached, blew soft waves of smoke into the air. Paula thanked me, and I thought maybe she wanted to say more, but she didn't, so I went back to where Becky and Linda slouched in the shade of the parked bus, comparing blisters.

GOING HOME, Linda sat next to me, and Becky was in front of us. A thin layer of dust coated my body, clinging to the sweat. Every window in the bus was down and wind roared through, but it wasn't refreshing, more like being sandblasted. Linda plucked her shirt off her sticky skin and blew down her front. "I'm staying in the shower all night," Becky said.

I craned my head to look around the bus. Paula sat by herself, toward the back, her feet propped up across the seat. I'd never thought about whether she was pretty. We usually talked about her big boobs or how Mr. Rhinehart's face turned bright red when she walked by him in the hall. We said things like, "She thinks she's so great," or, "Did you see what Paula Elam's wearing today?" I couldn't remember a time when she was like the rest of us, when we weren't talking about her. By fourth grade she was wearing a bra, the first girl who did. She pulled up her shirt and showed us at recess. For a while she wore slumpy clothes so you couldn't see much, but then one day in seventh grade she showed up at school in a tube top.

Linda looked at where I was looking. So did Becky. Linda spoke quietly, "Bet she's pregnant by the end of our junior year."

"That isn't nice," Becky said, but not as if she much meant it.

Linda shrugged, yawned, looked away, scrunched deeper into the seat. "It's how it is with those kinds of girls." She closed her eyes.

Paula turned her head and caught me looking at her. Her eyes narrowed, but then she lifted one hand. I half-waved back. "She's on my team," I explained to Becky, who had seen.

Becky said, "Do you really think she's done it with everyone?"

Without opening her eyes, Linda said, "For sure."

I glanced at Paula. You couldn't tell that from looking, just like you couldn't tell she had a dead baby sister or that I'd done it with Joe Fry.

Outside, cornfield after cornfield went by as the bus driver found every rut there was on the gravel roads. Gray dust floated through the windows, settling on the vinyl seats, on us. The bus wheezed. I thought about how warm that dirt had been in my hand, as if it was something alive instead of boring dirt dragged into Iowa by a glacier.

THE NEXT morning, instead of Aunt Aggy, Will drove me to meet the bus. She had set up her easel in front of Mr. Cooper's house, wanting to capture it in the dawn's light, "a trick I learned from Monet," she said.

She planned to surprise Mr. Cooper on his birthday with a series of paintings of his house.

Will was half asleep, clutching a cup of cold coffee left over from last night's supper. I didn't even know he drank coffee. I stared at him as he drove, wishing he would say something—complain about getting up early, make fun of the girls going to *Jaws* who shrieked when the head fell out—but he was silent except for a big yawn every so often.

Last year Mama drove us to detasseling in this same car. Now the seat and mirrors were adjusted for Will. Will's trash cluttered the back. Will paid for gas. I'd been the one finally to take Mama's hairbrush out of the glove compartment, strands of hair still snared in the bristles. I pulled them out and let the wind whisk them away, tossed the brush in the garbage can on the way into the house. It might have been easier if Mama had taken this car to the train tracks instead of Aunt Aggy's—this still felt like her car, though it wasn't.

I accidentally kicked my lunch, and the crackle of the bag sounded so loud and harsh that I had to make Will say something. "Maybe Aunt Aggy will be a famous artist someday." He couldn't pass up a comment like that.

"Maybe pigs will fly."

I laughed as if he had said something wildly funny, lightly punched his shoulder. After a few moments when he didn't say anything else, I tried again: "Too bad about Kathy Clark." As we'd passed on the stairs last night, Will had told me she'd dumped him, but he didn't say more than that.

He grunted, then said, "This coffee's pathetic." He reached his arm out the open window, spilled out the coffee, tossed the cup on the floor at my feet. "She can do whatever she wants. I don't care." Maybe he really didn't; he sure didn't look very heartbroken.

"What happened?" I asked, though I could guess—she got tired of him not calling her back, not paying attention.

"She, I—" There was a long pause as he let the car idle at the stop sign on West Street. "Forget it," he said, accelerating. "Not my type."

"She's so nice," I said. "And pretty."

"Look," he said. "She dumped me, it's over, so shut up. End of story. I'm not asking you a bunch of nosy questions about Joe Fry." He must have felt me glaring at him.

We pulled into the school lot. Will braked, leaned his head all the way back against the seat rest, took in a big breath. His chin looked prickly.

I squinted at the waiting school bus. Paula Elam stood alone, leaning against the bus, smoking a cigarette. She hadn't knotted up her hair yet. Her nose was sunburned.

Finally I said, "That's because there's nothing to ask. I could care less about Joe Fry." I put my hand on the car door handle, waited for him to say something nice—that Joe asked how I was, that Joe was a jerk—waited, pulled the metal thingy back, let the door creak open. I grabbed my lunch and got out into another ungodly hot day, then slammed the door shut.

He called through the open window, "Alice!" His head was still all the way back, and he didn't look at me as he said, "A girl got pregnant." It came out fast, as if he hadn't wanted to say it.

I looked over at Paula again. She blew smoke out of her mouth hard and straight. Suddenly I knew which girl.

Will said, "I wanted to tell you."

I thought of those hot whispers going into Paula's ears, not that Paula would make the mistake of believing them. I quickly said, "Everyone knows what Joe Fry's like." I even managed a short laugh.

"I wanted to tell you," Will repeated. "But you haven't been the same since Mama died."

What a stupid thing to say. "Nothing's been the same since Mama killed herself."

"Say 'died,' " he said.

"Say 'shut up,' " and I walked away fast, but he didn't get out of the car and run after me. Instead he drove off, and there I was in front of Paula. She looked at me slowly, up and down, like she knew something secret about me, not the other way around.

"You found a cigarette," I said. God, I was stupid. I thought I might cry, so I looked at her stomach, hidden by an old, untucked man's shirt with the cuffs rolled up. Probably her bank president father's. I imagined him saying something like, "That Joe Fry's no good; stay away from him." Or whatever fathers said to daughters; I wouldn't know.

She dropped her cigarette butt, smudged it into the asphalt with her foot. "Thanks for trying to help yesterday," she said.

"Well," I said.

She grabbed her hair with both hands, twisted it into a knot. "I'm better now. I'm fine."

Our eyes met. I could be wrong.

But when we were walking the fields, I heard her throw up three rows away from me as Linda complained about how sweat made her face break out.

THAT AFTERNOON, Becky, Linda, and I ate lunch together, scrunched in the narrow shade of an ancient, abandoned tractor. We were too tired to say much. We had gone through this field once, then come back, but Rod said there was another sweep before we'd be done. I was tired of how straight the rows were, how hot the sun was, how Linda had something to say about everything, how Doug Foltz had made himself the leader of our team and kept shouting to get a move on so we would beat the blue team.

I bit into the peanut butter sandwich Aunt Aggy had fixed last night, warm and limp, disgusting. Linda crunched carrot sticks like she was bored with every detail of the entire world. Becky held her can of half-frozen Tab partway to her mouth. I shoved the rest of my sandwich in the paper bag. "Gross," I said.

Becky finally raised her can of pop all the way to her lips, sipped. Then she said, "Cindi was going to get married this summer, but the guy changed his mind. This Saturday was supposed to be the day. The dress is still hanging in her closet."

"Who told you?" Linda hated when she wasn't the first to know.

"She did," Becky said. "She started crying when I was keeping watch while she peed. Don't tell anyone."

I said, "So why are you telling us if it's a secret?"

Becky tilted her pop can from side to side. "I tell you guys everything."

Linda nodded. "Me too. Absolutely everything."

I rummaged through my paper bag, found an apple, mushy from jouncing around under a seat in the bus; I bit into it anyway. Paula's laugh cut through the silence. "Me too," I lied. Paula Elam is pregnant. What was so hard about saying that to my best friends? I did it with Joe Fry. My dead mother talks to me. I listen to *Dotty King's Neighborly Visit*. My father is some man my mother picked up on a train and she didn't love him. Nothing means anything anymore. Oh, and, Linda, your mother's having an affair. I opened my mouth but no words came out.

Becky said, "What?"

"Nothing." A breeze picked up, rustled the corn leaves behind us into a soft whisper, but it drifted away before it could cool my sticky skin any.

Linda and Becky murmured about Cindi's called-off wedding, and I nodded in appropriate places, thinking of how different everything would be if right now Mama were at her job typing classifieds at the Shelby *Beacon* the way she was supposed to be. (Not that she liked working there—strictly a paycheck job, she had called it. Like detasseling.) Then Mama said, "There are more secrets in the world than there is corn," which reminded me of her dream about being lost in a cornfield, shouting as loud as she could but no one hearing her—and abruptly that breeze sent a chill down my spine and I was glad I hardly ever remembered my own dreams. I butted into Linda and Becky's conversation to ask if Cindi ever ran into the guy who was supposed to be the groom, but before we could talk that over, Cindi yelled, "Three minutes!" and three minutes later, we were trudging the fields again.

DAY FIVE, Saturday. By day five, you were tasting the heat like something fuzzy clogging your throat, jerking in a tassel-yanking motion when you were sitting still, slapping away imaginary corn leaves brushing against your arms, staring at a TV screen that wasn't turned on. As you trudged down the rows of corn, yanking one tassel after another, you couldn't remember your life before this or imagine it after. It was day five, nothing but endless cornfields.

The sky was that heavy, low-hanging gray that cracks open suddenly to dump out buckets of rain, then closes up, making everything stiflingly humid. Rod kept staring at the sky, pressing a little radio to his ear for weather reports. For some reason (pollen? Rod's bonus?), it was important that we finish this particular field today. After lunch, the clouds darkened, thickened, turned puddinglike. We weren't supposed to go out during thunderstorms because the seed company didn't want anyone struck by lightning.

Still, Rod sent us out. "One more row," he said, eyes hidden behind his mirror sunglasses. "We can do it."

Cindi frowned, but she was too perky to look angry. I thought she might mention the dangerous conditions, but she glanced at her watch instead, maybe thinking about her wedding that should have been taking place. She hollered, "You heard Rod. Go for it!"

Linda and Doug were deeply involved in an irritating pre-flirtation that involved constant repetition of the phrases, "Did not, did too, you and who else, don't you wish," so I went as fast as I could to get out of earshot. Lately I was the first to finish, not only on the green team but out of everybody, earning team bonus points, which thrilled Doug. People were starting to accuse me of sucking up to Rod and Cindi. But it seemed as easy to pick tassels fast as slow. If my destiny was to pick X million tassels, why not hurry through them?

"Did not—oh, right—maybe in your dreams," melted behind me as I focused on pulling tassels from cornstalks. I imagined I was grabbing Joe Fry by the neck and yanking his head out of his body—pop—dropping it on the ground, trampling it. *So sorry, Joe Fry. Was that your head I crushed?* It was entirely satisfying.

Paula was keeping up with me. I went faster, not wanting to talk, but she went faster too. I hadn't spoken to her since that morning I had realized she was pregnant. Pregnant with an actual baby. I sped up even more.

Paula called, "What's with you? You're a maniac."

"You are too," I said, not letting up.

She looked at the flat, gray sky. "I'm scared of thunderstorms."

That made me pause, one hand on a tassel. "You're kidding," I said.

"When it storms at night, my mother comes and sits on the end of my bed." She sighed, shook her head. "It's kind of stupid. But I actually feel better seeing her there."

Mama loved thunderstorms, and she would run into the backyard in her nightgown to watch, getting drenched with rain. She didn't ask what I thought about storms, if I was afraid.

Paula repeated, "I know it's stupid."

A low rumble rolled across the field; hot air pushed closer. It was going to be a big storm, the kind Mama liked best. She'd say, "It's nature crashing the world down around us." You couldn't tell her it was lightning, rain, or weather. She'd say, "It's like getting a peek at the other side," not explaining the other side of what.

Paula grabbed a tassel, yanked it downward, exactly what we weren't supposed to do. Several leaves ripped. She pulled down on another tassel, another. More thunder grumbled, and she paused to stare up at the sky. "My mom tried to tell me it's angels bowling in heaven. Ridiculous."

I thought of her baby sister being an angel in heaven, of Mama, of angels wearing ugly rental bowling shoes.

Paula pulled down so hard she shredded half the plant. None of it made sense—not dead people crammed in a place up in the sky, not a baby or a mother dying, not hearing a dead person's voice.

I yanked a tassel, a slashing movement that tore six or so leaves. She yanked another. So did I. Suddenly we were racing along our rows, damaging every cornstalk within reach.

"Male rows," she said, slightly out of breath.

We plunged into the "never touch" male rows with their perfect pollen and grunted as we slashed and ripped whole plants. "We'll get fired," I said, but that made us laugh.

"Who cares about seed corn?" she said.

"Rod and Cindi," I said.

"They're busy doing it back at the bus." More thunder, louder—not

just a grumble—filled the sky, and Paula let out a tiny screech. Then she
giggled, and we resumed our rampage. Hard to believe I was wrecking a
cornfield with Paula Elam. What if I really did get fired? I slowed down,
stopped. "How can you tell when someone's done it?" I asked.

She paused, unknotted her hair and shook it free. A bolt of lightning
jagged across the sky. When the thunder came, louder and closer now,
her shoulders jerked as if she'd been stung, but she didn't look away.
"Okay, what are people saying about me?"

"No one's saying anything." I didn't sound convincing, even to
myself.

"Liar." Her stare pushed hard, her eyes narrowed. "I hear what people call me—slut, tramp, worse. Think I care?"

I shook my head, but she knew I was lying.

Tears filled her eyes, overflowed. "This would never happen to you.
You're so lucky." She grabbed hold of a cornstalk and heaved it out, roots
and all, threw it on the ground, kicked it, kicked it again. "I'm knocked
up," she said. "At least pretend to be surprised."

What surprised me was how much I hated her—for being afraid of
thunder, for making me wreck the corn, for doing it with any boy who
called her up, like it meant nothing, for doing it with Joe Fry, for making
me feel like her because I had done it with Joe Fry too.

Lightning flashed; thunder followed more quickly, seeming to surround us. I suppose standing in the middle of a flat cornfield during a
storm wasn't the smartest thing. But I didn't move. "Who?" I demanded.
I held my breath, let it out slowly, silently.

She pulled up another cornstalk, kicked two down, and stomped a
bunch more. "Joe Blow," she said, ripping up more male stalks. "Doesn't
matter who. Just one of the creeps around here. One stupid mistake with
one idiot guy." She stopped with the cornstalks. Then she looked away,
spoke quickly and furiously: "I wish my mother was dead. She hates me,
says I ruined her life. Know what it's like hearing your own mother call
you those names?" She pushed her hair behind her ears. "You and your
friends. Everything's always fine."

"My mother's dead for real!" I shouted, and hearing those words in
the middle of this vast, empty cornfield turned them into something terri-

bly frightening. I raised my arm to slap her, but she grabbed my wrist, pressing her fingers so tightly I felt them in my bones. She grabbed my other arm before I could lift it, and I strained against her, but she was strong.

"Believe me, I know all about dead people," she said.

I stopped struggling, stared at the strands of hair pressed against her cheek. I was afraid she'd keep talking, equally afraid she'd stop.

"Nothing's been the same since Debbie died, and that was five years ago," she said. "Alls I did was set her in the crib. Everyone said it wasn't my fault, that it was something that just happened." She dropped my wrists, stood back as if now she wanted me to hit her. I knew what she was going to say next; I could even whisper the words with her: "So why'd it happen to me?" Then she put her hands over her face and started crying in noisy gulps that made her shoulders shake, and I didn't hate her anymore.

Lightning ricocheted across the sky. It wouldn't be long before the rain started. I put my arm around her shoulder. There was a knobby bone at the top, underneath my fingers. A baby was growing inside her. Paula sank to the ground, and I sat with her, my hand still touching her shoulder. I was supposed to tell her everything would be fine. But it didn't seem like it would be.

"God, I hate this thunder." She shook my hand away.

"It's just thunder," I said.

"That's what I hate," she said. "It doesn't mean anything. There's no reason."

"There's a reason," but if there was, I didn't know it. "Static electricity, I think." I was remembering back to a vague grade-school unit on weather. "Like rubbing a balloon against your hair." Her crying slowed, so I kept babbling: "That's how storms start. Static electricity. Just part of nature." Lightning shot across the sky, like someone was ripping it in half, as easily as a piece of paper. Thunder boomed. "Like on TV," and I imitated the Parkay commercial: " 'It's not nice to fool Mother Nature.' "

"Nature sucks." Paula sniffled, pulled her wrist across her nose.

Lightning cracked, and thunder instantly followed. "You can tell how far away lightning is by counting between the flash and the thunder," I said. "Divide by five, and that's how many miles away."

"That wasn't even two seconds," Paula said.

Rain suddenly pelted us, the kind of hard, fast rain that makes newspapers dredge up statistics from the 1800s for comparison. Rivulets of water gathered around us, spilled out in all directions. Lightning zapped so fast there was no way to count before the thunder; it was all one big blurry, flashy, crashing commotion. Rain ran down the corn leaves onto us, as the plants bowed and swayed in the wind.

Paula wrapped her arms around herself.

I tried pretending the lightning overhead was nothing more than fireworks. But one single flash of lightning, and we could be dead. I'd seen plenty of lone trees in fields from the bus window, charred and broken.

Paula shouted, "Should we run back?"

"Better not to stand up," I said. "Anyway, which side of the field is the bus on? Did they already drive around?"

"Probably left without us."

"They'd notice we weren't there." Like they'd notice if I was dead, struck by lightning. I imagined Becky and Linda sobbing at my funeral, Aunt Aggy falling apart, Will writing my name with Magic Marker inside his baseball cap, next to Mama's. Joe Fry . . . well, he'd just keep doing it with girls in his car, and soon enough Becky would find someone else to tell secrets to, and Linda would be in love with Doug Foltz, and Aunt Aggy would marry Mr. Cooper, and Will would be the ace for the Cubs, and Dotty King's show would come on the air every day like always. Could that be? Paula had said nothing was the same after someone died. Corn leaves lashed at my face and arms as the wind picked up.

Paula started to say something but broke off with a scream because it was the biggest lightning yet, almost simultaneous with the loudest thunder, as if both were fractions of an inch away. Rain streamed around us. The ground smelled dank and wormy. Pellets of hail dropped down, like someone heaving gravel. I closed my eyes, but that seemed to make the thunder louder. So I opened them again, tilted my head to look at Paula, who sat the same way I did: knees hunched up to her chest, arms wrapped around, head ducked. If Mama liked this so much—rain jabbing like needles, handfuls of hail—where was she?

Paula was hysterical: "We're going to die!"

"It's just a storm!" I shouted.

"They'll be sorry if I die," Paula said. "Saying I wrecked my life, wrecked theirs. Like I committed the crime of the century. My mother made a hundred phone calls figuring out what to do, and my dad's looking for a military school for girls. God—what if he finds one?"

"What's going to happen to you?" I asked.

She buried her face in her scrunched-up knees. Her shoulders started shaking again, and for a long time I stared at them. Why did I ask when I knew exactly what was going to happen? Girls who got pregnant went away and secretly had the baby. Then they came back and pretended it had never happened. That was just how it was.

The hail let up, but nothing else. Finally Paula said, "It's not so wrong, is it?"

"What?"

"What I did. Wanting, you know, to be in love with someone. Wanting . . ." Her voice trailed off.

Thunder tumbled and rolled around us. I said, "I did it with Joe Fry. I thought he . . ." I swallowed around the lump in my throat. *Cared,* I finished in my mind, *loved me.*

She was silent, and I couldn't decide if she hadn't heard me or was pretending she hadn't. I spoke quickly, "I can't believe they're not looking for us. Cindi's so—"

"Every time I think that exact same thing."

I swallowed again. "It was Joe, wasn't it?"

Wet, battered cornstalks whacked us, looking for a way to grab hold. I counted seconds randomly, divided by five.

Then Paula said, "Um . . . no. I mean, maybe. I guess what I mean is, I don't know for sure who." She pushed her wet hair away from her forehead, rubbed both cheeks with the back of her hand, took a deep breath, as if she was finished crying. "God, I want a cigarette."

I said, "It's not like it meant anything with Joe Fry or anything." I closed my eyes, leaned my head way back, let the rain beat me, pound me. I thought of Mama standing in the backyard as rain poured down, Mama that time staying upstairs while tornado sirens wailed and we yelled at her to come to the basement. It was all so long ago.

Paula said, "This rain is forever."

But it wasn't. Already the silence between the lightning and the thunder was increasing as the storm moved on. The rain would stop, the sun would shine, puddles would dry, corn would keep pollinating, we'd go back to detasseling. There'd probably even be a rainbow.

In the distance, Cindi's tiny voice called, "Alice! Paula!" I opened my eyes.

Paula draped one arm across her stomach, said, "This is a secret," and paused.

People would figure it out soon enough, but I said, "Promise I won't tell."

"Not that." She scrunched a handful of mud, flung it across the rows. I didn't think she was going to say more, but then words tumbled out: "This. That I really want the baby. I mean, I'm scared, but I was thinking maybe having this baby could be like if Debbie didn't die. Everything could go back to the way it was. Am I stupid?"

Anger jolted me—she could have a baby, but I could never find another mother—and I grabbed the cornstalk next to me, shook it so water flew off. It looked like every other cornstalk in the row, the field, the whole state. I yanked it out of the ground. Yes, she was stupid to think anything could ever go back to the way it was, but before I could say so, she said, "That's what I want more than anything."

The rain had lessened, but it was still coming, soft and gentle now, dripping down my face like tears. My mud-splattered clothes clung to my skin; even my underwear and bra were sopping. We both knew her parents would never let her keep that baby, that people weren't like rows of corn, all the same and replaceable come spring planting. Saying so would only make everything worse.

She said, "I have a feeling it's a girl."

I crossed my fingers on both hands, held them up. She smiled, crossed her own fingers.

And there was Cindi, muddy and wet. "Do you know how worried we were?" she said, hands on her hips. "Didn't you hear Rod call everyone back?" We stood up as Cindi went on: "You could have been killed. What on earth were you thinking?"

Paula said, "I don't know," the low, dull voice that made angry adults angrier.

"Alice?" Cindi turned the word into a very sharp question.

"I'm sorry." I tried to actually sound sorry.

Cindi glanced around, kicked at the torn cornstalks. "I should fire both of you."

"Don't bother," Paula said. "I quit."

"You can't quit," I said.

"Like anyone will notice I'm gone." She glanced down at her stomach, shrugged. "Probably best anyways."

Cindi said, "Alice?" my name a softer question than before. But I wasn't someone who quit detasseling on day five, I wasn't a girl who got pregnant. I shook my head. Cindi went on, "You could've been killed," and I started to mumble again that I was sorry, but she spoke over me: "God, I hate today." She crossed her arms, let out a huge sigh, then another one. "God." She blinked quickly, tears aching to come out.

Paula was looking up at the sky, at a tiny patch of blue. Either she didn't see that Cindi was about to cry or she was going to cry herself. Then Paula lifted one arm, said, "Over there," and Cindi and I looked to where Paula pointed at a perfect rainbow arcing out of the field.

Cindi shook her head, rolled her eyes. "Just what this piece-of-crap day needs, a rainbow." Her voice was raw and scraped sounding.

"Like magic," Mama whispered, barely a breath.

To Mama, a cornfield was an ocean, a rainbow magic. But actually, a rainbow was raindrops bending and reflecting the sun's rays, random nature, just like the storm.

"Magic," Mama insisted. "Why now? Why today? Why this field?"

Paula kept looking up, one hand visoring her eyes from the sudden sunlight, while soft rain continued to fall. I watched, too, longing to see what she and Mama saw.

THAT EVENING, the bus arrived back at the school later than usual because Rod made us finish the field after the storm while he sat in the bus. The drive was extra jouncy; roads were muddy, and gravel had shifted into new ruts. In town, branches were down, and we passed a tree split into a Y by lightning. A few cars parked along the square had cracked windshields, and men were nailing plywood over the broken front window of Duncan-Camp Hardware.

Paula was last off the bus, and she brushed by me, walking fast, heading toward the far end of the parking lot, to the line for the pay phone to call for a ride.

I jogged after her, calling her name. Finally she turned and stared until I blinked and looked away. "Um, what're you going to do now?" I asked.

She bit her bottom lip, then said, "Go somewhere and have a baby. Come back and pretend it never happened."

"But it will happen," I said. "It is happening."

"So? We'll all pretend it didn't." Her fake-cheerful voice turned angry. "Debbie's been dead five years, and here we are like everything's fine. Just forget about it, forget it all."

"I can't," I said.

"You will." She crossed her arms. "Next year—everyone detasseling the same fields. A new Rod and Cindi. High school slut gets pregnant. People die. Babies are born. It's what happens, what there is." She waved one arm wide, almost hitting me in the face. "Like stars in the sky, rain from clouds. Why fight it?"

Cars pulled into the parking lot as parents came to pick up their kids. The headlights startled me; it wasn't dark yet, only dusk, a soft, muted gray, but the beams seemed to cut Paula and me in half with their ragged bright light. I didn't feel like riding with Linda's or Becky's mom.

I started to speak, but Paula interrupted: "I hate the sun for rising every day. I hate that spring always comes after winter, and summer always comes after spring. I hate how everything is exactly the same when nothing is. Debbie's dead, your mother's dead—but as far as the world's concerned, so what." She walked away from me, got in line for the pay phone. "Time for you to figure that out." Then she pulled out her lipstick, quickly smeared it across her lips, rubbed them together, shoved the tube back down her shirt.

Linda's mom drove into the parking lot in her powder-blue station wagon. Linda flicked a wave to Doug Foltz, then slid into the backseat.

Becky opened the car door on the other side, scanned who was still here, maybe looking for me, then got in, slammed the door, and they drove away. I watched the taillights disappear around the corner.

Cindi came up behind me. "Long day," she said, looking at her watch. She should be married now, part of Mr. and Mrs. Whoever, not a girl hanging around a corn-detasseling bus. "What a storm. I can't believe you two were out in the middle of it."

"Yeah." She stood there, seemed to be waiting for more, so I added, "It was scary." My eyes were on Paula pulling a dime out of her jeans pocket, dropping it into the phone, dialing, talking to her mother like that was no big deal.

Cindi chattered on: "Lucky you weren't struck by lightning. A guy I knew was walking from his car to his house and got fried in the driveway."

Paula hung up the phone, then pressed the palm of her hand against her forehead, rubbed tiny circles into it as if she had a headache. Then she pulled a brush from her lunch bag, started brushing her hair section by section with quick, even strokes, the way Mama had brushed her hair. Paula took her time, as if she enjoyed what she was doing, as if she were brushing her hair for someone in particular. I thought about Joe kissing Paula. About how he and I both hated coconut. I wanted never to see him again. I wanted to see him right now. I hated him. And I didn't. Paula should have told me the truth.

"Is your mom coming?" Cindi asked.

"My mother's dead," I said, emphasizing the last word.

"Oh! I'm sorry," she said, and then she was silent.

The sky had deepened into a darker blue-gray. Five or six birds zipped overhead, hurrying to find a tree before night. There were only a few people left now. Cindi looked at her watch yet again. She was supposed to be walking down an aisle, supposed to be in a whole different life. Even when she found someone else to marry, she'd always wonder about this life, this guy. What if?

A shiny, white Cadillac pulled into the lot, and Paula walked over to it without looking my way, without waving good-bye. I wouldn't see her again for a long time, and when I did, sometime next year, we'd say nothing, pretending we hadn't talked in a cornfield, hadn't huddled through a storm. Even if this wasn't what we wanted, it was the way it was. Paula got in the front passenger seat, closing the door about as quietly as you can close a car door and still get it latched. And then the car drove away.

Well, what was I supposed to do? Run after it?

So I called Will, who said he'd drive over in half an hour, during his break at the movie theater. He didn't sound happy about it. I could've walked, but something about sitting alone in the parking lot seemed like a good way to end the day. I eventually persuaded Cindi I'd be fine waiting on the bench that some class—the year was scratched out—had donated as a class gift. Cindi said, "We're supposed to make sure everyone gets safely home."

"I'm fine," I said. "I didn't get struck by lightning, so it's my lucky day." I laughed, a goofy ha-ha that sounded fake, but she sort of smiled, and then she got in her perky red car and drove away, still single, still unmarried, the same except not the same.

I sat on the class gift bench and stared into the darkening parking lot. The cicadas were droning. Funny how I heard them every night but rarely saw them, maybe a dead one on the ground, but never a live one buzzing in a tree. The sound made me think of the end of summer.

Mama said, "There's something about thunderstorms." She spoke in that lazy way she had when she was talking to hear herself talk.

"You sure missed a whopper," I said. *Yeee-oooh, yeee-oooh, yeee-oooh.* Those cicadas could go all night long.

She said, "Know how many cornfields are on the way to Chicago?"

"A hundred thousand."

"It's not a real number," she said. "The point is, each looks the same as the one before it and the one after. Like you're not getting anywhere."

"You got somewhere," I said. "New York. You met that man." That man: What had he said to Mama, what promises had he made? *You're so beautiful. I'll love you forever. We'll live happily ever after.* I thought about Mama listening to that voice telling her those words on the train, wanting to believe them, as cornfields passed one after another, a blur outside the window. I said, "Things happened to you."

"There I was in New York, not a cornfield in sight. But I still felt like I was trapped in one." She sighed. "Nothing had changed."

"Everything had changed!" I cried. "What about me and Will? And being married?"

There was a long pause, and I started fiddling with the top button of my shirt—open, closed, open, closed—waiting, suspecting she was going to tell me something surprising, waiting—open, closed—until I had almost guessed what it was. Still, hearing the words was like ice shoved down my back—"I wasn't married, Alice"—and I jumped up from the bench, paced a few quick, long steps, spun around, paced back, and just sat down again, slumped, my anger and nervousness already gone.

Why had I always thought she was married? Probably because you were supposed to be married. Even Aunt Aggy, weird as she was, would marry Mr. Cooper one of these days.

For a few minutes, Mama didn't say anything. It was like if Paula came back to Shelby with her baby instead of alone. I mean, Mama wasn't supposed to show up pregnant, with a kid and no husband.

"Everyone assumed I was divorced," Mama said. "Almost as bad, but not quite."

Was what she'd done so 100 percent awful? Like Paula. She was more than the names people like Linda called her and more than the bank president's daughter: She was afraid of thunder, she had a dead sister. She had even tried to make me feel better by lying about Joe Fry. Paula's baby would never know these things—or anything—about her. "But why didn't you get married?" I asked.

"He had a wife in another city who wouldn't divorce him," Mama said.

I pictured this man—my father; it seemed important not to forget that—living happily ever after with his own wife and kids and dog, Mama alone in a cold, dirty apartment, no friends, no money, no—

"Not like that," Mama said. "I thought it was my chance to escape. Nothing else mattered." She gave a hollow, echoey laugh. "But I was still the girl lost in the cornfield. It seemed I couldn't change that."

Mama coming home on the train, right back to all those cornfields, pregnant with me. She could have left me then, but she didn't. I said, "I don't understand." Even as I started to speak, I figured she didn't want me to understand. I continued anyway: "Not any of it. Why you felt trapped. Who that man was. Why you came back." I waited, then said it: "Why you killed yourself." The words were barely there, nothing but cobwebs. The cicadas paused as I held my breath and kept perfectly still. A moment later, they started up again. There was something about them and cycles, something that happened every seven years. More of them, less of them. I didn't know.

The cicadas went on and on, until the rhythm of my breathing matched their cry, until my heart seemed to beat with them, until it seemed the whole world around me pumped and creaked exactly in time with the cicadas' *yeee-oooh, yeee-oooh,* as if they—lowly bugs that they were—somehow had been placed in charge of this night.

Paula would go away. Even if no one told us, we'd all know why. Girls who "went away" had babies. But when they came back, there was no baby.

Finally Will's headlights pushed into the dark parking lot. The radio was blaring the Doobie Brothers, "Black Water." Will's favorite group, so maybe he was in a good mood. But he snapped off the radio as I got into the car. Did he like this tense silence always between us? A moment later he said, "What a storm. Power was out all over town. No traffic lights even." He sounded just like the retired farmers hanging around the courthouse benches, picking apart every nuance of the weather like it was the only thing that mattered.

"I was in the middle of a cornfield during it," I said. "Me and Paula Elam."

He talked over me: "We got the movie going right before you called. Forty-five minutes late. Branches are down everywhere. Whole trees. I heard Hy-Vee sold out of candles and flashlight batteries."

I slouched down, propped up my feet against the glove compartment. "We thought we were going to get struck by lightning." Already that fear was fading—had we really thought so?

"That never happens in real life," Will said.

"Does too."

"Hardly ever."

"Which is different than never." I sat up, opened the glove compartment, stuck my hand inside. It was crammed with important car papers and gas receipts. If I hadn't thrown away that hairbrush, it would be right here. If Mama hadn't killed herself. I closed the compartment with a bang. "Remember how Mama kept a hairbrush in here?"

"No." His jaw tightened.

"You do too," I said. "She'd lean over and smush whoever was in the passenger seat when she pulled it out."

"If you say so." He reached for the radio, left his fingers on the knob for a moment, then turned it. A man with a slow, deep voice was talking about opportunities at Kirkwood Community College. Will turned up the volume.

He was so impossible lately because of Kathy. I crossed my arms, stared out the window. Broken branches. Tipped, lidless garbage cans. Shiny puddles. Leaves plastered to the road and sidewalks.

He tapped the steering wheel with his fingers and spoke over the radio ad. "They said something like three inches of rain fell in forty-five minutes. Breaks a record from 1906."

I said, "So? In a hundred years—or one year—this record will be broken. Or tomorrow."

Tap-tap-tap. I grabbed his hand to make him stop. "Suppose you're right," he said.

"Nature always wins," Mama whispered.

We were home. Small branches, sticks, twigs, and leaves littered the driveway; the car's tires crunched over them. Will turned the radio down to a murmur and spoke carefully: "I hear Paula Elam's pregnant." His fingers started tapping again—so incredibly annoying—but I didn't move. I wanted to shout that yes, I was sorry for what I'd done with Joe, he could stop bringing it up all the time, I'd learned my lesson. Tap-tap. He never listened anymore.

"Sounds like Joe Fry's problem, not mine," I said, trying to keep my voice from shaking. I got out of the car—bone tired, damp socks, every muscle aching—and trudged to the kitchen door, accidentally sloshing through a big puddle at the bottom step.

Someone had replaced the burned-out bulb in the porch light—maybe I had? I looked back at Will in the car, lifted one hand to wave. A breeze picked up, rustling the trees, knocking water off their leaves and down onto me.

A strand of hair blew against my mouth; I left it there, licked my lips so it would stick better, but the wind pushed it back out anyway. The car backed away, re-crunching the same sticks and leaves.

I stared at the water droplets on the back of my hand, tilted my hand sideways so I could watch them run downward, forming perfect little stripes, like bars on a prison. The wind roused again, rustling the leaves, so it's not like I was standing in utter silence though that's how I felt.

Sixteen more days of detasseling, give or take.

BIRTHDAY

ON the first day of school, Becky and I were standing at our locker when Linda came clunking up in new Candies that made her walk too slow. "Guess who's all of a sudden staying with her relatives in Minnesota?" She shifted her books from one hip to the other.

I said, "There aren't any relatives. Just say Paula Elam's pregnant."

Her breath came out in a huff. "How'd you know?"

I slammed the locker shut even though Becky's notebook was still in there. "Everyone knows." As I stormed off, I heard Linda and Becky say at the same time: "What's with her?"; "She's such a bitch lately."

Looked like being called a bitch by your friends meant no one was feeling sorry for you anymore because your mother was dead. I pushed open the door to the second-floor bathroom, stepped inside. Cigarette smoke hung in layers, but the room was empty. I coughed, stirred up some smoke with little wavy hand motions. Why did I come in here, anyway—she was gone. The bell rang, and I left.

About then, maybe a bit before, I started taking baths at night, twisting the hot-water faucet until it wouldn't twist farther. When the water reached the tub's rim, I would turn it off and watch steam rise from the smooth surface. Then I'd stick my foot in the hot water, jerk it out in pain, stick it back in for a second longer, jerk it out, on and on, until eventually my whole body was immersed. Every time I took a bath, I'd try to get in faster than the time before, hoping one day I'd climb right in and feel no pain.

Once in, I'd reread the official papers about Mama's death: accident reports from the train company, the sheriff's report, letters from the insurance company, Aunt Aggy's guardianship, various forms and certificates. These were important papers that Aunt Aggy kept in a bulging folder—not at all the kind of thing to read in a hot bath, which is why I took them in there with me, letting steam soften the pages in my hands. Mostly I was staring at all those official words the way a child looks at a dot-to-dot puzzle, amazed that numbered dots could add up to anything, let alone a picture of a dog, let alone the reason a mother would kill herself.

That was also about when I started lighting a match to watch the flame burn down to my skin. Then I'd flick my wrist to put it out. I'd do a book at a time—match by match, flame by flame, like Mama did when she lit candles. There were maybe fifty candles crammed on the sideboard, and when they were all lit, the dining room looked so much like a church that once I had asked what she was praying for. She had laughed, not in a ha-ha way, and said, "Anything." I bought her a lighter at Mott's drugstore, and she thanked me but kept using matches. Now I lit matches the way she had, though I blew mine out quicker because that flame really hurt when it got low. Maybe Mama saw me doing these things, but she never said what I'd expect: *Stop, be careful.* Or even, *Keep going.*

Part of it was that I liked watching the flame race to my finger, liked how my skin turned red in the scalding water.

The other part of it was that my sixteenth birthday was coming up. Everyone expected me to get a driver's license. I had passed the test for my learner's permit way back in January, but I hadn't driven since Mama killed herself in Aunt Aggy's car.

Sitting in a car was fine. Someone else driving was fine. But whenever I thought about my hands on the steering wheel, my foot pressing the accelerator, I saw Mama's hands on the wheel; Mama's foot on the gas; Mama gently bumping the car onto the train tracks, slipping it into park, pulling the key out of the ignition—according to the reports, the key was found in the dry weeds along the tracks—then twisting the mirror to check her lipstick as she waited for the train whistle. It would be distant at first, then closer, closer. Maybe shifting her weight, licking her lips, shutting her eyes. But not moving. Not jumping out and running. Like watching the flame burn the matchstick, your finger, your arm, then all of you and the rest of us too.

In Shelby, sixteen equaled a driver's license, which equaled instant freedom. Being sixteen was the "get out of jail free" card, never begging a ride from Will, no more waiting in a doorway for perpetually late Aunt Aggy to pull up. Walking nowhere. Linda started every sentence either with, "Doug said . . . ," or, "After Alice gets her license . . . ," and Becky passed notes in history, "Three more weeks!!," wreathed with smiley faces. Since I had the easiest access to a car, Becky and Linda had planned a string of weekend nights that all involved me driving: Friday-night football games (home and away), Saturday-night loops around the square, a road trip to Iowa City to wander around the campus flirting with cute frat boys.

I was supposed to be excited about turning sixteen. Instead, I ignored my homework and took a hot bath every night. I burned through more and more matches, so many I had to buy a box of a thousand at Duncan-Camp Hardware.

Also around this time, Aunt Aggy decided Mama hadn't killed herself but had been an innocent victim in a tragic accident. "The car stalled," Aunt Aggy explained. "Your mother passed out. The train didn't blow its whistle. The whole thing was a terrible mistake." She would start up on this during TV commercials, while washing dishes or folding laundry, coming upstairs, going downstairs, in the car, in the kitchen.

At first I challenged her with questions: What about the keys in the grass? Why was Mama out driving around so late at night?

Aunt Aggy had no answers. All she said was, "The thing is, it doesn't make sense the other way." She was right about that. But were you allowed to twist everything into a nicer story just because you wanted to? Still, it was hard not to see that now Aunt Aggy was crying less often, painting with brighter colors—portraits, no more dull still lifes—and had started frosting her hair with Clairol Golden Bluff, a change Mr. Cooper noticed and complimented.

She started worrying that because Mama had died in such a tragic accident, she should have negotiated more money for us. "That horrible train company," she said. "Making me sign release papers when I was in the deepest depths of my most desperate grief. I'll show them who they're dealing with." She set up appointments at lawyers' offices within a ninety-mile drive—here, Iowa City, Ottumwa, Cedar Rapids—and talked about going to Des Moines or St. Louis. "Whatever it takes to find the right man for the job," she said.

I asked to go along with her. "Good idea," she said. "We'll look like a team." That's not why I went. These meetings were like the steam in the bathtub, the scratch of the match. I wrote up notes and skipped school to go.

Aunt Aggy liked walking into those fancy (and unfancy) offices, carrying the rubber-banded folder of official papers, drinking coffee that secretaries brought, telling the story—how Mama was a perfect mother, a respected citizen of the community, how she left two sweet children, how Mama would never-not-ever park a car on train tracks on purpose, how the train company's team of oily-haired lawyers nagged her into signing papers, not giving her a heartbeat's time to skim over them. Sometimes the lawyers leaned back in their chairs, murmuring, "Interesting"; sometimes they asked Aunt Aggy for the name of the man she'd dealt with at the train company; sometimes secretaries photocopied the official papers. That's when Aunt Aggy tucked her damp Kleenex back into her purse, squeezed my hand, and smiled her I'm-so-brave smile. "Appreciate your time," she said, "I'll be in touch," and never was.

I didn't speak, just sat in the leather chair next to her—Exhibit A. The secretaries gave me coffee I never drank, and the lawyers watched me through narrowed eyes, as if picturing me in a courtroom swearing to tell the whole truth. They stared harder when Aunt Aggy told the story of the train wreck, to check if I was crying, to see how my tears would look on the stand. But I tried not to let my face change expression. I didn't want to go on the stand where you swore to tell the whole truth. The truth was, we had life insurance money, train company money, government "kids-with-a-dead-mother" checks, the leased cornfields, the house, and it's not like any lawyer—no matter how thick the carpeting in his office or how fancy the lettering on his business card—could make the train company bring my mother back.

So Aunt Aggy talked to the lawyers and I listened, letting her story sink deep into me until it almost sounded true, the way a child believes in fairy godmothers and witches after enough bedtime stories, and I imagined myself in a court of law swearing to her version, my hand on a Bible, telling the story exactly the way Aunt Aggy did, knowing which words to accentuate, when to dab my eyes with a crumpled tissue, where to sigh and let my lip tremble—like the way you learn over time how to tell a joke well.

SUNDAY MORNING Will was outside washing the cars, which was about the only chore he bothered to do. Sometimes I helped if he was in a good mood. Lately, his mood depended on whether the Boston Red Sox had won the night before. Will used to root for the Cubs, but just because Joe was a Boston fan, so was Will all of a sudden. He could go on for hours about Carlton Fisk and Yaz and Bill Lee and the Sox's chances of winning the World Series, and how Joe said the Reds couldn't hack the pressure, and what was so hot about the Big Red Machine anyway? I checked the Big Peach sports section of the Des Moines *Register*—yes, the Sox had beaten the Orioles and were three and a half games up, so I went out to the driveway. "The Sox won," I said.

He pointed the hose straight up in the air and squeezed the nozzle so water rained back down on us. "It's gonna happen, Baby Sister."

I grabbed a sponge out of the bucket of soapy water, started rubbing wide circles across the hood of Aunt Aggy's too-giant Cadillac (the car she had bought to replace the one Mama wrecked). Will set down the hose, grabbed another sponge, joined me. "What I wouldn't give to be in Boston," he said. "See them clinch it at Fenway. Just get in the car and go. Wouldn't cost much—we'd pack up a cooler of sandwiches, sleep in the car. So, gas money, tickets, some hot dogs."

I pictured me and Will driving through an endless ocean of cornfields, chugging up and over the mountains of Pennsylvania, the big cities and tall buildings rising in the east, pulling up in front of Fenway Park, feeling like finally we were somewhere. Everything would be fine: We would be the way we used to be, making jokes and Will spitting water at me through the gap in his teeth, me reading the maps, Will taking care of everything else—pumping gas, checking under the hood, adding oil.

Will stared into the distance like he was seeing the same things I was. "Two people could do that drive in a couple days."

Mama had left everything to head east. Until this minute Boston had been only a dot on a map. Now it was going to be a real place my brother and I would escape to. "Boston," I whispered to myself, "capital of Massachusetts." To Will, I said, "I'll have my license after my birth-day," and a tingly shiver jolted my whole body.

He wrung out the sponge, dunked it in the soapy bucket, let go of it so it filled with water and sank down. "I meant me and Joe."

I stood perfectly still, watched a line of soap bubbles melt off the car hood. *Me and Joe.* Like swallowing a heavy stone.

"You know Joe and I are both Red Sox fans."

If I said, *Don't leave me,* what would Will say? That he was going no matter what? I couldn't stand to hear him say that. "Anyway, there's school." My words were cold and fast. "Football. Your job. It's not like you're really going."

"Right," he said too quickly, as he squeezed and soaked his sponge again and again. "Just talk." His face closed up, the way it did when I brought up our father. Was Will ticking days off a calendar in his head? If it wasn't Boston in September, it would be Alaska in October, or Califor-nia in January, or the Cubs in June. Everything was always so easy for him—hopping in a car and just driving away, leaving me behind like I was nothing.

I rubbed Aunt Aggy's car hood, pretending to be interested in removing a blotch of bird crap. Stupid Joe Fry and his stupid Red Sox. Shelby and the Chicago Cubs were good enough for Will until Joe came along. I scrubbed harder, lifting away the last crusty speck.

"Anyway, you won't get your license unless you start practicing driv-ing again," he said. "Why'd you stop?"

I shrugged, kneeled to rub the front passenger side of the car, paying special attention to the silver strip running along the side. Didn't he know? Driving would be like holding the match between my fingernail and thumbnail to let the flame get closer, like plunging my whole body in the hot water. What would he say if I told him all that? Finally I said, "She killed herself in a car."

We sponged in silence. Then he said, "Aunt Aggy's lawyers think it was the train's fault. That it was an accident."

I pushed and pulled my sponge along the side of the car. It was clean, but I kept going.

"You know Mama liked to beat trains at crossings." He bent down, wiping the front driver side, and I couldn't see him.

I said, "The car was facing the train head-on."

He choked out one word: "So?"

I thought about Will getting in the car and driving away, leaving me. "The sheriff said evidence showed that the car on the tracks faced the train. That's not an accident." A minute later I said, "The key wasn't in the ignition. That's not an accident either." When he still didn't say anything, I stood up and said, "That's not," and then, louder, "it's not an accident, Will." I side-armed my sponge at the bucket. It missed and skidded along the driveway. I watched Will wipe the side of Aunt Aggy's car in smooth, even strokes.

He said, "Joe Fry doesn't ask about you. Not once. Not ever."

"Go to Boston!" I shouted. "Go to hell! I don't care!" He kept sponging the side of the car until I ran inside. I didn't leave my room until after supper, until after he'd driven off to his stupid job at the movie theater and it was too late to tell him it didn't matter if it was an accident or not since she was dead either way.

THE NEXT day Aunt Aggy and I had an appointment with another lawyer. As usual, she said, "He comes highly recommended," but actually she picked names at random from the yellow pages at the library. His name was James Thomas or Thomas James; "People with last names that are really first names should expect confusion," Aunt Aggy noted.

Aunt Aggy was afraid of her big, old, finned Cadillac, though she claimed it was the car of her dreams. Mr. Cooper had helped her pick it out from a used-car lot in Iowa City, so maybe it was the car of his dreams. She drove at least ten miles under the speed limit, keeping her hands knuckle white at the ten-and-two position, never looking away from the road. She wasn't good at turns, always swinging way out to make it around the corner. Driving usually required so much of her attention that it surprised me when she snapped the car radio off and said, "Joe's not around anymore."

Why did she pick now to be involved in my life? I scooched lower, pretended I was absorbed in my own important thoughts. I turned the radio back on.

She spoke above the Carpenters, all fake casual: "Did he break your heart?"

I wanted to lean against her shoulder and cry, sob until there were no more tears. *Of course he broke my heart*, I wanted to say. *Paula told me they're all assholes and she was right.* But we never talked about things like that. Instead of murmuring, "There, there," and telling me everything would work out, she would fuss that I had said "assholes." Some comfort.

I looked out the window. "I'm fine," I said. "I don't believe in broken hearts. Technically the heart is a muscle, and muscles don't break. Bones break and glass breaks and cars break down, but the broken heart is a myth made up by people who write sad books and make sad movies and sing sad songs." I watched a farmer riding a tractor across a field.

"Who thinks 'technically' when you're talking about hearts?" Mama whispered.

Aunt Aggy said, "Like any *artiste,* I understand about broken hearts, is all. If you have any questions." She sighed dramatically, ready with her long, involved stories about the alleged six engagements, about Mr. Cooper and his reluctance to get married even now that he couldn't use his crotchety old father as an excuse.

I said, "What about Mama?"

Aunt Aggy fiddled with the radio dial, pausing briefly on three or four stations before finally settling on one, which she turned to maximum volume. "Like everyone else, I suppose," she shouted over distorted classical music. "Breaking hearts, getting hers broken."

The man on the train (*my father*)? But Mama had claimed she didn't love him. So who? I asked, "Who broke her heart?"

Aunt Aggy started singing "dum-dee-dum" with the radio, pretending not to hear me when I asked again. Mama didn't say anything either, just sort of sighed, making me think there was a story, a glamorous, romantic, tragic, broken-heart story, not anything like my embarrassing Joe Fry story. I started to ask another question, but Aunt Aggy shook her head, said, "Not while I'm driving."

MR. THOMAS James seemed like he might be "the right man for the job." Aunt Aggy sat on the edge of her seat, her whole body tilting toward him, as if she'd topple over any minute. Her head bobbed up and down like a needle in a sewing machine, she was in such agreement with every word he said: He thought I was a lovely young lady; and Aunt Aggy was a fine woman who clearly wanted to do the right thing by her beloved, dead niece; and how unfortunate that he didn't have the pleasure of meeting Will, who sounded wholesome and upstanding. These things took at least fifteen minutes to get out because Mr. James used great quantities of the longest words possible. I had heard that lawyers charged by the hour, so judging by how long it had taken Mr. James to say nothing, I assumed he was filthy rich. The office was stuffy, so I let his words float over me as I stared at the line of windows behind his desk (all closed), wondering what the chances were that one might open up by itself. The view was boring, of the lot where Aunt Aggy had parked the car. A beam of sun glinted off the windshield, sending a squinty star of light into my eyes.

Finally, he asked Aunt Aggy to tell him about Mama and the "situation." I settled in my chair to listen, taking a deep breath at exactly the same time Aunt Aggy sucked in a deep breath and began: "You would never wish a sad death on anyone, but especially not poor, dear, sweet, kind, lovely Annie. She was in the prime of her life, a picture of health, just as happy as a lark. You couldn't find a more devoted mother, a dearer niece, a truer friend. Seeing a life like hers cruelly snuffed out is an immense tragedy; the immensity boggles the mind, truly it does. I myself am an artist, accustomed to dealing with immensity, yet . . ." She held out her hands, palms up, then clasped them together. The gesture and artist reference were new additions to the story; Mr. James seemed suitably impressed. Aunt Aggy continued: "When I think of poor Alice and Will, abandoned, orphans in the world—"

"Where's their father?" Mr. James asked. His pen scratched in the sudden silence that followed. Had no one asked this simple and obvious question before? Aunt Aggy's mouth hung open; it was like hearing that the shoe didn't fit Cinderella's foot. Finally Mr. James stopped writing, looked up, asked, "What about her husband?" I noticed a broad gold band on Mr. James's left hand. Of course he was married; there were two school photos on his bookcase of boys with buckteeth. It was normal to be married. He said, "Their father?," and tapped the pen point against the paper. For a moment no one spoke. It was like what would happen if I left the faucet on and let hot water spill out over the top of the tub.

"Well." Aunt Aggy didn't look at me. "He's no longer with us."

"Also dead?" Mr. James stared hard at me, as if I were responsible for this added misfortune. "Tough break."

Aunt Aggy cleared her throat, then relaunched The Story: how Mama was supposedly coming home from delivering a birthday cake— "one of her best, looked just like a wrapped gift, she'd been working on it all night; Annette wouldn't call a cake done until it was perfect . . . like an artist and a painting, I suppose"—and that her own car was in the shop for routine maintenance—"treated her car beautifully, oil changes and tire rotations like clockwork; the boys at the garage said they'd be delighted to buy that car if she was ever selling"—and that Mama was a bit distracted because the PTA nominating committee had asked her to run for president—"and she would've made a wonderful president: extremely organized and so good with people. Annie was a natural diplomat!"—and how poor Mama suddenly found herself on the train tracks with a train bearing down—"her last thoughts were extremely sorrowful, I'm sure, fearing she'd never see her two precious children again. Alas, not in this world, but, God willing, the next."

This is where Aunt Aggy fumbled a Kleenex out of her purse and dabbed her eyes. Every time. I'd heard her tell this story three times in one grueling day of appointments, and she cried at this exact spot each time.

There was only the scratching of Mr. James's pen. Then he tugged a handkerchief out of his pocket, blew his nose. "Hay fever," he muttered. If he wasn't the right man for the job, no one was.

Aunt Aggy went on—her favorite part was telling about the evil train company—but I was thinking about how none of the other lawyers had asked about my father. It was like all of a sudden asking, why was the sky blue? Some things you didn't think about. Some things were just there, part of your life and who you were, and I was a girl without a father. I had never been anything else, and Mama hadn't wanted to answer my questions about who he was: *Was he tall? Did he wear glasses? What was his favorite food?* But Mr. James—an important lawyer—obviously thought it was perfectly normal to ask about my father.

Suddenly Mr. James said, "What about you, Alice?," and he gave me a great big smile, the kind clowns paint on their faces.

The other lawyers hadn't asked me direct questions. I glanced at Aunt Aggy, who seemed to be preoccupied with picking tiny pieces of lint off her skirt. "Don't be shy, Alice." Then she leaned forward and whispered loudly to Mr. James: "Takes after her dear, sweet mother. Shy as a mouse."

Oh, brother.

"Let me phrase it another way," Mr. James said. "What are your feelings regarding the occurrence of your mother's demise?" He held a pen poised over a pad of paper. As the silence built up, he wrote something on the paper, underlined it once, twice.

On the side wall next to Aunt Aggy hung an important-looking, framed diploma with a gold seal and a lot of Latin words. Mr. James's name was written in curlicue letters: "Thomas Anthony James." I wondered if he had grown up as Tommy. It was hard to imagine anyone calling him Tommy now, not even his mother, because he seemed so official.

I looked out the window at the car. Aunt Aggy called it "butter yellow," but it was really just a pale, almost no-color, yellowy-beige. That was how she and Mama were, constantly seeing butter-yellow where there was dead-grass color. So maybe Mama would like Aunt Aggy's prettied-up story and I should keep quiet. But you didn't deliberately choose to park on train tracks if you were trying to be pretty, did you? If I were Mama, I'd say something right now. Like, *Aunt Aggy's story is stupid.* Or, *Aunt Aggy's story is true.* I waited a moment and thought Mama whispered, "But you're not me; I'm not you."

The silence felt like a heavy thing dumped in my lap. I pushed my hair behind my ears, sat up really straight, said, "I'm not shy, and neither was Mama."

Mr. James said, "Ahhh," and wrote down another word but didn't underline it.

Aunt Aggy stopped playing with her skirt lint, carefully said, "Perhaps 'shy' is not the exact word. Reticent." She drew out the word "reticent," trying to impress Mr. James.

Aunt Aggy and her happily-ever-after fairy tales would never get me to who my father was or why Mama killed herself. I took a deep breath, let the words spill out: "She parked her car on the train tracks on purpose. She knew what time the trains ran. It was her fault, not the train company's. Aunt Aggy is making it all up. No one would vote for her to be PTA president even if that's what she wanted to be, which she didn't. I mean, none of it is true, none of it's the way Aunt Aggy's saying." I wanted to add, *There wasn't even a husband because she wasn't married to my father,* but I had already said too much, and my insides felt shaky, like I might throw up, so I held my breath, concentrated on the diploma on the wall: Loyola University. I didn't want to look at Aunt Aggy, but my eyes slid: Her mouth was a tight, impenetrable line, and her fists had clenched around the loose fabric of her skirt, bunching it up to reveal a run in her panty hose that she had stopped with a dot of pink nail polish. I had a sudden, crazy idea that Mr. James could track down my father, make him come to Shelby to take care of me and Will. My breath puffed out all at once.

Mr. James set down his pen. It rolled across the piece of paper, along the desk, and onto the carpeted floor. He didn't pick it up. He leaned way back in his leather chair, back so far the chair squeaked, then said, "Alice, perhaps the incident didn't happen exactly the way your great-aunt describes. However, it may not be fruitful at this time to speculate as to what actually happened. What's important is to develop the evidence—which may end up being consistent with what you say or with what your great-aunt says or even may be consistent with something entirely different." He sounded as if he was reading straight out of a book. The room right before his office had been filled with shelves of boring-looking books; I supposed Mr. James had read every single word in each one. We must have looked confused because he added: "Ultimately, we can't know what happened." Then he sat forward in his chair, opened a drawer and pulled out another pen, started writing.

I stared at the law school degree. The words and his curlicue name blurred behind my tears. No one thought to give me a tissue.

"Let's return to the facts at hand." Mr. James looked at me, at Aunt Aggy, back at me. "What we're focusing on is justice, compensation for pain and suffering, lost income. The one person who knows exactly what happened on those train tracks is gone. So trust me when I say we can't know the exact, real truth—not now, not in a hundred years, not ever. But a court of law can answer certain questions: Was the train company negligent in maintaining the crossing? Was the engineer at fault? Were there circumstances beyond this woman's control that led to her unfortunate death? What is just compensation?"

Those were not my questions.

Aunt Aggy said, "You make it sound simple." Her fists had unclenched, so her skirt covered up the panty hose run.

He balanced the pen end to end between his index fingers, stared at it so hard you'd think it was stretching. Then he spoke quietly: "It is simple as long as you both understand that our purpose here is financial compensation; our purpose is not to find out what really happened."

Aunt Aggy looked down at her lap. Her hands were crossed one on top of the other, and she stared at them like if she looked away they'd disappear.

Finally I said, "Yes, Mr. James, we both understand. We're fine with that." My voice sounded like an adult's.

Mr. James did more talking, planning a "strategy," as I stared at the law degree until it became just a square on the wall. There were reports from the sheriff, reports from the train company. Men had scoured the

area for clues. The train engineer had given a statement. There were facts
all over the place, everywhere you looked, pages and pages of facts all saying the same thing: Mama killed herself. And once these men had
reached that conclusion, the papers got shoved into a folder and the
folder got dropped into a file drawer and the file drawer got locked up
and the key dangled off a ring with a bunch of other keys in someone's
pocket. And just like that, everything was supposed to be finished.

I DIDN'T think Aunt Aggy would talk to me on the way home, but right
after the radio news update about the crazy woman who had tried to kill
President Ford, she started up: "Did you see the way that lawyer kept
writing things down? I'd prefer someone with a better memory. He can't
help us. I made an appointment for tomorrow with a man up in Cedar
Falls. He comes highly recommended."

I slouched as far down as the seat belt would let me. I was tired of
lawyers. And everything else. What I wanted was simple, impossible.

Aunt Aggy said, "I think this next lawyer will be the one. His secretary—sweetest voice, like a baby doll!—told me he won a settlement of
five million dollars against the Greyhound bus company because a bus
backed over a six-year-old boy and smashed one of his little legs."

I looked at her hands, tight on the steering wheel. The car that had
been close behind us suddenly jumped into the other lane and sped by.
"What's the hurry?" Aunt Aggy said, which is what she said whenever
someone passed us, which was often. The other car got smaller. Soon it
would be a speck and then it would be gone. "Fifty-five is too fast, if you
ask me," Aunt Aggy added. "There's an energy crisis, you know."

I asked, "Why don't you ever talk about Mama unless we're in a
lawyer's office?"

"I talk about her all the time. Constantly."

"Not really," I said. "No one hardly does."

"I guess it makes me too sad," she said. "Remember, Alice, it's
like a—"

"Band-Aid," I finished. "And how come no one talks about that man
on the train?" I couldn't say *father,* not out loud, not to her.

She hummed a tune I didn't recognize, then said, "How are you and Will doing in school?"

What was worse: no attention or attention? I had thought for sure she'd be angry with me. "We're fine," I said.

Her face flushed. "I'm your guardian, you know. I can ask those things."

"So if I were dead, you'd stop talking about me?"

"You're not dead, thank God," and she briefly took one hand out of the ten-and-two position to pat my leg.

"If I were dead, you'd make up stories about me and pretend they were true?" I stared at a clump of black cows huddled in the shade of a billboard for the Capri Motor Lodge.

"You're not dead," she said.

"If I were."

"Don't say that, it's bad luck." We were going slower and slower, until she steered the car onto the bumpy, narrow shoulder along the road and came to a complete stop. She shifted into park, took her hands off the steering wheel, and folded them across her chest.

"Something wrong with the car?" I asked, though I knew she was just being dramatic.

She shook her head. The car's engine intruded into the silence between us. There was a big, ugly crow on a fence post, a clump of purple thistles just outside my window. She was about to yell at me—or start crying or threaten to fall apart. I had wrecked her story.

Instead she spoke normally as she stared straight ahead: "What you said in there, how it happened . . . how can you believe that?"

"It's true." A monarch butterfly skittered above the thistles, finally dipping down to land on one flower.

"Art has shown me there is more than one truth," Aunt Aggy said.

That would be fine if we were in the middle of a painting, not in a car on the side of an Iowa road. I said, "But that's how it happened. The reports . . ." My voice sounded weak, and I let it trail off, stared at the intricate black-and-orange pattern on the butterfly's closed wings, like stained glass.

Aunt Aggy unfolded her arms, grasped the steering wheel as if she wanted to shake it hard. "I know what happened. I asked HOW, how you could believe that. That's always been my question, Alice." Her face was still and hard, like the lone rock you see on the sidewalk that you're about to kick, then don't, not sure why not.

Why were the questions like that now? Ever since Mama killed herself. I had no answer for Aunt Aggy.

The butterfly opened its wings, fluttered away. I thought it would stop at the patch of thistles up ahead, but it kept going until I couldn't see it anymore. Fall and the first frost were practically here; that might be the last monarch I'd see until next summer.

Aunt Aggy sighed, said, "Cedar Falls is all the way up by Waterloo," and I realized I would never hear her tell that story about Mama again—and already I sort of missed it, like when you've been happily sitting in the bathtub and suddenly the water has turned ice cold.

We were mostly silent the rest of the way home. The only other thing she said about Mr. James was as we pulled into the driveway: "A smart man, very smart."

A WEEK later I was sixteen. I picked out a cake from Sugar-n-Spice Bakery, topped with sixteen red frosting roses. ("Three or four is enough for most people," the woman said when I placed my order. "Pink? Yellow?"; "Sixteen," I repeated, "red," because Mama made as many frosting roses as you wanted in any color.) Aunt Aggy invited Linda, Becky, and boring Mr. Cooper over for supper, her attempt to create a party though I told her I didn't want one. After supper, she unveiled a freshly painted portrait, and everyone recognized me despite my face being orange and my hair yellow. Becky gave me Love's Baby Soft bath powder with a great big puff, and Linda gave me Dr Pepper Lip Smackers. Before heading out the door as Joe's horn blared, Will tossed me a tiny baseball-glove key chain with one key: Mama's car.

Wonderful presents on a wonderful birthday. A bakery cake instead of Mama's butterfly cake was wonderful, and the macaroni and cheese—I added dry mustard, as Dotty King recommended—was also wonderful. Talking nonstop about getting my driver's license was wonderful, especially the part about how impossible it was to parallel park, and how the examiners marked you down if you barely grazed the curb with one wheel, and how Becky's sister took the test four times before she passed. Yes, it was all just so, so wonderful.

I blew out all my candles on the first try. Technically, that meant I would get my wish. Technically, my wish was impossible. But Mama's whisper tickled my ear later, as I scraped food off dirty dishes and into the garbage: "My baby girl's sixteen. Happy birthday." Was that supposed to count as having your mother with you on your sixteenth birthday? Did that count as absolutely anything at all?

THAT NIGHT, I woke up from a nightmare about parallel parking: I was backing in and twisting the wheel as hard as I could, but the car wasn't turning, so I crashed into a red Cadillac behind me. A policeman yelled, "I saw exactly what happened, and I'm writing it up in an official report." Every time I asked what happened, he shook his head and said, "It will be clear in my report." He kept writing on a piece of paper on a clipboard, though I begged him to stop. I had never actually parallel parked because Mama was terrible at it herself; she'd banged up a couple of cars trying to cram them into spots, and the insurance guy had called to tell her that if he saw her parallel parking anymore, he'd cancel her policy.

I thrashed around in my sweaty bed, flipped the pillow, hoping for cool spots. None, and none in the sheets either. I rolled onto my stomach, then my back. There was nothing to stare at on the ceiling, no cracks, no light fixtures, no shadows from the moon. I closed my eyes and saw the exact same nothingness.

Like being dead.

I opened my eyes, shoved aside the sheets, went to the window—not that there was anything to see, just the same old backyard I'd been staring at for sixteen years.

Any regular night I would reread an Agatha Christie mystery (I always forgot who did it) or open my history book (which never failed to put me to sleep in study hall). I grabbed a pack of matches and lit one, thought about running hot water for a bath. But it was my birthday. I shook out the match before it got down very far and grabbed the key chain off my desk. The metal of the key was cool, and I pressed it against my forehead until it turned warm, then flipped it to feel the other side, that jolt of cold metal. I thought about Will driving to Boston, Mama getting in the car that night, me going off in Joe Fry's Mustang, Paula Elam climbing into her parents' Cadillac; I scraped my finger along the rough, jagged edges of the key. If it wasn't for my nervous, flippy stomach, I would have thought I was sleepwalking as I pulled on jeans and a hooded Hawkeyes sweatshirt, then tiptoed down the stairs, through the kitchen, out the door, into the open garage, into the car, adjusting the seat and mirrors. I examined my sixteen-year-old face in the rearview mirror. It looked the same as it did yesterday, when I was fifteen.

"Turn the key"—and I did, not sure if it was Mama's whisper I heard or my own.

I hadn't been driving for months, but I went slowly, there was no clutch, and it wasn't like many cars were out at four in the morning. I tried to think about what Mama had said: "Like steering a cart down the grocery aisle."

Mama cleared her throat, said, "Never forget about other drivers. Assume they're going to do something stupid. Just because their turn signal is blinking doesn't mean they're really going to turn at that corner. And another thing . . ." She went on with the safety/seat belt/defensive-driver lecture I had gotten when she'd taken me to get my learner's permit. More information I didn't need or want from her.

As she gabbed about how smart it was to wait a second after a traffic light changed in case someone ran the light, I quietly undid my seat belt. When Mama was teaching me to drive, she would take me out early in the morning because there were fewer people on the road. She talked nonstop the whole time, her arm up against the dashboard so she could bang it when I did something wrong: braking too suddenly (bang); or, "That's a California stop, rolling through that way; make a complete stop at the sign" (bang).

The funny thing is, that wasn't at all the way she drove. She'd gun it down the hills, pass on curves and bridges, roll down every window so wind careened through, speed up when she heard the bell dinging at a train crossing—even if Will and I were in the car, jouncing us hard and fast over the tracks so our teeth were about to jiggle loose as the whistle narrowed in on us. We always turned to peek back at the train rumbling past, never said anything to each other about how close it was. "This is how I drive," she'd explained, "too late to change now." She was pulled over all the time but rarely ended up with a ticket; the cops who knew her saw fines didn't do any good, and the ones who didn't know her were charmed with a smile, a ten-dollar bill, and a promise to drive responsibly. "Driving like a bat out of hell is the one thing in my life I'm really good at," she always said. Once a couple of mothers from the PTA had come by and politely told her she was a menace and didn't she care about the safety of her children? Will and I overheard her tell them to mind their own business. Even though riding in the car with Mama was what we imagined a runaway roller coaster would feel like, it was hard not to notice that no one else's mother was being called a "menace," hard not to think about the time Becky and I were in the backseat and Mama had raced the train on her way to Garfield Park for a 4-H picnic. Afterward, Becky told the other girls that my mother was crazy because she had tried to get us run over by a train. Becky's mom drove us to 4-H after that.

So how could she be the kind of driver who pushed her car up to a hundred plenty of times but then droned on to me about all those stupid safety rules? The traffic light at Broad and East was red, and I deliberately drove through it.

"Alice!" Mama shrieked. "A red light means stop even if no one's there."

"What are you going to do, ground me?" I asked. "Take away my car key?" I pressed my foot on the accelerator and the car leaped forward. Fun! I made a screeching left turn onto Spring Street, gassed it so I'd really fly down the hill; my stomach went whoosh as we hit the bottom, then coasted up. I raced through the stop sign.

"This isn't like you," Mama said. "Doing dangerous things."

I never did dangerous things, but here I was, doing them. Air filled my lungs and I pushed it back out; my breathing felt strong and powerful. I could go to Boston, I could stay on a train and flirt with a man. Dangerous things were more than adding dry mustard to macaroni and cheese or insisting on sixteen frosting roses. "Where are you going?" Mama asked, her voice sounding the way I had felt those times when I'd looked out the back window, that rumbling train so close I could count the bolts on the boxcars.

That's exactly when I realized why I was out driving, what I wanted to do. I pulled a U-turn that wasn't tight enough since the car bumped up the curb and onto the Reineckes' lawn, then I flew back down the hill on Spring. Hard to believe I'd been afraid of driving.

Mama pelted me with questions—"Where are you going? Didn't you see that stop sign?"—but I was speeding through Shelby. I swerved around the lone car I came across, the driver an old man who had probably learned on a Model T. Mama shrieked for me to slow down, but I was getting the same gut jolt I got before dipping my foot in the hot water. Finally I screeched the brakes, then edged the car diagonally across the railroad tracks at Benton Street, waited for a minute.

The car seemed loud in the sudden silence.

Mama didn't say anything, so I twisted the key and the engine stopped. Talk about quiet—as if I was the only person awake in the whole world. I tilted the rearview mirror and watched my face. Here I was, here where my mother had killed herself.

Ahead of me was the sign that said "RAILROAD CROSSING" in big capital letters on crisscrossed boards. This wasn't one of those crossings where wooden gates went down when a train was coming—Mr. James had said that was in our favor. Also, he asked if perhaps the sign was faded and weather-beaten, hard to read. "These could be indications of negligence," he had said. But the sign was quite clear. Two words, four syllables, sixteen letters. You couldn't miss it unless you wanted to miss it.

This was one of those birthdays that was supposed to mean something: Boom, you're sixteen, so now you can drive. Other birthdays like that: Voting. Legal drinking. Social security. You blow out candles one day, and then something's supposed to be different.

A mother throws her car key out the window and everything is different forever after.

I said, "You missed my birthday." My voice almost echoed in the emptiness of the car. I didn't want to cry, so I repeated myself, louder: "You missed my birthday."

She coughed, then spoke quietly: "Well, but—"

"You missed my birthday, you won't see me graduate from high school, you won't be at my wedding, and my babies will have only one grandmother. Why didn't you think of that when you were on these train tracks?" I rolled down the car window. The lingering night air smelled heavy, like wet grass. She wouldn't make my prom dress or wedding cake, would never send me letters at college or accept my collect calls. How could I stand it?

"Did I explain to you what the blind spot is?" Mama asked. "How sometimes you can't see the driver next to you in your mirror?"

Like driving information was what I wanted. I thought about Mr. James and his Loyola law degree and how all that smartness didn't mean he was able to tell me what had happened here. I drummed my fingertips on the steering wheel. How long did Mama wait for the train? How much time did she have to think? What if there had been one minute more, one second—would she have changed her mind? Maybe the train was running early and if only it had been on time . . . or maybe it was late and that's why she didn't miss it. If she'd been in her own car, not Aunt Aggy's; if we'd had macaroni and cheese for supper, not pigs in a blanket; if it had rained that night, or hadn't rained the day before. I leaned my forehead against the cool metal of the steering wheel, clenched my fingers around it.

If I could just know one thing for absolute sure.

What had Mama thought about when she was here? In the cornfield with Paula, I might have been struck dead by lightning, but I wasn't thinking about anything grand or important, more like who Becky would share a locker with or if Joe Fry would come to my funeral. But Mama knew for a fact she was going to die—her key was out there on the grass. So what was she thinking about?

I rubbed one finger over the curvy parts of the key that stuck out of the ignition. I could ask her. But what if she didn't give the answer I wanted to hear?

I opened the glove compartment. Will kept matches in there for emergencies. He always had exactly what was needed in emergencies. I imagined him in Boston, building a little campfire in a park to heat up a can of soup. I rummaged around: Yes, there was even a can opener. Then I lit a match and maneuvered it so only the tiniest portion of cardboard was trapped between my fingernails. The flame flickered and waved, almost alive.

Maybe it was an accident. Mama waited too long—like letting the flame get you. Maybe something was wrong with the car. Maybe it was someone else's key in the grass.

I shook my hand so the match went out, tossed it through the window, and lit another.

When people were in movie or TV courtrooms, they always swore to tell the truth, the whole truth, and nothing but the truth—though Mr. James had said we'd never actually know the truth. I pictured us in an old black-and-white movie like *To Kill a Mockingbird*, crammed into a stuffy courtroom, everyone fanning themselves with newspapers, and Aunt Aggy on the stand, stating her occupation as "*artiste,*" swearing to tell the truth. Mr. James would give a tiny nod, and she'd start in on that story about Mama being PTA president, grabbing wads of tissue out of her purse, weeping until the jury started sobbing with her, even the men, and the judge would have the bailiff pass out Kleenex. By the end, everyone would believe that what Aunt Aggy said was the way it had happened. She would have sworn on a Bible that every word was true.

Then Mr. James would call me to the stand: "Alice Marie Martin."

Everyone would stare as I approached the stand (wearing clogs and the yellow dress from last Easter, or, if it was summer, my blue sundress with the spaghetti straps that tied at the shoulders). Clunk, clunk, even trying to tiptoe—maybe the judge would give a look to the bailiff, *Isn't she cute?*—and I'd shift my weight to get comfortable in the sweaty wooden chair. Out of nervousness, I'd confuse my right and left hands, and we'd chuckle about that, then I'd be sworn in to tell the truth, the whole truth, and nothing but the truth, so help me God. And Mr. James would ask, "Why did your mother kill herself?" Everyone would fan themselves harder, leaning forward so they wouldn't miss a single word. I'd watch one of those shiny green flies crawling across the corner of the judge's bench. But I wouldn't speak, and the spectators would murmur, and the judge would get impatient, say, "May I remind the witness that you're under oath?" in a booming Charlton-Heston-as-Moses voice, and finally I would say—

The match burned my finger and I shook it out, slipped my finger in my mouth. As if on cue, as if I really were in a black-and-white movie, I heard the glimmer of a train whistle. Or imagined I did. I mean, what were the chances? But there it was again, the low *wooo-ooo,* the faraway sound that made any lonely night feel that much lonelier, the sound Aunt Aggy made wishes on, the last sound Mama heard. I tossed the matches onto the floor, wrapped my fingers around the key in the ignition, but didn't twist. I didn't know for sure the train was on this track, that it was even coming this way. My heartbeat pumped loud in my ears.

Wooo-ooo. I closed my eyes to hear better. You'd think Mama (who had been lecturing me all night about safe driving) would say something like, *Get off the track, there's a train coming.* You'd think she'd be yelling at me.

There was something very pleasant about this moment when the whistle seemed to be getting closer, thinking that if I kept sitting here I wouldn't ever have to worry about parallel parking. I wouldn't have to watch the taillights of the car as Will drove away, I'd never see Joe Fry again, I wouldn't have to hang that ugly, orange-faced portrait in my bedroom.

There was no bell dinging at this train stop. No protective gate coming down. No flashing red light. Just that whistle—heading where? California? Boston? Chicago? That would be the last thing I'd hear, the last sound in my ears. And my heart pounding.

Mama wasn't saying a word.

My fingers were clenched around the key in the ignition. I could turn it. Or pull it out.

I had heard train whistles before, but maybe I'd never really listened, because I couldn't grasp how sweet and sad and lonely and perfect this one sounded, like music no one had written yet, like the way you feel when you see a butterfly dead in the front grille of the car, like the things you want to tell someone but can't. All that in one train whistle, and yes, why shouldn't that be the last thing to fill your ears and mind, that and your beating heart, your rasping, shallow breath; was this the only way to know one perfect thing, to have one last, final, true answer?

I stared at my face in the mirror, my face that looked like Mama's. Mama sitting here all alone. Why didn't I know? Why hadn't I heard her walk down the stairs? Why hadn't I kissed her when I went to bed? I didn't even have a bad dream that night; I didn't get up for a glass of water. I went to bed and slept through the night like everything would be exactly the same in the morning. Why didn't Mama come into my room and wake me up? I would have said something. One word might have been enough.

Still Mama said nothing.

A car horn blasted, and my head jerked away from the mirror. On the road behind me was Joe Fry's Mustang; he and Will were in the front seat. The horn blared again, long and hard and mean, exactly the opposite of the train whistle, like the difference between the moon and a light-bulb. Will was stumbling out of the car and Joe hung out the window hollering something I couldn't hear and suddenly I realized the sky was lighter—almost day—and that horn was going and the clattering train was bearing down, my God, and there was nothing about who would come to my funeral or the grand meaning of life or anything except starting the car with my slippery, sweaty fingers, pressing my foot down hard, harder—like pushing with a feather because nothing was moving—until finally the car lurched forward onto the road, and I swung the wheel way left to keep off the grass. Not until half a block away did I remember that I could brake. The train rattled by, the whistle not sad and lonely at all, but simply a warning, a sound you hear a million times without it meaning anything except that a train's coming.

As I let my breathing even out, I looked at my face in the mirror again, certain I'd see something different. In the mirror's background, the train hulked beyond me, its clatter filling the tiny space in the car. The caboose passed, the whistle floating into the distance, already gone, already somewhere else. My face was just my face.

I should've kept going because now Joe was coming over the tracks, screeching the brakes to stop next to me, Will's open window across from mine. Will stared straight ahead, his face pinched shut. A little muscle I'd never seen before stretched tight across his jaw. No way was I talking first. Finally he said, "What was that all about?" The words were as tight as that tiny muscle. He should be nicer. Didn't he know I had almost died?

If I jammed the gas pedal to the floor, I could fly home, run inside, and slam my bedroom door, shove Mama's makeup table in front of it so no one could come in. But then what? There would be Will, banging on the door, shouting, when all I wanted to do was disappear. I made my voice really quiet, like maybe he wouldn't hear. "I guess I needed to, you know, know what it was like."

"You're so fucking stupid!" He pounded his fist once, twice against the dashboard. "What if we hadn't seen you?" He crossed his arms hard against himself. "What then?"

The back of my neck got sticky with sweat. "I was about to drive off."

He said, "I can't always be responsible for you, Alice."

"I'm fine; I can take care of myself."

"Oh, obviously." He was breathing heavily, as if there wasn't enough air for him. For a scary minute I thought something was seriously wrong, but then his breathing slowed to normal and some of the tightness melted out of his face.

"Are you really going to Boston?"

He glanced at Joe. Joe tilted his head to one side, pushed on it with his palm.

Another long silence. A car drove past, slowing to stare at us but not stopping. The driver bumped over the railroad tracks as if it was no big deal. Will slumped all the way back in his seat, looked straight ahead.

Joe leaned toward me, asked, "So what was it like?"

Will glared at him, but it was the right question. I could tell Joe I almost peed my pants in the race to get the car started and off the tracks. I could say that not hearing Mama's voice when I needed it most was worse than what any train could do to me. How I was waiting for some grand vision but got none. That I had never seen greener grass and more beautiful trees than over here on the other side of the tracks, how I'd never noticed how fragile morning light can be. I could say I had never felt my heart pump more blood through my body, so much and so fast that the tips of my fingers tingled, as if they were on fire. But none of those things was exactly how I felt, not even all of them together.

Will said, "Both of you shut up," and he scrunched his eyes closed.

Right then it was an effort to remember that Joe had gotten Paula Elam pregnant, that he hadn't called me even once after that night—because I was thinking only of his car pulling up, his question that was unlike Will's angry lecture. I wanted to tell him no one yelled at me to get off the tracks, certain he'd somehow understand Mama's voice. But I said, "It wasn't what I thought. I mean, not that I thought anything. I didn't plan . . ."

Joe stared straight at me. "You faced death."

Will opened his eyes. "She didn't fucking face death; she was a stupid fucking moron parking a car on railroad tracks for kicks. Fuck it. Fuck you."

"Leave her alone," Joe said. "She's just trying to figure out shit."

Will snapped his head to look at Joe, then looked away. "No, you leave her alone." They were angry words, but he said them more in a scared way. No one said anything. No one looked at anyone else.

Finally I spoke, not sure if I was talking to Will or Joe or both or neither. "You saved me." Maybe that was true. Or not. I wasn't Mama; I would have driven off the tracks. But I guess we didn't know that, just like maybe Mama didn't know either until she was right there, listening to that whistle. "You saved me," I repeated.

"Stop it," Will said. "What if I'm not there next time?" I knew what he was thinking, as if he had said the words: like we hadn't been there for Mama.

"She's okay," Joe said. "There won't be a next time."

"Shut up," Will said. He got out of the car, started walking over to me. One day Will would leave. His shoulders slumped, and he was moving slowly, as if he were carrying something heavy and awkward. My brother looked older than I had ever seen him, like suddenly he was an adult, expected to take care of everything—including me—whether he wanted to or not. Then his face twisted and tugged as he unsuccessfully tried to hold in a yawn, and he looked seventeen again, my brother who would leave me one day. It didn't matter what I did or said or thought or wanted: He would leave. Maybe he was already partway gone, and I hadn't noticed until now.

I wanted him to feel better. "We couldn't have saved Mama. Even if we were there." It was what you were supposed to say.

"Shut up." He stood at the driver-side door, flicked his hand so I'd scoot to the passenger side, which I did. He got in, twisted the mirror back to its normal position.

"Hey, I'm sorry," Joe called.

Will turned, looked at me; he spoke so softly that I almost didn't hear him: "We'll go to our graves thinking we should have saved her. You know that."

His words took my breath away. The truth was like stepping straight into fire.

A FEW days later, Will taught me how to parallel park. There was a complicated system that he explained in great detail, something about lining up wheels and bumpers and seat backs. He drew a diagram with arrows on a scrap of paper he pulled off the floor. He stood on the sidewalk to guide me, shouting, "Cut the wheel now; other way; straighten out— straight, Alice! Damn it." He parked and unparked, telling me to watch how he lined everything up (he whacked the steering wheel for emphasis), but I was mesmerized by how smoothly the car melted backward into the spot, as if his mind guided it there, as if wanting to park perfectly made him park perfectly, as if (again) it was just something he could do that I couldn't.

"Come on, Alice," he said. "It's not like building a nuclear reactor. People parallel park every day."

"I hate them all," I said, trying hard to smile.

He sighed. "Okay. Take a break." He got out, walked to the passenger side, and I slid over so he could climb in. The seat was warm from his body.

We sat on East Street in the car he'd parked so perfectly in the waning sun. It was an embarrassing place to be learning parallel parking, since a few people were still walking in and out of Duncan-Camp Hardware, open late until seven-thirty on Thursday nights. A couple of men stopped to watch, like I was a show on TV, not a regular girl learning parallel parking. Will fiddled with his seat-belt buckle, flipping the latch up and down. "You know."

I listened to a cardinal calling from a tree across the street, very red, very loud.

Will continued, "Going to Boston was all talk."

"I know."

"I just want . . . something."

I nodded. "I want it too."

There was a traffic light up at the end of the block, and I watched it go from green to yellow to red to green over and over. I thought of Mama learning to drive, sitting in a car watching that same green-yellow-red pattern. You could admire the precision of it. Or you could let it make you crazy.

A clerk in a blue smock flipped the "Open" sign in the hardware-store window over to "Closed." Tears pressed against my eyes, and I blinked them away. I wanted to make Will promise never to leave me, never to leave here.

Will said, "Want to try one last time?"

"Okay," I said, but I didn't pull out. I closed my eyes and remembered the train rushing toward me, its whistle blowing, wind and heat and noise swirling, everything coming right at me, burning hot. Nothing would stop that train, not me on the tracks, not Mama. The report said the engineer had pulled the brake. But it was impossible to stop a train when it was going fast. (That was a question Mr. James had asked: "How fast? Certainly another area of potential negligence.") In the report, there was a chart about how long a train takes to stop, how many feet at how many miles per hour, like an algebra problem. I imagined that chart blown up, hung in a courtroom.

What it all came down to: Mama hadn't said one word to try to stop me.

And I hadn't said anything to stop her. Like Will told me—we should have saved her. In my mind, the ground collapsed and I was falling, falling, falling into blackness, unable to grab hold of anything, no end, because saying nothing didn't mean I wanted her to die.

Will said, "Here's your problem: You're driving with your eyes closed."

"Ha, ha," I said, my eyes still closed to hold back the tears.

"You didn't need me to say anything," Mama said. "You drove yourself off those tracks. You, Alice. You chose all by yourself. And I chose."

But she chose wrong. I wanted to tattoo the words into her forehead, shout them again and again.

Will sighed. "When you fall off a horse, you've got to hop back on."

"You're not me," she whispered.

She was my mother. She missed my birthday.

Will poked my shoulder. "We don't have all night."

So I opened my eyes, twisted the key, and did the short forward-backward twists and turns to maneuver the car out of the parking spot, pulled forward. The engine rumbled.

"Line it up," Will said.

I pretended I was lining things up, but what things? Line up where? It was stupid to make people parallel park. Maybe I could sign a paper promising never to do it.

"I missed your birthday," she said. "And I miss everything else about you and your brother. But still, you're not me. And sitting on train tracks won't make you me."

Nothing she said would ever, ever make me believe she made the right choice.

Her voice sounded distant and faint: "The simple truth is, not every choice gets the luxury of being exactly right or wrong."

There was a moment of silence, where the entire world seemed to hold its breath—Will because I was about to try parking for the nine-millionth time and I had to get it right eventually; traffic because the light ahead was red and there were no cars on the cross street; everyone outside had gone inside; the cardinal across the street flittered away; and me, holding my breath because I was on the verge of something—I didn't know what, like the feeling when I watched steam rise off the bathwater, but more, harder—and the whole world held its breath for that single moment before gently letting go. A car zoomed through the traffic light, the neon sign at Whit's buzzed on, and Will let out another gusty sigh, but for that one moment, that one instant of the kind of silence you rarely notice, I did know one thing—incompletely, yes; and I couldn't exactly understand or explain or remember what I knew. But I knew it.

I shifted the car into reverse; with Mama's "The simple truth is" filling my ears, I turned the wheel, lined up nothing, just turned until the car felt turned the right way, straightened it, inching backward, not thinking of anything except Mama's words, still backward, "The simple truth," swinging the wheel the other way, was in, all the way in; I pulled the car forward a tad; Will flung open his door, and I looked at the curb to see a good-enough gap of six inches.

"You did it!" Will cried. He held up both hands for a high-five, but I leaned over and hugged him instead, kept hugging through his embarrassment.

I could parallel park. I could do anything.

DRAMA

O more hot baths. No more matches. All that crazy stuff
ended after I got my driver's license, like turning off a faucet, no more
anger left to spill out of me. Mama was dead, and just as nothing I'd said
or done had killed her, nothing I could say or do would bring her back.
That was the simple truth.

Maybe I didn't feel like a normal person, but finally other people
seemed to think I was fine. Anyway, now everyone was busy gossiping
about pregnant Paula or if anyone could beat Kathy Clark for homecoming queen. I voted for her, wishing she was still dating Will.

Then, as president of the PTA, Linda's mother announced that Jefferson was going to put on school plays again, and *Our Town* was first. Dr.
Ellis, one of the language arts teachers, had agreed to direct, and Mrs.
Johnson said she'd assistant direct and handle ticket sales. So that was
another thing to talk about.

Dr. Ellis had taught shop before getting his Ph.D. and turning into a
language arts teacher. People whispered, "Midlife crisis," when he started
wearing turtlenecks and elbow-patch jackets, carrying around a pipe no
one saw him smoke. It was hard to believe he had been a shop teacher: In
class, he would read love poems in a sad, choky voice. He'd pause in the
middle of a sentence to look out the window and watch drifting clouds.
Becky considered shifting her love from Mr. Miller to Dr. Ellis but

decided she couldn't live without Mr. Miller's dimples. There was one tricky thing about getting along with him, though, to always remember that it was Dr. Ellis, not Mr., or you'd get lectured about showing proper respect for a Ph.D. in education.

Now Dr. Ellis held our fates in his hands: He would be casting *Our Town* and promised extra credit to everyone who auditioned. I was desperate for extra credit because I had skipped a lot of classes for those lawyer appointments.

Linda, Becky, and I talked about *Our Town* at the Friday-night football game, smushed together on a hard, wooden bleacher. Linda was planning to go for the lead, Emily, and wanted me to convince Will to try out for the male lead, George, explaining, "There's a kissing scene." As if Mrs. Johnson would let her daughter kiss a boy onstage with everyone in town gawking.

The crowd cheered, so we did, too, something about the defense, holding something, but I only paid close attention when Will (number 37) was on the field, on offense. Joe Fry (number 55) was also on offense, and every time I saw him bending over, I wanted to give him a good, swift kick. I wondered if he ever thought about Paula. I couldn't imagine what she was doing: sitting around with other pregnant girls who were waiting to have their babies so they could go home and be normal again?

The October night was unusually chilly and crisp; our breath floated in clouds when we spoke. It was the kind of night where you start thinking, *Snow*. The cheerleaders, wearing fuzzy mittens, bobbed in place between cheers to keep warm. Becky's mother had made us bring a blanket to stretch over our knees. My ears were getting cold because before the game we had met at Becky's house to try out her brand-new curling iron. We agreed that our hair looked great, but it meant no hats. I lightly covered my ears with the palms of my hands.

Becky said, "It's such a sweet play."

"But she dies." I had skipped to the end: Emily, dead, sitting in a cemetery.

"Just because she dies doesn't mean it's an unhappy play." One look at my stony face and Becky hurried on: "She comes back to life to relive one ordinary morning and discovers how beautiful the world is. That's the message—to appreciate life. The whole thing is adorable and so romantic." Clearly she also wanted to be adorable, romantic Emily. Probably every girl in school wanted to be Emily. Not me: I'd be happy with extra credit and some bit part, a sister or neighbor, with three easy-to-memorize lines. I wasn't a leading lady.

Mama butted in: "I was Emily."

I watched Will run and cut to the far side of the field, but the quarterback shoved the ball into Danny Kadera's stomach. He was instantly tackled. Linda sighed. She had started going with Doug Foltz after detasseling, but he'd sprained his ankle and was on the bench. She had expected to be dating a football hero. Also, Lily Pfister had stopped talking to her, claiming a real friend wouldn't date someone else's "one true love" (even if this "one true love" had dumped her). It was very dramatic—a screaming fight in the cafeteria; Doug's friends elbowing him; Linda's face bright red from trying to out-scream Lily; Lily heaving a lunch tray to the ground. I wanted to ask Linda if Doug was such a prize; maybe she wondered the same thing, since she wasn't saying he should play the lead opposite her. On the other hand, she had repeatedly told us the names of their four children: Doug Jr., Jeremy, Tracy, and Jill.

Mama repeated, "I was Emily."

On the field, it was one of those plays where everybody seemed to randomly smash into everybody else, but the crowd cheered. Becky pressed her fingertips to her nose, then to Linda's, checking to see whose was colder.

Mama went on: "Everyone said I was a natural. That I should go to Hollywood or Broadway. Know what it's like to hear an auditorium of people crying?" Mama was good at showy things: making desserts that were lit on fire, creating "atmosphere" in a room, sewing outfits that looked right off a magazine page. Riding away on trains with a handsome stranger. We had watched old movies together on TV all the time and talked about the stars—who was pretty, who was girl-next-door, who was tragic. Not once did Mama say anything about a school play.

Same bodies piling on each other. "Throw it to Will," I shouted.

Mama's voice got faster, more insistent: "The director was a new teacher just graduated from the university, hired last-minute after Mrs.

Stutzman had gallbladder surgery. He had lived a year in Paris, he said, and smoked cigarettes that smelled like cloves. Some of the girls were afraid of him; I never would've tried out if he hadn't told me to. Everyone said he looked like James Dean. Mr. Stryker, Mr. Roy Stryker."

Linda was staring at the bench, at Doug Foltz sitting alone with his crutches sticking up like empty flagpoles. You wouldn't link a movie star's name with his.

Mama said, "When you talked, he nodded a lot, as if you were saying the smartest thing he'd ever heard. In class, we read poetry out loud, and he called on me to read the most. 'Teacher's pet,' the girls whispered. He liked how I read is all. That's why he made me Emily."

The only other person I'd heard go on so much about a teacher was Becky talking about Mr. Miller. It was strange to think of my own mother having a crush on a teacher.

Linda grabbed my arm, startling me. "Promise you'll ask Will to try out. I'll die if some geek plays George." Becky let out a quick, hard "huunh," and glared, so Linda added, "If I get Emily." She flipped her hair.

Mama whispered, "You could be Emily. Don't you want to be someone else, escape the expectations and assumptions that weigh us down? For one moment have someone else's thoughts in your head instead of your own? To be someone else, not you?" She sounded passionate and convincing, though I wasn't exactly sure what she meant. I looked at Becky and Linda. They never thought about being someone else.

Linda was speculating that Doug's ankle would heal by the time of the show, so he should try out for some smaller part, like the milkman. I interrupted: "Why do you want to be Emily?"

"It's the biggest part."

Our team punted the football. It soared high in the air, a beautiful arc, before falling into jaggedy bounces at the end of the field.

Becky nudged me. "What part do you want?"

Linda tugged on the blanket, pulling it off one of my knees. "She just wants extra credit in Ellis's class."

The teams lined up as the cheerleaders chanted, "De-fense! De-fense!" Their waving pompons reminded me of wind skimming a cornfield, the way the tassels danced. The crowd shouted along, Becky and Linda, too, lifting their arms in time with the cheer.

I thought of Mama on the stage in front of everyone. A play—just words—couldn't really turn you into someone else, nothing could. Right? But I found myself softly saying, "Emily," repeating, "I want to be Emily." I yanked the blanket back, covering my knees all the way. Becky and Linda stopped cheering; Linda crossed her arms against her chest.

Even with the noise surrounding us, I felt a nervous silence tightening. Becky pushed her glasses higher on her nose. Finally she said, "This should be interesting."

Linda flipped her hair. She didn't look worried or interested as she stared at Doug Foltz some more.

Mama murmured something I didn't quite catch, about the earth being wonderful, and a moment later when I realized that was a line from the end of the play, when Emily was dead, a nervous chill tickled from my spine to my scalp, like a thousand quick pinpricks. Then Becky said she wanted hot chocolate from the boosters booth, and I jumped up to go with her.

I READ the play twice that weekend. Dr. Ellis had called it "a brilliant chronicle of life and death" in the audition schedule handout, and I had to agree. *Our Town* wasn't like what we read in English class, filled with symbols, like *The Scarlet Letter*, or too long, like *David Copperfield*. Thornton Wilder's words were beautiful and simple, easy to understand. I pictured myself asking the Stage Manager if people ever really realized life while they were alive, and the Stage Manager shaking his head, murmuring about how maybe the poets did. Then a pause as women in the audience pulled Kleenex from their purses, everyone overwhelmed by ten different emotions at once—none of which they'd ever felt until they saw me as Emily, delivering Thornton Wilder's perfect words. Oh, Mama was right; I just had to get Emily! What did Linda know about how precious life was? Why did Becky think she could understand the world's fragile traumas?

Will came into the kitchen, catching me murmuring at the imaginary Stage Manager, whose gentle, wise face was like Jimmy Stewart's in the late-night movies I used to watch with Mama. I was wringing my hands and smoothing the skirt of a nonexistent white dress when Will asked, "What are you doing?" He looked so grown up in his blue shirt and the striped tie he wore to the movie theater.

I pushed the script across the table. "You should try out."

He snorted. So much for Linda's dreams about kissing Will onstage and that set of unborn-but-named children. He said, "Since when do you want to be in plays?"

"Mama was in it. Aunt Aggy said she was good." Actually, Aunt Aggy had told me it was scary to see Mama up there, "like she was someone else entirely, not the girl I knew."

"I never heard about that," Will said.

"You don't know everything about Mama," I said. "Or me. I can be in a play if I want."

He tugged at his tie. There was a dark stain the size of a lima bean in the middle, probably popcorn grease. When it was busy during a kids' matinee, he was supposed to help the girls sell popcorn. He had a responsible job, he was the star pitcher, he played on the football team. My brother wouldn't think about being someone else. Would he? I stared hard at him, but he looked the same as always: tall, big, strong, cute; his hair over his collar now; the blue-green eyes that could sparkle or harden to ice. I wanted him to smile and show me that familiar, comforting gap between his front teeth. But his face was still and serious. Everyone said I looked like Mama. So who did he look like? It was that big question that never went away. What if I just asked, as if it was a normal thing to say? Would he stop for a minute, sit down and talk to me? Or be mad? I spoke fast, like I was asking something simple: "Do you ever wonder who our father was?"

He let go of his necktie. His hands dropped to his sides, balled into tight fists. I couldn't tell what he was thinking because his face looked tense and closed off.

"I mean, I wonder," I said, hoping to ease the awkwardness with more talking. "We could find him maybe." As if finding your father was a matter of checking the lost and found.

His hands unclenched before he nodded, slowly at first, then faster. "Sure, Alice," he said, wrinkling his forehead in mock thoughtfulness, his voice turning singsongy. "What a great idea. You go to California and see if he's a movie star. I'll check the baseball players. Could be our father is Carlton Fisk. Maybe Carl Yastrzemski. Or crazy Bill Lee. Maybe everything has been a big mistake and we should be living in Boston with our baseball-player dad right now, getting front-row seats and free hot dogs at the games."

"Stop it!" I cried, slamming my hand hard on the table. He had to wonder about our father—he had to!—so why couldn't he admit that to me? Though he was standing right in front of me, I felt that if I reached out to touch him, nothing would be there. I tried to be calm, but my voice shook: "One of those lawyers could find him, maybe."

"Right. What happens after we find our 'father'?" He put exaggerated finger quotes around "father" and was nearly yelling: "He's going to move in here and we all live happily ever after? Is that what you think?" He knocked a chair up against the table rim, then kicked its leg, sending the chair askew.

I straightened the chair. Will could be so nice, like patiently teaching me to parallel park, but then he could act as if I meant nothing to him. All I wanted was to hear him admit that he wondered about our father in the same desperate way I did.

Maybe he was afraid I was about to cry, because he sighed, looked up at the ceiling, then down at the floor. "Okay, what if we knew who our father was?"

"Then we'd know." We'd know why Will's hair was lighter than mine and his nose was pointier, why he was so good at baseball and I was the only one in the family who didn't like going barefoot.

He looked away, then spoke softly, as if they were the hardest words he'd ever had to say out loud: "It's not like Mama ran off to Timbuktu. If he wanted . . ."

To find us.

The words hung there, and I swiped one hand through the air as if I could knock them away. More than anything, I hated being a girl without a mother or a father, hated that my brother was the only one left and that he had changed: He didn't know what I was thinking anymore or try to answer my questions. I hated him standing there in that striped tie and blue shirt that he'd bought for his stupid job in the movie theater. But I couldn't say all that, so I said, "The Red Sox will never win the World Series because they're cursed."

"That's crap." He kept staring at the door, but he didn't move toward it.

"I read an article in the paper. They're cursed for selling Babe Ruth to the Yankees when the owner wanted money for a play," I said, certain that *Our Town* would easily be worth any baseball star. He didn't look at me, so I shouted, "So there!" a couple of times until I felt ridiculous for yelling at someone who wasn't yelling back.

He turned to me, smiled quickly, then tapped his hand on the script. "Break a leg."

"Huh?"

"It's how they say good luck in the theater," he said. "Mama said it before baseball games. So weird." He sighed. "But you know Mama." He tapped the script again and left.

LOTS OF girls were trying out for Emily, and quite a few for the mothers, too, the bigger, heavier girls, as if all mothers were big and heavy; Mama would love that. The potential Georges were mostly leading-men types, no one to worry Linda. Pimply Jerry Zaiser, captain of the debate team, bragged that Dr. Ellis had specifically suggested he try out for the Stage Manager, so he was a shoo-in, which upset the rest of the would-be Stage Managers. Linda popped a Tic Tac in her mouth every two seconds.

We sat in our usual clusters in the auditorium seats, slumping low, nervously thumbing the pages of our scripts, squinting to read in the dim light. Dr. Ellis handed out index cards for our names and the roles we'd like to be considered for. There were permission slips to get signed if we got a part; mimeographed ticket order forms for parents and relatives; a sign-up sheet for committees: costume, set, publicity, stage.

Mrs. Johnson was already assisting. She had brought a tray of homemade cookies that she passed, reminding people to take napkins, remarking loudly that crumbs attract mice. Broadway actors probably didn't eat oatmeal cookies before an audition or get lectured about attracting mice, so I refused. Mrs. Johnson said, "Never too early to watch your weight," and patted her trim belly with one hand. When she got to Dr. Ellis, she held the tray in front of him, then snatched it back as he reached for a cookie. She giggled, and he laughed. She offered the tray again, then pulled it back. He seemed to find this incredibly amusing.

Linda was hunched over, studying the open script in her lap. Her hair hung down the sides of her face like a curtain, and she held an unbitten cookie in one hand. Dr. Ellis had a laugh that was hard to ignore, like a goose, and it echoed across the auditorium as Mrs. Johnson yanked away the cookie tray yet again. Linda examined her script.

Becky whispered, "He's in a good mood."

He hadn't been during class that afternoon. He had yelled at us for not finishing our *Great Gatsby* worksheets, accusing us of being a bunch of lazy kids who were too young to appreciate the book's sad, romantic ironies. Then he snapped the chalk in half, told us to read until the bell rang, and stared at the clock harder than the rest of us.

Finally Mrs. Johnson held the tray still, and he grabbed two cookies in each hand. They both found that hilarious, and they laughed even harder when he crammed both handfuls of cookies into his mouth all at once. Talk about crumbs.

Becky whispered, "I don't think he likes me much."

"Me either." We looked at Linda, who was mumbling lines to herself, running one index finger along the page. A lot of things weren't fair.

Dr. Ellis stood up, pulled his pipe out of his shirt pocket, waved it around. "Okay, people! Let's get this show on the road." He goose-laughed at his own joke, then explained the audition process. They'd take it part by part, he'd read the cues, he might ask us to read other parts or he might not. "Be natural, be loud," he finally concluded. "Mrs. Johnson plans on selling every last ticket, so we'll need to project our voices all the way to the back row." Mrs. Johnson waved at her name. She wasn't as pretty as Mama, but still pretty enough to be in the movies, maybe as the star's best friend. I wondered if it bugged Mrs. Johnson that only big, heavy girls were trying out for George's and Emily's mothers. She had been the state pork queen when she was my age, though it was hard to imagine someone's mother ever being my age. Dr. Ellis shouted, "All the Emilys up onstage."

Two-thirds of the girls crowded up the side stairs onto the stage. We stood in a ragged line, sweaty and nervous, shifting our weight from side to side. Overhead lights sent heat and unflattering angles onto us as Dr. Ellis stared, chewed his unlit pipe stem, nodded his head, shook it, twisting his mouth in contorted, impossible-to-interpret ways. Then he asked Mrs. Johnson to collect our index cards and told us to sit down. We would read one by one. He called my name first.

Alone up there, I was surprised by how enormous the stage was. In the empty space around me, I was tiny, nothing. I sucked in a lot of air, let it out bit by bit, like a leaky balloon.

Dr. Ellis fumbled through his clipboard, poked around the nearby seats for his script. Mrs. Johnson handed him a thick folder, and he flipped through that. "Hang on, Alice."

I felt the other Emilys staring at me, thinking, *Too skinny, too ugly.* I took another deep breath. Maybe I was those things.

Mama said, "Don't be you. Be Emily. Be someone else," and she spoke with such intensity that I was startled. Like I could say, *I'm tired of being Alice, so I won't be her anymore.* Mama had to know that was impossible. Emily was a part in a play, words Thornton Wilder had written, a character. But in the same passionate voice, she said, "Grab your chance to escape, let your life be an unwritten book. We're not born who we are— we become who we are," and all my breath zoomed out. Who was she before she became Mama, my mother? Had I ever wondered about that?

Dr. Ellis barked a page number, started reading Mrs. Webb's line. It was the scene where Emily asked her mother if she was pretty, the kind of conversation girls around the world had with their mothers all the time. My guts twisted into a thick braid of nervousness, and when my line came out a whisper, Dr. Ellis shouted, "Louder!" I'd forgotten how to breathe, but I read my line again—louder—and he read more Mrs. Webb, turning Thornton Wilder's beautiful words into an ugly monotone, then me again, and my head felt light, floating somewhere far away, and the hot lights were suffocating. Mama whispered, "Let yourself go." Just as I was remembering to breathe, Dr. Ellis started to cough. Mrs. Johnson pounded his back with her fists; he croaked, "I'm fine," which made him cough harder, so she walked him up the center aisle to the drinking fountain in the lobby. You could bet no one would have a coughing fit when Linda read.

I thought of Mama looking out at the people filling these same seats, the parents of the kids I knew, only kids themselves when Mama said these exact same words. In fact, thousands of girls had spoken them, sharing Emily's longings and fears. Thousands of people in the audience had heard them, laughing and crying. The idea of it was amazing, and maybe writing a play was the most noble thing in the world.

"Disappear," Mama whispered. "Escape into words."

The lobby door swung open, and Dr. Ellis and Mrs. Johnson took their time getting back to their seats. She held his arm, as if he might launch into another coughing attack. As they sat, she said something we couldn't hear that made him laugh. Then he cleared his throat, said, "Okay, let's go," as if it had been me holding things up. He read Mrs. Webb in that awful monotone, and I stared at a point beyond the fire-exit signs over the back doors. The lights above me turned luminous and filled with warmth, the way the sun feels on the top of your head on a blue-sky afternoon when you and your mother are stringing beans, and you've got so many questions—are you smart? are you pretty?—and everything the world has to offer is shimmering ahead, and yes, this tiny moment is important, but not really—it's just one of a million that make up your life, and both of you are happy and careless, assuming a never-ending supply. Dr. Ellis kept up that monotone and said "super" when it was supposed to be "supper," but in the end, it was Thornton Wilder's words that I needed to make me Emily, and it was Mama reading Mrs. Webb, being Mrs. Webb. If Thornton Wilder were somewhere down there, slouching in one of the hard auditorium seats, he would suddenly sit up straight, knowing all those rewrites and late nights and crumpled pieces of paper were for this one, tiny moment when I, Alice, became Emily, asking my mama, "Mama, am I pretty, am I smart," the way I had all those times before, the way I thought I would keep doing for years and years.

Dr. Ellis said, "That's fine," and the lights were suddenly hard and hot; I was sweating, one fist clenched, absolutely exhausted, and everyone clapped and kept clapping as I walked down the stairs off the stage back to my seat; they clapped as I plopped next to Becky, rubbing my forehead with the heel of my hand, and clapped and clapped and stared at me as if they didn't know who I was anymore.

The clapping faded, and Dr. Ellis called the next Emily. I made the mistake of glancing at Linda. Her lips were nothing but a skinny line, and her eyes were narrow, but when she saw me looking, she smirked and flipped her hair. I could read what was going to happen as clearly as if it were written on the last page of the play.

On Wednesday the cast list went up: Becky had one line as Woman in the Balcony, and I had two parts, sort of: Mrs. Soames, the crackpot neighbor in the cemetery, and the understudy for Emily. Linda was Emily.

Also on Wednesday, Will skipped work at the movie theater; his boss called to see what was wrong. When Will didn't come home that night, with Mama's car missing, Aunt Aggy and I didn't have to say it—Joe Fry. But I woke to the phone ringing at three in the morning, and after I tiptoed out of my room to listen, all I heard was Aunt Aggy repeating, "You can't do this," again and again, her voice a notch higher each time until it was a squeak. Abruptly she banged down the phone but didn't let go of the receiver. Then she looked up to where I stood at the top of the stairs, listening, my eyes squinty from the downstairs light. She tugged at the hairnet holding in her pink foam curlers, snapping the elastic band against her forehead. The tiny sound echoed in the immense silence between us; I didn't want to hear what she was going to say. Then she covered her face with both hands, said, "Will's at a gas station on I-80 in Illinois." Those words made no sense to me, and I shook my head, not wanting to believe her. "What am I supposed to do?" She threw her hands in the air. "I didn't know he was going to run away—did you?" My feet were cold on the wood floor; I pressed the sole of one foot against my calf, switched feet. I kept shaking my head. It didn't exactly feel like a lie, but it wasn't the truth either, more like last night's disjointed dream you suddenly remember at lunch: Was it real? Did it happen? Was Will really gone? I had thought all that talk was that, merely talk.

Aunt Aggy knotted the belt of her robe. "What are we supposed to do now?"

I couldn't answer. All I could think of was my brother plunking dimes into a pay phone at a run-down gas station as trucks lumbered by, and how I was left standing here in my nightgown, with my cold feet, still shaking my head.

Finally Aunt Aggy sighed, like maybe she wished she could be someone else, but then she picked up the phone and called the sheriff.

I COULDN'T say the words, could barely think them. My brother had run away, Will—the baseball hero! the boy who used to date the homecoming queen! my perfect brother!—had actually run away. Because of the Red Sox and Joe Fry? Because he wondered about our father but couldn't say so? Because he was tired of telling people he was fine when maybe he secretly wasn't?

Whatever the reason, an awful loneliness hung over the next few days when I looked at the driveway and remembered that Mama's car was gone, or I didn't have to slump on the floor waiting for the bathroom to be free, or if I saw the box of Sugar Pops no one was eating. It was like those first long weeks after Mama died, expecting her to shake me awake, explaining that it was all a bad dream. I stayed home from school, telling Aunt Aggy I was sick. She didn't care.

I would go into Will's room, sit on the edge of his unmade bed, stare at the baseball players on the wall staring back at me. Reggie Jackson. Luis Tiant. Fergie Jenkins. Hank Aaron. A Cub with no name on the poster. They all seemed to be posed midsomething—midpitch, midhit, midthrow—their action never completed. Will's glove was missing, his bat, some T-shirts and jeans, underwear and socks. And his winter coat. I wished I hadn't noticed that. But I told myself Will would come home after the Red Sox won the World Series, that everything would be fine, that he was fine.

"He'll be back, I'm certain," Aunt Aggy kept saying, her bottom lip trembling, tears on the verge of falling. "This is different than your mother." But when I asked how she knew, she shrugged and said, "It has to be, that's how I know," which didn't feel very certain to me. I didn't mention the winter coat. She painted a portrait of Will that barely looked like him, though the dark browns and blurred sheen of grays were exactly how the inside of my head felt, scraped hollow and dry.

The sheriff filed a report, told Aunt Aggy that teen runaways were "problematic," made no promises. Will wasn't some "teen runaway," he was my brother who was gone—and why didn't the sheriff see that and do something, find a way to bring him back? But it was Aunt Aggy talking to the sheriff, not me, and she said things like, "If you hear something," and "I'm sure you're doing the best you can," instead.

When I finally went back to school, I thought for sure I'd find Joe Fry gone, too, but he was around the same as always, going to football practice, working on his car in the parking lot during lunch. I would feel him looking at me if we passed in the hall. One day in the cafeteria he slid into the chair across from me, next to Linda, who instantly scooted her lunch tray away from him. Becky mumbled something, and I sipped my chocolate milk through a straw. His voice sounded empty: "I didn't know he'd go for real." Joe was the one person who might understand how alone I was, and I was about to touch his hand, which was right in front of me. But Linda made a scoffing noise in her throat, and I remembered that night in July, so I looked down at the scarred, wooden table as I reached the bottom of my milk and kept sipping, letting the straw make that ugly, ratchety sound, until Joe stood up, shoved his hands in his jeans-jacket pockets and stalked away.

Linda said, "He's a big fat liar."

I set down my milk carton, nodded, hoped she'd shut up. She didn't: "I heard he bet Will twenty bucks he was too chicken to leave." Becky must have kicked Linda under the table because she was suddenly quiet.

I should've said, *He left because our mother killed herself and we're all falling apart in secret ways.* Instead I nodded again, said, "Joe Fry's an ass-hole," and enjoyed their surprise at hearing me say a word like that.

I told Mama that Will would never have left if she were still alive. "If," she said. "That short, sad word—the saddest," as usual, avoiding the issue. Will wasn't the kind of boy who ran away, who left just like that. Joe Fry maybe, but not Will. Clearly it was Mama's fault, though yelling at her didn't change anything—he was gone and so was she and I was the one left behind, alone.

I saved all the Red Sox articles and studied the tiny print of the box scores, stared at the grainy photos. Late at night I'd switch on the radio to find out if they had beat Oakland because, like the paper said, anything can happen in a short play-off series. How comforting to think of Will doing the same things, wherever he was.

After a while Mr. Rhinehart stopped calling for updates, and Aunt Aggy and I didn't catch our breath anymore when a car passed our house. Every day that dragged by made me feel worse. I didn't care about anything except the play and rehearsal. I liked the orderliness of the scenes, everyone talking in turn, saying the exact right thing. I liked knowing which words came next, who was supposed to speak. The play made sense when nothing else did.

I gave up doing homework so I could learn lines. I'd sit in the kitchen, Mama reading opposite me until I had memorized Mrs. Soames. It was a decent part—a gossipy hen, gushing inappropriately at the wedding, dead in the cemetery in the third act. Better than Becky's one line that she shouted from a seat in the balcony. Learning Emily was harder, but Mama and I worked through the first act—Emily at breakfast, Emily after school, Emily distracted from her homework by the moonlight and George. Mama read the cues perfectly, her voice brusque for Emily's father, romantic and uncertain for George, motherly for Mrs. Webb.

One night I was working on lines at the kitchen table, sitting in Will's chair because I couldn't bear to see it empty. Mama said, "I memorized the whole play. For years, those lines popped into my head as if I'd really lived in Grover's Corner. Like Thornton Wilder was writing about me."

"What other plays were you in?" I asked.

There was a silence before she said, "None," chopping that one word into tiny pieces in a way that made me want to ask why not. But she read a cue, then interrupted me when I started my line to say, "I kissed Mr. Stryker."

WHAT? What were you supposed to say to that? He was a teacher.

"Before rehearsal," she said. "I skipped biology to work on lines alone in the auditorium, only I didn't know how to turn on the lights. So I was sitting in the front row, thinking about how I was Emily, when he came in. I didn't say anything, but he spotted me right away, sat next to me, so close his arm hairs tickled mine. He told me about how the Parisians spent hours in sidewalk cafés talking—not about the weather, like people in Shelby, but about ideas, about love and passion. 'They're a restless people,' he said, 'not contented cows, chewing over the same old cud.' He stopped abruptly, afraid he'd insulted me. Did he think I was like them? I took the Juicyfruit out of my mouth and stuck it under the seat. 'No more cud,' I said, and he laughed, a great big sound. Then— was this bold girl really me?—I kissed him; he was ready, as if he'd been waiting. Afterward, he whispered, 'We won't tell anyone,' which of course I already knew."

It was wrong to kiss a teacher, wrong for a teacher to kiss a student. Wrong, wrong, wrong. Even Becky would faint if Mr. Miller actually told her he was in love with her. It was all so strange: Mama and a teacher in the ratty old auditorium, Mama chewing Juicyfruit. I'd always thought of her as just my mother, but here she was with this life, things that had happened before we knew her. Like a character in a movie.

"Afterward, all the time, he talked about us running away together," Mama said. "My heart would about stop when he said we should go to Florida and live in an ocean bungalow, or he wanted to see my hair shine in the Paris moonlight, or that in a past life we were Indian lovers in a tepee on the plains. Anyone who wasn't afraid of him was in love with him—students, teachers, the cafeteria ladies. Even a boy. But it was me he promised to marry. That was our destiny, our fate."

Mama—my mother—wanting to run off with a teacher. Did anyone else know this? "So . . . then, you . . ." It wasn't clear what I was supposed to say.

"It's not like I believed him." It was hard to guess from her suddenly casual voice if she had or hadn't.

I waited, stared down at the script, at Emily's lines highlighted with a yellow Magic Marker. What would Emily say? Of course, Emily's mother was normal. Good old Myrtle Webb, always telling Emily to eat a good breakfast and to be sensible.

Mama sighed. "It's not like I really thought I'd be his wife." Now it was clear—she was lying. "What happened, happened. There was nothing anyone could do."

As if that was the cue I'd been waiting for, I asked, "What happened?" My breath moved slowly through my body. There were no Strykers in Shelby that I knew of, so whatever happened couldn't have been good. I stared at Emily's lines, at all those words on the page, each carefully chosen by Thornton Wilder, word after word evaluated and tested and written in and scribbled out and written back in until he had *Our Town*, "a brilliant chronicle of life and death," until it was so perfect no one would dare add another word or take one out. All those performances, and every single time the last line would always be the Stage Manager wishing everyone a good night's sleep.

The kitchen faucet was dripping again, just enough so you noticed but not so much that you'd call a plumber. Will had promised he would fix it.

Finally Mama said what I was afraid she would say: "He died." Her voice shredded the words. "People thought it was a car accident. But I knew what really happened."

The print in front of me blurred. Emily had a lot of lines. What was I thinking, wanting such a big part? Mrs. Soames was enough, and besides, I got to wear an old-fashioned hat in the wedding scene. I pulled back one corner of the script, let the pages riffle down in clumps. Again. Finally I had to whisper, "How did you know?"

"He died the way James Dean did, and I never for a minute believed that was an accident," she said.

James Dean crashed his Porsche Spyder on September 30, 1955. Mama had told me the story many times. "In California, on his way to Salinas for a sports-car meet," I said.

"Men like that don't just die," Mama scoffed. "Men who control their destinies don't make wrong turns when they're driving."

Why would James Dean kill himself when his movie career was taking off? Why would Mr. Stryker? Or Mama? I glanced around the kitchen at the clock on the wall, the dirty dishes stacked in the sink, the calendar magneted to the fridge, a splotch of tomato juice on the floor.

"I stared out my bedroom window into endless darkness, didn't see a single star for months," Mama said. "What about our destiny, Paris, the ocean? What was I supposed to do now? I wasn't Emily anymore, wasn't the girl who was going to run away with Mr. Stryker, wasn't the girl who had kissed him in the auditorium or waited for him at the old cemetery after school. Who was I supposed to be?"

People were who they were, who they'd been. Like Linda, like Becky. "Are you one hundred percent sure it wasn't a regular car accident?" I asked.

"Listen to me," she said. "Men like that don't just die. Like my father's hunting accident."

Drip, drip, drip. I wanted to hit the faucet with a giant hammer. I spoke slowly: "He went out pheasant hunting. The gun went off."

Mama said the same words, but differently, more pointed: "He went out pheasant hunting. The gun went off. Think about it, Alice."

I picked at a hangnail on my thumb. Mama had claimed she didn't remember much about her father: He was a really good whistler, "he'd rather whistle than talk," she'd said, and he liked to tease her by popping out his dentures. He had died when she was ten. Aunt Aggy had pasted the newspaper clipping into a scrapbook: "Shelby Man Dies in Hunting Accident" was the headline. There were hunting accidents and car accidents all the time; people slipped in bathtubs and drowned. Plenty of people died from bad luck, without any control over their destinies at all. The hangnail tore off.

I shook my head, slow at first, then harder. It was impossible for me to believe what Mama said: because then how could she do the same thing to me? How could she, how? The question was like a mouthful of saltwater; your foot suddenly not finding the bottom of the pool; the powerful wind that rips the hat off your head, sending it skidding down the road, out of reach.

I closed my eyes and launched into Emily's words, soothing and comfortable, and then I became Emily, holding my breath, listening to the train up to Contoocook. I finished the whole play without Mama.

MRS. JOHNSON met privately in Dr. Ellis's classroom with each of the understudies for a big pep talk about our important role. She said careers had been launched when the star couldn't go on and the understudy took over. Maybe on Broadway someone might get sick or break their leg, but in Shelby, this show wouldn't go on without Linda. She'd thump around in a leg cast if it came to that.

Then, as if delivering good news, Mrs. Johnson announced that the understudies might give a Saturday-morning show for the grade school. I nodded, but who wanted to present the most beautiful American play ever written to a bunch of kids squirming on a gym floor?

"Any questions?" Mrs. Johnson looked out of place sitting at Dr. Ellis's cluttered desk, her hands folded together as if she was worried about accidentally knocking his important papers onto the floor. We had signed up for ten-minute time slots, so I was about to stand up when she said, "I wanted to play Emily way back when I was in high school."

I was startled, not only that she had changed the subject, but to think of her in high school, memorizing a locker combination, smiling at a boy (Mr. Johnson?) in the hall, maybe even upset that Mama was picked for the part of Emily instead of her.

"Oh, well," she said. "Water under the bridge. I was a freshman, too afraid to try out."

Hoping to prolong the conversation, I asked, "Afraid of what?" I mean, she had been state pork queen.

"Just young and afraid," she said. "Now I'm old and afraid!" Her laugh was twittery and nervous, birdlike. "Letting yourself go like that in front of all those people. It just seemed easier . . . not to. Your mother, though. She was wonderful. I'm sure she told you stories." Mrs. Johnson nodded, so I did too. "We had no idea she had all that in her. She kept to herself even back then; hearing more than 'hello' out of her was a miracle. Like a person gets only so many words. But there she was, up onstage, talking away, the perfect Emily. After she ran off, I was sure she'd show up in the movies. Oh, well. Things have a way of working out, don't they?" She abruptly glanced at her watch, gave me a "time to go" smile.

But I grabbed the sides of my desk with my hands, held on tight, as if she might drag me from the room. "I remember my mother telling me about the teacher who did *Our Town*."

Mrs. Johnson tilted her head, looked up at the clock. I followed her gaze, and we watched the second hand sweep away five seconds, ten. "Oh, we all had a crush on him." Ten more seconds. "I'd forgotten about Mr. Stryker."

"He died in a car wreck," I said. My knuckles had turned white, so I let go of the desk, flexed my sore fingers. What was I supposed to ask? *Did my mother think she was going to marry him? Did he really kill himself?* I tried to picture Mrs. Johnson's face if I asked those questions, but couldn't.

She was still staring at the clock. I noticed a sagginess under her chin, a thin frown wrinkle stretching across her forehead. "That was a long time ago," she said. "The Stone Age." Same twittery laugh. "Better get back to rehearsal." This time I stood up and left.

THE WORLD Series started Saturday night, and I watched the games on TV. The first two were in Boston, and I sat right up next to the screen, scanning the crowd scenes for Will. I stared at Carlton Fisk, Yaz, Fred Lynn, the others, wishing I could see our father in one of them. Will had the same honest, open face as Carlton Fisk. But Yaz was closer to the right age. And Luis Tiant was the most impressive with that mustache— though Bill Lee was the funniest, Fred Lynn the cutest. I wondered if Will was doing the same thing; and would we study every man that way for the rest of our lives?

THE WEEK blurred into learning lines, rehearsal, Red Sox versus Reds, making up excuses to teachers for unfinished homework ("That's not like you, Alice"). By Thursday I was so tired of it all, I skipped school. I told myself I was working on lines, but mainly I lay in bed, worried about the Series being tied, worried Will had run out of sandwiches from home, worried that there truly was a curse on the Red Sox, worried about the stupid umpire who made the bad call that cost us Wednesday's game, worried that Will had taken his winter coat because he knew he would never be back.

It was actually a relief to drag myself to rehearsal. Dr. Ellis started— as always—with stretching exercises where we stood in a circle and rolled our heads around, our necks snapping and crunching. Then we lay on the gritty stage floor and clenched all our muscles, then relaxed—again, clench and relax, again, as Dr. Ellis droned, "The human body has hundreds of muscles, and this exercise helps you identify each one. The body is the actor's most precious instrument." He said this every single day. Then we stretched as far and as hard as we could, from fingertips to toes, and released. Over and over, like we were rubber bands. For concentration, we were supposed to close our eyes, but I always kept mine cracked open, watching Dr. Ellis through an unfocused blur.

Usually Mrs. Johnson stretched on the floor with us, careful to keep her skirt tucked neatly over her legs, but today she stood next to Dr. Ellis on the stage, her arms folded against her chest. One foot was tapping, and she kept turning her head, as if someone she couldn't see was trying to have a conversation with her.

I heard the auditorium door creak, then whoosh shut—it was one of those doors that was fixed so it couldn't slam. The footsteps down the aisle were fast and heavy, clearly not a kid's tennis shoes. "I'm not interrupting, am I?" called a hearty male voice. I lifted my head to see, almost pressing my chin to my neck. Mr. Johnson. "Thought it would be fun to watch play practice," he shouted, settling into a seat in the third row. He was the only man in town who wore a tie every single day, because he was the mayor. When he gave us rides, he asked with fake concern how I was, and when anyone else got out of the car, he'd say, "Be sure to say hi to your folks for me," and with me it was just, "Good-bye." I slammed the car door extra hard at that because he was always telling Linda the door would drop off its hinges if she wasn't gentler.

"Dad, why are you here?" Linda said. She didn't sound very happy, but probably her voice was tight because we were in the clenching part of the exercise. Talk about lucky—her mother was practically running the play, and now her father came to rehearsal because he couldn't even wait for opening night.

Dr. Ellis and Mrs. Johnson glanced at each other. A big breath gusted out of Dr. Ellis. Then he said, "Delighted, Mr. Mayor. We're warming up."

"Please, Mr. Ellis, call me Jim," he said, all cheerful. "Just want to see firsthand what my favorite PTA president's up to these days."

Dr. Ellis was equally cheerful: "Well, then. Call me Roger."

"I believe in setting an example by giving our fine teachers the respect they deserve," Mr. Johnson said. "If that's okay with you, Mr. Ellis."

Was it my imagination or had he accentuated "Mr."? I waited for Dr. Ellis to correct him, but he merely told us to relax our muscles. In the silence that followed, Mrs. Johnson giggled, and I was surprised by the echo.

Dr. Ellis said, "And stretch. Two . . . three . . . four . . . five."

The auditorium chair squeaked noisily as Mr. Johnson shifted around.

Mrs. Johnson looked at her watch. "Can we get on with it?"

Dr. Ellis said, "Stretch. Two, three, four, five," counting too fast.

"We're already stretching," Jerry Zaiser said.

"So relax," he snapped. "Two, three, four, five," again, too fast. Half of us were stretching, half relaxing.

Mr. Johnson said, "I won't disturb you. Not a peep out of me!" The chair squeaked and squealed, almost like a pig.

Dr. Ellis clapped his hands several times. "Let's go, people," and everyone sat up, blinked, let the dizziness drop away.

Mrs. Johnson was staring straight up at the lights and curtains and the tangle of ropes that coordinated everything. The pleats in her skirt were flattened, not crisp and precise.

Mr. Johnson's chair squeaked again as he gave a big wave to Linda. "Hi, honey!" and Linda waved back, a quicker, tinier, embarrassed motion.

Mrs. Johnson hissed, "Pay attention!," and glared at Linda, who opened her script, moving her lips as she went over lines.

"Okay, let's go!" Dr. Ellis clapped his hands again, as if we were a pack of dogs.

The boys set up rows of folding chairs. We were working on the third act, the scene in the cemetery where all the dead people—including me, Mrs. Soames—were sitting around, being dead. It made me think of Mama sitting in a folding chair on a bare stage, being dead for real. I didn't like the part at the very end, where George goes to the cemetery and starts crying and Emily just stares at him because he doesn't understand.

Dr. Ellis fussed because we had forgotten who was supposed to sit in which row, which chair, and as he sorted us out, I watched Mr. Johnson's fingers on both hands drumming the armrests at his side, his right hand going fast, his left going slow. Mrs. Johnson perched on one of the empty cemetery chairs; the script was balanced on her knees, and she jumped when Dr. Ellis said her name, so the script tumbled to the floor. She picked it up, rapidly flipped pages, stirring the air enough to lift her bangs off her forehead.

Then Dr. Ellis reminded us that the dead people in the cemetery must be calm and matter-of-fact—"the dead and the living have different concerns." Mr. Johnson interrupted him midsentence: "Where's the drinking fountain?" His smile looked like it had been cut out of construction paper and pasted onto his face.

Dr. Ellis slowly turned and stared at Mr. Johnson. He smiled back that same fake smile, saying, "Sorry, I didn't hear you," though how could he not have?

Linda pointed to the back of the auditorium: "Right through that door." Mr. Johnson didn't get up, and Linda added, "To the left, Daddy," still pointing, "go left once you're through the door." She made little jabby motions with her hand.

Mr. Johnson stood up, letting his chair squeak and bang. He took the long way out to the aisle, knocking his knees against every single seat—*thunk*. There wasn't a way to walk through that row any more noisily, and we all fell silent, watching him. His footsteps thumped up the aisle, and he pushed hard on the bar across the door so it swung way open, as far as it would go. Then it slowly whooshed shut. Something was going on.

Dr. Ellis let out a big breath, almost as loud as the whooshing door, and Mrs. Johnson sighed sharply. "Okay then," Dr. Ellis said. "Let's start with—" But the door popped open, and Mr. Johnson thumped back down the side aisle, knocking one hand against each seat back, whistling off-key in a loud, echoey way. Again, you couldn't help but watch him.

Mr. Johnson cut across the auditorium through a row of seats, bumping each chair, grabbing each seat back, and he reached the middle aisle, then thudded down to the front row, sat down. In the tight silence, Mrs. Johnson suddenly shrieked, "What do you think you're going to see?" Her voice easily projected all the way to the last row of the balcony. "Leave us alone!," and she hurled her script at Mr. Johnson—no mistake, no way you could say, *Oops, it slipped.* All the pages fluttered open as it shot through the air, then fell at his feet. He kicked it away, and it flipped shut.

No one else moved. When Mr. Johnson spoke, his voice was the softest it had been the whole time, but we all heard: "Cunt." Then he walked up the center aisle—quietly—and left through the main door, which closed gently behind him. I stared at the red exit sign above the door because I didn't want to look at Linda or anyone else—especially not Mrs. Johnson.

A moment later, Dr. Ellis said, "Rehearsal's canceled."

"No it's not," Mrs. Johnson said, shoving Linda toward the center of the stage. Linda stumbled, almost fell, grabbed Jerry Zaiser's arm. "Go ahead, honey." Mrs. Johnson had the same "perfect mother" voice and smile she used when she was holding a tray of cookies.

Linda hadn't let go of Jerry.

"Start," Mrs. Johnson snapped. "Go!"

Linda flipped her hair, opened her mouth, but her shoulders started to shake as she began to cry.

"Say a goddamn line!" Mrs. Johnson shouted. Everyone started shifting around, staring up at the lights or over at the auditorium chairs or at the exit signs or straight down at the polished wood of the stage floor, listening to Linda's half-choked sobs until finally Mrs. Johnson said, "Alice, here's your big break." She grabbed the script out of Dr. Ellis's hand, flipped through some pages. What was I supposed to do?

"Be Emily," Mama said.

Would Linda hate me? Would I care if she did? My folding chair screeched as I stood and slid it backward. Linda rubbed her forearm across her face, then turned and bolted up the aisle, through the door. People seemed like they couldn't decide whether to stare at the door or at me.

I didn't know the third act very well, but I started by saying, "Good morning," which wasn't quite right but close enough, the beginning of dead Emily back home for her twelfth birthday, with the Stage Manager watching. I thought of how many times I had said "good morning" to Mama; there was no way to say that simple line and make it mean everything it did. Maybe Thornton Wilder was a genius, and maybe he knew small towns and their secrets. Maybe he wrote a thousand drafts of this play before settling on these words; and maybe even by some miracle he was right, the dead could come back if they wanted to; and surely it was true that living people didn't properly appreciate life. My chest tightened until it was almost impossible to breathe.

The world overflowed with those lines, those tiny, single moments. How Mr. Johnson felt saying that word. How I felt hearing it. Mr. Stryker kissing Mama's lips, tasting Juicyfruit. The smell of Joe Fry's car. Rain pouring on the cornfield. Parallel parking. The way Aunt Aggy's oil paints glistened on canvas. Crushed Cherry lipstick.

All that, yet Mama chose sitting on a cold folding chair on the bare stage, staring at the imaginary stars as the lights went down and the curtain closed. My mother, my own mother, didn't think of me when she made that choice. Could mere words—or anything—ever explain that to me? That she would never again laugh as we danced at the sink to "Crocodile Rock" while washing the supper dishes or never set a stack of five vanilla wafers—my favorite—on top of my book as I studied at the kitchen table the night before a test? Or toast marshmallows on a fork over the gas burner so we could have s'mores in the winter? Who would do those things with me, for me? Who would remember how much I loved vanilla wafers?

Mrs. Johnson must have been talking to me, because she snapped, "Your line," maybe not for the first time, and instead of giving me the beginning and waiting to see if I'd get it, she read the whole thing and her next line and my line after that, and she kept on reading, getting louder and louder, until Dr. Ellis shouted, "Sandy!," and she shut up. She stared at the lights again, the tangle of ropes and pulleys and weights.

The line that came next was on the tip of my tongue, something about being happy just for this moment, but I didn't say it.

Dr. Ellis said, "Rehearsal's canceled." He glared at us, pointed to the exit, until people slowly began filtering toward the back of the auditorium, grabbing jackets and books, carefully stepping over Mrs. Johnson's script that lay splat on the floor. I lingered, the last to leave, Dr. Ellis saying, "Don't take all day, Alice," as he headed over to turn off the houselights. Partway up the aisle, I knelt to tie my shoe, listening to his footsteps clunk across the stage and back. Mama urgently whispered, "Look, Alice, look now," and I saw the two of them—Dr. Ellis and Mrs. Johnson; Roger and Sandy; not a teacher, not a mother, but a man and a woman—standing on the stage, knotted together in a tight embrace, entwined in a long kiss, her hands pressing his shoulders, his fingers tangled in her hair, holding the back of her head, the footlights burning on them, making their shadows huge, and Mama whispered again, "Do you see now how secret most lives are?," and in front of me the two lovers embraced, but in my mind I saw Mama, a girl my age, before she was my mother, secretly kissing Mr. Stryker in this same auditorium—one of the many things I had never seen or known about my own mother now vivid, as if in a sharply focused snapshot.

It was wrong, obviously, but watching that kiss, feeling it, something also seemed right, and for a moment I couldn't say that anything anywhere was for sure. The door wasn't noisy when I finally tiptoed through it.

REHEARSAL WAS canceled the next day; a substitute teacher in for Dr. Ellis let us work on our *Great Gatsby* worksheets in small groups, so we gossiped about what had happened yesterday. Linda wasn't in school;

Becky said she had called but the phone rang and rang. When Dr. Ellis returned on Monday, he announced that Linda wasn't going to play Emily after all, and weren't we lucky to have such a well-prepared understudy? There was more: Sadly, Mrs. Johnson wouldn't be helping out, and we were told we'd certainly miss her enthusiasm and marvelous spirit.

Becky whispered that she had overheard her mother talking on the phone: Mrs. Johnson had moved into the Seville Apartments in Iowa City, taking the three younger kids, but not Linda. "The apartment complex has a swimming pool," Becky added, as if mothers who ran away from their husbands shouldn't be so lucky. Maybe if Becky had seen the kiss or knew what I knew about Mama, she could believe that Mrs. Johnson was someone more than Mr. Johnson's wife and Linda's mother.

And the day after that, Linda came back to school, flipping her hair, telling us school plays were "ridiculous make-believe," and that now she was busy at an important after-school job in her father's office. She transferred out of Dr. Ellis's American literature class and dumped Doug Foltz in a five-second conversation in the cafeteria, in full view of Lily.

The Red Sox were behind, two games to three, in the World Series, and game six had been postponed for three long, dragged-out days because it was raining buckets across New England; everyone was waiting for the big game six, waiting for the nor'easter to blow over, waiting. I imagined Will standing in line all night with everyone else who wanted those precious tickets or sitting in Mama's car as rain sheeted the windshield, staring at the gray, unfamiliar world around him—missing Iowa, missing me, or maybe missing nothing. Finally it stopped raining that Tuesday. The game was on Channel 7, and I watched every minute of it, sitting cross-legged on the couch, squeezing the pillow in my lap, too tense to eat the popcorn I'd made, gasping when Fred Lynn crashed into the center-field wall and didn't scramble up right away, relieved when he was fine, even staying in the game. But Luis Tiant just didn't have his stuff, and the score shot up to six-three Reds, until Bernie Carbo's magnificent three-run homer tied things up in the eighth inning. In all that staring at the TV I couldn't find Will in the stands, and I didn't see that man somewhere out there who looked a bit like Will and a bit like me. It was such an off chance that I would, a miracle even to think it. But a pinch hit, two outs, three-run homer to tie the game was almost a miracle, too, so I understood why people loved baseball, and I kept scouring the stands, all my fingers crossed.

It was nearly midnight when Carlton Fisk slammed the ball out toward the Green Monster in left field, and we all watched him dance along the first baseline, waving his arms, so desperately wanting to keep that ball in fair territory, wanting to make it a home run instead of a foul, to turn it into the game-winning run, and he did all that as everyone in Boston—including, I hoped, Will—screamed and cheered and went wild with happiness, and the Red Sox won! The announcers said it was the best game ever, a classic, that there had been nothing like it and maybe never would be again. When the phone rang right after, I ran to answer— it had to be Will. But Joe Fry shouted, "Did you see that?," and I shouted back, "Oh my God," and he said, "Jesus fucking Christ, Alice, he was there, he saw that, I know he was there," and for one second I thought of the man who was my father, and who's to say he wasn't there or wasn't somewhere watching that game? It was a moment where you could believe absolutely anything, even Joe Fry mumbling, "Sorry I'm such a jerk," before hanging up.

OPENING NIGHT. I sat in front of the mirror in the makeshift dressing room putting on my Emily makeup, looking so much like I was concentrating that everyone left me alone. I even heard Jerry Zaiser say, "Don't disturb Alice—she's getting in character," a phrase he had picked up from an episode of *The Odd Couple.* I drew on more eyeliner.

If Mama were here, she'd tell me to break a leg.

Aunt Aggy was bringing Mr. Cooper to opening night, "like the kind of dates they go on in fancy cities," she'd said. "We're quite the artistic family these days; Mr. Pablo Picasso himself would be impressed. A painter, an actress." And she smiled so sweetly I couldn't tack on: *a dead mother, a boy who ran away.* She dredged up an old, rusty pair of opera glasses, and she kept urging Mr. Cooper to bring his "pince-nez," so in some ways I was wishing they'd stay home, but also I was glad someone was going to be there to watch me.

A girl's voice cut through the blur of chatter: "The auditorium's packed!"

Dr. Ellis clapped sharply. "Ten minutes, people!" he yelled, pushing his hands through his hair.

I put on red lipstick too bright to wear in real life, but it was okay because stage lighting washed you out. After that incredible game, Boston had ended up losing the World Series, and everyone was saying they had known all along that the Cincinnati Reds would pull it out in the end, but wasn't it a great series, the best? I just wanted Will to come back. I wanted to walk out on the stage and look into the front row and see his face. In a movie or play, that would be the ending.

But once I got out there, I didn't see him in the front row or any-where, and he didn't come backstage afterward either. Aunt Aggy and Mr. Cooper did, with a dozen roses—the first time I ever got a bouquet from a florist (funeral flowers didn't count). Aunt Aggy kept saying, "Wasn't she absolutely divine?," and Mr. Cooper nodded his head and repeated, "Divine," enough times to satisfy her.

Dr. Ellis was practically crying as he told us we were superb, that we deserved our standing ovation, on and on, as if he was giving a farewell speech. (Which he was: Monday after the play, the substitute was back, filling out the rest of the semester while the school looked for a new lan-guage arts teacher. I tried to remember what he had told us but couldn't because I had been admiring my roses, trying to think of what Dotty King had said to put in the vase to keep them fresh: sugar? lemon juice? We heard he went to Iowa City, and his wife threw everything he had left behind out in the front yard, in the rain.)

Becky whispered that Joe Fry had been in the balcony, two rows away from her. "Alone," she added, with a meaningful look.

No Linda. No Mr. Johnson. No Mrs. Johnson.

But what I would remember most was one moment in the third act. Emily was saying good-bye to the world—to clocks ticking and sunflow-ers and coffee—about to tell the Stage Manager that the earth was too wonderful for anyone to realize. In that quick moment, I thought about clocks ticking and sunflowers and coffee—and the fuzzy mittens the cheerleaders wear at cold Friday-night football games and the way newspaper rips all ragged when you're trying to tear out an article about your favorite team—and kisses. I looked over at the cemetery of folding chairs, and for one small second, I felt Mama sitting there, her hands folded in her lap, that crooked smile, her eyes shining. She looked straight at me. But it wasn't like the play when George visits the cemetery and Emily is unmoved. It was how a mother looks at her daughter in such a way that the daughter will understand for the rest of her life that yes, one person thinks—no, knows, KNOWS—that yes, she IS pretty, yes, she IS smart, yes, absolutely yes. The kind of moment that is impossibly short yet also forever, and that tear trailing down my cheek could have been mine or Emily's or Mama's. By the time I sat in my own cemetery seat, Mama had vanished. If she had really been there.

Three days later, Will came home, rumpled and smelly, heading straight for the refrigerator, an ugly, half-healed burn across two knuckles. I couldn't sit still, following him, hanging up his coat, moving aside the paper bag of dirty clothes he plopped on the table.

The first thing he said was, "I was there at game six. I saw Fisk's home run. I was there." It was all he talked about, that and getting Carlton Fisk's autograph on a crumpled napkin and actually talking to him for a minute: "I told him I played baseball, and he said, 'Good luck, son.'" Will had missed so much school that he had been kicked off the football team, he was about to flunk most of his classes, they'd put him on academic probation, and there was talk that he'd have to go to summer school if he expected to graduate. But he didn't care. "That one moment was worth it all," he said, "worth everything."

Yes. Mama should have remembered that.

PIE

WILL had all kinds of stories about being in Boston—dodging cops to secretly set up his pup tent every night in a park near Fenway, scrubbing pots at a seafood restaurant where after-hours the waitresses watched him eat his first-ever whole lobster ("like wrestling a turtle"), the flat-sided hot-dog buns at Fenway, how people knew he was from somewhere else by the way he talked. Aunt Aggy didn't like hearing these stories; she'd snap, "I'm glad some people think it's fun to run off and scare everyone half to death," and Will would laugh, not caring at all about how worried we had been.

Mostly he talked about Boston when we were alone, like driving to school. "I was halfway across the country, Baby Sister. That's far." He said that often, like there was something about it he couldn't quite believe.

Twelve hundred miles. (I had measured on a map.) "I didn't think you'd come back," I said. *Like Mama*, was the unspoken rest of the sentence.

He looked uncomfortable, brought up lobster again, how to suck meat out of its tiny legs. We were at school, and he pulled into a parking space off by itself.

Maybe my hair was wavy like Mama's, but he was the one who had run off the way she had, who had left me behind. "So why'd you come back, anyways?" I asked.

He cracked his knuckles, first all together, then one at a time. "I guess." He paused, then the words came in a rush: "I guess I'm not really someone who can leave like that, though I . . ."

Tried? Wanted to? Wished I were? Any end to that sentence was scary. I nodded as if I understood completely, crossed my fingers that my brother was back for real, for good.

THANKSGIVING WAS coming up. At Thanksgiving, Mama used to be a traditional, normal mother, making mountains of traditional, normal food. You'd think she'd be the kind of person who'd say frog legs for Thanksgiving could be fun, but she was turkey and gravy all the way.

Mama kept her Thanksgiving information in a big accordion file splattered with gravy and turkey grease: master lists of groceries to buy; recipes ripped from *Family Circle* and *Woman's Day*; notes on timing the turkey; how much butter, oil, and broth for basting; cookbook page numbers to consult. There was a section for new recipes under consideration: ten ways to make cranberry relish; rolls—Parker House, cloverleaf, high-as-a-kite; stuffing recipes with exotic ingredients no one would think to shove inside a turkey—chili peppers, collard greens, wild rice. There were articles on what to do if your gravy was lumpy, thin, greasy, or salty; a canned pumpkin label with a scribble, "This brand!!"; a section on leftover turkey (soup, tetrazini, creamed, à la king, croquettes, potpie). It would be absolutely impossible, unthinkable, to have Thanksgiving without that folder. But I couldn't find it anywhere.

I pulled cookbooks off the shelf, hoping maybe the folder was jammed behind them. Aunt Aggy watched and said, "Those recipes don't matter."

Sure. She'd fry up hot dogs. I stacked the cookbooks: two different copies of *Joy of Cooking, Betty Crocker's Cake and Frosting Mix Cookbook, Better Homes and Gardens, Festive Dishes for Entertaining,* and so on. No one had looked at them since Mama died. Scraps of paper marked various pages: meat loaf with cornflakes that Will had for his birthday supper, cold dill soup we had poured down the sink, cookies we rolled out and cut with cookie cutters every Christmas, angel food cake for bake sales, three-bean salad for picnics, chocolate cake with the batter we licked off the beaters.

One of the *Joy of Cooking* books had two red-ribbon page markers attached to the top, like a Bible. One ribbon was at a page with recipes for possum and beaver tail. The other ribbon marked homemade marshmallows. That was Mama—happy to spend time making marshmallows when a normal person would go to the store and buy a bag for fifty cents. Or to mark a recipe that required asking the butcher at Hy-Vee for two pounds of beaver tail—how embarrassing.

The other copy of *Joy of Cooking* was beat up, its blue cover splotched with crusty splatters, dark rings, and a couple of burned spots. Dog-ears marked some of the yellowed pages: Meat Shortcakes, Mashed Potato Salad, Eggless Prune Whip, Broiled Sardine Canapés—checkmarks on things you wouldn't make (or even eat) nowadays.

Aunt Aggy opened *Betty Crocker's Cake and Frosting Mix Cookbook,* tapped her finger on a page. "This cake is frosted like a piece of candy corn."

I didn't need to look. "Mama made that cake three Halloweens ago when I stayed home from school sick. She warmed ginger ale and let me lie in her bed, and she painted my toenails with Ruby Jewel nail polish while you and Will answered the door for trick-or-treaters. We gave out Milk Duds that were a rip-off because each box had only two pieces, but they were Mama's favorite."

Aunt Aggy's brow wrinkled up all raisiny; she said, "I don't remember any of that, not even the cake."

I remembered which saucepan Mama used to heat up ginger ale for sick people—the tiny yellow one that was the only survivor of an old matched set from the Sears catalog (the frying pans got their insides burned black, Will used the big pot for creek minnows, and the handle had fallen off the medium pot). Mama knew I liked drinking from a teacup and saucer because that was when I was reading mostly books about England, where people had tea at five o'clock. She had set a tiny box of Milk Duds on the saucer, and I slid the candy onto my tongue so the smooth waxiness melted and the caramel dissolved, making those two candies last forty-five minutes. Every detail of that Halloween was in my head forever.

Aunt Aggy looked at the book, then set her hand flat on the page, blocking out the picture. She spoke quietly: "You'd think I couldn't forget a cake that looks like candy corn."

"Doesn't matter." But it seemed to me it did.

She said, "Let's drive up to Iowa City and eat Chinese food for Thanksgiving."

Was she insane? "Who eats Chinese food on Thanksgiving?"

"People who live in China," she said, trying to coax me into a laugh. She would erase everything if she could, like pulling off that Band-Aid she was always talking about. If only it were so easy.

"Don't you want Mama's turkey?" I asked. "Mama's pumpkin pie?" Pumpkin pie was my favorite dessert in the whole world, but Mama refused to make it any time except Thanksgiving—no matter how much I begged. "Pumpkin pie means Thanksgiving," she had said. "It makes the day complete."

Aunt Aggy sighed. "Mmm . . . cranberry relish. I think she used vanilla."

There were thousands of recipes in that stack of cookbooks, none of them the ones we wanted. Vanilla in cranberry relish? How were we supposed to know that?

Aunt Aggy closed the cookbook with the candy-corn cake. "We'll manage."

Manage by running away? Manage by painting pictures that now didn't look like anything except blobs of color? She should at least pretend to help me look for the folder; she should do something. I pushed the stack of cookbooks, sending them skidding into a messy jumble on the floor. When Aunt Aggy gave a Mrs. Johnson fake smile and said, "Hungry Man makes a nice turkey TV dinner," I didn't respond, just walked upstairs very slowly, then slammed my bedroom door. I leaned hard against it until the overwhelming urge to cry passed. Then I sat at my desk and stared out the window at the blank backyard, where every twig and leftover leaf, every blade of grass was brown and shriveled.

I had already asked a bunch of times. "Where's the Thanksgiving folder?"

Mama said, "Remember when Will accused me of putting BBs in the mashed potatoes because they were lumpy?" She laughed, all tinkly and silvery, as if she was in the room.

I said, "He spit out the lumps into a little pyramid on the side of his plate."

"Remember when you dared Will to eat the turkey heart and we caught him throwing up in the bathroom?" Mama said. "Remember when I found that maple syrup from Vermont that cost more than Log Cabin but made the sweet potatoes so much better?" Her voice had moved into that dreaminess it got whenever she talked about cooking. It was never "just supper" with Mama.

"Well, how am I supposed to make those sweet potatoes if I don't have a recipe?" I tossed a chewed-up pencil at the wastepaper basket. It clattered in, so I threw another that hit the wall, leaving a mark. "I don't even like sweet potatoes." But we might as well call off Thanksgiving without them. And the two stuffings—classic in the turkey (that we all ate) and "experimental" in a pan (that only Mama liked—pecan oyster; chestnut sage; apple rye—something different every year). And watching Mama drape the turkey with butter-drenched cheesecloth. Racing Will every time the oven door opened because whoever was first got to baste. The *ch-ch-ch* of Mama's knife chopping celery and onions; the ping of cranberries dropping into the colander to be rinsed. And breathing the kitchen air, that mix of roasting turkey and the neck simmering on the back burner and frying onions and melted butter and biscuits and pumpkin pie—and winding through it all, knitting everything together like the secret ingredient, Mama's White Shoulders perfume. That was Thanksgiving, every last delicious detail, like a movie you want to watch again and again.

EARLY SATURDAY morning, I went to the grocery store to buy pumpkin-pie ingredients. Back home, I was sitting at the table, working my way through a bowl of Cap'n Crunch, studying cookbooks, when Will came downstairs. He looked rumpled, partly asleep.

"Hey, Baby Sister," he said. "Find that cereal recipe in a cookbook?"

"For your information, I'm practicing pumpkin pie for Thanksgiving."

"Thanksgiving?" He stretched out the word, landing hard on each syllable. "What do we have to be thankful for?"

I looked up at the kitchen clock on the wall: 10:35. That was no surprise because the battery had worn out ages ago, leaving the clock stuck there.

He grabbed a handful of Cap'n Crunch from the box, let pieces drop from his fist into his mouth as he spoke: "When I was in Boston, I thought I saw Mama. There was a woman walking in front of me, swinging her purse the way Mama did when she was in a good mood, wearing a thick red sweater, a turtleneck with those twisty ridges, you know, those sweaters Mama liked."

"Cables," I said, but I could barely speak, remembering Mama in her thick red sweater; "crunchy," she had called it.

Will reached for another handful of cereal, dropped it in his mouth, and I watched him chew for what felt like a long time. Finally he swallowed, then said, "I ran to catch up with her. When I did, I couldn't remember what Mama's face looked like."

I stared at a Cap'n Crunch crumb clinging to his top lip. Forget Mama's face? No. That wasn't possible, couldn't happen. Not in eight months, not in eight years, not ever. My whole body felt heavy, as if carved from stone, and blinking was a struggle, breathing; so was looking away, looking back. The crumb was gone, licked off maybe, fallen. "We're talking about Thanksgiving, not Boston," I said.

"It was like looking in a mirror but seeing nothing." He stared at the clock.

I followed his gaze and snapped, "It needs a new battery." Something reminding us of Mama was everywhere—even that ugly clock. She had bought it at a garage sale for ten cents.

He grabbed the cereal box, reached in, and rolled shut the wax-paper bag. Then he tucked together the cardboard flaps, like he was suddenly very worried about stale cereal. His voice was subdued; maybe he wasn't really talking to me: "I think that was the first time I believed she was gone forever."

Abruptly, I said, "You never even sent me a postcard. How was I supposed to know you were coming back?"

"Look, I'm here, aren't I?" He rubbed cereal dust off his hand and onto the tablecloth. His face looked hard, like cold glass.

I pushed away my cereal bowl. All I wanted now was pumpkin pie and turkey. "Thanksgiving will be fine once I find Mama's recipes." The old *Joy of Cooking* was open to the piecrust recipe, and I jabbed my finger at it. "This is the pie," I said, standing up as if I knew what I was doing.

"I don't like pumpkin pie," he said.

"You ate three pieces last year."

"Did not."

"Remember? After dinner, when we were carrying dishes to the sink, you dropped the sweet potatoes," I said. "Potatoes and glass splattered all over the floor, and Mama teased, 'No pie for you.' After we did the dishes, Mama whipped the cream and brought out the pie, and you said, 'Thought I don't get any.' She said, 'It's unconstitutional to deny your son pumpkin pie on Thanksgiving.' Everyone laughed—even Mr. Cooper's boring father—and Mama cut you an extra-big piece smeared with tons of whipped cream. You said, 'We learned in history class that the Constitution guarantees two pieces of pumpkin pie on Thanksgiving, maybe three.' And Mama said, 'If you can eat three pieces of pie after that meal, you never have to wash another dish.' And I said, 'Unfair! What if I eat three pieces?' And she said—"

"Make your stupid pumpkin pie," and he bumped into a chair in his hurry to leave.

I finished that conversation in my head: She said, "Alice, if you eat three pieces of pie, your stomach will explode, making a bigger mess than those sweet potatoes on the floor." We all laughed, and I had thought, *This is the best Thanksgiving ever.*

I turned pages to find the pumpkin-pie recipe, past grape pie, custard pie, jelly pie. Maybe this wasn't Mama's exact pie, but the kitchen would fill up with pumpkin smell like a regular Thanksgiving.

"Piecrust is tricky," Mama said.

"I cook fine," I said. "Macaroni and cheese, pancakes, tuna casserole."

Mama said, "There's an art to piecrust."

Art was the *Mona Lisa*, not a pie. A pie was reading a recipe, following directions. I flipped back several pages, read out loud: "'Rules for making piecrust. All your ingredients should be very cold. Ice water is a must.' That's art? Think I can't make ice water?" Okay, so there were two more full, tiny-print pages about piecrust—just crust, nothing about fillings. But lots of information meant the recipe was precise, so you would end up with perfect crust. "Why do people say 'easy as pie' if it isn't easy?"

"I don't know—why?" Mama said, like I'd asked her a riddle.

I took the cookbook to the counter, started dragging out the flour bin, the saltshaker, baking powder, the big beige bowl, the flour sifter. I read the recipe again—actually, it called for cake flour.

Mama said, "Regular flour works fine."

The recipe said "or bread flour," but cake flour was listed first, so I found Mama's Swans Down and scooped some into the measuring cup.

"Level it with a knife," Mama said. "That's how to measure flour."

Nothing in the book about that, but I remembered helping Mama with cookies and how she dragged a butter knife over the measuring cup to get a perfectly flat top. Then I dumped my flour into the sifter, started sifting away, raising a white cloud. The handle made the exact squeak I remembered from when Mama stood in the kitchen sifting. I liked watching flour fall into the bowl, making a soft pyramid.

I added salt and baking powder—"Level the spoon against the edge of the can," Mama said—sifted again. "Skip that sifting if you're in a hurry," she suggested.

The recipe didn't say what to do if you were in a hurry, so I kept sifting.

"Baking powder in piecrust," Mama said. "Interesting." Clearly she wanted me to ask why that was so interesting, but I didn't care; the recipe said, "1 teaspoon baking powder." I shook the sifter over the sink to knock out the excess flour. Then I turned on the faucet, about to hold the sifter under the water, when Mama shrieked, "Don't get it wet!" I froze, and Mama added, "Never wash a sifter. It will rust."

It's not like the cookbook said anything about sifters. Dotty King talked about why sifting was important but had never warned us about wet sifters. I turned off the water.

I measured the lard and butter and divided the slippery lumps into two parts like the recipe said—Mama mumbled something about tiny cubes, but since the book didn't say anything about that, I plopped one part onto the flour. This wasn't so hard. I started imagining the pies I'd make—regular ones like apple, peach, cherry; and the weird ones in the book, jelly, sour cream, transparent, molasses. My pies would be as famous as Mama's cakes.

Next, the book said to "cut" the shortening in with two knives or a pastry blender. I knew what a regular blender was, but not a pastry blender. And were you supposed to use butter knives, steak knives, or big chopping knives?

Mama started to say something but I interrupted: "I can do this myself," thinking, *If you wanted to make pies for Thanksgiving this year, then*— I grabbed two knives out of the silverware drawer, started slicing the lard and butter in the flour. But lumps stuck to the knife blades. I was supposed to do this until the mixture looked like cornmeal, not that I thought cornmeal looked much different than flour, and then "cut" in the rest of the shortening until the dough was in pea-size lumps.

I read ahead, hoping the recipe would get easier—"Be prepared with ¼ cup ice water." I ran cold water into the ("Glass," Mama whispered) measuring cup up to the one-quarter line. Mama said, "The ice will mess up that measurement."

Another thing the book didn't mention. Three pages of directions and nothing was clear. I banged an ice tray against the side of the sink until cubes fell out, dropped them into the water. The level rose to one-half cup.

"Let the water get cold. Then take out the ice and remeasure," Mama said.

"I know." I picked up the knives. I had chosen the one book that had a million words of instruction but still couldn't tell me exactly what to do. My armpits were sticky with nervousness.

I stabbed at the shortening again, remembering from the "rules of piecrust" on the previous page that everything was supposed to be cold. The butter had been on the table since Aunt Aggy's breakfast toast. Why didn't the recipe say "cold butter" right there?

I scraped shortening off the knives, saw a note above the rules for making piecrust: "Beginners often forget to **preheat** the oven." So I twirled the oven dial to 450, the temperature for pumpkin pies, according to the chart.

Mama said, "I usually do 425 and turn it down after fifteen minutes."

"This book says 450." Actually, I wanted to throw the book across the room. Even if I figured out this cutting thing, there were directions coming up like "blend the water in lightly." What did "lightly" mean? And, farther ahead: "One can produce superior piecrust by using a fork to lift the ingredients, thereby spreading the moisture evenly throughout. Equally fine results can be achieved by using a spoon, or working the dough very gently with the fingertips." Fork? Spoon? Fingers? Which?

Mama said, "There are as many ways to make piecrust as there are cooks."

I dropped the knives, and they clattered in the bowl. Nothing looked like cornmeal; the lump of butter was gooey soft; the recipe said I should chill the dough for twelve hours, which meant I'd be rolling it out at midnight; and the fork-spoon-finger issue wasn't resolved. "I want to make it your way," I said.

She started talking fast: "For apple pie, I use the cheese piecrust; if I need to put together a pie fast, I go with the hot water piecrust; if it's a fruit pie, I double the basic recipe and roll out two extra crusts to stick in the freezer; if it's—"

"I just want pumpkin pie!" I shouted. The moment of silence was welcome. "Like you made. I mean, I know there's one brand of pumpkin you like best. I bought Libby's. Is that it? And I know there's an exact recipe, one I could follow. Where's the Thanksgiving folder with the real recipes?"

I let my head fall way back. That clock still said 10:35.

I tossed the knives into the sink where they slipped partway down the drain. I wanted to switch on the disposal and grind those knives into dust, but if I did, there would only be a screechy clank, then the disposal would break and no one would get around to fixing it. So I fished out the knives and set them next to the sifter on the counter. I dumped my piecrust into the sink and listened to the disposal chew.

I WASN'T in the mood for school on Monday. In fact, school had been dragging all semester. I was free from chemistry but had been "rewarded" with Mrs. Lane's advanced, honors biology because my grades last year were good. Fewer formulas but too many diagrams of cells, though I was decent at drawing them. Gym class was a horrible abyss of volleyball. And the substitute American lit teacher skipped the rest of *The Great Gatsby* to make us read *Moby-Dick*—though mostly she talked about whales becoming extinct. Grades seemed pointless. A, B, C—did a letter really tell me how smart I was?

"This isn't like you," teachers murmured when they passed back my C papers, my D+ quizzes, and maybe now I understood a little bit what Mama meant when she had talked about wanting to be someone else. Just because I had always been good at school, did I have to be that way for the rest of my life? What if I was tired of studying, of school, of everything?

Monday morning was dull and gray, the endless beginning of an endless week. On the way to school, Will purposely ran over a dead squirrel instead of swerving to miss it. Then, between second and third periods, Becky spilled a whole can of Tab in our locker, mostly over my notebooks. When I ran to get paper towels from the second-floor bath-room, Donna Slade was wearing jeans with a peace sign Magic-Markered on the butt, just like Paula Elam, and I thought about asking if she ever heard from Paula, but I didn't have the nerve. When I got back to the locker, Becky had gone to her chemistry class, leaving the mess for me. Instead of cleaning it up like I was supposed to, I slammed the locker door and decided to skip study hall and go sit in the car where no one could bother me.

The cold car was peaceful. I just stared at the brick school building, coincidentally in the opposite direction from where Joe Fry's blue Mustang was parked. I turned on the radio, keeping Dotty King low—a sound but not too much of a voice—and I watched frosty breath float out of my mouth, watched the windows slowly steam white, and thought easy, random, drifty thoughts. It would've been nice if I were a smoker; I liked the idea of sitting in the car, blowing smoke rings the way Mama did. She had said they helped her think. Lately, Linda talked about smoking. She claimed she was going to be a "social smoker" when she was old enough to go to bars; according to Linda, women looked sexiest holding a clear drink with ice and a cigarette. She wasn't around as much lately because she visited her mother in Iowa City every Saturday; "All we do is shop," Linda said, "she'll buy me whatever I want." Becky was impressed, but I knew Linda didn't mean it as a good thing. She never mentioned her father or Dr. Ellis, and I wondered if maybe Linda would be relieved if Becky and I would simply ask the questions we had: *Is your mom dating Dr. Ellis? Does your dad still hate them? Are you sad?* But it was easier to let Linda talk on about her new crush, Danny Kadera, who played on the football team instead of just riding the bench like Doug.

The background to my random, drifty thoughts was Dotty King's voice bubbling up into excitement, back down, back up. She was always so happy about something—a new way to fix meat loaf, getting ketchup stains out of a lace tablecloth, what to do with the leftover juice from a can of peaches, how to attract cardinals to your bird feeder. It was like Mama's smoke rings, one thing after another rising from out of nowhere, Dotty King's recipe for chocolate-marshmallow icing; and the way Mama used to sit and stare and smoke until her bedroom was hazy; and that a paste of cornstarch and water removes spots from wallpaper; and Mama lying on her bed for hours, not saying one single word even when you asked a question right to her face, just lying there as the room got darker until all you could see was the tip of her glowing cigarette as you walked by; and how peanut butter gets gum out of your daughter's hair; and how Will, Aunt Aggy, and I each had to know Mama was deep into one of her moods again—you could see it, like a curtain covering a window—only no one would say anything, not even to each other, and why not?; and how hyacinth bulbs should chill in the fridge for eight weeks before you plant them; and on and on, into a peaceful, random timelessness, Mama's sad smoking, Dotty King's tricks for pudding, me remembering last year's Thanksgiving when Mama mashed twenty-two potatoes so we'd have leftovers . . .

Had I drifted off to sleep? There was an insistent tapping on the passenger window. I leaned over and rubbed away the condensation, certain I'd see Mr. Rhinehart demanding to know why I wasn't in class. But it was Joe Fry. I felt my jaw tighten, then I rolled down the window a crack, said, "Will's not here." That whisk of cold air bit into my nostrils as I breathed it, waking me up, so I added, "I think he has French this period."

Joe got into the car, cold air swooping as he opened and shut the door. He rolled up the window, leaned his head back, let out his breath in a quick, white column. We hadn't spoken since that game six night, ages ago, and I rarely thought about him. Joe Fry was just a guy my brother hung out with, someone who skipped a lot of classes, number 55 on the football field—soon not even that, since the last game was next week. He said, "This isn't like the train tracks, is it?"

I felt my face turn red. Another thing ages ago. What had I been thinking back then? "Just bored with school."

He grunted, as if my comment was too obvious for words. Quite the sparkling conversation. If only he wanted to know how to choose the freshest blueberries—I could tell him to look for plump berries with that whitish coating Dotty King called "bloom." Or if the icing on his cinnamon rolls was cracking, "then add a bit of light corn syrup," Dotty had said. Those were things I could talk about, things I knew. I said, "Too bad about the Red Sox."

"I lost twenty bucks," he said. "But what a series. Next year."

"Next year." Not that I really thought so, that curse seemed too real. Though I guessed the answer, I asked, "How come you didn't go to Boston?"

He shrugged, as if Boston was nothing, nowhere. So I was right: Will hadn't told him he was going either. Will had decided in secret, all by himself, without telling anyone. I should have been happier finding out that Will didn't like Joe Fry more than me, but it was like seeing that flattened squirrel on the road, mad at myself for feeling sad.

Joe shoved his hands in his jacket pockets. "So you're sitting out here doing nothing?"

I wished I had turned off the radio. It was low, but I could make out Dotty King's cheerful voice saying you want the hot pudding to coat your spoon.

"I've got some pot," he said.

"No thanks." Everyone knew I didn't smoke pot.

"Sure? Well, let me know." Joe pushed his hands down harder into his pockets. I noticed myself staring at his lips, thinking about that time when I kissed him, so I looked out the window. It was supposed to snow today. The air outside had that feel, on the verge of something. His lips had been soft, warm; they'd probably feel perfect in a cold car on an about-to-snow day.

"What are you thinking about?" he asked.

I certainly couldn't say, *Your lips.* So I said, "Everyone in America sitting around their dining room tables on Thanksgiving eating pumpkin pie." Everyone except my family, and Paula's family maybe, Linda's family. I added, "Like it's no big deal, like it's normal."

"What's normal?"

"You know, normal," I said. "What everyone does."

"It's just a word," he said. "What does it really mean?"

"It means . . . normal." I was looking at his lips again, so I jerked my head around, fiddled with the blinker. "Regular. Usual. What's supposed to be."

He said, "Sure you're okay?"

"I'm fine," I said, but I started to cry, not little drippy tears, but loud sobs, the noisy, messy kind you'd give anything not to be crying in front of the boy you did it with that one time in the summer. I leaned my forehead against the steering wheel. I felt so stupid, which made me cry harder. I tightened my grip around the steering wheel until my nails dug into my palms.

He pushed aside my hair and set his fingertips on the back of my neck, a gentle tickle, like the way rain on the roof sounds when you're half asleep. Yes, Joe Fry was a good—no, incredible—kisser and yes, he had a tiny idea of why I really was in the car, but also he got Paula Elam pregnant, making her leave. I shook my head, knocked his hand away, said, "I'm fine. Just a bad day in biology. That Mrs. Lane expects us—"

"What's fine?" He put his hands back in his pockets, stared straight ahead.

"Fine is fine!" I shouted. "It's how I feel! Stop asking stupid questions. Just leave me alone." That wasn't what I meant to say, though I wasn't sure what I did mean to say. He slid out of the car, slammed the door. I watched him stalk through the parking lot to his Mustang, then drive off alone.

The bell rang—time for biology class. I turned up the radio. Dotty King said, "Puddings must be stirred constantly while they're cooking. Never let them boil. Remember those two things for perfect pudding every time. That's all you need to know."

Of course. Dotty King would make perfect pumpkin pie; she could tell me how to make piecrust without all that mumbo-jumbo about art and forks versus fingers. She'd just say right out, "Use your fingers." Or, "Use a fork." I imagined her gleaming-white kitchen, her recipes alphabetically organized in a row of matching file cabinets lining a wall. Pumpkin pie would be a matter of looking under "P." I grabbed my biology notebook and a pen, started scribbling a letter on a dry, clean piece of paper:

Dear Mrs. King: I love your show! My mother [I debated briefly between "died" and "killed herself"]—*killed herself, so I have to make Thanksgiving dinner, but I can't find her recipes. I tried making pumpkin pie on Saturday but got confused. All I want is to know how to make piecrust. I know ingredients are supposed to be cold and you're not supposed to wash sifters. But I still can't make piecrust. What's cutting in shortening? What's a pastry blender? What's—*

I ripped the paper out of the spiral notebook, crumpled it, and tossed it into the backseat. The letters she read on the air asked one question ("How do you keep graham crackers from going stale?"), not a million.

And if they mentioned dead people, they were normal dead people like grandmothers who had died of old age.

It was practically Thanksgiving, and the only thing that mattered was Mama's pumpkin pie.

I turned the car key, reached for my seat belt. I had just enough time to get to Iowa City and catch Dotty King at the radio station before her show ended. Joe Fry had slammed the door hard and angry when he got out of the car. Those questions—*What's fine? What's normal?* One thing normal was sitting at a table with your family on Thanksgiving, eating pumpkin pie with whipped cream, and everyone laughing at something that wasn't all that funny but that seemed funny right then. That was normal; that was fine.

PLENTY OF people in Shelby thought Iowa City was nothing but a town of radical-lazy-commie-longhaired-hippie university students. But some people appreciated Iowa City. Mama liked the downtown bustle of shops and restaurants and how you could walk along the streets and no one would say hi because no one knew you; and how the guy scooping ice cream at Baskin-Robbins was getting a Ph.D. in something exotic like anthropology. Mama had always talked about being a student at the university, saying things like, "You start out a student, and when you're done you're something else: philosopher, historian, chemist." Course catalogs sometimes came for her in the mail, but that was as close as she ever got. I liked Iowa City, too, especially football season, with the black-and-gold banners on all the store windows and the big yellow mums with the letter "I" in the center that the pretty sorority girls pinned to their wool jackets.

Mama would take me up there to kill a Saturday afternoon a couple of times a year. We always went to lunch first, then a movie. Lunch was at the Kresge's dime-store counter. We sat side by side on sparkly red vinyl stools that spun all the way around, and Mama ordered for us: "Two grilled cheeses, two orders of French fries, one coffee, one hot chocolate." The waitress behind the counter wore a hairnet and a little cap on the back of her head; her uniform was turquoise with a white apron, and she looked like she was about a hundred years old. She always said, "Coming right up, dearie." The grilled-cheese sandwiches came on a paper doily in a red plastic basket and were cut on the diagonal, with an edge of cheese oozing from each half. One sandwich was always a little burned, and Mama took that one. The French fries were crinkle cut, in a separate basket. The drinks were served in cones that slid into a tan plastic cup holder with a round handle barely big enough for Mama's finger to fit through. A star of whipped cream floated on my hot chocolate, and the waitress gave me a short brown-and-white-striped plastic stick that looked like a straw but wasn't, so I could stir the cream until it melted. I pretended my hot chocolate was coffee, as Mama made up stories about the waitress's life, about the man three stools away who'd ordered a fried bologna sandwich and Seven-Up, about the two ponytailed students smoking and leaning close in the corner booth. Mama said we couldn't make up stories at home because we already knew everything about everybody. Now and then I wondered what the hamburgers tasted like or the fried bologna sandwich, but I never said so to Mama.

After lunch she'd take me to a movie. The Englert was glitzy, with pink lights surrounding the yellow marquee and velvet curtains across the movie screen, but we preferred the smaller, boxier Iowa Theater. Sometimes the movies at the Iowa were French with subtitles, and I pretended reading the dialogue didn't bug me because those were Mama's favorites. We sat in the front row, sharing a box of Milk Duds, and watched all the credits afterward—"Those people are important too," Mama said, so we'd see who the "best boy" was and the "gaffer."

The drive home always felt too quick. Mama barely talked, and the car filled up with so much cigarette smoke it was like being trapped in the middle of a dark, sullen cloud.

Now, I was at the traffic light where if you turned left you headed downtown—toward Kresge's and the Iowa Theater—and part of me wanted one of those grilled-cheese sandwiches, wanted to spin around on a red vinyl stool like I did when I was with Mama. But Dotty King's show would be over soon, so I went straight instead, stopping to ask directions at the Skelly by Pearson's drugstore; the man pumping gas told me Dotty King's radio station was just outside of town, beyond City

Park, that I'd see the tower once I got down the hill on Dubuque Street. He didn't ask why I was going there—not like in Shelby, where people would want to know why you were going to a certain place.

I was calm when I pulled up to the small brick building, but as soon as I put the car in park, my heart jumped when I thought of talking to Dotty King in person. So I stared at the station, which wasn't a whole lot bigger than a house, shaped exactly like a square. One lone window near the double doors. If it weren't for the red-and-white tower jabbing the sky, I would have thought the gas station man had lied.

I kept the car running as Dotty King explained that soaking raisins for ten minutes in warm water or fruit juice would plump them up for the "best oatmeal-raisin cookies ever." I practiced what I was going to say, getting through, "Hi, I'm Alice," before staring at the cars in the parking lot, trying to pick out hers. It couldn't be the blue Ford with the dented fender because Dotty would rather die than drive around with a dented fender. The white Buick next to me seemed likely, not a speck of clutter in the backseat and the maps in the door pocket were folded in precise creases.

On the radio, Dotty King started to sign off: "We're about out of time, but I must thank my loyal listeners for sending those recipes for green-tomato cake. If you remember back, Mrs. Elmer Metzger of Swisher told us every year her granny baked a green-tomato chocolate cake for her September birthday, using up those last tomatoes off the vine, and Mrs. Metzger wants to carry on the tradition for her first grand-daughter, born September fifth. God bless you! Those recipes are com-ing—how I love a happy ending! Let's wind up another episode of *Dotty King's Neighborly Visit*. This is yours truly, Dotty King, coming at you live on KXIC-800, thanking you for listening, thanking you for being you. Bye-bye!"

I turned off the radio, the car. Instead of hopping out, I watched Interstate 80 beyond the station, trucks and cars whizzing by, heading east and west. It was the same road Will had followed to Boston. The gray sky pressed low to the ground—snow for sure. I should get out of the car and go inside, ask for Dotty King, get the recipe for piecrust, hurry home. Will was going to be furious that I had taken the car. I stared at my face in the rearview mirror, checking that nothing was stuck between my teeth. Putting on lipstick would fill time, but I didn't have any. Finally, I got out of the car, gently pushed the door shut. My footsteps were loud on the pavement as I walked across the parking lot to the doors lettered with KXIC.

"There's more to pie—to cooking—than a recipe," Mama said. "It's not just half a cup of this and a teaspoon of that."

"Maybe it's art to you, but for normal people, it's just making supper." My hand was on the knob when a short woman barreled through the door, practically knocking me down.

"Close call!" she exclaimed, like it was my fault for standing where I was. She adjusted the cat's-eye glasses that were askew on her nose. Even after that, her face somehow looked crooked. Her plaid coat had enormous gold buttons that were shiny enough to show me my rounded, upside-down reflection. She balanced a thick blue binder on one hip, shifted it to the other and back again.

"I'm looking for Dotty King," I said, hoping this wasn't her, certain it was.

"You're not from the IRS, are you?" But then she laughed, said, "In the flesh," giving a smile so big and toothy I thought of the wolf in "Little Red Riding Hood." She should've been taller. Or younger. Or not wearing a coat with such big buttons. She should've been someone who hugged you. "Don't be shy," she said, still smiling. "I don't bite."

"In the spring I wrote you a letter asking about orange juice," I started.

"I remember!" she said, and nodded so hard her glasses went crooked again. "Thanks for writing. Orange juice is an important topic."

Remembering my letter was a good beginning. "Now I have another question."

Dotty King looked at the sky, lifted one arm. "I thank God for loyal listeners like you, sweetie; you listen with your grandma? That's the darlingest thing! Want a picture? We've got plenty right inside at the front desk, signed and everything. They're free! Bet I got one right here," and she reached into her binder and pulled out a large black-and-white photo that she handed to me. "Brr, where's that sun today? I know it's going to snow. My bum knee beats the weatherman every time! Boy, do his feathers ruffle when I tell him that!"

I looked at the photo, at her. She looked about a million years younger in the photo.

"Already signed, isn't it?"

I held it out so she could see where she had written, "To one of the best listeners in the world! Hugs—Dotty King."

"Well, then," she said, talking through that big smile. I imagined her smiling the whole three hours of her show. "Bye-bye, sweetie," she said, heading toward the parked cars, high heels tapping. "Tell your grandma thanks for listening. You know my listeners are the best in the world!"

"Wait!" I called, jogging after her. "I don't have a grandmother. And I skipped school to drive here from Shelby."

Dotty King jerked up one arm so her coat sleeve slid back a bit, and she looked at a tiny silver watch. "Not enough hours in the day, that's the God's honest truth. Quick, tell me why you drove up here. Want me to speak at your school assembly? My wonderful assistant schedules those things, Carla—sweet gal, organized from A to Z. She'll help you out."

"I have to know how to make piecrust," I said.

"You skipped school for piecrust?" She was still smiling, but her eyebrows jumped, practically touching her hair. I waited for her to ask why so I could tell her about Mama and the recipes, but she said, "Ever hear of letters? Still, here you are and the rest is spilt milk. Go on inside and Carla will look up a recipe from the files."

She turned, about to walk to the cars, but I grabbed her sleeve. The fabric was thick and nubby. "Listen to me," I said, realizing there was no way she remembered my orange juice letter. "I have to make pumpkin pie for Thanksgiving."

She shook her sleeve loose, said (still smiling), "Carla will get you a packet of recipes lickety-split." She put her hand on mine. Her fingers were cold—because we were standing outside and it was November, about to snow any minute, and there was a wind blowing that I hadn't noticed until now, and cars and trucks whisked by on the highway beyond us. But I'd been sure Dotty King would have the kind of hands that push your hair off your hot forehead when you're sick, when you're sipping warm ginger ale, and the beige blanket with the really soft stuff sewn on the edges is pulled up to your chin and you're lying on the couch pretending to read an Agatha Christie mystery, but really you're just lying there, book upside down on your stomach, eyes half closed, wondering when the chicken soup in the kitchen will be done, listening to the knife turn carrots into small pieces, half asleep, imagining yourself snuggled in a wave of Mama's chicken soup smell. Right then is when someone comes in and whispers something comforting you don't quite hear, then smooths hair off your forehead. Dotty King's icy hand wasn't like that at all.

She kept talking, sounding more like her radio show as she got going: "Sweetie, get those recipes from Carla, and what you need to do is wash your hands in cold water before you start. Cold hands, cold heart, they say—but I say, cold hands, flaky pastry! Keep a light touch—toss it with a fork, or, if your fingers are cold, then go ahead and use them. Be sure—"

"I don't want a bunch of hints about cold hands. I want to know exactly how to make piecrust. Just one-two-three." Wind scraped my face, making my eyes water.

"Sweetie, read as many recipes as you want, but pies are marvelous, tricky things. The only way to make one is to make one—then another. And another." She slid back her coat sleeve again, looked at her watch. "That dentist absolutely won't wait another minute," and she walked to the blue Ford with the dented fender, calling back, "Just bake your pie, sweetie; dive in and get your hands dirty. That's the secret to good cooking, not being afraid to get your hands dirty. Actually, that's the secret to a whole lot of things if you think about it." She plopped the binder on the hood of her car, reached into her coat pocket for a pen, and pulled a piece of paper from the binder, looked at it, flipped it over, and started writing. "Just—dive—in—get—your—hands—dirty," she said as she wrote. "I'm putting that on the show—if I don't lose this scrap of paper, ha! My best ideas are from my wonderful listeners. Tell your grandma she'll hear about our heart-to-heart. 'A young friend,' I'll call you—yes, that's lovely—'a young friend visiting from Shelby.' We won't mention skipping school. What the hay—tell me your name." She kept writing without looking up.

"Alice," I said. *Ka-chunk, ka-chunk*—my heartbeat sounded too loud, but there were things I had to say: "I don't have a grandmother; I've never had a grandmother, not even for one day of my life. And if you really remembered my orange-juice letter instead of faking that you did, you would remember my mother is dead—she killed herself." Had I really said all that? But I wanted her to hear me, to say she'd come over on Thanksgiving to make turkey and pumpkin pie and that everything would be right, exactly the way I remembered.

She finally stopped smiling as she stared off at an invisible point in the distance, somewhere far beyond the cars and trucks on the highway. Now she looked even less like her photo. Maybe she was going to cry. But she started talking, slowly at first, then faster, and all smiley again: "We should do a show about piecrust, what with Thanksgiving on its way. Carla can pull the files on pumpkins and—" She held that silent smile so long I almost thought her face had frozen. Then she said, "Sweetie, both our mothers died too young—gone when we needed them, still gone—and there's no way around that," and I wanted to hug her or touch her arm or tell her about Mama, but then she went back to her radio voice: "Mincemeat—nothing like a truly great mincemeat! And sweet-potato pie! Anyway, you've been a wonderful inspiration, Allison. You're a doll! Bye-bye!" she said, and slammed shut her binder, went around to the driver's side, got in. She revved her car for a minute, then backed up too quickly, twirling the wheel with one hand, the other giving me one of those movie waves, where your hand stays still and the fingers flap up and down.

I watched her car until I couldn't see it anymore. The wind picked up, cutting through my coat, and I shivered as I stood alone in the empty silence of the parking lot. I let go of the photo in my hand; it slid across the asphalt, lodging against the back tire of the white Buick.

I had driven all this way and still didn't know how to make piecrust. Or know anything else except that Dotty King wasn't any better off than I was just because she knew things like how to wrap pipe cleaners around metal hangers so your clothes won't slip off. It seemed a good time for Mama to say something, but she didn't. She knew a lot of things too: all those makeup tips, driving instructions, how to make pie. I remembered her lying all alone in that dark room, the tip of her cigarette the only bit of light, like a tiny pinprick in the blackness. Maybe no one knew anything when you got down to it.

I shivered again. The last thing I wanted to do now, or ever, was go to Kresge's and find out that our grilled-cheese sandwiches were rubbery or that the stools screeched when you spun them. I tilted my head back and looked up into the gray sky, thought about all that unfallen snow up there, waiting to drop down.

DRIVING HOME, I watched the tiny snowflakes swirl in the beam of my headlights and smack up against the windshield, getting swept away by the wipers. The Eagles played on the radio; before leaving the parking lot, I changed the automatic preset button from Dotty King's station to the station that played "all the hits, all the time."

I was humming, lulled by the blowing snow, trying not to think about Dotty King and those crazy coat buttons, when Mama broke in: "I ripped up the recipes in that folder."

"What!" The car swerved, and tiny stones from the shoulder of the road pinged. I yanked the car back onto the road. I'd know how to make the sweet potatoes with the fancy maple syrup, never re-create her pumpkin pie. Thanksgiving was ruined forever, gone. What had Will said, like looking into a mirror and seeing nothing? That was how I felt. I didn't even want to hear her explanation.

"Right after last Thanksgiving," she said.

So she had known then that—I stared at my knuckles, whitening from how tightly I was gripping the steering wheel. I pressed my foot hard on the accelerator, lifted it when the car jerked to eighty.

Her voice was flat: "I ripped up one and kept going. Tiny, tiny pieces. I couldn't stop until all the recipes were gone. But here it is, Thanksgiving again, recipes or not."

The car was practically steering itself. I was like one of the snowflakes outside—falling, falling, falling. Didn't Mama like Thanksgiving? Didn't we have a great Thanksgiving last year? Will dropped the sweet potatoes. We ate three pieces of pie. Everything had seemed perfect. I counted the snowflakes that landed on the windshield.

Mama whispered, "You have no idea."

I kept counting in my head, hypnotic, soothing, reaching the low two hundreds. I didn't want to think of one single thing except how many snowflakes hit the windshield.

Mama spoke again: "It's not your fault. This has nothing to do with you." There was a pause, then Mama sighed, which meant there was more. Did other people, did everyone have this many secrets? It struck me that maybe they did, and I lost track of my counting, waited for Mama to speak. After another moment, she began: "Mr. Stryker drove to Iowa City for Thanksgiving dinner with friends. I begged to go along though it was ridiculous to think I might. I was good at excuses about why I was home late, why I'd stayed after school, but no lie would satisfy my mother about something as big as Thanksgiving. Our meal was dull and drab—like anything I had to do that didn't involve Mr. Stryker—but finally it was almost over. Mr. Stryker had called pumpkin pie 'the most sacred part of Thanksgiving.' That's how he was, turning pie into something magic. But with that first bite, my stomach twisted, like wringing out a wet rag, and the inside of my throat squeezed shut; after the moment passed, I set down my fork, asked to be excused. My mother—who had not one ounce of patience for sickness—told me to finish my pie, that it was shameful to waste food, especially on a day of thankfulness. She cleared away the dishes and said I had to stay until I finished. Like I was four years old. I was furious, so I sat there, her letting me—we were both stubborn beyond belief—until nine-thirty that night, when the principal called, going alphabetically down the list of students to tell them Mr. Stryker had died in a car accident earlier that afternoon."

Right then I could've vomited up every pumpkin pie I had ever eaten.

Mama sounded almost angry, the words tumbling out fast: "He had a birthmark shaped like Spain above his right ankle. I knew his shirt size, shoe size, height, weight. He had an imaginary friend as a boy, a cowboy named Tex, and he got a collie for his tenth birthday that he named

Snickers, after the candy bar; Snickers still lived with his mom and dad in Muscatine. 'Great dog,' he told me. 'She'd love you.' For God's sake, all that was gone, but I had to act like everyone else—sad, yes, but I couldn't cry the most. Couldn't protest the gossip about some heartbroken girl-friend in Iowa City. I was used to covering up and lying, and anyway, things felt blurry. I wasn't sure myself what was real, what wasn't: Emily, yes; car crash, yes; but the ocean? Our destiny? Tex? None of it made sense. How a man like that could die."

No one who is loved should die. That was simple. I watched the snowflakes zooming in at me. Was Mama right to keep Mr. Stryker a secret? I thought of Mrs. Johnson: that phone call I had overheard, Mr. Johnson saying the bad word, the kiss I'd seen. What kept those things from disappearing like the snowflakes on the windshield was the fact that Mrs. Johnson was living in the Seville Apartments in Iowa City right now. Her secrets weren't secret anymore, so that years from now I could say, *Remember when Linda's mom ran off with that teacher?* and Becky, still my friend, would know; she'd nod and laugh and agree: *That was wild.* Wasn't that how to hold on to things?

Mama sighed again. "I was always so lonely."

That silence, her cigarette slowly moving through blackness—the only way to know she was there sometimes. Was your mother supposed to tell you she was lonely? I was relieved when she went on talking about Mr. Stryker:

"It was a week after his memorial service. I got to working my way through *Joy of Cooking*, starting with pumpkin pie, page 505. That's when I remembered exactly what was real: the smell of pumpkin pie. Like cold water in my face. Finally my mother had enough of pies and me taking over her kitchen, cooking more food than we could possibly eat, and weeks and weeks where I didn't say a word. Not that there was much talking in that house anyway. But, 'I give up,' she said, and Aunt Aggy promised all I needed was a change of scenery, a simple trip to Chicago. They had no idea. Finally I could disappear, escape for real."

I shook my head hard, as if that could snap the jagged pieces of Mama's story into a single, neat, orderly line. Impossible. Mama was so sure about everything—the dog, the birthmark, the Juicyfruit gum. But could I believe any of the rest of it? Did Mr. Stryker really plan to run away with Mama? Was his car crash an accident or not? So I said something that should have been easy: "I always thought you liked to cook."

"I do," she said.

"But cooking makes you remember such an awful thing."

"Yes." Her voice was calm. "The way you still want pumpkin pie, even now."

This conversation felt like sand slipping too fast down an hourglass.

Mama said, "What's more scary than remembering is forgetting."

Will in Boston forgetting Mama's face. I hadn't wanted to hear such a thing was possible. "We could've had apple pie on Thanksgiving. Apple's good." But I was lying: Apple didn't compare to pumpkin.

Mama said, "Everyone has the right to eat pumpkin pie on Thanksgiving. Check the Constitution." She laughed, and I thought of the sudden flash of her brilliant, wide, crooked smile, her white teeth framed by red lipstick.

I smiled myself as tears edged down my cheeks. Eating pumpkin pie would always make me think of our last Thanksgiving together. And of Mama sitting at the table, not knowing the phone was about to ring. And of Dotty King's photo that barely looked like her. And this crazy year, desperately driving an hour to learn how to make piecrust. Pretty soon there'd be something else pumpkin pie would remind me of, and something else, until Thanksgiving—and pumpkin pie—and cooking—and the broken clock on the kitchen wall—and the squeak of the sifter—and how a lone cigarette looks piercing the dark—would be a jumble of everything, good and bad, the way snow piles up on the ground so you can't tell one flake from another.

AUNT AGGY announced that this year Thanksgiving was going to be a team effort. "Like it or not, we're going to have fun," she said, grimacing, slapping her fist into her palm a couple of times. We had no idea what to do in the kitchen, how to make a whole Thanksgiving meal. But not doing anything was more frightening.

Nothing was a hundred percent wrong, but nothing was right: Will carved the (overdone) turkey and knocked one of the drumsticks on the floor. The Jell-O mold from a recipe on the box wouldn't unmold so we had to scoop it out in glops with a spoon. My *Joy of Cooking* gravy had lumps that I fished out before anyone noticed. We ran out of butter, and Mr. Cooper choked on a burned Pillsbury pop-up crescent roll. Aunt Aggy spilled half a pot of coffee when she was reaching for the salt. No one remembered that the tablecloth needed to be ironed, so it was a mass of wrinkles. The wishbone accidentally went down the garbage disposal. I burned the top of my hand while taking the turkey out. The potato water boiled over twice. I yelled at Will because filling the baster with water and squirting me once wasn't funny and doing it three times really, really wasn't funny.

Aunt Aggy insisted on setting a place at the table for Mama, as if Mama were here. She spooned up food, dabbed a bit of everything on a plate, set the plate at Mama's seat, unfolded the napkin and laid it across the empty chair. Will and I looked at the napkin, looked at each other, said nothing. Thanksgiving had come—without Mr. Stryker, without the recipes, without Mama. And like it or not, it was going to come again next year and the year after. It was hard to sit at the table, facing food that ranged from tasteless (at best) to just plain bad, feeling hypnotized by Mama's plate: gravy forming a skin, potatoes getting crusty, turkey edges shriveling, Jell-O melting into a red liquid pool. Every time Aunt Aggy glanced over at that plate, she murmured, "So sad," and Mr. Cooper nodded gravely. This was the woman who wanted the whole world to rip off its Band-Aids? The woman who strolled around town in an artist's beret, oblivious to snickers and stares? Who painted a canvas pure green and told me with a straight face it was a picture of the soul of a blade of grass?

Aunt Aggy pushed food around on her plate, not eating much; Mr. Cooper reached for the mashed potatoes, spooned some onto his plate, then hers, as if he knew exactly what she wanted. Which he did: She ate a big forkful of potatoes, then another. (Will had mashed them and there were just enough lumps so you knew they hadn't come out of a box.) I suddenly hoped Aunt Aggy and Mr. Cooper would get married someday. I hadn't thought about Aunt Aggy being lonely, but of course she was and maybe she always had been. I felt like Dotty King for a moment, staring off at the invisible point, finally seeing something that had been right in front of me. I needed to remember that about Aunt Aggy, no matter how weird she seemed. So when we cleared the dishes, I was the one who carried Mama's plate into the kitchen and carefully scraped the mess of congealed food into the garbage disposal when no one was watching, then slipped Mama's plate in with the stack of others waiting to be washed.

I had started that morning already worn out, so by the time we finished the dishes, I could have fallen asleep standing at the sink, wearing rubber gloves. But Will said, "Where's the pumpkin pie?"

Aunt Aggy was ripping the last bits off the turkey carcass, dropping them into a Tupperware container. She said, "Alice is too tired to whip up cream for her pie right now."

I knew what she meant. We had made it through the meal; why press our luck?

Will picked at his teeth with his pinkie nail. "It's not Thanksgiving unless there's pumpkin pie."

Oh, brother. Like a piece of pumpkin pie could turn this shambles into a real Thanksgiving. That was asking a lot of the poor pie I'd managed to pull together. It was hidden, covered by a dish towel so no one could see how horrible it was. A deep crack—more like a crevice—divided the pie in half. A film of brownish, sticky, watery gunk had accumulated on the top overnight. The middle of the filling looked runny but there was an overdone circle of hard darkness rimming it. Then the piecrust! That was too thin, so there had been holes in the bottom and sides that I'd tried to patch with extra dough—filling had leaked through, creating black, burned spots you could see through the Pyrex pan. The edge was overdone and crumbly, and I didn't have enough dough to make a pretty rim the way Mama had, so I'd just poked fork prints into it. In fact, it had been tricky getting the crust centered evenly in the pan, so about a quarter of the pie barely had any crust rimming it. Overall, it was the kind of pie that was only good for one clown to smash into another's face.

"No, no," Mama whispered. "It's beautiful. You'll see." Obviously she had missed that Grand Canyon crack.

Will went to the cupboard and pulled out a stack of plates, opened the silverware drawer and got a knife and forks. He slapped the plates around the places at the table, four of them. No plate "for Mama" this time. Aunt Aggy clutched Mr. Cooper's arm; he patted her shoulder. Then Will went around the table again, setting out forks. "Where's the pie, Alice?" he said. "I smelled it baking yesterday."

"I threw it away."

"Liar." He stared at the counter until he spotted the towel-covered pie behind the toaster and carried it to the table. "I never liked whipped cream," he said.

Actually, he loved whipped cream. We all absolutely loved whipped cream. No matter how much Mama had whipped, we ran out.

Aunt Aggy nodded. "What's whipped cream anyways?"

"Cream," Mr. Cooper said, shrugging. "Whipped." He led her to the table, pulled the chair out for her, then sat down himself.

It was going to be a horrible moment when that towel came off. Overdone turkey was one thing. The food page of the newspaper printed funny articles about how turkey was always overcooked and jokes about how dry it was. And bad side dishes didn't matter because there were so many of them—so you ate more potatoes, extra stuffing, another spoonful of beans. But pie. That was it. That was Thanksgiving.

"Serve it up, Baby Sister," Will said.

"Are you really hungry?" I asked. Didn't anyone understand I'd never again have that folder of Thanksgiving recipes, never?

Mama said, "You made a pie without that folder. Your own pie by yourself."

Will whisked off the dish towel like he was a magician. Everyone went, "Ohh," all at once and said things like, "It looks delicious," and, "Yum," and, "Ahh."

Okay, so it didn't look like one of Mama's perfect pies. But we ate the whole thing then and there, right out of the pan, no plates, ate every bit of filling, scraping up every crumb of crust, and Will made us laugh for the first time all day, not fake getting-along laughter but real laughs, when he licked the pie pan and put it back in the cupboard, said, "Beats washing dishes." And when I was clearing off the unused plates, Mr. Cooper seemed to sum up everything, that first Thanksgiving without Mama—the first of all the rest of them, the beginning of a long forever—when he said, "I sure can't believe we ate a whole darn pie like that. I'll never forget it. What a day."

TREE

WILL had stopped talking about Boston—no more stories about rotaries and lobsters and Carlton Fisk. At first I was relieved because each time I heard, "When I was in Boston," I felt that stab of *I left you; I could leave again.* But hearing nothing was actually worse, all of us pretending everything was back to normal, though Will wasn't doing any of the work he'd missed in school, he hadn't fixed the leaky faucet or put up the storm windows, and even after Coach Thorbeck got the academic probation lifted, Will didn't go out for basketball, though he'd been a starter since he was a sophomore. And he couldn't hide the icy chill in his eyes, telling me that though his body and car and winter coat were here in Shelby, his mind remained somewhere distant, a place beyond me.

Finally, one afternoon I blurted out, "You never talk about anything anymore." We were in the kitchen; I was spreading mustard on my bologna sandwich, and he was swigging chocolate milk out of the carton in front of the open fridge.

He stopped drinking, read the side panel of the milk carton for a moment, then spoke abruptly: "Is it really so awful not to have a father?"

That wasn't the kind of question I was expecting. I kept sliding the same smear of mustard along the bologna, back and forth. Could he tell

I'd been thinking about Boston and the night Carlton Fisk hit the home run, that I wondered if our father could do something magic like that? That though I never mentioned him, I thought about who he was, why he hadn't come looking for us, how we didn't know one actual fact about him, almost as if he wasn't real. The color of his hair—his name—his job: I just longed to know one thing that mattered, one thing that could make him my father instead of the man on the train.

Will put the milk back on the top shelf, closed the fridge and leaned against the door, slouching down so we were almost eye to eye. He didn't blink. "What's the matter, Baby Sister?" he said. "Think you're the only one around here with questions?"

I set the dirty knife in a greasy frying pan left to soak in the sink, realizing too late that if I wanted to cut my sandwich now, I'd have to get another knife dirty. Would anything ever feel normal again? I stared out the window above the sink, at an abandoned bird nest balanced high in the leafless branches of the apple tree. All summer we'd never seen that nest up there. I couldn't lie, not about this. "Yes, I do think it's awful. It's lonely and it's awful."

"I knew you'd say that." He pulled open the refrigerator, stared inside. The yellowish light on his face made him look tired. He picked up a piece of cheese half wrapped in crinkled foil, turned it over in his hand.

"Don't you think so?" I asked.

He returned the cheese, kept staring inside the refrigerator, like something was supposed to be there but wasn't. "Of course," he said, casual now. "But maybe it's not the worst thing that could happen to someone."

I thought of Mama, so maybe not the absolute worst, but definitely 9.9 on a scale of 1 to 10. How could he not agree? I picked one example, though there were many: "Don't you wish there'd been someone to go with you on Cub Scout camp outs?"

"Can you imagine Mama in a sleeping bag?" A moment later he laughed, as if he were actually thinking of something else, not Mama, not our father, but something I would never understand. One shoulder shrugged. "So I went camping alone."

"Everyone else has a father," I said. And mother.

Will closed the refrigerator, turned to look at me, his eyes narrowed, a scowl twisting his face. "We have a father. Just not here."

I stared out the window again. How did that bird nest stay up there when it was nothing but twigs and grass? One gust of wind might fling it to the ground.

Then Will said, "I think I remember him one time carrying me to a window and he stood holding me in the sunlight."

I waited for Will to go on, to tell me absolutely everything. Finally I looked at him, prompted, "And?"

He shook his head. "That's all."

Everything was lonely and awful. I shouted, "You were a little baby! You can't remember that!" He couldn't.

Will raked his fingers through his hair, shook his head again, harder. "He's just a man, Alice. Probably nothing would have been very different." I could tell he was trying to convince himself.

He had actually held Will, but I had nothing. I looked at the nest again, drew in a deep breath and tried to sound neutral, not angry or hurt: "I never thought you'd leave me."

"I'm not going anywhere. I'm right here."

Not really, I almost said. But he wouldn't understand what I meant. So I nodded, bit into my sandwich as I watched him leave the kitchen, walking fast, not looking behind.

So, Will was on my mind, and Aunt Aggy and her ridiculous paintings. She had convinced Mr. Breer to display them at the White Front Café, writing tags to accompany the paintings: "Loaned by the artist, price negotiable, commissions welcomed," with her name and phone number so everyone knew it was her.

But my real worry was getting through Christmas when we were still wrung out from Thanksgiving. Everything about Christmas was horrible: Grocery-store Muzak's endless, flutey versions of "Little Drummer Boy." Radio deejays who couldn't get enough of "Jingle Bells" sung by barking dogs. Linda (who was convinced that her parents would get back together for Christmas) wearing tinkly jingle bell earrings every day. Christmas was noisy and jolly, cute and bright. There wasn't a day I didn't want to put my hands over my ears and scream.

Mama had said Christmas transformed everything—a pine tree into a Christmas tree, paper-wrapped boxes into presents, an old man into Santa Claus, a baby into a savior. "Like magic," she had told us.

Of all the things Mama had done that meant "Christmas," my favorite was how Will and I hung a dozen special, snow-white candy canes on the just-decorated tree. Then, on Christmas morning, each candy cane was striped. "Magic," Mama whispered to us, and she meant the candy canes, yes, but also the way simple, everyday things were transformed on Christmas morning—the smell of coffee floating like a cloud; how stray pine needles pricked our cold, bare feet as we ran into the jumbled-up living room; even Aunt Aggy's ratty blue terry-cloth robe with the worn spots in the elbows—it all was magic, just like the candy canes. Eventually I was old enough to realize that Mama had simply replaced the white candy canes with Hy-Vee striped ones, but I nodded anyway, every year, when she whispered, "Magic."

Now, Will, Aunt Aggy, and I couldn't even talk about Christmas; our conversations were vague, spiraling into mumbles—"Should we send cards?"; "I don't know, should we?"; "I don't know"—ending with shoulder shrugging, sighing, staring at the ceiling. So when Aunt Aggy brought up the Christmas tree one night after supper, we started our shrugging-sighing-staring routine. But Aunt Aggy was determined: "It's Christmas, and that means a tree." She tugged at a loose thread on the sleeve of her blouse.

A moment later, I said, "I like how pine smell fills the house."

Aunt Aggy finally yanked the thread free. "Someone has to decorate it."

The cardboard box of ornaments was in the basement: goofball ornaments Will and I had made in school that Mama refused to throw away—potpie-pan angels, clothespin reindeers, twig stars, thread-spool snowmen; colored balls individually wrapped in Kleenex so they wouldn't knock together; twisted strands of blinking red lights. Mama was the one who remembered things like which potpie-pan angel was Will's and which was mine; she told the story of every single ornament as she pulled it from the box, the pipe-cleaner Santas she had made when she was eight, the four-foot-long gold-painted macaroni garland she and Aunt Aggy had strung together the year her father died, and so on.

Will tapped his fingers on the table. "Should I bring up the ornaments?"

"The needles are so messy," I said.

"Lots of vacuuming," Aunt Aggy said.

We sighed, almost in unison, and Aunt Aggy poured more milk in her coffee. Her spoon clinked against the side of the cup, disturbing the tense silence. Then Will said, "Tinsel all over the place."

But Mama had always said, "What's a tree without tinsel?" At Linda's house, they hung tinsel one strand at a time, but Mama threw handfuls everywhere, front and back, top branches and bottom. Not a spot on the tree was bare, not a branch didn't shimmer. "Look what a little tinsel can do," she'd say. "This is every tree's secret fantasy, to look like this."

"Tinsel clogs the vacuum cleaner," Aunt Aggy said. She sighed and uncrossed her arms; Will looked at the ceiling, crossed his.

I stared at some crumbs on the table. Even if we had a tree, there would be no white candy canes turning striped overnight. And that was what Christmas had always meant.

The next day Aunt Aggy came home with a tree tied to the roof of the car. "Someone had to do something," she said, sounding angry as she wiped her boots on the mat. The tree stayed on the car overnight. The next morning I kind of felt sorry for it and wrestled it off the car, not realizing how heavy and awkward it would be. Then I slowly dragged it into the house, knocking over chairs and piles of newspapers, scraping the walls, leaving a trail of needles. I pushed the armchair into the kitchen to make space in the corner where we always put the tree, next to the window that didn't lock right. The empty corner looked bare, and the idea of a Christmas tree was suddenly so stupid that I left the tree lying there on its side, branches poking up every which way like a big, dead, bloated porcupine in our living room.

Later, I stayed upstairs and listened as Aunt Aggy and Will struggled to get the tree into the stand: "Turn that bare part in back"; "Darn thing's crooked." When I went downstairs the next morning, there was the tree, crookedly propped against the wall, bare and unornamented. That's how it stayed because we had used up every last speck of Christmas spirit getting it in the house and standing. It was an ugly tree, with a big bald patch where some animal had chewed away branches; it didn't reach the ceiling like normal trees, and if you brushed against it, wads of dry needles sprinkled down. No one daydreamed in front of it, listening to Christmas records. In fact, half the time we forgot we even had a tree, banging into the chair that had been moved near the kitchen table, squawking, "Why's this chair here?" before remembering why, and we only brought up the tree to say things like, "Probably the ugliest tree at the lot," or, "Still hasn't tipped over." I thought Mama might rise to the tree's defense; she was a sucker for the sad, lonely-looking trees, always wanting to buy them all. But she didn't defend it, didn't agree it was ugly—didn't say one word about the tree, about Christmas, about candy canes.

The tree was perfect for this Christmas—which made us hate it even harder.

FINALLY, IT was Christmas Eve day, and Linda, Becky, and I were doing last-minute shopping at Duncan-Camp Hardware, the only store still open downtown. Actually, it was just me shopping, since they had already bought their thoughtfully selected, perfect presents ages ago. In one hand I held a pair of garden gloves specially designed to use when pruning roses; in the other was a lemony-smelling patio candle that supposedly repelled mosquitoes. "Which for Aunt Aggy?" I asked. I had dug both items out of the jumble on the bargain table in the back of the store.

After a moment, Becky said, "It's the thought that counts."

My thought was, the faster the better. I'd already decided on a Super-Chamois for Will to use when he washed the car. Then I had told Becky and Linda to pick out Charlie Brown ornaments—Linda chose Lucy leaning on Schroeder's piano, and Becky wanted Snoopy sleeping on his doghouse. I was embarrassed because they saw that the ornaments had been marked down 50 percent, but even Linda was too polite to mention it because she felt sorry for me. They both did. None of us even liked Charlie Brown. Becky said, "I'll hang this on my tree every year and think of you, Alice," and I felt worse for buying on-sale, babyish presents at the hardware store.

Becky answered my question with, "Gloves," at the same time Linda said, "Candle," then they laughed awkwardly.

I wasn't the only pathetic one. In with the groceries Will had bought last week were two boxes of Russell Stover candies wrapped in Hy-Vee's green-and-red-striped gift paper. He snatched them out of my hand, snapping, "What?," though I hadn't said anything. I had noticed the display near the front of the store, but buying prewrapped candy had seemed too sad even for this hopelessly sad Christmas. Right now, though, Russell Stover seemed a million times better than pruning gloves or a stinky candle.

Linda said, "Next year, you should do your shopping in Iowa City like I did. My mom took me to Things & Things, where the college girls go." (She had given me and Becky each two bottles of Mary Quant nail polish, emerald green and bright red, which, Linda said, the lady at the store told her had been featured in *Mademoiselle*.)

"What do Christmas presents mean anyways?" I said, checking the price tags.

Linda half-frowned. "Don't be such a Scrooge." As if her mother wasn't still living in the Seville Apartments. As if people weren't talking about how her father stopped by Whit's Bar practically every night now. What did she have to be jolly about? I wanted to heave that candle across the aisle, into the display of fake Christmas trees all decorated with the same twinkly white lights.

Becky pushed her glasses up her nose, something she did when she was nervous, and said, "Well, I'd say gloves last longer than a candle."

Linda nodded, said, "Yes, but a candle—"

"What do you know, Linda?" I spoke quickly, meanly. "You think your mother's coming back. Sure she is. Like Santa's a real, live, fat guy who slides down chimneys."

Linda gasped, a sort of choking sound, like something inside her was being strangled. Becky looked from me to Linda, Linda to me. They were waiting for me to explain, apologize the way you were supposed to when you said something cruel, even if it was true. But I said, "Christmas is stupid."

Linda bit down hard on her trembling lip. I still wasn't sorry; in fact, I hoped I had wrecked her Christmas the same way mine was wrecked. She didn't have a right to be so happy. Her voice was shaky: "My parents will so get back together. Christmas is a time of miracles."

"Oh, brother," I said. "Christmas is a time to buy a bunch of junk for people who don't like what you bought. Like green nail polish and pruning gloves." I couldn't stop: It was every angry feeling I'd had since April gushing out all at once. I tossed the gloves in my basket, on top of the chamois and the Charlie Brown ornaments and started walking fast to the front of the store, trying to get away. I wasn't someone who said mean things for the sake of being mean. Becky caught up and yanked my arm so hard I almost fell backward.

"What's with you?" she asked. "You're not acting right."

Her forehead was wrinkled with I'm-worried-about-you lines, which made me more angry, thinking of her mother at home frosting the cookies they had baked this morning, and her family singing carols around the piano tonight. At her house there was a big, tinselly, blinking tree everyone had helped decorate. Linda—standing behind Becky, playing with the fringe on her scarf—who should have been like me, instead was perky and joyful, certain her mother would drive down from Iowa City with a carload of presents and a couple of her famous fruitcakes. And she probably would—that was the thing about Linda and her life and everyone else's life except my own stupid, miserable life—things worked out for them. "Your mother's never coming back!" I shouted at Linda.

"At least I have a mother!" she shouted right back, then immediately said, "I'm sorry. I didn't mean it."

But of course she did, we both did. She kept tugging her scarf fringe, waiting for my apology. It was confusing: My heart was pumping too fast, as if I was still mad, and I wanted to cry, but also I felt very calm, almost peaceful, that feeling of watching a pond smooth itself after someone has thrown in a rock. What Linda said, what I said—the words kept swirling through my head, as if they needed to be spoken. In the silence, the bells on the hardware-store door jingled.

"Okay." Becky took a deep breath, let go of my arm and patted my shoulder. "Both of you, stop it. Alice, Linda and I are very sorry your mother passed away—"

"Killed herself!" It was like standing at the edge of a vast, endless canyon, the way I felt the echo of those words come back at me, almost like hearing my voice for the first time.

"Alice?" It was Joe Fry, heading up the wrench and screwdriver aisle.

My stomach heaved, as if I were going to throw up.

Linda's face was so pale her pink blush stood out like streaks of Magic Marker. But when she heard Joe's voice, she smirked at me before waving at him, flipping her hair to make her jingle bell earrings tinkle festively.

"Hey." Joe rocked back a bit on his boot heels, looked above our heads.

"Merry Christmas," Becky said, filling the awkward silence.

"Yeah, Merry Christmas." He stood next to me, close enough that the outside air clinging to his jeans jacket made me shiver. "What're you guys doing?"

Linda beamed her flirtiest smile. "Helping Alice Christmas shop."

My face turned hot as Joe glanced in my basket. What kind of loser went Christmas shopping at the hardware store? He picked up the chamois, said, "These give a great shine." He rubbed his thumb against the cloth, then dropped it back in my basket.

"We decided not to do much for Christmas this year," I explained. Saying "decided" made our inaction seem planned. "I mean in terms of gifts. No tree. Like that."

Linda's words bubbled into the conversation: "But Christmas is a beautiful holiday, the season of miracles." She sounded fake, like a TV commercial, and her earrings tinkled again. "It's a shame when someone can't enjoy the spirit of Christmas and won't even put up a tree."

"You have a tree." Becky spoke as if I was a sulky child needing encouragement.

"Not a regular Christmas tree," I said. "It's ugly."

Becky said, "Still means Christmas. And what's wrong with a chamois?"

"A chamois's cool," Joe said. "Beats underwear or socks."

"Socks are the worst!" Linda squealed. She playfully poked Joe in the ribs. Then, tinkle, tinkle, and she went off into a long, supposedly funny story about when she was nine, unwrapping box after box, each containing a single kneesock, until she matched up ten pairs. I could barely pretend to listen.

Mama didn't give presents like socks. Even when we wrote up Christmas lists of things like Barbie dolls or tea sets or Monopoly, we got the things she wanted: rock-tumblers, pastel crayons, candle-making kits. On Christmas morning, she'd be the one opening the rock tumbler box after it had been unwrapped, reading the directions out loud, looking for the best place to plug it in. I was more interested in adding my new state of Iowa charm to my bracelet, but Mama's voice was so excited, so insistent, that the rock tumbler became a little less weird. "We can make jewelry," Mama said. "Tie tacks. All we need are ordinary rocks. Look at these pictures." She unfolded the color brochure and stared at each panel as if she had found the secret to the world inside a nerdy rock tumbler from the Sears catalog. "Nice," Will or I said, already forgetting whose gift it was supposed to be—it was clearly Mama's.

Linda was starting another story, but I interrupted: "I'm paying for my stuff," and practically ran up front, toward the cash register.

Joe's footsteps clumped behind me, and my heart beat hard and fast for a moment. "Wait up," he called.

I stopped by the snow shovels. Another thing we ignored—shoveling snow. After the first storm, it just piled up; people's boots packed the snow on our sidewalk into a slippery, narrow pathway; you could feel the glares as people passed our house, the only house on the block without Christmas decorations, the only one with piled-up snow, the only one with a mother who had killed herself. Eventually, in a warm spell, the snow melted.

Joe looked at a point off in the distance. With anyone else I would've thought it was nervousness that made him fold and unfold his arms across his chest, but Joe Fry didn't get nervous, certainly not around someone like me.

I shifted the basket from my left hand to my right, then reached out and touched the smooth wooden handle of a snow shovel. Last year there was a storm that started at midnight and dumped down two feet of snow. Mama woke up Will and me, and we put on our boots and coats, then hurried outside for a big snowball fight at four in the morning, the patio light making our shadows huge in the lingering darkness. The world felt empty and still, purely white. Without saying so, none of us wanted to interrupt that magical feeling, so we kept silent, pelting each other with snowballs without saying a word, as the snow fell fast and thick through the dark. We didn't go inside for a long time though we were soaked and tired. But finally Will went in, then I did, then Mama was last. She cooked up a big pot of oatmeal sprinkled with brown sugar, and we drank hot chocolate, still barely talking. Afterward, we crowded on top of her big bed—even Will—and dozed as the sky brightened into morning, until it all felt like a dream. I never told anyone about that snowball fight; it seemed too hard to explain why Mama might be awake at four in the morning instead of asleep like other mothers.

That snow had stayed on the ground for weeks after. I often caught Mama staring out the window at it, a shut-down look on her face, as if she didn't want anyone to talk to her. I wondered what she was thinking, though I never asked.

Joe's voice startled me: "It's not anything, but this is for you." He reached into the pocket of his jeans jacket and pulled out an acorn, which he held in his open palm.

I picked it up with my thumb and index finger. It was big, about the size of a dime gumball, but just an acorn that anyone could pick up off the ground, the kind you'd kick along the sidewalk while you were talking and not even notice. I looked more closely, rolling it between my finger and thumb, wishing there was a way to really feel the perfect, even brownness instead of merely seeing it, because it was the most precise shade of brown. The scallop design on the cap was exact and symmetrical, not a scallop crammed too tight or too loose, each scallop perfectly shaped, each where it was supposed to be.

He didn't look at me. "I've had it for a while. You know how you put your hands in your pocket and feel that thing that's always there, like a thread or a penny? That's this acorn."

There was a movie-ticket stub in my winter-coat pocket from last year when Mama and I saw that Japanese romance at the Iowa Theater, and I wasn't about to throw it away, at least not until my fingers had rubbed and frayed the paper into nothing. "I like it," I said to be polite, but suddenly I did like that acorn. As kids, we threw acorns at each other in the fall; girls cracked them open with rocks and served "pioneer dinner" to dolls; boys chased the squirrels that were busy burying them. Acorns were everywhere. I stared at the one in my hand as if I'd never really seen an acorn before.

He said, "I found it on your mother's grave."

My fingers tightened around the acorn, and I squeezed so hard it almost spurted out of my grip. I wanted him to look at me but he didn't.

"I see her grave pretty often," he said.

Oh, of course. The cemetery was where he took girls—Paula Elam, Dara DeWitt. While they were doing it, the acorn had ground into his back like the pea in the fairy tale about the princess, so Joe jammed it into his pocket, forgetting about it until today. Even as I thought that, I hoped he would say something so I'd know none of it was true.

He spoke so quietly, I had to lean in to hear: "Ever since—well, there's something about places that mark someone who's gone. Graves. The World War Two plaque at the post office. Even those old trophies in the case at school. People should have something to show they were here." Joe folded his arms across his chest one last time. He seemed taller than I remembered, and I thought of him catching that baseball last July, saving Will's no-hitter. Of course he wouldn't care about jingle bell earrings. He was someone who looked at graves, who understood that people, even mothers, died and left and that you couldn't have any hope at all that they might change their minds and come back, the way Linda's mother could.

Maybe it wasn't so wrong to do it if it was with someone who knew all that. I felt awkward, so I looked at the speckled tile floor, the layers of muddy boot prints, said, "I like the acorn."

"It was one day in September," he said. "There's no oak tree nearby, but that acorn was right there. I remembered you said your birthday was in September. I don't know if you want to plant it or keep it in your pocket or throw it in a drawer or what."

I slipped the acorn into the coat pocket with the ticket stub. "Is it lucky?"

"Lucky?" He stood perfectly still, as if moving would wreck something. "It is what it is. An acorn."

"I mean, the way people carry a rabbit's foot," I said. "Or a lucky penny. Aunt Aggy has a bottle cap from when she was twelve years old that she says is lucky."

"An acorn is a huge oak tree inside a tiny seed," he said. "That's better than an old bottle cap."

I tried to imagine a boy giving Linda or Becky an acorn. Linda would drop it on the ground in disgust, kick it away. Girls like Linda and Becky got necklaces from boys, and, eventually, diamond rings, sparkly jewelry they showed off to girls like me. You couldn't say, *Look what a boy gave me,* and pass around your acorn.

"Why not?" Mama asked.

Why not? What would happen if people stopped kicking acorns off the sidewalk and picked them up instead? If people actually saw the oak tree waiting inside?

"Magic," she whispered. Maybe that answer was good enough for a child wondering about candy canes, but at my age no one really believed in magic. My question to Joe came out abruptly: "How did you know my birthday was in September?"

"You told me," he said. "That night."

We had never talked about that night, and just hearing him say the phrase made my breath feel quicker, my heart louder, but neither of us spoke; we stood there until he grabbed a snow shovel handle. His voice started casual but ended up slightly choked: "Think we'll have a white Christmas?"

Oh, brother. "Maybe." Christmas could be plaid for all I cared.

He let go of the snow shovel and pulled me into a sudden tight, lumpy hug, kissed the hair at the back of my neck, then tilted my head, pressed his lips against mine, and what was this supposed to be? We were so close the metal buttons of his jeans jacket pressed into me where my coat was undone, and I smelled some sort of dark, piney aftershave. Was this real? Was it? But then he stepped back, hands still holding my face, and I demanded, "What does that mean?"

His hands dropped to his sides. "It was a kiss."

"I know that." Did Becky and Linda see? They were going to ask a million questions—and I didn't have one single answer.

There was a pause—I felt us both holding our breath—then he pointed to the ceiling and said, "Mistletoe," and way up high, by the fluorescent lights, was the tiniest scrap of plastic mistletoe, half a branch that someone had probably hung last year and forgotten about. I faked a laugh, said, "Mistletoe," like I'd known from the beginning that that was all it was, that Joe Fry didn't kiss for real.

He pressed two fingers against my lips. They were impossibly warm given the fact that it was December and he wasn't the kind of guy who wore gloves. He said, "Merry Christmas, Alice," and walked toward the front of the store. When I looked up again, I saw it wasn't mistletoe at all, it was a dangly cobweb someone had missed knocking away. The bells on the hardware-store door jingled. I took a big breath, stuck my hand in my pocket to feel the acorn. At least that was definitely real.

Becky and Linda hurried up, our fight forgiven. Words fluttered like confetti: "What'd he say—you look funny—where'd he go—what happened anyways?," all normal questions, but how was I supposed to answer? Something important had happened, but was it the kiss or the acorn or neither or both? If I told them, Linda would announce that the acorn was stupid, and Becky would be certain the kiss meant true love. Maybe it was strange that Joe had walked around for three months with an acorn in his pocket. I couldn't picture Will giving an acorn to Kathy Clark when they were going together. So I said, "He's a weird guy," and stalked to the cash register, plunked down my basket. Mr. Duncan wore a red Santa cap, and he was overly jolly as he rang up my stuff, asking if we were naughty or nice. Becky giggled out of politeness, so he gave each of us a foil-wrapped chocolate Santa, as if we were children.

The store bell jingled as we pushed through the door; "Merry

Christmas, girls!" Mr. Duncan called after us. He followed us to the door and flipped the "Open" sign over to "Closed," snapped off the lights. It was gray and shivery outside, and I was sorry I had walked, sorry there was no one to give me a ride home. We huddled on the corner of the town square; the windows of the White Front Café looked dark and blank; so did every other store lining the square. The courthouse in the center felt abandoned; usually there were a couple of old guys warming the benches on either side of the steps, but there was no one. Even Whit's looked locked up. Everyone was home, getting ready for Christmas. Not a single bird perched on the World War I memorial statue, the place felt that unnaturally empty.

Linda glanced all around, the way she did before she was about to tell a secret. "I heard Paula Elam is home for Christmas."

"Pregnant?" Becky's mouth hung open for a minute, and white, frosty breath swirled out of it.

Linda nodded slowly and grimly, looking just like her mother. "Isn't that wild?"

I was supposed to agree and help them chew apart Paula, who probably just wanted to be with her family on Christmas. Instead I looped the handles of my shopping bag up on my arm, buttoned my coat. It wasn't like I wanted to mention that Mama had come back to Shelby all pregnant with me. I pulled the ornaments out of the bag and handed one to Becky, one to Linda. "Merry Christmas."

Becky started to speak: "Oh, Alice, please don't be—"

"I'm fine," I interrupted. "Merry Christmas."

"I'm sorry about before," Linda murmured.

"I'm fine," I repeated, louder, more firmly.

Finally something else moved as five or six sparrows flew overhead. We watched until they were gone. Then Linda sighed, looked at her ornament. "This is really cute."

"Merry Christmas." I was one of those dolls with a string in her back saying the same thing over and over: *Merry Christmas, Merry Christmas.*

The streetlights suddenly switched on early, probably because the sky was so gray. I stared up at the lights, at the tired, old, silver-snowflake decorations that had been hanging in downtown Shelby every Christmas since I could remember. They looked like they'd been mashed flat all summer in someone's garage.

Becky said, "Want to come to my—?"

"I've got to get home." There was a long pause. They had been my friends for ages.

"Okay," Becky said. "Merry Christmas."

"Merry Christmas."

"Merry Christmas," Linda said.

"Merry Christmas," I said for the millionth FUCKING time, and then finally, finally they started walking toward their houses, and I watched them for a minute before I headed off toward mine. Partway there, my hands got cold, even through my mittens, and I stuck them in my pockets. I couldn't feel the acorn because of my mittens, but it was there.

AT HOME, Will was slowly putting away groceries, while Aunt Aggy darted around the kitchen, constantly in the way; every sentence verged on screaming. You could tell she was enjoying getting worked up, like she needed to yell just for yelling's sake. "They're predicting a colossal ice storm!" she shouted. "On Christmas Eve!" as if the weather cared about which day it was on the calendar. "Of all the—! How will we get to St. Mary's tomorrow morning?" This was the first I had heard about going to church; I'd assumed it was one of those torturous holiday things we had "decided" to skip.

Will tossed a pack of bologna into the refrigerator. "Drive, like always." He gave me a quick, tired smile, like he was glad to see me, though he was always the best of any of us when it came to handling Aunt Aggy's breakdowns. He edged around her to stick a few boxes of Kraft macaroni and cheese in the cupboard.

All her fingers beat rapidly on the counter. "The roads will be a sheet of ice. We'll crash the car. We'll die!"

"We'll be fine," he said, impatience edging into his voice. "Half the time those weathermen are wrong anyway." He bent to put some Palmolive under the sink, then started flattening the brown paper bags.

"Not Channel 2," she said. "Dale Hartman's never wrong."

Will sighed, pounded a wrinkle in the bag with the bottom of his fist.

I leaned up against the doorway. "Are we really going to church?"

"Of course," Aunt Aggy said, all outraged, as if we were church regulars. In fact, the last time we had been there was for Mama's funeral. "It's Christmas, which means we're going to church."

"Yeah, well, Christmas means a pretty tree with ornaments and presents and stockings and Christmas carols, and none of that is happening around here," I said.

"We have to do something—don't you understand?" Aunt Aggy whirled around and opened side-by-side cupboard doors, then slammed them shut with a big wham. "Your mother always went to church on Christmas. It's the least we can do."

Church never seemed to mean anything to Mama. She had given me and Will the basic Catholic background—baptism, first communion, CCD, confirmation—but when I had asked Mama why we didn't go to church on Sundays like everyone else, she'd said, "Church is for people who can't find God through their own imaginations," which made no sense to me at the time but meant we could sleep late on Sundays and eat pancakes for breakfast.

Church on Christmas morning was a different matter. "It's important for you kids," she always said, though we insisted it wasn't. But she'd say, "A lot of people really believe in all this. Maybe things are easier if you do."

I wanted to ask if she believed—obviously not much, or we would've been going to church every week. But maybe a little, because why else did we go on Christmas?

Last Christmas morning we were late; Mama led us up the center aisle, her head motionless and her eyes forward as we marched to the empty seats way up front, sliding across the long pew as everyone behind us watched, their eyes pricking into my back like needles. Even Father Carroll seemed to pause, staring as if trying to place us. I slouched low into the pew, Will also. Not Mama—she sang loudly and was the first to pop up when Father Carroll said, "Please stand." Afterward, instead of sneaking out the side door, Mama dragged us through the main doors and jostled

through the crowd to shake hands with Father Carroll. "Merry Christmas,
dear," he'd said to Mama, and somehow, the way he said, "Merry Christmas," seemed to mean something deeper than the way other people said it.
It was like that moment when we were singing "Joy to the World" and the
stained-glass windows of the saints jumped alive as sunlight pushed
through them, sending spots of red, purple, and blue dancing on the white
walls, along the pews, sliding up the side aisles, and I remembered exactly
the sound of Mama's voice joining in with the choir's, singing, "Let heav'n
and nature sing, let heav'n and nature sing . . ." Was that exact moment
God or was it sunlight? Was it the thing that could put a huge oak tree into
an acorn, then leave that acorn on my mother's grave for Joe Fry to pick up
and give to me the day before Christmas?

Aunt Aggy seemed to have arrived at the end of a long, breathless
speech: "If we go to midnight mass tonight, we'll beat the storm, and do
what your mother would want. I'm your godmother, after all, responsible for your spiritual growth." She inhaled deeply, gave her head one final
nod, her finger one last shake. "I'll call Mr. Cooper." Off she went.

Will looked worn, like an unelasticky sock you should throw away.

"It's just church," I said.

He slumped down into a chair, halfheartedly drummed his fingers
on the table a couple of times.

I watched from the doorway. "Are you all right?"

"What would be wrong with me?" He gave a quick, short laugh, like
a bark. "I just wasn't thinking we'd have to go to church. Where does she
get these ideas?"

But he would drive us anyway, and compliment Aunt Aggy on her
blouse, whisper something in my ear that would make me laugh. He was
so perfect, my brother. Everybody liked Will. Maybe he had run off to
Boston to see a couple of baseball games, but like he'd told me, he was
here now, and he wasn't going anywhere. I lingered, hoping he'd want to
talk. Instead he reached for the sprawl of newspapers on the table and
flipped the pages of the Shelby *Beacon*, stopping to read the high school
sports report.

So I went upstairs to wrap my presents. All I found was old birthday
paper with clowns on it. Needless to say I didn't bother with ribbons or

bows, and I shoved the presents under the tree, with the two Hy-Vee Russell Stover candy boxes from Will and the sweaters and jeans still in shopping bags from Aunt Aggy. There were also a couple of awkwardly large, flat, square packages wrapped in cut-up grocery bags and too much tape. Paintings. (I was hoping for an all-black canvas titled, *Soul of a Miserable Christmas*.)

The tree was dark and bare and off center; it would have toppled over long ago if it hadn't been leaning against the wall. Mama would hate this sad, ugly tree as much as I did. But even she wasn't saying much about Christmas—or anything. I missed her. A ring of dry needles circled the tree; I scuffed them with my shoe, grinding them deep into the carpet.

AUNT AGGY, her best fake smile plastered across her face, announced that Christmas Eve was going to be fun. It wasn't. We ate oven-fried chicken and box mashed potatoes in complete silence, all of us staring as hard as we could at one tiny point of nothingness. After supper we sat at the table while the TV droned in the living room, no one getting up to change the channel or turn it off because no one wanted to be anywhere near the Christmas tree. Time passed slowly, divided into fifteen-minute commercial breaks.

Finally, we went upstairs to get dressed for church.

Then Will headed out to warm up the car. I stared out the dark window, next to the front door. Weatherman Dale Hartman kept his perfect record: Sleet had started to fall. Already the sidewalks and street were shiny-slick, and I heard the tiniest tapping at each window. Aunt Aggy was upstairs finishing her makeup; seeing Mr. Cooper (who was meeting us at church) required an extra layer. This must be the worst Christmas in the history of mankind.

Mama said, "I thought you liked the rock tumbler."

Now was not a good time to talk about rock tumblers. "It was fine," I said.

"It turned rocks sparkly and beautiful," Mama said. "Ordinary rocks became extraordinary."

She had made necklaces and bracelets that she actually wore in public. Rings. Barrettes. She glued rocks from the rock tumbler on ballpoint pens, key chains, on a money clip she carried in her purse. People commented all the time, things like, "What an unusual necklace," mostly not meant as a compliment. She'd say, "Dug up this rock when I was planting petunias," or, "Found this in Will's shoe after a day at the creek."

I pressed my nose against the cold window, breathed out a white patch of fog. Had Mama always been going around doing weird things like wearing rock-tumbler jewelry? Even when she was my age? When Linda's mother was my age, she was crowned Iowa pork queen at the state fair; she'd shown us her scrapbook. Of course, now she was living in the Seville Apartments in Iowa City, without her family on Christmas, so apparently being pork queen—and normal—didn't mean you had all the answers.

"I was pregnant when I was your age." Mama's voice was crisp and precise.

I swiped away the smudge of fog with my hand, squinted out at the icy sleet raining down. "I'm sixteen. You were seventeen when you ran away on the train, and Will hadn't been born then." There was a silence. "So, you couldn't have been pregnant when you were my age. I mean, I know what you're saying, but it's not exactly—" I stopped talking. Sleet tapped at the window.

"I was pregnant when I was your age," she repeated. "No one ever knew."

There it was. Mama, my mother, had done it with Mr. Stryker, just as Paula Elam—and I—had done it with Joe Fry.

She continued, very matter-of-fact, like commenting on the weather: "I was only pregnant for two months, and then I wasn't. In one instant I was a mother, then in another instant I wasn't. Poof."

"What happened?" I asked.

"I wanted the baby, if that's what you mean," Mama said. "Desperately."

"Wait," I said. "No one ever knew?" At least she should've told Mr. Stryker; maybe then he wouldn't have . . . died like that.

Or. No. She had told him. "Oh, Mama," but the word—her name, who she was, Mama, all of it—sounded wrong. This was too much to piece together. "Mama," I said again, more insistent.

"I wanted to be someone else." Now Mama's voice had turned slow, sad, quiet, tentative. "I thought maybe I could be a mother."

I brushed the cold, dark glass with my fingertips. Unless you were right up close to the window, you couldn't see outside; instead, there was only my own reflection. "Being a mother isn't like being Emily," I said.

"You don't understand!" Mama cried.

Being a mother wasn't Linda naming the imaginary unborn children she planned to have with every boy she met. Sometimes it was Mrs. Johnson with her (supposedly) perfect family. And sometimes it was Paula Elam. But my mother thought it was a part in a play—and that you could simply walk offstage when you got bored.

I could punch my fist through the glass pane right now. It would hurt, there'd be blood, I'd scream, Will and Aunt Aggy would come running; maybe I'd spend Christmas in the hospital, and the nurses would murmur, "Poor girl," when they fluffed my pillows.

The silence felt very heavy, tangible, like dark velvet curtains to push aside, or thick air locked away in an unused attic. It was stifling; I couldn't breathe, couldn't move, couldn't think. I spun around, away from the window.

"Listen to me," I said, then said it again because I liked the sound of the words: "Listen to me. Whatever else you've done, whatever other secrets there are, whoever you are or think you wanted to be—the fact is, you ARE a mother. You're my mother and Will's mother. That's all there is to it."

"Oh, Alice," Mama said, the words soft and strange. "Not exactly. But, yes, my darling, that's how simple it all should be," and suddenly Aunt Aggy flurried down the stairs, muttering about her coat, her perfume, whether she should wear snow boots, the icy roads, what a good boy Will was, how pretty I looked, my coat, why I wasn't wearing snow boots, the part in my hair that wasn't quite straight, her purse, was the oven turned off?

Then we were in the car, off to church. I sat alone in the backseat of Aunt Aggy's big boat-car, huddled deep into my coat as Will maneuvered down the dark streets. Thank God it was late enough that everyone had turned off their Christmas lights for the night, and our undecorated house—the only one in town, it felt like—didn't look so barren. Even old Mrs. Lisk had managed to tie red bows around her tree trunks. Will said, "Roads aren't too bad yet."

"Slow down," Aunt Aggy snapped, though he was going one mile an hour maybe. "And please put both hands on the wheel."

He simply did what she said, like he was too tired to talk.

It took an eternity, but finally we got to St. Mary's. The parking lot was packed because of all the extra people like us who only showed up for holidays, so Will let us off at the door and drove around the block to find a parking place. I had a sudden fear that he wasn't coming to church, that he was going to disappear again, he'd been so quiet lately. But that was silly, and anyway, there was Aunt Aggy, grabbing my arm so I could help her up the stairs, complaining she was sure to break a hip, leg, and arm what with the sheets of ice everywhere.

The church was crammed with sleepy-looking people in clunky snow boots and thick coats, bodies overflowing out of pews. Up front, choir members yawned head-splitting yawns, setting off waves of copycat yawning. A couple of babies yowled, their cries echoing and bouncing off the walls; an old man hacked and coughed. And the stained-glass windows remained blank in the darkness.

Mama's funeral rushed back at me: too many people; the air warm and humid with body heat; that angular casket up in front for everyone to stare at, as hard and polished as the pew I sat in; Will, arms folded, not crying, and me wanting to be tough and certain like that, sobbing; the tissue Aunt Aggy set on my knee—I gave my head a hard, violent shake to stop thinking about it.

Aunt Aggy tramped up the main aisle, craning her head this way and that as she searched for Mr. Cooper. I waited in the back, leaning against the bulletin board; after too many jolly people whispered, "Merry Christmas," to me, I figured out that keeping my eyes closed would prevent that. If Mama were alive, we'd be at home sitting around a pretty, tinsely tree, and Mama would say something like, "Christmas-tree light flatters a woman," and I'd be eating a chunk of homemade fudge, letting each chocolaty nibble melt in my mouth, feeling warm and drowsy and content, half-listening to the conversation and the silences between the conversation; looking at the tree, at the white candy canes, knowing they'd magically turn striped by morning. And then—

"Merry Christmas, Alice."

I scrunched my eyes tighter, pretending I hadn't heard, but there it was again, along with a nudge in my ribs: "Merry Christmas, Alice." So I opened my eyes to see Paula Elam, big and bulky in an overcoat that I guessed was originally her father's. She smiled, lifted her arms straight out so the coat tightened against her belly, whispered, "My parents thought they could hide me. They were sure no one would be out in the storm. Pretty funny, huh?" She stuck her big belly out even farther, patted it. "They're upstairs looking for seats in the back corner of the balcony where they can shove me before anyone sees I'm here." She laughed. It was pretty noisy near the doorway where we were standing, what with all the "Merry Christmasing," the door opening and closing, murmurs about the storm, but Paula's laugh rose above the commotion. People turned to see who was laughing but quickly glanced away when they noticed her.

I stared at her stomach. It was a baby, a real baby. "Um, so how are you?" I asked, looking up at her face, flushed pink, rounder than I remembered. I thought about hugging her but was afraid her stomach would get in the way. Plus, I barely knew her.

"Saint Joseph's Home for Girls is more like Saint Joseph's prison," she said. "I'm crawling out my window onto the roof at night to get a smoke. Nuns and pregnant girls everywhere you look. Can't remember the last time I kissed a boy, let alone . . ." She pulled a lipstick out of her coat pocket, lined a bright red smear across her lips, then bared her teeth.

I pointed to my front left tooth; she licked away the lipstick smudge.

"How's everything?" she asked, like we were regular friends trying to catch up. Like I was supposed to say, *Aunt Aggy's still wearing the beret and her paintings are getting stranger and Mr. Cooper still hasn't popped the question; Will ran away to Boston and he's back, but he didn't go out for basketball. It seems like he barely talks about anything, and what should I do about that?*

"Fine," I said.

"How's your Christmas?" she asked, then answered: "I know. Sucks. After my baby sister died, my mother chucked every Christmas ornament, Christmas stocking, record, tablecloth—you get the idea. Then she informed my little-kid cousins that Santa was fake. More people hate Christmas than you'd think." She swooped out her arms. "You'd be surprised."

If only Paula were the kind of person you could call up and invite over. She'd probably laugh at the Christmas tree, make me see that it was goofy instead of ugly.

The organist started the first notes of "O, Come All Ye Faithful," and the choir and congregation launched in as the priest and processional walked up the aisle. I stood on tiptoes and spotted Aunt Aggy halfway up the front, turning and waving one arm. The empty space beside her didn't look big enough for a cat to squeeze into, so I waved back, meaning I'd stay here, then I looked away so she would stop with the windmilling. Still, I was glad she hadn't forgotten about me; I imagined Will sitting in the car, deciding between east and west. "What about your family?" I asked Paula.

She whispered, "Screw them; they're happier without me around. No way I'm sitting in that cruddy balcony. Like locking crazy Paula in the attic when company comes." She laughed softly, but with a sharpness that made me wonder if she was angry or sad or both. Her eyes were hard, like gray stones. I'd never noticed the color of her eyes. For a minute she looked straight ahead, then she hissed, "Stop staring. I'm not an animal in the zoo." Tears glittered along her bottom lashes.

I shifted my weight, jammed my hands in my coat pockets, rubbed my fingers over the acorn, the ticket stub. The things I wanted to ask would only make her more mad: *Do you hate Joe Fry? Do you miss Shelby? Even with a dead sister, is Christmas normal now?*

She leaned closer, still looking straight ahead, whispered, "Do you believe in miracles?"

Linda's singsongy, fake talk about how Christmas was a time of miracles felt a million miles away from Paula's hoarse question. Paula didn't mean Mrs. Johnson moving back from Iowa City; she meant a real miracle, like loaves and fishes or water into wine. My words were quiet, hesitant. "What would be a miracle?," though I guess I knew one answer—a dead woman's voice.

Her whisper turned into another angry hiss. "Think about the biggest miracle of Christmas. Like a baby—my baby—being the son of God."

Wasn't it wrong to say something like that in a church on Christmas Eve? But no bolt of lightning struck us down, no roof caved in, no devil rose in flames to snatch our souls.

Paula went on: "I mean, why'd God pick Mary? Couldn't someone like me have a miracle in my life? Is it wrong to want something?" Paula folded her arms across her stomach, like she was trying to hug herself. I rolled the acorn between my fingers. Paula tightened her arms. She was having a baby, a real baby.

"That's a miracle," I said, pointing to her stomach.

"A married lady having a baby is a miracle," she said. "Me having a baby is a problem."

"Paula, that's a baby inside you," I said. "It could grow up to be anything. President. Movie star. Millionaire."

She turned to look at me. Her face didn't move. She was prettier than I remembered. If you didn't know who she was, you'd say, *There's a pretty girl*. "I don't get to keep this baby," she said. "You know that."

I nodded. Should you want a baby when you were sixteen? Did having a baby—and being a mother—really make you someone else the way Mama had hoped?

Paula kept looking at me until her face dissolved into tears. "What if it grows up to be another awful, slutty girl like me? What then?"

"That's not who you are," I said. "Just because. . . " I trailed off, watching Paula's mother push through huddles of people. Everyone turned to stare at her after she passed, and a low whisper seemed to follow her. If Mrs. Elam noticed, she didn't show it on her face. She wore a beautiful white wool coat that Becky and I had admired often in the window display of the Fashionable Miss Shop; it was so expensive looking—soft and fuzzy, like a pulled-apart cotton ball—that we didn't dare go in to check the price tag. And here it was on Mrs. Elam. She wasn't smiling as she whispered to Paula, "We were wondering what happened to you." When she noticed me, her eyes gave a quick flick, as if she wasn't a hundred percent sure who I was. And certainly she didn't know Paula had explained to me about her dead baby sister. "Christ, have mercy," she repeated with the crowd.

"I'm fine," Paula said as tears rolled down her face.

Mrs. Elam rested her hand on Paula's elbow. "We have a seat upstairs for you, honey. You shouldn't stand this whole time, not in your condition."

Paula's arms were still wrapped tightly around her body, around her baby.

Mrs. Elam's hand slid upward, onto Paula's shoulder, patted her. She murmured, "Lord have mercy," along with the congregation.

Paula wiped her wrist across her cheeks, but the tears kept coming. Even with that bright red lipstick, she looked like a little girl wearing someone else's saggy coat.

The choir started singing "Glory to God in the highest," and Mrs. Elam's mouth moved with the words, though no sound came out. Right then I saw that whatever Paula might say or think or do, Mrs. Elam would stand there forever—forever!—just waiting for her daughter.

In a sudden whirl, Paula turned and hugged her mother, noiselessly sobbing into her shoulder, lipstick smearing that expensive white coat as she burrowed her face in her mother's arms. Mrs. Elam stroked Paula's hair and moved her lips to the words along with everyone else.

Why wasn't being my mother enough for Mama?

I had to look away, and when I looked back, I saw Will at the doorway. The tip of his nose was red and his hair was wet with sleet (he never bothered with winter hats). I half-lifted my arm, but he had already seen me, and he started threading through the clusters of families crowding the back, slowly coming toward us, staring down at his feet.

Paula stepped away from her mother, looked all around as if she was surprised by something. Then she nodded yes to an unspoken question, and Mrs. Elam rested her arm across Paula's shoulders, gave her a tight, never-let-you-go squeeze that made me like Mrs. Elam so much I thought my heart would explode. That white coat was ruined: Red streaks jagged the shoulder, collar, and part of both sleeves. You couldn't cover those stains with a scarf even if you tried, and even Dotty King had said lipstick stains were forever. "Merry Christmas," Mrs. Elam whispered to me before leading Paula up the winding balcony stairs, each one creaking twice, and I imagined their feet side by side, climbing the stairs together, Mrs. Elam's hand resting on her daughter's shoulder all the way. I didn't have to be up there to see Paula with her swollen face and big belly and smeary lipstick and red-rimmed eyes squeezing into a pew with her mother and father, her two sisters, their bodies pushed close and warm, and Paula cozy in her dad's old coat, back where she belonged.

Now I could answer one of Paula's questions: No, it wasn't wrong to want something or to look for the extraordinary in the ordinary, to hope to find that. A rock tumbler was a fine present.

"Merry Christmas, Alice," Mama whispered. "My darling daughter."

I caught my breath; her voice suddenly felt that close, and I spun around, searching the crowd for her face, for the red wool scarf she wore wrapped around her neck when it was cold.

Just then Will reached me, leaned up against the wall, close enough that I could smell Tic Tac on his breath, hear a soft gurgle in his stomach. I was so grateful for his presence; I wanted to fling my arms around my brother, hold on tight, never let go. Instead, I matched my breath to the rhythm of his, and for the first precious minutes of Christmas, Will and I stood side by side as Father Carroll talked about whatever he talked about, waiting for the choir to sing Mama's favorite, "Joy to the World," so we could sing along as loud as we could.

WILL WOKE me up the next morning, the same way he had awakened me all the other Christmases before, by tiptoeing into my room and balancing on the very edge of the bed, bouncing lightly until I rolled over and looked at him through my half-open eyes. He was morning rumpled and wrinkled, yawning, but bouncing up and down on my bed, hard, excited about something, all jittery, as if he'd been awake for hours. He

seemed so happy, so much like himself again, that for half a second I
almost forgot that this wasn't a normal Christmas. But I remembered.
"Too early," I whined, yanking the covers over my head.

Will said, "I want to show you something."

"Did Santa bring me a pony?" I said from under the blankets.

He didn't laugh. "Look at this," he said, and got off the bed, his
footsteps heading across the room. I pushed the covers away; he was
standing at the window, his back to me, arms crossed. Sunlight glinted in.
It must've been seven-thirty, eight o'clock—too early to face a bad day.
"Look," he said again.

I got out of bed, hurried across the freezing floor, and, arms crossed
tight for warmth, looked out the window. The world was encased in a
brilliant, glittering layer of ice: all the trees, the leftover brown leaves
blown up against the fence, the fence, each individual blade of dried
grass, the patio, the picnic table, each saggy branch and twig of the apple
tree, the empty bird nest, the leftover stalks jutting up out of the garden,
the tomato cages, the tangle of dead bean and morning-glory vines twisting up the fence, Aunt Aggy's rosebushes, the clothesline poles. Everything outside shimmered and glimmered and glowed and sparkled;
bright sun reflected off every surface, scattering bits of light.

Blades of grass were individually wrapped in ice—like glass, like
sugar coating—each separate from the rest, as if this was the way you
were really supposed to see a lawn: blades of grass, each unique, each
gleaming and wonderful and special.

I had seen these trees out my window a million times, but never as
splendid as this.

I looked at Will, wanting him to say he was happy, needing to hear
the words to make this moment real.

He hadn't moved.

A quick wind set the scene swaying and sparkling, like the shift of a
kaleidoscope.

I was afraid to step away from the window, afraid this beautiful
world would disappear (as indeed it would—sunlight; warmer weather;
people walking across the grass, footsteps crunching the icy blades, arms
knocking branches). But right now, it was all here in front of me.

Was an ice storm a miracle? Or was it just an ice storm, just weather, just what happened when raindrops fell into colder air, turning into sleet? Was this the world as it truly was? Was this what Mama saw when she pulled a rock out of Will's shoe, even before she dropped it into the rock tumbler?

"Merry Christmas, Baby Sister," Will said, sliding his arm around my shoulder, pulling me close into the warmth of his body.

THE HUMAN BODY

I DECIDED that a new year was a good thing. The calendar on the refrigerator wasn't the one Mama had hung, with pictures of European castles; it was a brand-new calendar I had picked up free from Hy-Vee, showing scenes of Iowa wildlife: bunnies, deer, quail, blue jays. There was a thick layer of fresh snow on the ground that Aunt Aggy and I shoveled off our sidewalk and driveway, each of us commenting about how the exercise felt good, and the brisk chill of the air—but we really meant that it was nice to see our house looking normal again, like the other neatly shoveled houses on the street. It was the bicentennial year, a once-in-a-lifetime occurrence to set apart this year from last. And Aunt Aggy said finally the country could put Watergate and Vietnam behind us, and look ahead to a presidential election. Most of all, though, I could think, *My mother died last year*, which sounded far away, like something that happened once, distantly, barely. All because of 1976 instead of 1975.

Mrs. Johnson had not returned to Shelby at Christmas to get back together with Mr. Johnson, but Linda claimed she would eventually: "If she leaves the apartment now, before the lease is up, she'll lose money. It's a big legal thing." Maybe I looked doubtful because she added, "I saw the lease with my own eyes, Alice. I'm not making this up." Linda never said her mother was "gone" or had "moved"; instead, she only used the word "away," like Mrs. Johnson was visiting her sister in Marshalltown.

If you messed up and said "gone," Linda would correct you icily: "My mother is away, for your information, not gone."

And Paula Elam had disappeared again, almost as if she'd never really been here, though I couldn't forget her hoarse whisper in the church, her mother not caring about those lipstick stains on her expensive white coat.

Other notable events of Christmas vacation: Aunt Aggy removed her paintings from the White Front Café, complaining that no one in Shelby appreciated art. "More proof that genius goes unrecognized," she told me as she stacked the paintings against her "studio" wall. Mr. Cooper was seen leaning over the glass counter where the diamond rings were at Pender Jewelers, but it turned out he was only getting his watch repaired. Will got back his job at the movie theater when Billy Dodds, who had replaced him, got fired for borrowing ten dollars for gas from the ticket money. I snooped in Aunt Aggy's closet and found her scrapbook. The headline about my grandfather definitely read, "Shelby Man Dies in Hunting Accident." In fact, the word "accident" was used nine times. Mama's response: "I know what I know." And then, like always, Christmas vacation was over before we were ready.

ON THE first day back at school, Linda and I were standing outside the biology lab, waiting for the bell. It didn't pay to go in early: Mrs. Lane might tell you to water the plants in the greenhouse or lug microscopes out of the storage closet, then complain about how you were messing up. Like, if you were watering the plants, she followed along, pressing the dirt with her thumb, saying, "More, please"—"please" meaning "you idiot." She had a way of talking that clipped off the pleasant sounds of any word, and she tossed around "chloroplast" and "cytoskeleton" like we were supposed to know them offhand. Everyone was afraid of her, even Mr. Rhinehart—he never made her chaperon school dances or monitor a lunch shift or advise a club, and she was allowed to bring her cat to school if it stayed in the greenhouse—which it didn't; often during class it jumped on her desk or climbed onto the overhead projector. She was always puttering around in her precious greenhouse, startled when the bell rang and the classroom filled with students. She had grown up in Shelby; "Peculiar," Aunt Aggy reported. "Pockets filled with crickets and dried-up plant leaves even in grade school."

On the other hand, she'd written, "Potential to develop the mind of a scientist" on one of my lab reports. She hung my paramecium poster in the front of the class, complimented my neat handwriting when labeling "vacuole" and "mitochondria" and the rest. (Her writing was as tiny as a typewriter's.) She could say the word "dead" in class without staring at me; Mrs. Lane just said "dead" like she was saying "photosynthesis." And she had been the only teacher to send us a note after Mama died: "So sorry to hear of your Devastating loss." I liked that capital "D," though, of course, it was grammatically incorrect.

The bell rang, and we filed into the classroom. Mrs. Lane stood at the chalkboard, wearing her white lab coat and ratty tennis shoes. There was a rumor that she didn't wear clothes under the lab coat, but once I saw her in the lunchroom buying a carton of milk and she had on a shapeless yellow dress. She didn't ever call roll. It seemed she didn't care if she knew our names; she never used them. Mrs. Lane stared as we jumbled into our seats, stared hard, harder, until we were quiet. Then she launched in: "The next phase of our study is animal biology. Leaving behind the world of plants and single-cell organisms, we plunge ahead to ask the most basic questions of animals and, ultimately, ourselves: How do we function? What is our place in the world? Who are we?"

I doodled in my notebook. I would miss the plants and paramecia, the drawing and labeling with colored pencils. Class periods melted away as we stared into microscopes, looking deep inside plants, comparing what we saw to the pictures in the biology book, copying our visions into lab notes. It was the only homework Aunt Aggy wanted to look over, but she kept asking me the titles, as if the drawings were from an art class. We labeled things like "phloem" and "xylem" in roots, stems, and leaves, until finally the system made perfect sense: how roots connected to the stem, the stem to the stalk of the leaf, the leaves themselves; phloem carrying food, xylem carrying water. How weird to see Aunt Aggy's houseplants and think of a philodendron making food, photosynthesis, cells at work.

An unhappy murmur arose from the class. "Gross!" Linda's face puckered. Obviously I'd missed something. Mrs. Lane's hands were on her hips, her head cocked to one side. The murmur grew stronger, shifted into groans, whispers, pens tapping tables.

I nudged Linda. "What?"

"Dissecting frogs," she whispered.

Mrs. Lane spoke loudly: "It's shameful that not until this year has the school board—in its infinite wisdom—included dissection as a vital part of the advanced biology curriculum. Budget concerns indeed. Well, the point is, we're making the most of this wonderful opportunity now."

Will used to bring frogs home from the creek, keeping them in a bucket, an old window screen balanced on top so they couldn't jump out. He dug up mud to put in the bucket, carefully arranged rocks, dropped in crickets and flies and bread and hamburger—but no matter what he did, the frogs died after a few days and we buried them in the backyard.

Linda raised her hand and asked, "If I get a note from my mother, can I be excused from frog dissection?" Other heads nodded, mostly green-gilled girls.

Mrs. Lane crossed her arms against her white lab coat. "How do you expect to develop the mind of a scientist with that attitude?"—her most stinging insult. "I fail to comprehend denying yourselves this opportunity to further your knowledge. That is the human quest: to seek knowledge, discover answers—and within the framework of those answers, ask bold new questions." She continued, but I went back to doodling.

Mama had let Will keep the buckets of frogs in his bedroom. He hoped they would croak at night, but they never did.

AS SOON as we sat down for supper, I asked Will, "Did you ever cut open a frog?"

"That's hardly dinner conversation," Aunt Aggy said. She had fixed hamburgers and Tater Tots, one of her best meals. She bragged about the secret ingredient in her burgers, which was only garlic salt. Mama had mixed in at least a dozen different spices, but I'd have to admit that Aunt Aggy's tasted more like real restaurant hamburgers.

Will shook his head no, chewing, in a hurry to get to the movie theater. He was working practically every night now and both weekend
matinees. Aunt Aggy complained that Mr. Clough was working him half
to death, but Will seemed to want all those hours, as if he was trying to
make up for running off last fall.

"We're going to dissect one in biology," I said. "Linda thinks it's
disgusting."

"I didn't cut up animals in school," Aunt Aggy said. "What on earth
does anyone learn from that?"

"The frogs don't know you're cutting them up," Will said. "They're
dead." He took another bite of his hamburger. "Like this dead cow we're
eating," and he opened his mouth wide to show his half-chewed meat.

Aunt Aggy dragged a Tater Tot through ketchup and popped it in
her mouth. "Can we please talk about the weather?"

"People eat frog legs," Will said, swallowing.

Aunt Aggy groaned. "Enough."

"They're just frogs. Who cares?" Like he hadn't ever in his life
dropped bread into a bucket, murmuring, *Please eat, please.* He said,
"Gotta go," shoved the rest of his burger in his mouth, and left, still
chewing.

A moment later, I said to Aunt Aggy, "He misses playing basketball.
That's why." What I meant was that if Will were playing basketball, he'd
be the big star again, and Kathy Clark would like him. Everything would
be fine.

"Basketball," Aunt Aggy said, half a question.

I shrugged, no longer interested in supper. My half-eaten hamburger sat there until Aunt Aggy pulled her napkin off her lap and neatly
draped it over the plate, which felt like the respectful thing to do.

A FEW days later, I was in my room staring at the pages about frog dissection: "Dorsal View of the Superficial Muscles," "Ventral Views of the
Viscera." I didn't know the word "viscera," but judging by the drawing,
it meant guts in the most guttish way, like the junk that oozed out of a
squished bug. Soon I'd actually be looking inside a dead frog, touching

the bile duct and spleen, drawing pictures with colored pencils, getting a grade.

I had touched dead things: fried-up moths in the light fixtures, a garter snake Will accidentally ran over with his bike, leathery baby birds, doves Mrs. Felper's cat left in our yard, squirrels on the road in front of the house, scaly fish before Will cleaned them, frogs from the creek, mice, a baby rabbit. Mama.

Aunt Aggy's red-rimmed eyes had filled with another round of tears when she told us it was our last chance to touch Mama. We were at Moore's Funeral Home, everyone talking hushed and whispery, as if we were in a library, but with sniffling and nose blowing and the whoosh of Kleenex being tugged out of the box. Aunt Aggy was crying, the way you were supposed to at a wake, so people patted her shoulder and said, "There, there," or they clicked their tongues and pulled her in close, murmuring, "A shame, a tragedy, an awful thing." Those words were easy to say. But I felt those same people looking at me and Will, thinking, *A mother who died and left behind her children. What mother does that? What kind of children are those?* Will and I barely said anything to anybody, not like Aunt Aggy, who thanked everyone over and over for coming, who announced, "What a tragedy," in every conversational lull.

Perfect, strong Will didn't cry. *Who doesn't cry at his mother's funeral?* When Mrs. Lisk or Becky's mom or Kathy Clark or anyone started mumbling to me about being sorry, I closed my eyes the way little kids do when they want to be invisible. I imagined I was invisible. I imagined I was somewhere else. I imagined Aunt Aggy was the dead one. Opening my eyes was like feeling my skin getting peeled away.

"Your last chance," Aunt Aggy repeated. *Who's afraid to look at their dead mother's body?* Will stalked off, clusters of people stepping apart as he pushed through them; the front door opened and closed. Would this feel less real if I walked away? I shut my eyes, imagined I could be the one who left. But where could I go to escape this—all of it, her body, that echoing question, *What kind of mother?* Will should understand that. I half-thought about going after him, bringing him back, but Aunt Aggy touched my shoulder, said, "Don't be afraid. She looks just like you remember. Mr. Moore did a nice job." Aunt Aggy had taken a photo and

Mama's clothes in to the funeral home; she had picked out the casket and the hymns for the church and had done just about everything as if it was nothing more than planning a big party. She squeezed her fingers deep into my shoulder. "Honey, I know you'll be sorry if you don't," and she sounded so certain.

So I walked to the back of the room where the casket was. There were a million bouquets of flowers to pass, a million staring eyes, a million whispers: "She's so brave—poor thing—a tragedy," and then I was there.

Mama wore her violet Easter suit with the white blouse, though in real life she would never lie down in that dress because it wrinkled so easily that she hadn't even liked sitting in it. The makeup on her face was too much or not enough or colors that another woman would choose. Her hair looked shellacked.

I closed my eyes, then opened them.

Her hands were folded across her chest, fingers laced, and I put my hand on top of hers. I had touched those dead things and now I was touching my dead mother. My mother was a dead body.

No. I slammed shut the biology book. My hand rested on the cover—veins and muscles and bones, blood pumping through it. I clenched it into a fist, pounded the fist onto the book once, twice, so the desk rattled.

Mama said, "Do you really think of me as gone?"

"I don't see you anywhere in the room," I said, looking around.

"Does that mean I'm not here?"

"I touched your dead body," I said. "You're dead." That was a fact, that was inescapable science.

ON MONDAY there was a big jar of frogs on Mrs. Lane's desk; she was so excited that she had started class before the bell rang. Linda and I came in as she was passing out trays that looked like cake pans except the inside bottom was black and spongy. Linda poked her finger into it. "Gross," she said.

"Did you get a note?" I hoped she had, so I wouldn't hear "gross" every two seconds.

She poked the tray again. "Mrs. Lane said I shouldn't live my whole life escaping tough things by getting a note."

I almost liked Mrs. Lane for saying that. She was a true scientist—no-nonsense, factual.

Mama said, "Cut apart a frog and stare at its heart and brain, but that won't tell you how a frog feels when the sun warms its back."

I doubted that Mrs. Lane ever wondered how a frog felt about anything.

Linda flipped her hair. "I might tell my dad to get her fired."

"It's just a frog." I stared at the jar on Mrs. Lane's desk. The frog bodies were elongated, stretched like used-up rubber bands. The jar was the same as the jumbo-size mayonnaise in the picnic section at Hy-Vee, as if Mrs. Lane had gone to the grocery store and put pickled frogs in the cart along with her tuna and cat food.

"This is very sharp." Mrs. Lane set a sheathed scalpel on our table, then she began talking to the class in a syrupy, dreamy voice I had never heard her use before: "People, you're embarking on a beautiful scientific journey. Never fear science, though it involves messy things like dissecting frogs." She gestured broadly with the hand that held the scalpels. "Science is the quest to expand mankind's knowledge. That's all—but of course, that's everything."

I was usually afraid to ask questions in biology, but I suddenly spoke up: "Where did the frogs come from?"

She went on, ignoring me. "With this journey come answers—yet answers bring more questions, which means our scientific journey is never complete." She paused, glanced at me, spoke in her regular, clipped voice: "Questions about the scientific journey?" She didn't care about my question.

I asked it anyway: "Where did the frogs come from?"

She set her hands on her hips, so the scalpels she held stuck out like flagpoles. "Chicago."

I swallowed, asked again: "I mean, were they living in a creek eating flies before someone caught them and stuffed them in that jar?"

People in the class rustled, suspecting that this would be more interesting than any scientific journey. Murmurs rose from various points in the room; heads nodded. Linda's foot nudged mine under the table, warning me to shut up.

"A creek?" Mrs. Lane looked like she wanted to jab that handful of scalpels into my forehead. She spoke loudly: "Throughout history biologists have performed experiments on the frog. In 1628, English physician William Harvey's studies with frogs led to the discovery that blood flows in a continuous circuit, away from the heart in the arteries and toward the heart in the veins. Marcello Malpighi, an Italian botanist, in 1661 used the microscope on frogs to discover capillaries connecting arteries and veins. Throughout history, the lowly frog has provided mankind with answers to important questions." She walked to the chalkboard, started writing names and dates, a sure sign that something would be on a test. Everyone except me copied "Malpighi—lungs/capillaries—1661" and the other names and dates; the room filled with scritching of pens on paper, chalk on blackboard. I had lots of questions, but looking at frog guts wouldn't answer a single one.

Mama said, "What do names and dates tell you? What do they really mean?" as Mrs. Lane talked about some Italians who figured out how to make batteries thanks to frogs.

I rolled my pencil across my empty notebook. It was a Dixon Ticonderoga number 2 and needed sharpening. Names and dates were very important. But I didn't write any down.

Mrs. Lane told us about a German teacher and his student who jabbed needles into live frog nerves in 1833. ("Gross," Linda whispered.) Mrs. Lane made it clear she held little hope any of us would be as smart as the German student.

"How does a frog feel when the sun warms its back?" Mama murmured. "How does a girl feel as she looks out a train window watching buildings melt to cornfields, returning to that place she never wanted to see again? What does the sound of a train whistle cutting across every night do to her? How does she feel when she looks for the proof that she was loved and there's nothing?"

I rolled my pencil with one finger. I remembered pelting Mama with snowballs in the dark morning, Mama and me making strawberry jam one summer and learning to fox-trot on paper footprints while listening to the "You Can Dance" record from the library, Mama ordering grilled cheese at the Kresge's lunch counter, Mama basting the Thanksgiving turkey, Sunday mornings eating a stack of Mama's pancakes. Becky's mom complained about things like inflation and the price of hamburger going up a dime, not cornfields and train whistles. To her, "magic" was only a word for children.

"How does that woman feel when she reaches for the man who's gone? When cornfields surround her like an endless ocean to drown in?"

How was I supposed to know all that about my mother? It was too much: I swooped my arm across our table, knocking the dissecting tray onto the floor in a big, satisfying clatter that made Linda jump. Everyone looked up, and Mrs. Lane slipped the piece of chalk into her lab coat pocket, crossed her arms, said, "More silly questions about creeks? If you aren't prepared to approach this class in a scientific manner, I suggest you drop out and save us all some time." She tightened her lips, but it didn't seem like she cared if I left or stayed. Had she forgotten writing "fine work" on my paramecium poster?

I sat perfectly still as Mrs. Lane watched me through narrowed eyes, like I was nothing but a speck on a microscope slide. Everyone stared. Finally, I picked up the dissecting tray, put it in the exact middle of our table. "When do we get our frogs?" My voice was teeny.

"Now." Mrs. Lane opened a desk drawer, pulled out a pair of rubber gloves that snapped as she tugged them over her hands. She unscrewed the jar lid, and a sweet, medicinal smell seeped into the room. Someone coughed, someone else. "Bring up your trays so I can give you a specimen," Mrs. Lane said. No one stood, so she added, "These frogs won't bite; they're deader than doornails," and she stuck her hand into the jar and dredged up a frog. Droplets dribbled off the frog's dangling foot, collected on the floor in a tiny puddle that Mrs. Lane swiped with the bottom of her shoe. Finally she walked to the front lab table and dropped the frog belly side up onto Cathy Hershberger and Kathy Clark's dissecting tray. Then she pulled another frog from the jar like it was nothing worse than grabbing toast out of a toaster. She pointed at me and Linda.

Linda nudged the tray toward me. "You go."

"I'm not afraid of a frog." I grabbed the tray and slowly walked to the front of the room. Mrs. Lane plopped a frog on the tray. She barely looked at me before plunging her hand in the jar for another one. I stared at the frog's brownish belly, its arms flung upward as if to say, "I surrender," the big hind legs sprawled wide.

Mrs. Lane barked, "Next!"

I carried the tray straight-armed, as far from my body as possible. What a way to end up: high school students cutting you apart, misidentifying your lungs and spleen, copying off Mike Brenneman who was good at science, handing in a report written the night before, dropping your body in the garbage—and not remembering a single thing about your heart or liver, not knowing anything about you. I set the tray in front of Linda.

She leaned in close. "Let's name her Christine." Christine Beecher was the girl Danny Kadera, Linda's crush, had started dating. Linda gave the frog a quick jab with the edge of the still-sheathed scalpel. "Like a voodoo doll." She tapped the edge of the scalpel against the frog. "Right now Christine's getting a stomachache," and when Linda poked the scalpel harder into the frog, I yanked her hand away.

"Stop it," I said.

"It's just a frog," she said.

Everyone had a frog, so Mrs. Lane screwed the lid back onto the jar. "Pushpins for securing the specimen's legs are up here," she said. "Today we'll make our opening incision, pull back the skin, explore the muscles. Each team member should draw what they see, labeling the major muscle groups as seen in Figure 14-3, in Appendix D. Dissection instructions begin on page 472. Questions?"

How did these frogs die? What kind of frogs were they, what species?—we'd had a whole unit on phyla, classes, and orders, but these frogs were nameless. Were they mothers and fathers? Were their lives happy? Why did these particular frogs—out of all the frogs in the whole world—end up dead in a jar?

No one spoke, so Mrs. Lane continued, "Stomach side up for the ventral view. Dig those pins in—if they're just through the webbing your specimen may shift."

Linda went to get pushpins from the bowl on Mrs. Lane's desk, ending up in a conversation with Mike Brenneman that required a great deal of hair flipping. I assumed Linda's interest was related to Mike's perfect science grades.

I stared at the frog, still not touching it. Mama's skin had felt cold, not cold like an ice cube or snow or your toes when you don't wear boots, but cold like emptiness, like if blankness had a texture. Like what was left where something used to be. The way you feel at night when you wake suddenly and don't know where you are, where anyone is, who you are. Her fingers were laced together, and as I stood there with my hand on top of hers, I let the murmurs and stares and whispers swirl away like water down a drain, until I stood in perfect, total silence.

I set my index finger on the dead frog's stomach, pressed gently, expecting it to be stiff like Mama, but it was more like a half-wet sponge. Impossible to believe that this frog had ever felt the sun on its back.

Linda dropped a bunch of pins onto the lab table; we watched them roll. Several spilled onto the floor. "We're supposed to pin Christine's legs," she said, sitting down.

I massaged my forehead. "Stop calling it Christine. It's a frog."

"Calm down, Alice. I know what it is."

I jammed a pin into the frog's top left foot. Like a thumbtack in a bulletin board. I pressed as hard as I could, then pinned down the remaining feet. "Here's one frog that's not hopping away." I pulled the safety cap off the scalpel, touched the blade tip to the frog's throat. It barely pierced the skin, like a pinprick without the single drop of blood.

"One dead frog is nothing," Mama said. "A thousand train whistles are less than a whisper. Ten thousand tears aren't a drop."

Linda read from the book: " 'Make a midventral cut in the skin from the jaw to the cloacal opening. Extend the cut along the ventral surface of the limbs and remove the skin.' What's ventral?"

"They're saying slice it open," I said and drew the scalpel along the length of the frog. I expected it to shudder, but it was only an empty, dead body.

Linda peered over my shoulder. "What do you see?"

I eased aside the skin with my thumbs; surprisingly, it slid away like chicken skin. A dead body, just an empty, dead body, like Mama. Next thing I knew, I was flat on the floor with Linda's and Mrs. Lane's faces huge in front of me, the whole class buzzing, my head throbbing, my arms and legs heavy. "You fainted!" Linda shrieked, whacking the inside of my wrist. She fanned one hand in front of my face, almost hitting my nose.

Mrs. Lane was calmer; it was her cool fingers on my forehead. "Better see the nurse."

I barely knew where I was. Everything felt too bright, too close. "I'm fine," I said.

"People who faint are not fine." She told Linda to walk me to the nurse's office and hurry back.

The halls were quiet, the floor still shiny from the Christmas-vacation polishing the janitors had given it. My head hurt, and my thoughts were squeezed from somewhere distant; everything took a long time: The hall was endless, each footstep an effort; my cold fingertips didn't seem part of my body; even Linda's chatter was far away: "What was it like? Were you faking? Maybe we won't have to cut up the frogs. I bet you could sue. So, what was it like?"

Finally I said, "Like being dead! Is that what you want to hear?" I sped up. The nurse's office was around the next corner. I'd only been there once when Becky was too embarrassed to go in by herself to get Tampax.

"I'm just asking," she said, jogging to keep up. "I never fainted."

We turned the corner. Up ahead, Joe Fry bent over the drinking fountain, his long, dark hair draping forward. I slowed, stopped, and Linda bumped into me with a noisy "ouf." Then she said, "You're supposed to go to the nurse's office." She sounded like her mother.

Joe looked up, rubbed water drops off his lips with the back of his wrist, wiped his wrist against his thigh. He was either coming in or going out because he wore his jeans jacket. I'd never thought about him in class, hunched in one of those awkward, too-small desks, taking notes, worrying about a pop quiz. "What's going on?" he asked.

"We're going to the nurse's office. Alice fainted, if you must know." Linda tugged my arm. "Come on."

"How are you?" he asked.

I was about to say, *Fine*, what I always said, but I wasn't fine. I had fainted. My head hurt. My mother was dead. Fine, fine, fine. What a stupid word it was—clunky, in the way, like a heavy cement block to hide behind.

He asked again, "How are you?" It was a real question, not simply what you say to someone. In fact, I realized he hardly ever did things just because you should do them.

My voice felt loud and strong in the empty hallway: "I want to get out of here," not sure if "here" meant biology, school, Shelby, or something beyond, trusting Joe would know what I meant.

Behind me, Linda whined, "Alice! You're not supposed to do that!," as I walked to Joe, then she said, "What about the nurse?" and Joe pushed the drinking-fountain button so water spurted up, let it go, waiting for me, and Linda said, "What should I tell Mrs. Lane?," and there I was, next to Joe who pulled his car keys out of his pocket, jingled them a bit in one hand, and I left Linda behind as Joe and I headed to my locker so I could get my coat.

When we were in a landing on the stairwell, that's when he stopped, turned toward me and framed my face with his hands (which were warm) and kissed my forehead once, twice. My heart beat faster, harder. I felt blood push through my veins. My breathing quickened. The imprint of his lips lingered on my skin, the way a match glows even after it's been blown out.

JOE DROVE; we ended up in Iowa City, sitting in the car in a parking lot overlooking the river, barely talking. There was a path along the river's edge, footprints crisscrossing through the snow. The sun's light was weakening, fading, like the sheen of milk coating an empty glass. Everything seemed without color—snow, sky, the ice-sludgy river. Even the trees, shadowy, a clutter of branches, were simply dark, not quite black, not quite brown. The light slipping away made me want to shout, *Stop!* But who would I be shouting at?

Joe said, "Was it because of the frog?"

Fainting. That seemed long ago, something that happened somewhere else.

"I don't know." But I knew exactly. It was Mama, Mama's body, dead like the frog I had been about to cut open. Mrs. Lane had probably never fainted in her life. Clearly, I didn't have the mind of a scientist.

"Is that the kind of mind you want?" Mama asked.

Why not? It was a world of answers and reasons–why and things you couldn't argue with. If you cut open a frog, you saw what was in the book: Figure 14-3 in Appendix D.

Mama's voice was encouraging, leading me to the answer she wanted: "Don't you ever want to see beyond what's there?"

I remembered the scientists Mrs. Lane talked about, men who had opened frogs and ended up discovering how blood veins worked and inventing batteries. There were no batteries in Figure 14-3.

"With answers come more questions," Mama said.

Mrs. Lane had told us that same thing. I hated that. There should be an end, a final answer, a moment of "This is it."

"There isn't," she said, and I caught my breath for a moment, the way you feel when something sounds true though you don't understand why.

Joe stared out the front of the car. "Amazing light."

I never thought about light being amazing, but when I looked out the window, I saw it could be. I answered his question: "Something about all those dead frogs crammed into a jar. No one cares about them. They're just frogs." Mrs. Lane would say that a scientist wouldn't think twice about dead frogs in a jar. But Joe didn't say that. Joe didn't say anything.

We sat in silence as pale pink slid in, rimming the horizon, like the inside of a seashell.

I said, "Will used to bring home frogs from the creek. When they died, I buried them. I mean, out of respect. It's what you do, even for a frog."

Joe nodded, staring out the window as if he'd been hypnotized. No one listened to me, no one in the whole world. As if the words coming out of my mouth didn't exist. I wanted to bang him on the head with a dissecting tray to get his attention. Instead I blurted out, "I'm breaking into the biology lab to get the frogs. I'm going to bury them."

He turned his head, didn't blink. I thought he was going to say, *You can't do that*, but he said, "Easy to get in through the greenhouse. That flimsy door. One good kick and you're in."

I wasn't someone who kicked in greenhouse doors. "I was kidding."

Joe said, "I'll help you."

I shook my head. "It's talk, I'm just talking."

"We should bury them. Like you said, show some respect."

"You just want to break into school."

He lifted one shoulder, gave a tiny smile. "That, but not only that."

The pink had melted away, and the sky was gray, purple, almost night. The day was on the verge of being gone.

"Like it matters to frogs," I said. "Like they know."

He spoke quickly: "I wish I went to her funeral. But Will and I weren't hanging out then, and you were . . . Fuck." A moment later: "I was afraid to go."

The light was gone, and just like that it was night.

I opened the car door, let it hang wide. Cold air whisked in, and the fog started melting off the side windows. Air should have a distinct color so you could see it; maybe that was one thing I liked about cold, because for once I could feel air, so I knew it was there. Didn't anyone understand that I had been afraid too? I tapped the plastic dome on the car ceiling. "How come the light doesn't come on?"

Joe set his hand on my sleeve, said, "What was it like?"

"What was what like?" I felt stupid sitting there with the door wide open like I was going to storm away, but that's not what I wanted. I didn't even know what I wanted. What I wanted was not to want anything.

"Her funeral." His voice was so soft that I almost didn't hear him.

I opened my mouth but instead of speaking I watched frosty air swirl out. I never talked about Mama's funeral. Not with Aunt Aggy, not with Will, not with anyone. As if saying the words would make it too real. But that was the thing: It WAS real. It was. My mother was gone, voice or no voice, and maybe some day I would figure out why she had killed herself and maybe I wouldn't.

"Start at the beginning," Joe said. "Or wherever you want to start."

I looked at his hand still on my sleeve, his grip surprisingly light yet steady. Then I closed my eyes. "At the funeral home, there was a box of pink Kleenex on the table next to the roses from Becky's family. The organist was late and the singer started without him, and his feet pounded like hammers up the church stairs to the balcony. The pen they set out so people could sign the visitors book was from Farmers and Merchants Bank. I had a little canker sore on the tip of my tongue that I kept pushing up against my tooth to make it hurt." I told him how at the wake, Mrs. Johnson took Polaroid photos of each flower arrangement and wrote on the bottom who had sent it so we could write thank-you notes later (which we never did); about Mr. Gould, Mama's boss at the *Beacon*, with his arms folded hard against his chest the whole time, staring at the carpet, letting cigarette after cigarette burn all the way down in an ashtray; in the church basement, afterward, how the clock was an hour off because no one had moved it forward from daylight saving time; how stiff and dull her dead body was, the difference between touching a tree and touching a wooden table. It felt good hearing all those things I'd never said before, feeling words pour out of my mouth as if they'd been waiting for the chance. I told Joe about Mama's body in that box, that box going into the cold, dark ground, clods of dirt and shovelfuls of mud and worms and grubs dropping down on top of her—burying her—like that was a normal thing to do, which maybe it was if it was anyone else in there, not your thirty-six-year-old mother, not Mama. How Will left, afraid of looking at her, afraid to touch her dead body, but Aunt Aggy said I should, so I did. How I held on to Mama's hard, dry hand—though I was touching her, I wasn't; though she was there in front of me, she wasn't. I had never seen so clearly how two opposing things could both be true, something I didn't understand until I heard myself say it that way to Joe.

Joe listened the whole time, without saying a word. Finally I said, "All day it felt like I was waiting," and I opened my eyes and finished: "For her to say good-bye." Then I stopped talking, wondering if Joe could understand hoping to hear one word from a dead person.

He leaned over me and pulled the car door shut. It felt quiet all of a sudden without me talking, without the wind blowing in. He said, "It's unfair." Then he put his arm around me and we leaned close together, warming each other, staying still until all the windows were fogged again, until the sky and the river were the same perfect black.

JOE WAS right: The greenhouse door was flimsy. I was terrified alarms would blare, janitors would swarm in, the sheriff would pull a gun, or the crazy cat would attack us. But nothing like that happened: Joe kicked the door, it swung open, we walked inside. We had brought a flashlight from the car, but the greenhouse was infused with a purple glow from a set-up of Gro-Lights in the corner ("Pot?" Joe whispered, checking. "No such luck."), so it was easy to maneuver the cluttered aisle, stepping over the clay pots and bags of soil, the watering cans and misters, a coiled rubber hose. Beyond the greenhouse, the classroom itself was dark. We stood for a moment in the doorway, letting our eyes adjust, and I thought about all the chapters of all the books I had read, teachers warning, "This will be on the test." What would it feel like to stand up there, everyone in the class thinking you had all the answers?

Joe turned on the flashlight, flicked the beam from corner to corner, creating a kaleidoscope of shadows and shapes that made the room seem magical. "Where are they?" he whispered.

I touched his hand that held the flashlight, guided the beam around the room until I spotted the dissecting trays, covered with dark sheets of plastic, lined up on two of the back lab tables. "I'll get them." I took a deep breath that I held for as long as it took to stack the trays, trying not to think about dead bodies, about guts hanging out under the thin plastic. The stack was awkward, and I walked slowly, my head turned away, though there was no escape from the smell. Joe kept the light at my feet, so I could see where I was going.

"They stink." He nodded at the trays balanced in my arms.

"Formaldehyde." I hoped he didn't think Mama's body had been stinky. Aunt Aggy had sprayed on White Shoulders perfume, but it hadn't smelled the same.

"Anything else?" Joe asked, forgetting to whisper. His voice felt out of place. He walked behind Mrs. Lane's desk, picked up a mechanical pencil he stuck in his pocket, flipped the pages of her desk calendar, pulled open a drawer.

It was unbelievable that I was holding a dozen dead frogs. But a lot of things were unbelievable. I shifted the trays in my arms, shook my head, whispered, "No," said, "no," then again, as loud as I could without shouting: "No." I wanted my voice to bounce and ricochet like a cartoon character shouting into a canyon, but it didn't.

Joe laughed. "You've never done anything like this." He sent the flashlight beam up to the ceiling, illuminating water spots and warped tiles. "So, what was your mother like?"

The light slid along the walls; I caught a glimpse of my paramecium poster. This should be an easy question to answer. "She was nice and loved to cook."

"And lay moping in bed too much." Mama's voice was rhythmic, as if she was reciting a well-known nursery rhyme. "And smoked more than she should have. You know those things are true, Alice."

"Made the best macaroni and cheese," I said. "Pancakes every Sunday. She was fun."

"Suffered terrible insomnia," Mama said. "Was jealous of anyone whose picture was in a magazine. Loved the way tall buildings shaded city blocks, the clatter of the subway pulling into a station. And fried rice at a tiny place on Canal Street, in Chinatown."

There was no Canal Street in Shelby, no tall buildings. I talked louder: "She liked to wear scarves and dress up." This wasn't right—Mama sounded like a list, not a person. "And she wore high heels to PTA meetings." Mr. Stryker, the baby, the hunting accident. Staying up in the kitchen the night of the tornado. Driving way too fast. The constant cloud of cigarette smoke surrounding Mama. I added, "Her favorite color was red."

Joe pointed the flashlight at my face; I squinted, then twisted my head. "Stop." He snapped off the beam so the room went dark.

After a moment he said, "Your mom sounds great."

"Too bad you didn't know her," I said. Those words seemed to echo, and suddenly I remembered we had broken in, we weren't supposed to be here. "We should go."

He took some trays off the top of my stack, then we walked back through the greenhouse, to the car. My fingers got cold because I had stuffed my mittens in my pocket, and I almost slipped on a patch of ice at the foot of the stairs to the parking lot, but otherwise everything was fine. I hadn't known it would be so easy to break into school. I didn't even feel guilty, maybe because we were stealing frogs, not microscopes or film-strip projectors.

Once the trays were stacked on the backseat floor, we got into the car and Joe pressed the accelerator so it roared, turned the defroster fan as high as it would go, made the car roar again. I wanted to feel dangerous, like Bonnie and Clyde, as he peeled out of the parking lot, but all I felt was sad.

"Let's take them to the cemetery," I said, though he hadn't asked. He didn't look my way, and he still wasn't looking at me as we pulled into the rutted, snowy driveway of the old cemetery outside town. The car jounced and slid; Joe stopped but left the engine running. I said, "My mother always liked this place. That's why they put her here."

"She's not here," Joe said. "Just her body."

"What about these frogs?" I snapped. Burying the frogs didn't seem like such a great idea now. The cemetery was covered with snow; we didn't have a shovel, and even if we did, the ground was frozen. I stared out the dark window, thinking about how Mama was over there, her stone sticking up through the snow, nothing on it but her name. And right over there was where I'd done it with Joe in this same car. And there was where I'd stared out at the cornfield on the day she was buried. Once Joe had said people should have something to show they'd been here, but a gravestone didn't seem enough. I turned on the flashlight, shone it out the window but couldn't see anything.

Joe reached back his arm and brought a tray forward, half-balancing it on the top of the steering wheel. He lifted one corner of the plastic sheet, peered underneath.

I grabbed the other side of the plastic, yanked it off, pointed the flashlight beam at the frog. It was all mangled and peeled-apart-looking, like a green grape without a skin. No one would see this pulpy mess and think, *Frog*. There were a bunch of labels: "Pectoralis Major," "Cutaneous Pectoris," "Deltoid," "Sartorius." "We're doing muscles first," I said.

"All those fancy words for a frog?" Joe said.

"Mrs. Lane told us research on frogs helped scientists discover batteries."

Joe touched a leg with his fingernail. "So many muscles in one frog. Amazing."

"That's how it can jump." Probably Mrs. Lane could explain the exact function of each muscle and how they all worked together; I half-remembered a picture in the biology book of a frog jumping in slow-motion, a diagram explaining that the back legs thrust the frog through the air while the front legs helped absorb the shock of landing.

He set another finger on one of the side muscles. "Gracilis Minor."

"The human body has over six hundred different muscles." That was also from the biology book. I remembered because that had sounded like too many to me. How could something with six hundred muscles— not to mention a brain and nerves and blood veins and so on—stop working and die? Six hundred muscles should mean something.

Joe said, "I heard it takes fifty muscles for one kiss."

I kept my face still, thought about scientists researching in a lab: counting, kissing, counting. I could kiss Joe again. I could kiss him again and again, and maybe I'd forget about the frogs and the cemetery and Mama. But he laughed, and I said, "You made that up."

"It should be true," he said.

Mama whispered, "I could tell you about things that should be true."

There was already so much she'd never told me. "I can't believe my mother is dead," I said and stared off in the direction she was buried.

He set one hand on my knee, and we sat in silence for quite a while. Medical students cut open dead people—calling them "cadavers" to be polite—so they could poke around inside Mama and label her heart and lungs and stuff. But could they find out why she killed herself, who she was? I shivered, though the car was running, the heater blasting warm air.

After I had touched Mama's dead body, I ran into the funeral home bathroom and scrubbed my hands with pink soap that smelled like old-lady perfume. The water from the hot faucet didn't warm up, and my hands turned cold and numb. *This is what it would be like*, I thought, *if—* But Mama couldn't feel anything anymore, and my hands could be a block of ice and I still wouldn't understand what it meant to be dead. Only what it was like to be left behind. I snatched my frigid hands out of the stream of water, rubbed them hard with a bunch of rough brown paper towels. I pressed my fingers against my cheeks, the back of my neck, knowing my own body heat would warm them eventually. Even so, I had never before felt more suddenly, totally, forever cold.

I broke the silence abruptly: "What are we supposed to do with these dead frogs?"

"Let's stick them in Rhinehart's mailbox," Joe said.

"It's not a joke!" I yelled.

"What do you want to do?" he asked.

"What do I want?" My voice shook, and I hoped I wouldn't cry. "I want them to come back to life, and I want to take them to a pond where they'll feel the sun on their backs as they catch flies, and I want them to live happily ever after." I pushed his hand off my knee, crossed my arms.

"The mailbox thing would be easier." A moment later, he added, "And what about after happily ever after . . . ?" His words trailed away.

"Right. They die." I got out of the car, started walking through the snow, breaking the light crust. I wasn't wearing boots, and snow wedged down the sides of my tennis shoes. I called, "Maybe burying them in snow is like taking them to a pond." Snow was frozen water, water was a molecule formed by hydrogen and oxygen atoms. Coming down to science in the end seemed like the right thing to do for frogs that had died in the quest to expand mankind's knowledge. I added, "Anyways, it's better than a jar or a dissecting tray. It's the best we can do." We—the people left behind with our questions. Me and Will. Mrs. Elam and Paula. Mama. Even Aunt Aggy in her weird way. I swished my foot in the snow, creating a hole I pretended was shaped like a tiny pond. The snow was about six or eight inches deep, but I didn't want to reach the bottom; the frogs should rest on clean white snow, not last year's grass. The air was so cold it hurt when I breathed it in.

Joe turned off the car.

I kept digging. One car door opened, another (neither closed), the dissecting trays clattered lightly, and Joe's footsteps crunched the snow, slowly coming toward me. I bent down, pushed on the thin layer of snow at the bottom of the shallow hole with my mittened hand, packing it down, smoothing and evening it.

"They say no two snowflakes are alike," Joe said.

"Is that actually true?" Why would each snowflake be different, why would science bother making snowflakes beautiful? Most people didn't even like snow.

He shrugged, his hands filled with a stack of trays, the flashlight tucked into his armpit, its beam cutting straight across the dark night. "Why not?" he said. "No two people are the same. No two sunsets. Probably no two frogs."

He bent, and I reached for the first frog. I pushed the plastic sheeting to the ground, started tugging the pushpins out of the frog's feet. There wasn't enough light to read the muscle identifications. I pulled one mitten off with my teeth and picked up the frog. Paper labels fluttered to the ground. The frog's body was stiff in my bare hand, cold, dead, empty—a different form, the way water could be frozen into snow or heated into steam or examined under a microscope to look at paramecia and all those other one-celled organisms—and I stared at the frog for a moment, at the cut-up insides. You could see a frog in a pond and never know all those incredible muscles were right there under the skin. You could see a frog jump and never, ever wonder how.

The hole I had dug looked inadequate, but I set the frog down inside it, gently, with great care and attention.

THE NEXT day, Mrs. Lane expressed her disgust at the "childish prank" that "set back science," and compared the person who'd done it to people who wouldn't listen to Galileo, the people who didn't believe Columbus. If Mrs. Lane, with her meaningful looks at every single person except Mike Brenneman, was trying to make the "guilty party" confess or break down in tears, it didn't work. People stared at their desks; Linda didn't even whisper once. I was very calm. Mrs. Lane's rant was like the sound of airplanes buzzing in the sky. No one would suspect me because I simply wasn't the sort of person who did that sort of thing.

But after the bell rang, as we were leaving, Mrs. Lane asked me to come by after school for a "brief chat." I was certain she heard my heart suddenly thump, but I just nodded.

When I returned to the biology lab after my last class, Mrs. Lane was in the greenhouse, ripping off bits of a cheese slice and dropping them on the floor for her black cat to snatch up. I cleared my throat, and she said, "Yes, there you are." How could she turn me in if she didn't know my name? I took a deep breath, preparing to deny everything: I was at the movies and my brother could vouch for me because he was head usher. I ran through the points that showed how much I loved science and the scientific journey: my paramecium poster, the A on my last quiz.

The cat twisted itself around her legs, then rubbed against mine. "Aren't you Mr. Loyalty?" Mrs. Lane said, and it took me a moment to realize she meant the cat. She tore off another scrap of cheese, dropped it. The cat bolted away from me, licked the cheese up off the floor. Mrs. Lane popped the rest in her mouth, quickly chewed and swallowed, said, "Into the lab, please," and she walked past me, leaving me to follow. She sat behind her desk, motioned for me to sit at the very front lab table, which I did. Someone had etched "I LOVE GINA" into the varnish, so long ago that it had darkened with dirt and age and was as clear now as if it had been written with Magic Marker.

She stared at me.

I stared back as long as I could, then I looked down at "I LOVE GINA." A branch tapped the window in an uneven rhythm.

Mrs. Lane rolled a pencil back and forth along her desk with one index finger. Finally she said, "I could have you suspended from school."

Obviously this was where I was supposed to say, *For what?* and protest my innocence, remind her about my wonderful paramecium poster. Instead I mumbled, "I know."

She continued, "Or drop you from this class."

I would never have a scientific mind. Scientists had questions that could be answered by chopping up frogs. My questions could never be answered. Why, why, why—it was the relentless tick of a clock; the breath entering my lungs and exiting; the sound of my heart—why, why, why, not even a question anymore, but a word, a way of being, something always and forever there.

Mrs. Lane went on: "Do you understand that all I have to do is order another jar of frogs from Chicago? The world is filled with dead frogs."

I imagined stacks of dead frogs, piled like snowdrifts along the side of the road after the plow's been through. How many frogs had died in the whole history of the world?

She said, "So, my question is, are we really talking about frogs?" She picked up the pencil, jabbed it upright into a can of pens and pencils on her desk.

I rubbed my finger across "I LOVE GINA." A thud came from the greenhouse—the cat jumping down from somewhere. How many muscles did a cat have? Less than a human, more than a frog, three hundred, say. You could look it up. I'd seen in the biology book that people dissected cats. Scientists thought they were so smart, ripping everything open to see how it worked. I spoke suddenly: "You don't even know my name or who I am."

Considering that we had been talking about frogs and now we were talking about names, she didn't look all that surprised as she nodded slowly. She was going to drop me from the class, get me suspended, maybe even expelled. She said, "Your name is Alice Martin."

There was a silence, then some clinking in the greenhouse as the cat knocked against clay pots. "How many muscles does a cat have?" I asked.

"Five hundred," she said.

"A frog?"

"Nearly two hundred."

"What about a human?" I asked, to check that she wasn't making up numbers.

"Six hundred." Her brow furrowed, and she looked very serious, almost sad. "The question you really want to ask cannot be answered. We've been pondering that question since the beginning of time—poets and scientists, peasants and kings. Maybe frogs, too, for all we know."

I looked at the table. Who was Gina? Who had loved her and carved those words? Did he still love her? Or was she a vague memory now, someone remembered as a random thought while drifting to sleep? "It's not fair," I said.

"True," Mrs. Lane said. "But on the other hand, it's the most fair thing there is because we all die, Alice. All of us. Flies. Trees. People."

There was a long silence. "I LOVE GINA." If those words weren't written here on the table, I wouldn't be wondering who Gina was, who the boy was. How could fairness feel so achingly unfair?

Mrs. Lane cleared her throat, startling me, and I glanced up at her, waiting for what she would say. I had an irrational hope that she was seeing inside my head, reading my thoughts. But her words didn't comfort me, though she sounded almost apologetic: "From a safe distance, one can find a certain beauty to such biological destiny."

Our eyes met and locked; neither of us looked away or blinked. Mrs. Lane was so smart that she had to know no possible distance of time or space could ever show me that "certain beauty" in Mama's death.

She opened her mouth, then closed it, nodded, and dropped her gaze to examine a spot on the sleeve of her lab coat. "I had your mother in class, you know," she said.

Where'd she sit? What grade did she get? Was she smart? So many questions to ask. I hesitated, worried I would pick the wrong one, then asked anyway: "What was she like?"

Mrs. Lane sighed. "What does a teacher know about a student? She got Bs, wasn't late to class, handed work in on time. The usual. You tell me what your mother was like."

It was impossible to answer that question without going back to that list of favorite colors and foods I had recited to Joe. Until she died, she had been only my mother, not someone to describe or understand. We sat in silence; even the cat had stopped roaming around. Mrs. Lane rubbed one fingernail on her sleeve.

"We think we know people." Her comment felt unfinished, but she peered closely at the yellowish spot on her lab coat, scraped at it, didn't speak.

I thought about that boy carving Gina's name into the desk. Did he have these kinds of questions? Or was he happy enough just to have loved Gina? I asked, "Do you remember a teacher from a long time ago—Mr. Stryker?"

Mrs. Lane looked up. "Haven't heard that name for a while."

"My mother talked about him, said he was like James Dean."

Mrs. Lane laughed, sort of a hollow sound that I couldn't remember ever hearing in class. "Girls back then were desperately searching for James Dean. Mr. Stryker had just started teaching, so we barely knew him. Maybe he was like James Dean—who could say he was or wasn't?"

"He died in a car crash," I said.

"I remember." Mrs. Lane nodded, spread her fingers wide in front of her on the desk. Her nails were bitten down and ragged. "A shock for the kids, finding out people actually die. A shock for all of us, of course. Here one day, not here the next. That sudden. Why is it such a terrible surprise every time, though intellectually we recognize death as our inevitable destiny?" She slid her hands close, laced the fingers together, watched me intently.

I could never answer that question, not in a million years, not even if I had the IQ of a genius, and I wished she would stop staring at me in that intimate, knowing way. Finally, I asked, "Are you going to expel me?"

She shook her head, her face softening, turning dreamy. I remembered the way Mama's face would look gazing out the window at mountains of snow, planning all the things we were going to do in the summer: learn calligraphy, read palms, buy an opera record and sing along. We did those things—but Mama still stared out the window, Mama thought up more things to do, Mama reached for another cigarette. That's how she was, and whether her favorite color was red or blue didn't really matter.

The cat started making that throaty "eh-eh-eh" noise cats always make when they spot a bird through the window. Mrs. Lane sighed again, looked at me with immense sadness, said, "He's a house cat, but it's in his blood, this wanting to hunt, the need to kill." She stood up, glanced toward the greenhouse, rubbed her palms on her lab coat. "I can keep him locked indoors for all the days of his life, but he'll still dream of the wild outside, long for tail feathers in his claws and the neck crunching between his teeth. It's who he is." She walked into the greenhouse.

Who he is.

I listened to Mrs. Lane coo to her cat, talk unintelligible baby talk, her voice dropping into a whisper, and the cat responding with a rumbly purr. Or maybe I imagined that last bit because that's what I wanted to hear.

THAT NIGHT, after Will and Aunt Aggy were asleep and the house was very quiet, I sat at Mama's makeup table in my bedroom and stared into the mirror. I tried to hold my face perfectly still, not moving even one of those six hundred muscles in my body, but of course I was breathing, my chest rising and falling. I took a deep breath and held it; in the mirror, I looked perfectly still. But my heart—a muscle—was pumping blood through my arteries and back through my veins; close up I watched my pupils widen in my eyes, controlled by a muscle. Then I blinked, using more muscles; nerve endings in my skin were registering that the room was chilly though I wore a sweater, that the sweater was itchy; my stomach and intestines and all the organs down there that I couldn't name were digesting the meat loaf and baked potato I had eaten for supper. It was amazing how all this was going on without my being aware of it, amazing.

I let my breath gust out. Scientists could explain how blood flows and what happens to food after you swallow it and what happens when you cut your finger so it doesn't get infected. They could explain all sorts of things. And they could tell you that someone died because their heart stopped working or because a blood clot went up into their brain or because too much blood flowed out of them. There were countless reasons why the human body might stop working. But reasons-why weren't the answer to "why."

In the mirror, I watched myself raise my eyebrows, a questioning look, the look Mama gave when she didn't quite believe a story you were telling her about, say, how the vase in the living room had gotten broken. The look that meant, *Oh yeah?* My eyebrow muscles tightened and shifted, along with the muscles on my temples. I smiled so that more muscles moved: cheeks, lips, chin, a little bit of my neck. Then I frowned, tilted my head, brought my hand to the side of my face, leaned my head down into it, blinked rapidly. I circled my other arm all the way around, and I got up and jumped up and down, swinging my arms, moving my neck, locking and unlocking my fingers, twisting my waist from side to side, shrugging my shoulders, flexing my ankles—a crazy dance that made me feel every muscle I could think of, every muscle I knew, around and around I danced and hopped and wiggled and jumped and twisted and bounced and spun, until I flopped backward on my bed and lay there, staring up at the ceiling, panting slightly, my lungs pushing out and sucking in invisible air. I said, "Alice Martin, you're alive. You have six hundred muscles in your body, and you're alive." It didn't even feel strange to be talking to myself.

DANCE

M RS. LANE suggested I help her around the lab after school on Tuesdays and Thursdays. I assumed it was sort of "an offer you can't refuse," payback for stealing the frogs, but she never mentioned that. Nor did she lecture me about developing the mind of a scientist. In fact, we didn't talk much at all, just worked side by side misting and watering plants, pinching back branches, mixing up a special blend of potting soil that she'd written out on an index card like it was a treasured family recipe, planting seeds in tiny peat pots. The silence between us was like the air in the greenhouse—warm and cozy—and it was easy to forget about the drifts of snow outside, the windchill factor, when inside it felt like spring. Mrs. Lane always said, "Hello, Alice," with a glimmer of a smile when I showed up at 3:10 sharp. Even the cat usually looked up from its nap, blinking its sleepy yellow eyes. I liked Tuesdays and Thursdays. I liked school again. And Linda and Becky weren't driving me crazy anymore. If only Will were normal, everything would be about as fine as it could be.

But Linda told me Will had turned down each of the four girls who'd asked him to the barn dance—a goofy, fun, girls-invite-boys square dance in the gym where people wore overalls and silly straw hats. I pretended I knew that already and quickly made up a reason why, but that night I waited until Will got home from the movie theater to ask him about it.

"Why aren't you going?" We were in the kitchen; he was eating fingerfuls of leftover macaroni and cheese out of a Tupperware container.

"Don't want to," he said.

"You liked it last year." He and Kathy Clark had been voted cutest couple, no surprise because last year Will played basketball, and the night before the dance he had swished in the buzzer shot to beat the Ashton Chiefs, our biggest rival. And Kathy Clark was Kathy Clark—pretty, sweet, smart, best guard on the girls' basketball team, said hi to everyone no matter who they were. Even Linda couldn't find a reason to hate her. But this year Will wasn't playing basketball, for whatever reason, and everyone knew Kathy Clark was crazy over wrestler Tim Lundquist, who probably was going to win state. "Kathy was so nice," I said. "Sometimes don't you wish you were still going out with her?"

"I'm not," Will said.

"But why did—?"

"Drop it." He jammed the last bit of macaroni in his mouth, talked through it: "I blew it with Kathy Clark, and it's over. It's not like missing the barn dance is the end of the world. I don't see you racing off to ask Joe Fry. So worry about your own problems." He wiped his hands on the bottom of the tablecloth, then loosened his movie-theater necktie, pulled it up over his head. He walked into the living room. I heard the TV come on, loud, then louder.

That was a laugh and a half, Joe Fry square dancing in the gym. I took the empty Tupperware to the sink, ran cold water into it. (Dotty King may not have been everything she was cracked up to be, but she was right that soaking cheese dishes in cold water, not hot, led to easier cleanups.)

I had never been to a school dance. On those nights, I'd play crazy eights with Mama and Aunt Aggy, supposedly to console me, but Mama was the one sighing, twisting clumps of hair around one finger, acting like she was the lonely one without a date. So I had to be cheery, crack dumb jokes, let her win, tell lies about how I didn't care about school dances. On those nights she smoked more than usual, reapplying her lipstick after every cigarette though it was only me and Aunt Aggy to see her. Later, I'd dump out the overflowing ashtray, watching all those red-ringed cigarette butts fall into the garbage can.

Mama spoke suddenly: "School dances . . . what if you look across the room and there's, say, Dick Troy wearing a coat and tie, and suddenly he's not the same boy who chucked an apple core at you in the cafeteria? What if, at that moment, on that night, while they've got that song on the record player, you see Dick Troy in a way no one else has seen him before? The way he was meant to be seen?"

Dick Troy was the mailman. He wore a dopey blue uniform, drove a mail truck, read the backs of postcards, and flipped through magazines before shoving them in mailboxes.

Mama said, "Possibilities. That's the magic of school dances."

Magic again. And in the Jefferson High gym. "So how come you never went on dates?" If I asked her that when she was alive, she'd say something like, "I'll date when Prince Charming shows up at the door, or James Dean," which was the answer I wanted to hear, that things would stay the way they were, with the four of us. After a while I asked just to hear that same answer, the way kids read fairy tales over and over again. But what if Mama had gone on dates? Now, thinking about it, the idea of Mama at a movie with Dick Troy was as weird as Joe Fry square dancing. I tried to picture a man knocking on our door, Mama rushing downstairs in a swirl of skirt and perfume, kissing me and Will good-bye. Then the door opened. Who was there? I asked again, "So how come you never went on dates?" You'd think she would want to be in love, want that magic she was always talking about.

She didn't answer; all I heard was the TV, Will laughing at an old *Gilligan's Island* rerun. A minute later, I went to see what was so funny. I sat on the couch next to him, asked, "How come Mama never went on dates?"

He didn't take his eyes off the TV. "Never thought about it."

"I wouldn't have cared," I said. "I mean, if she was happy."

"I'm trying to watch this," he said. "Anyway, can you imagine Mama on a date?" He laughed again, leaned closer to the screen. "I can't even think of it."

Mama on a date, in a car with a man, sharing popcorn at the movies, sending someone a valentine. Why couldn't I see that?

WE STARTED our square-dance unit in gym class, practice for the barn dance. We had been square dancing since fourth grade, so we knew what to expect. There were benefits: No gym suits. No shower after. No stringing up volleyball nets.

But there were drawbacks, like a record called "The Grand March." Boys lined up on one side of the gym, girls on the other, and we paired off as we marched in time to the music. To combat the shifting line as boys jostled to match someone good like, say, Kathy Clark, Mrs. Kay shouted, "Ladies, step forward," so you couldn't count out who you were going to end up with. Inevitably, I got a sweaty-palmed dud or someone who sneezed into his hand a lot.

As Mrs. Kay dropped the needle on the record, I figured out I'd end up with Owen Steff, a sophomore with a perpetually runny nose. Mrs. Kay started clapping her hands, calling, "Yee-haw," while Coach Thorbeck glared.

Owen's hand felt like an old banana peel in mine. Mrs. Kay shouted, "Ladies, three steps forward!" and I was suddenly faced with Brad Claussen, the one boy in school who could be called my ex-boyfriend, though we only went out for seven weeks (two because of my guilt about the gold-chain necklace he had given me for my birthday). Now, we wouldn't even say hi in the hallway.

We marched up the center of the gym, holding hands as lightly as possible, then matched up with three more couples, making our square complete: two senior boys, two giggly sophomore girls, Doug Foltz, and Kathy Clark. Doug rolled his eyes at all of us, said, "Square dancing sucks," and stared at the clock on the gym wall. Brad yanked away his dry, chapped hand and gave Kathy a smile that showed off his dimples. She said hi to everyone, then told me she'd been seeing Will a lot at the movie theater.

"He likes working there," I said.

Brad butted into our conversation: "Bet he gets free popcorn."

I nodded, stared off at the bleachers so he wouldn't feel encouraged to make any more comments.

"How about free pop?"

I'd forgotten how raspy Brad Claussen's voice was, like sandpaper scraping. "Yes, free pop," I said. "And he can go to the movie for free on his night off. That's everything free." Kathy laughed, and Brad gave me a cold look with no dimples.

Mrs. Kay started demonstrating a new move with Coach Thorbeck that involved a lot of dipping and twisting.

Brad sidled up to Kathy. "Speaking of everything free, Paula Elam's coming back," and I hoped I hadn't heard him correctly, but Kathy's smile froze on her face, so I knew I had.

Anyone who wasn't as nice as Kathy would've said, *That slut,* but she said, "How do you know?" repeating it a couple of times, though you wouldn't expect a girl like Kathy Clark to give someone like Paula Elam a second thought.

"Her sister told me," Brad got in before Mrs. Kay bellowed, "Everybody!," and we shuffled ourselves into square-dance formation, one couple as each side of the "square." Doug jumped into the head-couple position, dragging along one giggly sophomore. She had a hard time keeping straight her left hand from her right, so our group was a total mess; somehow after "allemande-left with your left hand, right to your partner, right and left grand," I ended up holding hands with Kathy.

As Doug fussed at the sophomore about her screwup, Brad rasped, "Paula's having the baby in Iowa City. She wouldn't sign the adoption papers."

Kathy looked at me, looked away. Her voice was icy now: "Nobody cares."

Brad said, "The guy the baby's gonna look like cares."

Joe Fry. I gave Brad a hard shove, but he just laughed and made a big show of brushing off his arm where I had touched him. "What's your problem, Alice?" Seven weeks of my life wasted on him.

"Shut up," Kathy said, probably the first time in her life she had told anyone to shut up. She turned to me, whispered, "Does Will—?," but then Mrs. Kay started bawling us out for not paying attention.

Paula was coming back—with a baby in her arms, not just a lump in her stomach. Joe couldn't ignore a real baby. During "Blackberry Quadrille," I scratched Brad's wrist with my fingernail so hard he yelped. "Watch it," he snarled.

"Watch yourself." The minute I got home that gold chain was going in the trash.

Kathy Clark wouldn't look at me or Brad. And she kept messing up, though we'd been doing these dances since fourth grade. They weren't hard, just a matter of following the voice on the record. Honor your partner, honor your corner, swing, promenade, right-and-left, do-si-do, allemande-left. I liked how those simple moves with their funny names added up to a dance, how you did a grand-right-and-left, grabbing hand after hand, working your way through the square, always meeting your partner at the end. Promenade home—head back to your space with your partner. It was simple and organized.

Mrs. Kay clapped her hands. "Time to learn a new dance—'Swing Like Thunder.' "

Coach Thorbeck slapped his palm on the bleacher and barked: "Listen up. One mistake and someone gets killed," which made the dance suddenly interesting.

Mrs. Kay said, "We'll skip the steps we know and practice the grand finale, swing like thunder," and she walked over to our square. "Girls, into a circle and grab wrists. Now, loop your linked arms over the boys. Duck, boys. Boys, cluster in and put your arms on each other's shoulders." As usual, there was the grumbling that arose whenever the boys had to touch each other, but Mrs. Kay prodded us into a close, tight circle held together by our intertwined arms. "Very good," she boomed. Coach Thorbeck set the needle on the record; amplified clicks filled the gym. I was pressed between Doug and Brad; across from me, Kathy stared at the ground.

The music started; Mrs. Kay tapped one of her big boat feet (size eleven—once we had peeked at a pair of shoes in her office) and snapped her fingers. The man on the record called out for do-si-do and grand-right-and-left, the safe, simple moves we had learned way back in grade school, and Mrs. Kay yelled above the music: "When he says 'swing like thunder,' boys step in and start spinning clockwise. Girls, hold on! When you get going fast enough, your feet lift off the floor and you'll fly! Gotta be strong, boys."

"No wimps!" Coach Thorbeck shouted.

"Now!" Mrs. Kay lifted one arm. "Swing like thunder!" and the music got twangy-fast, and after some confusion about which way was clockwise, our circle shuffled around as Mrs. Kay called, "Faster!," and my arms strained and the muscles in Brad Claussen's neck ridged like a thick cord, and we kept spinning uselessly as Mrs. Kay called, "Lift your feet, girls!" then, "Let yourself go!" All I could see were the boys' eight feet, close together, taking tiny baby steps, and my feet stumbling along after them. Coach Thorbeck yanked the needle off the record and the thump of our tennis shoes on the wooden gym floor was embarrassing. We slowed down, stopped, broke our circle; I shook out my wobbly arms.

"You boys are wimps," Coach Thorbeck shouted, shaking his head in disgust.

Mrs. Kay glanced at the instruction booklet. "Girls are supposed to go flying."

"Flying smack into the wall," Coach Thorbeck said. It was nothing new to see them bicker; they were ten years into a feud over scheduling gym time for basketball practices.

Mrs. Kay marched to the record player and dropped the needle back onto the spinning record. "Everyone!" she said, clapping her hands as the music started. "Yee-haw!," and we went through the steps we knew. When the man on the record called, "Girls link up, boys duck under, everybody now, swing like thunder!," we linked and twisted and spun, and my group was a thumping, hulking mess, but the girls across the gym started shrieking. We all watched as their legs lifted off the ground, rising almost parallel to the floor. Then someone lost her grip, and just like that they tumbled and crashed, knocking into another group, falling and skidding along the polished wooden floor. Coach Thorbeck nodded with grim pleasure, his "toldyaso" as clear as if he had spoken the words.

The girls brushed dust off their clothes. No one had cried yet, but Laurie Shubatt was rubbing her elbow, blinking real hard.

Brad Claussen murmured to Doug, "They weren't swinging a bunch of cows."

Kathy whacked his shoulder. "Real men could make us swing like thunder."

Doug flexed his shoulders and slowly stretched his arms above his head, looked at how his muscles bulged in T-shirt sleeves. Then he said, "Cool," loudly, firmly, that single word pronouncing a challenge for the boys of Jefferson High: Real Men got the girls flying, Real Men could swing like thunder. Everyone started talking at once, wanting to try again, even Laurie Shubatt.

Mrs. Kay called, "People, people," but we chattered on, louder, out of control, until Coach Thorbeck whistled shrilly through his teeth and we all fell silent. Mrs. Kay abruptly said, "Class dismissed," though we had five minutes left. As I was walking to the locker room to change out of my tennis shoes, Kathy caught up with me. She spoke in a low, strained voice: "What does Will think about Paula coming back?"

"Why would he care?"

"He wouldn't—never mind." She hurried ahead, catching up with some other seniors. Her voice blended with theirs, something about the barn dance, Friday's basketball game in Fairfield, a crack about Mrs. Kay's big feet. The usual things.

Oh my God. Will. I stood by the bulletin board outside Mrs. Kay's office and stared at the fading magazine pictures showing the four basic food groups. I reached up and tore down a photo of a basket of rolls, crumpled it, dropped it on the floor, kicked it.

I couldn't say the words, couldn't.

I watched Kathy across the locker room, how her brown hair swung back and forth, how straight and even her shoulders were. She was one of those girls who'd gotten a patchwork rabbit fur coat for Christmas. Linda too; I had tried hers on though I hated those ugly coats. So did Linda; she said, "I only asked for it to see if they'd get me anything I wanted."

Could I pretend this wasn't true? "Kathy!" I called as loud as I could; my voice ricocheted off the rows of metal lockers. "Kathy!" Compared to my shout, Mrs. Kay's big voice was a whisper. Kathy whirled around, embarrassed, and we stared at each other as everyone watched, the locker room oddly silent. "What's with her?" someone murmured, but then the gossip about the barn dance started again, the discussion of how Chuck Bates rubbed his arm against girls' boobs when he did allemande-left.

Kathy hurried over to where I stood, leaning up against the bulletin board. My hair caught on a thumbtack and I yanked it free. I could hardly breathe. She dragged me by the arm into the empty showers. I listened to a drip-drip from the far showerhead, stared at a wad of hair in the central drain, at mildew on the wall directly across from where I stood, at a crusty washcloth draped across a towel rack. It could be that what I was thinking was wrong.

She set her hand on my arm; I pushed it away. "I thought you knew. He said he was going to tell you." She sounded awkward and hesitant, as if she'd never actually talked about this to anyone before.

I shook my head. But I should've known. My own brother.

"I'm sorry," she said and tried again to touch me; I backed away. She crossed her arms. I crossed my arms. We were like two people in a mirror. The first bell rang.

"But you were his girlfriend." She stood opposite me, and I thought of the square-dance call "honor your partner" where boys bowed, girls curtsied.

"He got really confused, Alice," she said. "I mean, after your mother . . ."

She looked away from me; I watched the muscles of her throat tighten as she swallowed once, twice. Then I finished her sentence: "Killed herself."

"That was hard for him."

My voice rose, making my angry words batter the drab tiles, echo across the small room: "It was hard for me too!" Will was supposed to be fine, helping to rescue baby birds and driving us safely through the ice storm on Christmas Eve. Instead he was hiding enormous secrets and running off to Boston. Like he was a stranger. What was he going to do now? I took a big step forward, putting me close enough to smell Kathy's Love's Baby Soft, the same perfume I liked. For a moment I stood right in front of her, inhaling our scent. Then she stepped back, lifted her hands as if in surrender. "I thought you knew," she whispered before turning and knocking against the rolling basket where we were supposed to drop dirty towels, hurrying away from me.

The second bell rang. I was late for American government. The gym locker room filled with more girls, the sixth-period gym class; they giggled and talked while putting on their tennis shoes, lockers slamming, the door to the gym whooshing open and shut. I heard Becky complaining about a quiz in chemistry. No one saw me, and soon the locker room was quiet again, only the faint notes of "The Grand March" penetrating the walls.

What would it be like to be Kathy, knowing this awful thing about your boyfriend, not telling anyone for all those months? She was so pretty, always so nice and happy. How could she have kept that horrible secret?

The drip seemed to be getting louder; I reached up and touched the showerhead with one finger. Doing that didn't really stop the ice-cold water, only diverted it so it rolled down my hand, soaking into the edge of my sweater sleeve.

Will wasn't supposed to do things like that. Not Will, not my brother. He hadn't cried at Mama's funeral, and I had thought that was so brave and strong of him, so perfect. But maybe it wasn't. Maybe it was just . . . lonely.

"You couldn't have known." Mama's whisper felt intimate in this small, enclosed space, like silk on skin, the flicker of a shadow. "You couldn't have known," she repeated.

Her favorite color was red. Will had that gap between his front teeth that I loved. Was everything I knew so tiny and ultimately meaningless? It was like something solid and heavy whacked me in the stomach, once, twice, it wouldn't stop until I bent and threw up. Afterward, I leaned to turn on the shower, watched the water hit the floor and wash down the drain. Then I hurried out of the locker room, leaving the water running, and I walked all the way home without my coat or books.

AUNT AGGY was upstairs in her "studio." I had even started calling it that instead of "Mama's room." What with the half-finished paintings stacked along the wall and the smell of oil paint and turpentine, there wasn't much of Mama left anyway. The easel was set up, but Aunt Aggy was staring out the window that faced the backyard. I cleared my throat a couple of times as I stood in the doorway, but she kept looking out the window, chewing on the wooden end of a paintless paintbrush.

What I had found out from Kathy was another big secret to keep, like Mr. Stryker and the train and Joe Fry. How many could one person have? But telling Aunt Aggy would mean I'd have to hear the words, say them. Finally I asked, "Are you painting?" A canvas was propped on the easel, and as usual, this picture didn't look like anything I could see. Eggs in a nest maybe. A giant coat button. A really weird flower.

"Valentine's Day present for Mr. Cooper," she said. "I'm calling it *The Most Ultimate Essence of Love*." She took the paintbrush out of her mouth, stared at the bitten end, then launched into a one-sided discussion of pink versus yellow versus blue.

I alternately shook my head and nodded, soothed by her rambling. Maybe I could forget about Will in her avalanche of artistic theory and paintbrush waving—"if you listen to Picasso . . . Degas asserted . . . Gauguin conjectured . . . ," as if they had all been chatting on the phone the other day, and it went on until she abruptly interrupted herself to say: "I'll probably never be married. There, now I've said it." She blinked quickly, stared down at her suddenly still hands.

I was surprised. For at least three years she had been referring to herself in public as Mr. Cooper's eventual fiancée. And if he wasn't going to marry her, who would? He actually hung her paintings on the wall. That had to be the "ultimate essence of love." I said, "You know Mr. Cooper loves you. He's shy."

She wrapped all her fingers around the paintbrush, and I thought she was going to snap it in two. But she set aside the brush, smiled brightly, fakely. "I know. Ignore me and my twinges of despair. Artists are *très* moody." Then she tucked a strand of loose hair up under her beret. "Your friend's father was over here asking questions," she said, and I stared at my knuckles, which turned whiter as I tightened my grip on the door frame, thinking she meant Paula's father, until she said, "Linda," and I let go of the door frame.

Aunt Aggy stepped closer to the easel, peered at the painting. "She's gone, so's her mother. Her father was half crazy, asking did I know anything, did you know anything. I guess the landlord in Iowa City said she gave notice over the weekend with time left on her rent check. Now all four kids are gone."

Becky told me Linda called saying she had the flu and would we take notes for her? "Where'd they go?" I asked.

"Nobody knows." Aunt Aggy kept staring at *The Most Ultimate Essence of Love,* tilting her head from side to side, like a metronome.

"Are they coming back?" My voice was louder with each word, with each unanswered question. "How could they just leave?"

Aunt Aggy said, "That sweet Sandy Johnson—first to organize a PTA bake sale to raise money for band uniforms, those gorgeous rosebushes she babied. Now she's a divorcée on the lam with her kids. Next thing you know she's robbing banks like Patty Hearst." Aunt Aggy unscrewed the cap off the tube of paint. The sun suddenly emerged from behind a cloud, and a square of light shone through the window. Dust particles glittered and swirled and spun. "You think you know someone," she said. "Goes to show."

Like Will. I thought about how maybe he and Paula had gotten drunk at a party, or she happened to be walking through the school parking lot at the same time. Or maybe he called her up. Paula with her lipstick and her dead sister.

Aunt Aggy squeezed an inch of red onto her palette, wiggled her brush in the paint. It was all so crazy, all of it, and though Aunt Aggy said, "I can paint and talk at the same time," I went to my room and flopped facedown onto the bed. The words from "Swing Like Thunder" spun through my head, mixing with "Will and Paula, Will and Paula" and "Linda-Linda-Linda."

Linda was supposed to be homecoming queen and Henry County pork queen and marry whoever asked her first and have two girls and two boys—she had their names picked out. But now Linda was gone, on her way to California, Chicago, New York, Paris. I rolled over and looked at the dusty globe on the bookcase.

Mama said, "The world is tiny; there's no escape."

I stared at the globe, at big sprawling China. "Escape from what?"

"Who you are," she said.

Did people in China kill themselves? "You're my mother," I said. "What's wrong with who you are?"

"The magic is finding someone who sees who you really are, that person you want to be. When you find someone who loves you. Like that boy?"

Joe Fry wasn't the kind of boy girls were supposed to fall in love with. His hair was too long, and he drove too fast; he probably wasn't planning to go to the University of Iowa or Iowa State, but he wasn't going to farm either. Who knew what he was going to do? Boys like Brad Claussen—whose father owned the feed-and-grain store—were boys to fall in love with.

"You can love any kind of boy," Mama said.

Without meaning to, I murmured, "Roy Stryker."

Her voice was flat, final: "He died. He left me."

So did you—but I couldn't bear to say it out loud. I had loved my mother so much but that wasn't enough. I carefully said, "You know, there was no guarantee you two were going to get married and live happily ever after."

She said, "No one gets that guarantee. Not even people like Dick Troy."

I stared up at the ceiling. An old cobweb swayed from side to side in a breeze I couldn't feel; it was hypnotic to watch its back-and-forth movement, like dancing to silent music. I probably watched for ten minutes. But finally I stood up on the bed, stretched as tall as I could, jumped a little, and knocked the cobweb loose.

"What about Will and the baby?" I asked. "And Paula? What am I supposed to do?" Where was Mama with all her advice now? The room stayed very, very quiet, the way it was in the biology lab when I worked with Mrs. Lane. I let the silence fill me. I had loved Mama as much as I could. I wasn't her father or Mr. Stryker or anyone but me, and, yes, I had loved my mother absolutely as much as I knew how.

· · ·

WILL DIDN'T come home for supper, and I was almost happy not to see him, practically crossing my fingers that he had run away again, escaping this big mess. The turkey potpie—usually my favorite—was glops of paste going down because all I could think of was how eventually Will would tell me that what I had heard was true. And then what would I say?

After I washed the dishes and swept the floor, I watched five minutes of TV, called Becky, who had just left for basketball practice, dialed Linda's number and let the phone ring thirty times, wandered upstairs to stare out my bedroom window, went downstairs to look out the kitchen window. "You're worse than a cat!" Aunt Aggy exclaimed, watching me pace from the living room to the kitchen. But I couldn't stand the quiet house any longer: I had to ask Will, had to hear him tell me what had happened.

So I borrowed Aunt Aggy's car and drove to the movie theater. *Barry Lyndon* was playing, which Becky, Linda, and I had seen last week. Linda had mentioned her mother only once: "My mom's freaking out because she's gained ten pounds since Christmas. Maybe I'll get the clothes that don't fit her." Nothing that hinted at kidnapping.

I waved at the ticket booth, where Mrs. Arn was rubber-banding a handful of dollar bills, and walked inside the theater. The movie had already started, so the lobby was empty, except for Will sweeping spilled popcorn by the drinking fountain. Susie Hill was working the concession stand; she had the popcorn machine running, and fluffy kernels overflowed the kettle, filling the lobby with a buttery smell and such rapid-fire popping that Will didn't hear me until I was right next to him. "Jesus Christ, Alice!" He dropped the broom, which clattered against the drinking fountain and banged onto the floor. "You scared me."

There was no door to the theater, only a curtain, so once the popcorn stopped, it was easy to hear the previews. Something that sounded like a car chase. I leaned over and picked up the broom, which I held on to, swinging it back and forth. If only during the grand march Mrs. Kay hadn't said, "Ladies, three steps forward," I would've been with Owen

Steff, I wouldn't know what I knew about Will, and I wouldn't be here wondering what to say.

Will held out one hand for the broom, but I kept swaying it from side to side. He gave me a look like he wanted to smack me, like he was suddenly too old for anything fun, and for the first time I realized that my brother was going to be a father. Paula's baby was related to me.

I took a deep breath, stared at the broom handle, at all the chips in the black paint. "I heard something about Paula Elam today."

He put his thumb on the drinking fountain, pushed the button so water arced up. We both watched it. Then he said, "She's coming back."

"You know?"

He pulled his hand away from the drinking fountain. People in the theater laughed. "I called her on Christmas."

I took my hand off the broom; it balanced for a second before falling onto the floor. Neither of us reached to pick it up.

"We've been talking since then." Will stared at the popcorn stand. Susie was wiping the counter clean with long, smooth strokes, running the rag over the same spot, probably trying to eavesdrop. Her brother was a policeman in Iowa City. Her other brother worked on the farm with her father. "What do you want me to say?" Will's words came out choked.

I was hypnotized by the nice, even rhythm of Susie's arm. I could watch her wipe that counter forever. But she walked over to the popcorn machine and sprinkled salt over the mound of popcorn, stirring it with a metal scoop. "So it's true?" I whispered.

"I wanted to tell you," he said. "But when it happened, you were . . . we were . . ."

The theater felt silent. Even the movie was suddenly quiet—I imagined a couple kissing, a close-up turning them huge and fake on the screen. How could I not have known? "When?" I demanded. I could guess what he'd say because I could say the same thing: Last summer, one night, it just happened, our mother's dead.

"Does it matter?" he said. "A bunch of times. She—"

Susie interrupted, calling, "Alice, want some just-popped popcorn?"

I tried to sound cheerful: "No thanks."

"Anyway, now you know." He tried to smile, then bit his lip, crossed his arms, uncrossed them, seemed unsure of where to put them, like maybe there was something wrong with how they were attached to his body. He went on: "Sort of a relief, I guess. Not telling anyone didn't mean it hadn't happened, that Paula wasn't . . . Even after she left, she wasn't gone, if you know what I mean. This is better, I guess, everyone finally going to know. At least it's real now, not like some crazy nightmare."

I would never forget this moment or anything about it—the broom, the popcorn, the drinking fountain, *Barry Lyndon,* how I felt hearing him say, *I called her on Christmas.* My brother. Will.

He said, "I think maybe we're going to get married."

"You can't do that," I said, and the words sounded stupid. Who would stop him? "Joe told me about the scout from the Chicago Cubs. And what about the Boston Red Sox?"

He ignored me. "Paula and I talked about it, and that's what we want."

"What about the Red Sox?" I repeated.

He sighed. "There are twenty-five guys on the Red Sox. Out of all the guys in the country, in the world. I never thought for a minute I'd play baseball for real."

Yes, he did—so did I. "How come you never told me any of this?" I slapped the drinking fountain with my open palm, and he grabbed my hand, held on to it before I pulled free.

He scowled. "There are things you haven't told me. Like Joe Fry." He crossed his arms hard against his chest, pinning down and wrinkling his necktie. I wanted to reach over and tug it loose.

I wished he would call me "Baby Sister," his affection safely disguised as an insult. But he was right; we both had our own secrets now, each one putting another mile between us, like two cars driving fast in opposite directions. My voice rose: "But what are you going to do?" Susie glanced up from the popcorn counter.

He stared at me silently, unmoving, until the tension lines eased from his face. Then he spoke quietly: "I'm going to marry Paula and work at the movie theater and be a father and a husband."

I couldn't believe he used those words: *Father. Husband.* He was a boy, a brother. "You went to Boston once," I said. "Go back. She'll never find you. We'll both go."

"I'm not going to Boston," he said. "I tried doing that—I can't." I had never seen my brother cry, not even at Mama's funeral, and there he was, slumping against the drinking fountain, tears sliding down his cheeks, one after the other. He didn't even wipe them away.

I stared at the broom on the floor, at the popcorn strewn across the black-and-white-checkered carpeting. Nothing was how it was supposed to be: Mama, Will, Linda. "Why?" wasn't a question that made sense. "Does Paula love you?" I asked.

He said, "I thought about that baby going out into the world, thinking he had no one, and I couldn't stand it. Like us. How could I do the same thing?"

It all made sense when he said it that way. But still, nothing made sense.

He wiped his cheeks with the edge of his sleeve and picked up the broom.

So this was it. He was leaving me for real.

I said the first mean thing I thought of: "I can't believe you let everyone think it was Joe Fry."

His face hardened back into the face of a boy who never cried. "I never said he did it. Everyone thought exactly what they wanted to think, including you. Admit it." He started sweeping, pulling popcorn kernels out from under the drinking fountain, drawing them into a pile on the carpet. "I've got to get back to work," he said, as the broom scratched rhythmically. "I'm a father," and he gave a half laugh, and yes, technically he was, but as I watched him moving the broom back and forth, all I saw was my brother.

EVERYONE AT school seemed to have a tough time deciding which rumor was juicier: Linda running away/being kidnapped/joining a band of gypsies or Paula giving birth to her love child/Mr. Rhinehart's baby/Will Martin's kid. Versions varied greatly depending on who was the one doing the telling. As the last person who had actually spoken to

Linda, Becky got lots of attention. By third period she was claiming Linda
had called from a truck stop in Kansas. Luckily, people stopped gossiping
about Will if I was around.

Kathy Clark wasn't in gym class. We did "Swing Like Thunder"
again, and as we spun, the other girls in my square squealed as their feet
flew off the ground, but my feet stayed on the floor, stumbling and
trudging along. Then Pam Kessler's hand slipped, and she flew out of the
square, smashing into the bleachers so hard that she got sent to the
nurse's office. After that we half-heartedly did "Virginia Reel" and "Dive
for Oyster, Dip for Clam." Neither gave girls lumps on their heads,
though no one's feet flew up in the air either.

As we headed to the locker room, Mrs. Kay boomed, "Barn dance
next Saturday! Invite your beaux!" Hearing that made me crabby because
I knew I'd spend dance night playing crazy eights with Aunt Aggy and
Becky. The idea of Joe Fry square dancing was ridiculous.

Mama whispered, "Are you in love with him?"

Could she shut up about that? I didn't want to be in love with any
boy—but especially not with Joe Fry. I shoved my gym shoes in my
locker, slammed the door, snapped shut the lock and spun the numbered
dial, zero to thirty-nine.

Mama said, "More than air to breathe, sometimes what you need is
the right kiss."

The locker room started filling with girls from the next class,
including Becky, who sat by me, watching as I spun the lock dial around.
Finally she asked, "Will Linda come back?" She asked a couple more
times, but I ignored her. Could she just shut up too? People left other
people behind all the time. Finally I looked up from the white numbers
on the black dial and said straight out, "No one knows," though that
wasn't what Becky wanted to hear. She walked away. The second bell
rang, and I lined up the zero with the tick mark, gave it one last spin, and
left without looking at what number it ended on.

WHEN WILL confessed the whole story about Paula, Aunt Aggy nearly
had the breakdown she'd been threatening all these years. She hyperven-

tilated and hiccuped all at once. After she breathed into a paper bag for ten minutes and could talk again, she yelled that he was grounded forever, which must have sounded as ridiculous to her as it did to us, because then she shouted, "What else am I supposed to do?" Will sighed, shook his head, and walked out of the house, leaving the door hanging wide so cold air blew in. A minute later the car started up and he was gone. Aunt Aggy crumpled the paper bag, burst into tears. There was nothing to say. I went to close the door. "Don't lock it," Aunt Aggy said through her sobs, "in case he forgot his key."

I sat at the kitchen table that night, waiting for him, all the Agatha Christie mystery paperbacks I owned stacked next to me. I was rereading the last chapters, where everything was revealed. The gardener did it. The wife. The man with the limp. It was always so obvious when it was explained and you saw all those clues you had missed.

The sky through the window was lightening into gray when Will came through the door, car keys dangling in his hand. When he saw me, he shoved them in his pants pocket and sat opposite me, where he'd be "head couple" if we were lined up for a square dance. He put his hands flat on the table, stared at them. So did I, thinking of those hands throwing a no-hitter last summer.

He said, "Paula and I talked to her parents. It's all settled: We're getting married and after I graduate, Mr. Elam is giving me a job in the bank."

Married. Job. Bank. Will wasn't actually leaving Shelby. But he was getting married. Married.

Will swished one hand in front of my face. "Hello?"

"Congratulations," I said, what you were supposed to say when someone got married.

"It wasn't so awful," Will said. "I mean, her dad was mad, but later he told me he wanted someone to follow him into the bank, and none of those girls was going to."

"That's good," I said. "I guess."

Will smiled very quickly, almost shyly, as if embarrassed. "When I left, he said, 'Good night, son.'"

What was I supposed to say to that? He wasn't Mr. Elam's son. My voice was harsh: "I guess you're going to live with them in that nice house and eat steak for supper and drive to the bank with Mr. Elam in his Cadillac?"

He looked away. "Yeah." That was a million times worse to hear than anything Brad Claussen had said or Kathy Clark in the locker room or Will in the movie theater or Will telling Aunt Aggy.

"You should've stayed in Boston," I said, not sure if I meant it.

"I couldn't. I'm not like that." He closed his eyes. "I wish I knew if I'm doing the right thing."

The kitchen was so quiet I wanted to scream just so it wouldn't be quiet anymore. But when Will said, "I miss Mama," that urge disappeared.

"Almost a year," I said softly.

"My baby won't know her." Then he whispered, "Why did she do it? I always thought she was so happy."

In the dark, the refrigerator bumped on, whirring lightly. Did everyone's life lead to one question that had no answer? I turned over his hands and rested my palms in his. His skin wasn't chapped or sweaty, but warm and smooth. Had I ever touched my brother this way? "You're doing the right thing," which I said though I didn't know if he was or not—said especially since I didn't know.

THE BARN dance was the night before Valentine's Day. As predicted, Becky, Aunt Aggy, and I were sitting around the kitchen table getting ready to play crazy eights. ("Better than old maid," Becky muttered as she sat down.) Mr. Cooper was picking up Aunt Aggy for their day-early Valentine celebration, Saturday being a more festive day than Sunday, and she kept reminding us: "Only got a half hour, girls." She hadn't finished *The Most Ultimate Essence of Love* (though I couldn't tell), so she had bought Mr. Cooper handkerchiefs on which she had embroidered *X*s and *O*s for kisses and hugs. "Not the same as a masterwork, but . . ." She shrugged. "True art will not be rushed."

I shuffled, noisily flicking the cards down, then arcing them into a bridge. Mama had taught me that. "Just like Vegas," she had said, as if she were an authority.

Becky (who had seen plenty of Aunt Aggy's masterworks) asked, "How do you know what you've painted if it doesn't look like something specific, the way a picture of a horse looks like a horse?" I couldn't tell if she was just being her usual polite self or seriously wanted to know.

"It looks like how you feel," Aunt Aggy said. "Anyone can draw a picture of a horse."

"Not me, I'm terrible at drawing," Becky said.

Aunt Aggy spoke louder (she hated interruptions): "The point is, art is no longer mere imitation. Take *The Most Ultimate Essence of Love*. No one understands what love is. Certainly not *moi*." She flicked a crumb off the table, then snapped, "Those cards are certainly shuffled, Alice," so I dealt out eight cards apiece. "Artists explore the mystery; we don't define it."

Becky took off her glasses, carefully wiped the lenses on the bottom of her turtleneck, taking a long time polishing them. She looked pink-faced and embarrassed, sorry she had spoken. I didn't blame her. Maybe if Aunt Aggy stopped lecturing us about art and simply said, *I hope and pray Mr. Cooper proposes tonight*, we could relax a little.

"You start," I said to Aunt Aggy, hoping to get her involved in the game and avoid further talk about painting and the essence of love.

She still seemed a bit sulky as she flipped over the top card on the deck, but she exclaimed, "Clubs! My lucky suit!," and we got going, slapping down cards, making jokes, laughing, eating popcorn (teasing Aunt Aggy because she had accidentally sprinkled it with garlic salt instead of regular). It was the night it was supposed to be. Except that nothing was how it was supposed to be anymore.

Mr. Cooper was late. Aunt Aggy pretended she wasn't staring at the clock—not that the clock was telling her anything useful, because it still needed a new battery (since the fall). It was driving me crazy that every time she looked she saw 10:35 but didn't seem to notice.

Finally, just as Aunt Aggy gleefully slapped an eight on top of my eight, there was a loud knock on the front door. She stood up, grabbed her purse and the handkerchiefs (which she'd stuffed inside an old heart-shaped candy box), tossed her last two cards on the table. "Bye-bye, girls," she said, her voice a hundred notes higher than usual. Tap-tap went her shoes on the kitchen floor, turning to thumps on the carpet in the living room. "Hell-ooo!" she called as I heard the front door swing open. "Happy-Valentine's-Day-a-day-early!"

"I'll make nongarlicky popcorn," I said, standing up.

Before I could get to the stove, Aunt Aggy was back, glaring at me. "That boy."

My heart practically spun around. "Joe?"

Becky clapped her hands. "Like a white knight rescuing you!"

Aunt Aggy said, "More like a two-bit hood if you ask me, the kind that breaks your heart," and she sat down, picked up her cards. "Do you know what you're doing, Alice?"

"I think it's romantic!" Becky bounced in her chair, almost as excited as when Mr. Miller absentmindedly said hi to her in the school cafeteria.

Aunt Aggy stared at her cards as if she could see the future mapped out in them. I didn't even care if she could; I spoke loudly: "You're wrong about Joe!"

"You have to understand," she started, but I ran from the kitchen to the front door, yanked it open. There was Joe, arms folded across his jeans jacket, leaning up against the side of the house, covering the numbers of our address. The tips of his bare ears were pink from the cold. I wanted to jump in his arms and let him twirl me around; I wanted to kiss him forever. But I didn't even know what to say and it seemed like he didn't either. A cold wind whirled into me, making me shiver.

Finally he said, "Thought we were going to the barn dance."

"Barn dance?"

"Remember asking me?"

How could I forget asking someone to a dance? But then he laughed, and I gave him a friendly little shove. "Liar. I almost believed you."

"Want to go?"

"School dances don't seem like your kind of thing."

He shrugged. "Maybe not. But if we go, everyone will know."

"Know what?" I asked, almost a whisper, afraid of what he was going to say, wasn't.

He reached for a piece of my hair, rubbed it gently between his fingers and thumb. "You're pretty," he said, not answering my question at the same time he answered it.

"Come in while I change clothes." I opened the door wider. "Take over my crazy eights hand." I was joking, but that's what he did while I ran upstairs to put on a clean pair of Levi's, my blue blouse, a bra without worn elastic, and real lipstick that I slid on my lips while sitting at Mama's dressing table, looking in Mama's mirror. The color, light pink, was called Sugar-Bare. My lips felt thick, as if smeared with jelly leftover from toast, and my hand was going to wipe off the lipstick, when my elbow knocked into the Kleenex box. I grabbed a tissue instead, kissed it while I thought of Joe Fry, looked at the circle of my lips on the tissue, then back in the mirror.

Something was still missing, so I sprayed Mama's White Shoulders into that little hollow at the base of my neck and watched the liquid glisten before evaporating. Was I pretty?

Mama murmured, "You're beautiful."

I kept watching myself in the mirror. I smiled, looked pouty, smiled again. "Doesn't count. You're supposed to say that." I tilted my head one way and another.

"Only someone who loves you can see you how you want to be seen."

I had never thought of Mama as a woman who longed to sit across from a man over supper. She was just Mama, who wore red lipstick everywhere, even to Hy-Vee; and baked the best cakes in town; and thought every book report I wrote for school was brilliant. My mother, Linda's mother, were mothers, not girls on dates. But was that my fault? I was her daughter who loved her—but always and only the daughter— and that would never change, no matter what I found out about Mama. "I wish that had been enough for you," I said.

It seemed as if something fluttered in the mirror, but when I glanced behind me, nothing was there. "Anyway, I'm not ready to be in love," I said.

"It's not like a picnic to get ready for," she said. "It just sweeps you away. Then anything can happen."

Anything can happen. I felt a tingly chill nip along my neck, either fear or anticipation, I couldn't be sure.

"No!" she cried. "Don't you see? After Mr. Stryker, how could I love someone knowing it won't last forever? Knowing they'll break your heart, they'll leave, they'll die?"

"Well, I think you just have to," I said, watching my lips in the mirror as they framed the words, almost as if it was someone else talking, someone much smarter who happened to look like me. "You just have to," I repeated, enjoying watching myself talk in the mirror. Then I closed my eyes, said, "You shouldn't have given up, Mama." My heartbeat quickened, but I was right: what I said and saying it. I opened my eyes and there I was in the mirror.

Joe was waiting. I picked up the perfume, sprayed a bit more on my neck, my wrists.

Mama whispered, "You want him to smell you a room away."

I looked at myself one last time in the mirror, then left. Though I wasn't in there anymore, I was sure my room smelled of White Shoulders, of me. That was how it was with Mama—you could always smell where she had been, the room she had just left, as if she liked to linger.

Downstairs, Becky gave me a little hug and whispered, "Bet he kisses you!"; Aunt Aggy told me to be careful, then added, "You should listen to people who know what they're talking about," but couldn't she see I was tired of listening, that going with Joe was something I wanted to do, something that felt right, no matter how it worked out? I told her I'd be home by midnight and kissed her cheek.

Joe helped me slip on my coat, and he even opened my car door, like the boys in *Seventeen* magazine. Mr. Cooper came up the road as we were backing out of the driveway; I waved to him, and he was so surprised that he waved back despite his usual shyness. I tried to see if he looked ready to propose, but Joe was driving too fast.

Joe said, "I haven't been to a school dance."

"I guess they're fun," I said. "My mother . . ."

He slowed the car, pulled a pair of battered gloves out of his coat pockets. "What about your mother?" His voice wasn't tight the way other people's voices were when they said things to me like "Your mother."

"Was always nagging at me to go," I finished.

"Well, we should go." We were at the stop sign on Gilbert where you turned left to get to the school. He pulled his gloves on. Then he went straight instead.

I hunched down in my seat, crossed my arms, stared out the window as we drove around the square downtown, taking the corners too fast. The hardware store had hand-lettered signs in the window: "Snow-Blower Sale," and a man in a plaid jacket with the collar up was walking into Whit's Bar. Then we were out of downtown, heading to Prairie du Chien, I assumed, to the cemetery. I bit down on my lower lip, feeling some of the lipstick come off on the back of my teeth.

He asked, "All this time you thought I was the one with Paula Elam, didn't you?"

"No," I said. "Not at all. Never."

"Doesn't matter."

"I didn't." We passed the Johnsons' house; there was a porch light on, but no other lights and no cars in the driveway. I still wouldn't look at Joe.

"Your brother's amazing to do what he's doing. Lot of guys wouldn't."

"Would you?" I asked suddenly. "Never mind." If he said yes, I wouldn't believe him. If he said no, I'd hate him.

He said, "You don't ever really know unless you're there. People are braver or stupider than you'd think, or both."

"So is Will doing the right thing?"

"What do you think?"

I finally looked at him at the same time he turned to face me. In the dark, I felt him watching me, anticipating my answer. I said, "I don't know. I mean, his whole life will be different now. Forever."

He nodded, turned his gaze back to the road. "So's the kid's life. So's hers. So's everything. It's all connected."

I thought of everyone else back in the gym, square dancing with their partners. It was such an organized dance, with the rules and calls and the right way to do things. Like when that sophomore girl had put in her right hand instead of her left and that one tiny thing messed up the whole dance until we were just a tangle of partners looking at each other across the square instead of promenading home.

Joe went on: "Or maybe nothing's changed. Since it wasn't anything before, who's to say something's changed? The future's the future, only what we think will happen. But hardly anything happens the way we think. And the past—we make it up afterward. Two people remember everything different. You look at it that way, and all we've got is the present. That's the only thing that matters, the only thing we half understand." He banged the steering wheel with one hand.

No matter what, I liked that he said things no one else did. I asked, "Did you know about Will all along?"

He shrugged one shoulder. "That way you know something without anyone having to tell you."

We were passing Dane's Dairy, where Mama used to take us for ice-cream cones in the summer and they still sold milk in glass bottles. When I was younger, I had imagined going there with my missing father, talking and staring at each other over double dips. Mr. and Mrs. Dane had been married for sixty years; there had been a big article in the *Beacon* about their anniversary party. I said, "Where are we going, anyways?"

He seemed surprised. "Just driving. Thought you liked that."

I uncrossed my arms, watched his face in the dark. He stared straight ahead at the road, then reached over and put his hand on my knee. I put my hand on top of his hand. I could do it a million times and never feel as close to someone as I felt to him right that second. I said, "I thought it was you with Paula. I'm sorry."

"People believe what's easiest to believe," he said. "That's always how it is."

For several miles, I felt a peaceful silence between us, like an enormous, round moon hovering just above the horizon on a winter night, the kind of moon you want to wrap your arms around and hold on to. But next thing you know, it's already climbed to the peak of that cold, black sky, beyond reach, remote once again, distant. So I didn't interrupt the quiet, though I had more questions: *Why didn't you tell me about Will? Why did you let me think you were the one with Paula?*

Then he spoke: "We could drive to Canada if we wanted. This road takes us north."

"Canada!" I sat up straighter, startled, and he took his hand off my leg, put it loosely on the steering wheel. That silence had seemed so comfortable to me, but all along he had been thinking about Canada.

"My brother's up there," he said. "You know, the draft thing."

No one talked about it much anymore, but the night after getting his lottery number, Joe's brother packed up and left. His family got a postcard. It was about as sudden as what Mama had done. No wonder Joe liked markers of where people had been. "He can't ever come back, can he?" I asked.

"He likes it up there," Joe said. "Good hunting. Fishing. A girl-friend. He sent me a picture of her sitting in front of a tent in the woods."

To never come back. All I could say was, "Sounds great." I wasn't very convincing.

Joe's eyes stayed on the dark highway. "Says he can get me a job in the restaurant where he works."

"You're going to Canada?"

"I mean, if I want," he said quickly. "He was just saying. If that's what I want."

The dashed yellow lane dividers in front of us turned into a solid stripe. *Do not pass.* Then dashes again. *Pass with care.* "Canada," I said. "That's another country."

"It's just up the road. So not completely like another country. They speak English." He was talking too fast, like saying something you've never said out loud before. "But if it isn't Canada, it's somewhere. I'm going somewhere."

The car suddenly seemed stuffy, and I rolled down the window all the way, letting wind romp through. My hair blew all around in a big clockwise circle, ending up in my mouth, across my eyes, a tangled mess.

Finally, he called over the wind, "You knew that, didn't you?"

I wanted to shout as loud as I could: NO!—but he was right. I did know that.

. . .

WHEN WE were almost at Cedar Rapids, we turned around and drove back. We talked about school and teachers, and whether anyone had discovered the dead frogs in the cemetery, things like that.

Back in Shelby, he braked at the stop sign where we could either go to my house or to the school. It was late. The dance was probably over. It was just a school dance, really, the same people I saw every day square dancing in the gym. What was magical about that? The car rumbled. Two dogs barked back and forth, a low, deep bark and a higher, quicker bark. "Turn," I said finally.

He did, and we headed toward the school. The parking lot was still pretty full; two couples pushed through the gym doors, and light spilled onto the snowy grass. Joe and I walked up the stairs to the double doors, and he pulled one open, held it as I walked through. Even inside the hallway to the gym, where the trophy cases were, you could hear that the music was louder than when we were in gym class, and people were shouting, "Yee-haw!" I recognized "Hinky Dinky," an easy dance we had learned all the way back in grade school.

Joe turned to me and sang along with the record, " 'Hinky dinky, parlez-vous,' " and I laughed.

We passed a couple of sophomores in overalls making out by the drinking fountain. The boy was so absorbed in what he was doing that he didn't notice he'd leaned up against the bar that made the water spurt, and the back of his overalls was soaked. Joe rolled his eyes, smiled at me, and grabbed my hand.

We walked into the gym: bales of hay all along the foot of the bleachers, big tempera-painted signs that said things like, "Party Till The Cows Come Home!!!," folding tables with red-and-white-checked tablecloths, a scarecrow with a "Mr. Rhinehart" name tag. All that, and everyone wearing overalls and straw hats and bandannas and flannel shirts, but it was still a gym. They couldn't hide the basketball nets. No one had taken down the gym mats. Under the smell of hay was the smell of sweat.

Why had I wanted to come here?

We peeled off our coats and dropped them onto a bunch of others piled on the bleachers. "Hinky Dinky" seemed to have no end. I didn't look at Joe.

Everyone was dancing and laughing, do-si-doing, grand-right-and-lefting, bowing. It was so goofy. Didn't they know we were in the gym? Didn't they see that these dances were silly?

"Alice," Joe said, and when I turned my head, he kissed me—not a we're-friends kiss, not a gotta-do-this-to-get-sex kiss, but the kiss you don't realize you've been waiting for until that exact moment you're getting it. I wanted it to last forever because I knew right then that it might be the best kiss I would ever have—but it was already over.

He slipped one arm around my shoulder as his foot tapped to "Hinky Dinky"; " 'Hinky dinky, parlez-vous,' " he sang, and my foot started tapping in time with his.

Kathy Clark walked by hand in hand with Tim Lundquist. "Hi, Alice," she said, with her big, bright, nice smile. "Someone left from our square—you can join us if you want." Joe and I followed her to the other side of the gym, getting there just as the music ended.

"Last dance!" Mrs. Kay fanned herself with one hand. "Everyone on your feet!"

The last dance could've been anything—"Birdie in the Cage" or "Texas Star" or a million different dances—but Mrs. Kay said, " 'Swing Like Thunder,' " and everyone whooped and stomped the floor.

Kathy was flushed, her feathered bangs spiky with sweat. It could've been Will lining up with her as head couple, but it was Tim Lundquist. For now. Come spring or summer—or next week—it might be some other boy. That was the chance you took, and maybe the only thing to do was not think about that, at least not now, not when the last dance was about to begin.

Mrs. Kay set the needle on the record, and after a few seconds of scratchy silence, twangy music filled the gym.

We went through the beginning steps, the easy moves we had learned so long ago and had been doing all our school lives: do-si-do, allemande-left, right-hand star.

My lipstick had been bitten off, and you could only smell my perfume if you pressed your nose against my neck, but I felt beautiful. And

Joe. Joe looked good square dancing—gray long underwear tight across his chest, untucked flannel shirt hanging open, faded Levi's, scuffy boots, wearing what everyone else wore but wearing it better. And then what I saw beyond the clothes: the boy who missed his brother, who picked up acorns off the ground.

I was about to say something—the perfect words we would always remember—when the man on the record called, "Girls link up, boys duck under, everybody now, swing like thunder!," and we grabbed hold of each other, held as tight as we could. The boys spun fast, faster, tightened our circle and whirled, and suddenly my feet lifted off the ground, and I couldn't stop laughing, and Joe cried, "Alice! Look at you! You're flying!"

TIME

J O E wasn't my boyfriend the way it usually worked, standing at my locker between classes or saving me a seat at lunch. Instead we went for long drives in his Mustang and we talked. We didn't go to the cemetery, but we went other places. I told him I wasn't going to do it again right away, but there were other things we did. Becky would ask, "So is he your boyfriend or what?" and I'd say, "Or what," until she stopped asking.

He told me about his brother, showed me the Swiss Army knife he'd left behind for Joe and explained how he carried it everywhere because that's what Johnny had done; how Johnny had mailed him the last two hundred bucks he needed to buy the Mustang. Joe would be gone one day. If not to Canada, then to somewhere else far away. I could understand now how people left—sometimes suddenly—and calendar pages continued to turn from winter to spring, spring to summer. It was simple, yet of course it wasn't, not when you were the one left holding on to a Swiss Army knife or acorn or makeup table. That was why I liked to hear Joe talk about his brother: His voice lingered over the words, he spoke slowly and deliberately, sometimes with his eyes closed, as if he were seeing his brother's face, as if Johnny were right there with us. At those moments—Joe's breath floating white and frosty, bluish moonlit shadows slipping across the snowy cornfield—I could almost see Johnny, too, though I barely remembered what he had looked like.

Will drove up to Iowa City a lot to visit Paula, sometimes going with the Elams (he called them Larry and Mary Pat); most of the time, though, he went by himself. Paula was fine, he told me, staying with a family friend. "She keeps rereading that Dr. Spock baby book," he said. "You should hear her talk about croup. Like she's a real mother." He sounded amazed but also terrified. I did what I could: baked peanut butter cookies for Paula, didn't complain that he was hogging the car, pretended I hadn't found the spring-training baseball scores deep in the tiny print of the *Register*. The baby still wasn't real, not all the way. But at least it wasn't going to be an enormous secret for the rest of Will's life.

Mrs. Elam was arranging the wedding, a small ceremony for only family after the baby was born. Will didn't care ("All I do is show up on time"), and when Paula called to ask me to be her maid of honor, she told me she didn't care either. "She takes over everything," she said. "And face it, this isn't Barbie's dream wedding. The main thing is the baby. God, I hope it's a girl." *What about love*, I wanted to ask, *till death do us part*, as sentimental as that might be? It wasn't as if Will felt those things for Paula either. She guessed what I was thinking: "Maybe this isn't how it's supposed to happen," then mocked the jump-rope chant: " 'First comes love, then comes marriage, then comes the baby in a baby carriage.' I've got it exactly backward. But I keep telling myself there's more than one way to do anything. Right?"

Mr. Cooper had not proposed on Valentine's Day. So the day after, Aunt Aggy proposed to him! "I know the man," she'd said when she told me what she had done, "all he needs is a little push." He didn't answer for a week—to take her mind off it she painted six nearly identical pale pink masterworks, each with a thick black X through the middle—then he told her he wasn't 100 percent sure he loved her. According to her, she had calmly said, "That's the point of love, you ninny. There's no one hundred percent sure—it's not a math test! But you get married anyway. Like jumping off a cliff," and he had told her he wasn't about to jump off any cliffs either. "So I ripped away the Band-Aid," she said to me later, "and told him life was too short to be afraid of cliffs. Good riddance—he was holding me back, keeping me from fulfilling my potential as an *artiste.*" But she still burst into tears any time she heard his name, and no one was allowed to use the phone the entire week after his refusal in case he was trying to call to beg forgiveness.

He returned the paintings she had given him, stacking them in the garage one afternoon when she wasn't home so that she almost ran over them with the car when she pulled in. Now she was painting practically nonstop, gigantic canvases of black and purple squares. "The colors of a bruised heart"—and the way she said it sounded sad, not crazy.

It turned out that Linda was living with her mother and the other kids in an apartment in Cedar Rapids. Mrs. Johnson was a secretary at the same insurance agency where Dr. Ellis now worked selling life insurance. That wasn't a very exciting end to the story, but I respected Mrs. Johnson. Running away was the easy thing to do, leaving behind a gnarly mess of unanswered questions and confusion, like none of it existed. Maybe there was something brave about being a secretary in Cedar Rapids or marrying Paula Elam. Mama staying on the train was exciting—but Mama coming back to Shelby was brave, though she never saw it that way.

Then Mr. Johnson resigned as mayor and moved to Cedar Rapids to be closer to the kids, and Mr. Neff became mayor. Linda sent Becky and me a couple of letters on hot-pink stationery that said word for word the same thing she used to talk about: how cute the boys were at her new school. At the end: "Visit as soon as you can," and she underlined "soon" five times. Becky and I talked about driving up there, but we never went.

Kathy Clark became my new biology lab partner because her partner, Cathy Hershberger, dropped the class after flunking the second test. Kathy Clark never said, "Gross," no matter what was under the microscope, and she took her own notes instead of copying from mine. It was as if Linda had never lived here: She was gone the way a rock sinks down into the bottom of a pond.

Mama had been dead for almost a year. A year used to feel close to forever—birthday to birthday was an endless stretch of time, Christmas to Christmas even more so. Now, what did a year mean? It was a long time but really barely any time at all. It was nothing and everything, all the pages of a calendar, but less than a speck, actually.

. . .

MAMA'S BIRTHDAY was in March, but she had always refused to celebrate it. Of course that baffled me and Will because we loved how Mama fussed over us with special birthday cakes and one present for each year of our age. But she would say something like, "Another year gone. What's so happy about that?" No cake, no presents, no goofy hats, not even singing "Happy Birthday." If we made her cards, she read them, but then we'd find them in the trash later. "You must want presents," I'd say, and she'd tell me that what she wanted couldn't be bought. Back then, I thought she meant our love—what a normal mother would mean. It was hard to imagine not liking your own birthday, but half the time Mama wouldn't even mention her birthday until after it had passed.

Given all that, I wasn't sure what to think when Will told me Paula's baby—which is how I still thought of it—was due on Mama's birthday. We were sitting in my room, one of the few times he was home, one of the few times he wasn't locked in his room, record player pounding out the Doobie Brothers so loud the words blurred to nothing. Next Thursday was the day. I had checked the calendar.

He asked, "Don't you think Mama would like that?"

"She'd be thirty-seven," I said. Not very old. Aunt Aggy had turned fifty-three in February. Even that—more than half a century—wasn't actually very old either.

Will turned away, and started fiddling with a tassel on one of my throw pillows. Mama had made that pillow for me; it had just appeared in my room one day. All of a sudden there were a bunch of new pillows everywhere in the house. Then there weren't any more; Mama must have gotten tired of making pillows. Everything with her was abrupt like that. Candles, tulip bulbs, fancy French sauces: A million things came and went. Only now did I notice that about her.

Will said, "Paula wants to name the baby Summer."

"Summer?" I said. Of course the baby would get a name. But I had assumed they would name it after Mama—Annette or Annie, Andy if it was a boy. Even Linda, with her four baby names all picked out, would name a baby that was supposed to be born on her dead mother's birthday after her dead mother.

"It's crazy." Round and round that tassel went as Will's finger twirled faster. "I tell her, what if it's a boy? You can't name a boy Summer. She says it's a girl."

Watching that tassel spin was making me crazy, so I grabbed the pillow, hugged it to my chest, pressed my face down into the worn corduroy. Did a name matter? I wouldn't have been a different person if Mama had named me Jill or Rhonda or Michelle or Moonbeam. Still. My voice came out muffled: "You should name the baby after Mama." Babies were named after living and dead people all the time. After grandmothers and fathers and buddies-who-died-in-the-war. It was what you were supposed to do to make sure you didn't forget, to keep that dead person with you.

Will said, "That's worse than Summer," and he stopped. I looked up. For a moment he sucked the inside of both cheeks, and his face looked oddly caved in.

I wanted to force him to say the thing he didn't want to. "What's worse than Summer?" I asked. "What?"

"Forget it," he mumbled.

"What?" I threw the pillow at him. It bounced off his chest and dropped to the floor. We both stared at it. I thought of Mama cutting the fabric, pinning the pieces together, carefully guiding the edges through the sewing machine, stuffing batting inside, stitching it shut with a needle and thread. Admiring that pillow for one second before tossing it on my bed, then immediately starting another, then another. "Naming a baby after someone who killed herself? Is that worse?"

He kicked the pillow hard across the room, right into the leg of the dressing table.

I spoke slowly: "She's our mother. Not just someone who killed herself. Our mother."

"I know who she is," Will said, a challenge, a warning to say no more, telling me to pick up that pillow and arrange it neatly on the bed, to talk about the weather.

Actually, he didn't know the first thing about who Mama really was:

the train, Mr. Stryker, the dead baby. Was this the moment to tell him everything?

He went on, his voice calm on the surface but shaky underneath: "It's simple. She was our mother, we loved her, now she's passed away. End of story." He became very absorbed in tugging at the cuffs of his flannel shirt, yanking them, pulling them down as if they were long enough to reach over his fingers. He was like the little boy he once was, fussing about a scratchy sweater, fidgeting at supper.

We both had been through the same year, the same exact amount of time. I asked, "Do you really think that's all there is to it?"

"Yes!" He let go of his sleeves, and his hands fell down to his sides.

Baseball hero. Brother. Boy girls had crushes on. Now father and husband-to-be. He shouldn't need me telling him nothing was simple.

But knowing and saying were miles apart. We had never talked about it, not really, not in the deep-down way that mattered, not once in this whole long year. So now I said it: "She was our mother. She CHOSE to leave us. Is there anything simple—or even understandable—about that? Is 'why' a question that will ever get answered?" I felt a dizzy rush in my head, like when you stand up suddenly, as I heard my own voice saying those words that were so difficult to admit. But I had spoken them out loud to Will. There they were.

Will got up and walked out the door. A minute later, "China Grove" thumped on, shaking my windowpanes. I closed my door, but that noise was still there, drowning out everything.

THAT NIGHT Paula called to tell me her mother had bought the maid-of-honor dress and wanted me to come try it on some day after school. "Is it cute?" I asked.

Static crackled on the phone. "Doubt it," Paula said. "She loves baby-blanket pink, which should tell you everything."

I twisted the phone cord around one finger, let it twirl loose. No one was around to hear. So I asked, "How come that day in the cornfield you didn't say it was Will?"

"Who would believe that?"

She was right.

"It's weird how things work out," Paula said. "How he sort of ended up saving me and the baby, when none of those other assholes would have ever gotten married."

We had a poor connection; in the pause, I heard a snip of a distant voice, a woman saying, *I've always added a bit of mustard.*

Then Paula said, "I mean, I know he doesn't exactly love me the way it is in the movies, but there's this baby now, our baby. She's real. Every time I put my hand on my stomach, there she is. Isn't that amazing?"

I guess it was. Lots of things were amazing if you took the time to think about them. I was about to ask her another question, but she interrupted: "This baby," then stopped. Again the tiny, staticky voice cut in: *About twenty minutes, till they're good and tender.* I waited for Paula to finish her sentence, which finally she did: "All I know is everything will be different now. And I'm not leaving her alone, not even for one second."

I remembered her sister dying in her crib, Mama's baby. "Lots can happen in one second," I said.

She sort of laughed. "It's stupid, I guess. Like I can watch over her forever?" She laughed again. "Hey, did you hear that lady talking about cooking? Think she hears us too?"

"Oh sure," I said and wondered what Paula would say if I told her about Mama's voice. Maybe she would know what I meant and say something like, *That's the thing about dead people—if they're gone, how come they never really go away?*

But I didn't tell her about Mama's voice. Instead, we gossiped a bit about Linda, then Paula had to hang up the phone because she was calling from Iowa City, which counted as long distance, and every minute cost a fortune. We hung up right as the mustard woman was saying that some people put celery seed in potato salad though she had never done that herself. I liked hearing those voices floating around, their conversation going on even after Paula's and mine stopped, as if the whole thing with Mama's voice wasn't totally impossible.

. . .

WILL STILL wasn't talking to me because of what I had said. But he hadn't officially kicked me out of the wedding, so I went over to the Elams' house after school to try on the dress and mark the hem. Becky, who had been to three weddings, had already warned me: "Brides want to be prettiest, so they pick ugly bridesmaid dresses." I argued that Mrs. Elam, not Paula, had selected the dress, but Becky said, "Think she wants you looking better than her own daughter?"

The Elams lived on Park Street, in a big house on the corner where both Mr. Elam and his father had been born. They'd owned it forever, like the bank. Before I could ring the bell, Mrs. Elam flung open the door as if she'd been watching me through a crack in the curtains. She looked tired; tiny lines radiated out from the corners of her eyes and her lipstick was creased, as if it had been on her lips too long. She said, "Hello, dear," and as I stepped inside, she added, "Call me Mary Pat," as if she had practiced the words.

I didn't think I was old enough to call adults by their first names, but I said, "Okay."

She held out her hand for my coat, wet with rain, but when I gave it to her, she didn't seem to know what to do with it; she bunched it up in her arms. There was a lemony smell to the house, as if she had recently polished the furniture. I shifted my weight from foot to foot and wished she would stop staring at me. So I glanced around, trying not to appear nosy.

A lavender, zippered garment bag with "Fashionable Miss Shop" in curvy letters was draped over a chair in the living room. I'd never owned anything from the Fashionable Miss Shop. Mama had made most of my clothes: "Better quality for less money," she'd said. "More style. You don't end up twins with everyone else in town." She hated when I'd beg her to buy me a red plaid kilt because girls at school were wearing red plaid kilts with green sweaters, white kneesocks, and loafers. "Don't you want to dress like an individual instead of the herd?" she'd ask, and I'd nod yes, though I meant no. That was one good thing about Aunt Aggy— she didn't care what clothes I bought as long as they'd been marked down at least twice. So despite Becky's warning, a full-price, "store" dress was exciting, no matter what the color.

I thought Mrs. Elam would offer me a Coke or something, but she didn't. A radio played in another room; I couldn't make out words, but I heard the jingle of Dotty King's station. I wondered all of a sudden if Mrs. Elam hated Will, me, my family, if she had invited me over here to yell at me. But she looked sad more than anything, the deep sadness that shows up in your eyes even when you're smiling. Seeing that made me more nervous than the possibility of her yelling at me. It wouldn't be hard to step into the living room and grab the dress, take it home and hem it myself. Finally I said, "Thanks for the dress."

She said, "I guess we're related now."

I barely knew her; the last time I had seen her was Christmas Eve, when Paula had smeared lipstick all over that beautiful white coat. "Thank you for buying the dress." I remembered too late I had already said that.

"You kids have had a tough year," she said. "Your mother. Now this." She looked down at my coat, and I hoped she wouldn't spot the missing button. I kept meaning to search Joe's car for it. She gave her head a quick shake, plopped my coat on top of another on the rack, said, "Guess we don't have all day." She grabbed the garment bag off the chair in the living room, ran down the zipper and slid back the plastic, pulling out a pale pink dress the color of frosting roses. "Like it?" She pressed it flat against my body.

I nodded to be polite. The dress was several silky layers, with puffy sleeves, a not-too-low scoop neck, and satin ribbons that tied in back. It was something a six-year-old would beg to wear, a princess dress. For sure Paula had nothing to do with picking it.

Mrs. Elam said, "Paula will love it; I just know she will." She handed the dress to me, then reached for one of the dangling satin ribbons, rubbed the end between her finger and thumb. "You'll look absolutely lovely," she murmured, letting the ribbon flutter loose. "Try it on in Paula's room. Up the stairs, first door on the right. I'll get my yardstick."

Paula's bedroom was decorated in pink: matching pink rose bed-spreads on twin beds, window shades bordered with fuzzy pink ribbon and fringe, a floor lamp with a hand-painted rose on the shade, a tumble of pink pillows, pale pink walls. The desk and dresser were white with pink drawer pulls. It was hard to imagine Paula in all this pinkness. Did Mrs. Elam know her daughter one tiny bit?

The room had an empty feeling, like no one had slept there for a long time.

I kicked off my shoes, pulled off my sweater and dropped it on the flowered bedspread, then scrunched my jeans downward, stepped out of them. The rumpled jeans on the floor looked more like the real Paula than anything else in the room. There was even a pink teddy bear amid all the pillows. I imagined Mrs. Elam finding that teddy bear on a shelf in a store, buying it to surprise Paula; "the perfect touch," she might have said. Did Paula roll her eyes at it, annoyed at merely the thought of a pink teddy bear? Then did she plunk the bear on her bed, secretly liking that her mother had picked it out special for her and her pink room? Because why else would it still be here?

I pulled the dress over my head, found the sleeves. I couldn't reach all the way backward to get the zipper to the top, and doing the bow in the back was awkward; I retied it twice, but both times it ended up crooked.

Afraid to sit down and wrinkle the dress—which felt soft and silky against my skin—and expensive—I walked over to look at the things on Paula's dresser, waiting for Mrs. Elam and her yardstick. There was a piggy bank from Farmers & Merchants Bank; a dried-up palm from some long-ago Palm Sunday mass; a jewelry box, the kind with a tiny ballerina spinning inside and a pink velvet lining (not that I opened it, but I used to have the same one); and a framed black-and-white photo-graph of a baby in a white cloud of net and lace. Debbie. Her face was scrunchy, as if she had been crying right before they snapped the picture. I had picked up the photo to look more closely when Mrs. Elam came in. She carried a yardstick in one hand and a "tomato" pincushion in the other, like the one Mama used to have, with a little sawdust-filled straw-berry for needles that always ripped off and got lost. Mrs. Elam's straw-berry was still attached.

"Don't you look lovely?" She set down the yardstick and pincushion so she could run the zipper the rest of the way up, and retie the ribbons into a fluffier bow. Then she saw that I held the photo. "That's Paula," she said quickly.

"I thought it was Debbie." I set the picture back in the same place, as close to its original position as I could. My wrist bumped the jewelry box and, abruptly, a couple of tinny notes came out.

A moment later, she said, "Paula told you about Debbie?"

I turned to face Mrs. Elam. Her eyes had filled with tears, and she was staring at the photo. "I'm sorry that she, um, died," I said.

"We don't talk about Debbie." She blinked rapidly and swiped the back of her hand across each cheek; she had to do that a few more times before she got all the tears whisked away. I glanced around but saw no Kleenex to offer her.

I didn't know what to say, so I repeated, "I'm sorry."

Mrs. Elam dragged Paula's desk chair into the middle of the room. I climbed onto it, stood up straight. In our uncomfortable silence, the empty bedroom seemed filled with all the years of unspoken words about Debbie. If Debbie were alive, she'd simply be another kid skinning her knee, crying for a cookie, asking for a bedtime story. Mrs. Elam set the yardstick on the chair, and I grabbed the top, held it steady. The tiny threads dangling off the dress tickled my bare legs. She started folding under the hem, but it didn't seem like she was paying attention to what she was doing, just sort of fingering the pink fabric, folding it and letting go. She didn't pin it. Her face was too still: She looked like she was thinking about all those days of not talking about Debbie, as if she could remember each one exactly. Mrs. Elam murmured, "Don't move," and slipped a couple of pins between pursed lips.

Didn't so much silence make you feel alone?

"Now you understand," Mama said, but it wasn't a victory, more like revealing the final, saddest secret of all.

My mother had lived her life in silence—something I had never known. Was she telling me not to do the same thing? My heart was loud, pumping against my chest.

Mrs. Elam lifted her head; maybe she was listening to my heartbeat too. She took the pins out of her mouth, jammed them into the pincushion. "Is that the phone?" Sure enough, there was a distant ring from downstairs, just the shadow of a sound, and she set the pincushion on the bed and hurried from the room.

I stood on the chair, still holding the yardstick, and looked around. The room was as spotless as a room in a magazine picture; a speck of dust that drifted in here could barely settle on a piece of furniture before Mrs. Elam would whisk it away with a feather duster.

Mr. Rhinehart had told me I would be fine after one year. Like something magic was supposed to happen right after that 365th day ended and you were on to the 366th. But it didn't work that way, not for Mrs. Elam, not for Mama, not for me or for anyone.

Raindrops pattered against the window, the fifth day in a row of cold, hard rain. It felt as if the sun was never going to shine again. People were joking about arks.

I heard Mrs. Elam's footsteps downstairs but she didn't come back to Paula's room. The raindrops turned harder, streaking the glass with quivery lines of silver.

I stared at the yardstick in my hand. Three feet. Thirty-six inches. Divide each of those inches into halves and quarters and eighths and sixteenths. Real life could never be so precise, so exact. I lifted one knee and broke the yardstick with a swift crack, splintering it across the nineteen-inch line, then dropped the pieces on the floor. Mrs. Elam might understand about hating neat lines dividing everything in orderly increments.

Mrs. Elam's footsteps hurried up the stairs, but she passed Paula's room, kept going down the hall. I climbed off the chair and peered out the doorway. She was heading back to me, almost running, hitching her purse strap up on one shoulder. "The baby's on its way!"

"But it's not supposed to come until Thursday." Mama's birthday. Today was Tuesday.

"Babies don't have calendars." She laughed, squeezed my shoulders in a distracted hug. "Got to run. The girls, my mother's—where is . . . ?" she said, talking to herself. "We'll finish up later." Then she clattered down the stairs. "Will's already there; tell Aggy!" she called before the front door opened and slammed shut.

Even with the rain pounding, the house was suddenly quiet, and I became too aware that this wasn't my house. I stepped back into Paula's room, nudged the broken yardstick under one of the beds, then pushed the chair back to the desk.

The baby was real.

I stared out the window at the rain like I had never seen such a thing before, water dropping endlessly out of the sky. I was someone's aunt, related to Paula, even connected in a strange way to Mrs. Elam and this pink room, the pink teddy bear. I smiled to think of it, Mrs. Elam choosing this dress, telling me I looked lovely. She didn't know how awful this dress was, how wrong—so little-girl pink, the puffed-up sleeves like basketballs—but I could forgive her and like her anyway.

If I wore the dress home in the rain, it would be wrecked. So I reached my arm around my back, trying to grab hold of the dress zipper, which started in exactly that place you can't reach yourself. I grabbed the fabric from over my shoulder and scrunched it upward, desperately feeling for the zipper thingy.

Mama cleared her throat. The sound was sudden, like stepping on a stick in the dark, that moment where your breath quickens, thinking someone else is there.

I was still struggling with the zipper, worming my fingers along my back. She cleared her throat again, softer and more tentatively, and instead of waiting for her to speak, I said, "Tell me." *Tell me how lonely you were, how afraid, how sad; tell me why we all ended up how we did.* I repeated, "Tell me, Mama. Please."

Mama said, "Your father was the one who picked your name."

Finally I reached the zipper, just barely, and tugged downward. Cold zinged my back as my skin was exposed to the air. That was the last thing I thought she would say.

Mama said, "He wanted a little girl named Alice, after his grandmother who raised him. He talked about wanting you before you were born, before we even knew about you."

My father had seen Will, but I was born in Iowa. I lifted off the dress—chills kept knocking along my spine; I reached to pull on my sweater, jeans, shoes. He chose my name; he had wanted me; I was named after his grandmother, me. It wasn't the least bit important, but to be polite I asked, "What about Will?"

"My idea," Mama said, knowing it was important.

I picked up the dress, rubbed the soft fabric between my finger and thumb. Will had his eyes maybe, or his way of throwing a baseball. I had his smile or his fear of heights. There were ways he was here though he wasn't here. But something was missing, something wasn't quite real, and I took a deep breath, held it for a moment, then let it out as I demanded, "Who was he?"

After a moment that felt longer than it probably was, Mama gave me the answer: "Robert Smith. Bob."

My father's name was Bob; Bob Smith wanted a little girl named Alice. Suddenly the dress felt heavy in my hands. "There must be a million Bob Smiths," I said. Bob Smith, Bob Smith—words that were my father but weren't. Who was he? I'd never find him, even now that I knew his name. Even an expert lawyer like Mr. James couldn't possibly track down the one single Bob Smith who mattered. I had wanted to know who my father was, and now I knew: Bob Smith. I should feel satisfied, but I didn't. "Why wouldn't you ever tell us about him?" I asked.

Her voice shook: "Gone one morning. No note, no call. I never knew . . ."

I finished for her: "Why."

"Why," she whispered.

I wanted to be sitting down, but I didn't want to move.

"That's exactly who he was," she said. "Exactly."

"To you," I said. "To you, he's another man who left. But to me, he's my father." I barely noticed myself slipping the dress onto the padded hanger, squishing the billowing layers into the garment bag, dropping the whole thing onto the pink bed, zipping the bag shut. If everything could stop for just one second, maybe I could figure it out: Mama, my father, the baby, Debbie, Will, Joe, Linda, the whole world. Just one second. I closed my eyes, tight, hard, until I saw a sudden splash of yellow stars.

How did my mother die with no one knowing all those things about her?

The rain beat at the windows, sounding louder with my eyes closed, like it was desperate to get in. I finally opened my eyes, but it was just rain, the same as the four days before.

If Mama just would've . . . something. *Been someone else* was the answer she had come up with. But who could live in that kind of fairy tale—trapped in time, the unchanged ending, no one growing old, the princesses good, the princes brave, the stepmothers always wicked? Look at everything that had happened in only one year to me and Will and Aunt Aggy.

I went to the dresser and stared at the photo of Debbie. Would she have been a cheerleader or a girl who smoked in the second-floor bathroom? Someone who was good at math or wasn't? A wife? A vet? A movie star? A mother? The only way to answer those kinds of questions was to keep living. My fists clenched, my eyes crunched shut, my shoulders tensed—every part of my body felt tight and angry. "You're my mother," I said. "Why wasn't that enough for you?"

"I love you and your brother," she said.

"You left us."

"People always leave," she said. "People die."

"You chose to die!" I shouted.

She continued as if I hadn't spoken. "But do they really go? Am I really gone?"

A branch knocked against the window, and I jumped, startled, opened my eyes. The slippery plastic bag slid off the bed and onto the floor. I picked up the dress, draped it over my arm. I couldn't be mad anymore; she was right. Anyone could look around the room and see Mama wasn't here. But she wasn't gone either, just because she was dead. That was both sad yet immensely comforting, like Paula's pink teddy bear or sitting at Mama's dressing table or Will having a baby that was related to me.

"People are supposed to run out of time," Mama said. "But for me, time was endless infinity that stretched out into black, blank emptiness with no end, unbearable pain, unbearable nothingness, until one more minute was too much. You can't imagine, Alice. You can't know. It's no one's fault. There is no why."

I shifted the dress to my other arm; the plastic crinkled. We had never talked about these things, none of us, not once. But they were real, whether we spoke of them or not. Mama wasn't fine—no matter how hard I wanted her to be like every other mother. Our silence was a heavy, gray rock plopped down where we all could see it, too gigantic to push out of the way. I thought of that pinprick of light, her cigarette glowing in the dark of her bedroom.

Mama said, "Finally, all I saw was blackness. All I heard was nothing."

"You should've told me." My whisper almost disappeared in the emptiness of the strange house.

"Why?"

Why? Why? I tossed the dress onto the bed. "So I'd know," I said, helpless.

"But I'm your mother," she said. "You have to understand that there are things you'll never know."

"I can't believe that," I cried, though what she said was true and even forgivable.

The rain coming down was relentless. Finally, I walked down the stairs, took my coat off the hook, slipped it on. I waited for a moment, but the only things I heard were rain, the radio that Mrs. Elam had forgotten to turn off, in the other room. No words, just fuzzy sound. I left the house, pulling the door quietly behind me, and ran through the pouring rain to the car.

THE MINUTE I told Aunt Aggy about the baby, she shoved aside the canvas she was working on and immediately set a fresh white one on the easel. "An artistic rendering of birth," she said, and squeezed a thick squiggle of lime green paint across the canvas. Then she smeared the paint with a butter knife. "Everything will be all right," she declared. "I have that feeling. Now and then there's a day or a minute or a half second, and this is that exact half second, and right now I know everything will be all right." She gazed at the array of paint tubes. "Sometimes you know things without knowing why. Like the way I know to use green instead of orange." Then she squirted out another green line, crushing the paint tube in her hand, the way you're not supposed to squeeze toothpaste.

I had never thought of her crazy painting as anything more than being dramatic. Serious artists didn't check out books from the library, didn't slop paint on a canvas with a knife from the kitchen drawer and call it a masterwork. Not to mention that beret. She had to know she wasn't a real artist. I said, "But all it is is a green swirl."

"Maybe that's what you see on the canvas," she said. "But I see my life: the words I can't say, the feelings I don't understand, the thoughts I didn't know I had. I see myself." Her face reddened; she looked away, embarrassed. "I've never told anyone that before. It's silly." She pulled off her beret and tossed it onto the chair, then flopped down right on top of it. "I suppose I haven't had the most exciting or glamorous life. Maybe a lot of people wouldn't have considered it much of a life at all, growing up in this dinky town, never enough gumption to get up and leave, waiting around for a crazy old coot to figure out if he was in love with me. But I still see every minute as a precious gift."

The chair squeaked as she shifted. She wasn't looking at me; her face in profile seemed perfectly still, as if it was carved from smooth marble. What did being an artist mean, anyway? My voice wobbled as I said, "You should tell that to Mr. Cooper."

She shook her head, pointed at a stack of canvases in the corner. "It's right there. All anyone has to do is look." She shook her head again, then stood up, flashed a bright smile. "My muse is calling!" she chirped, and she jammed the beret crookedly on top of her head.

I reached over and straightened it. Then for quite a while I stood in the doorway, watching her fill that empty canvas with vast, random swirls of lime green paint.

WILL HAD begged Aunt Aggy not to show up at the hospital, afraid she'd fall apart in some messy way in front of the Elams. She had agreed, since she hated hospitals anyway. So we hung around the house and waited for the phone to ring with news about the baby. I read a chapter for biology, watched the Channel 2 news, wrote out a Spanish exercise, and threw away all the moldy stuff in the back of the refrigerator. I knew time was moving because I did all those things. But it felt like only a few minutes ago that I'd been standing on the chair in Paula's pink room listening to Mrs. Elam's footsteps on the stairs.

Every so often Aunt Aggy popped her head out of her studio to shriek, "Is that the phone?"

I tried imagining Will at the hospital, waiting with the Elams. In the movies, fathers paced hospital corridors, gulping coffee from cardboard cups. Movie fathers also smoked a lot when they were waiting for babies to be born. I couldn't picture Will with a cigarette in one hand, smoke swirling around his head. Was he pacing? Chewing his nails? Sweating? I wanted to be there, drinking vending-machine coffee, pacing and sweating.

So why not go? That was exactly what Mama's voice would say to me.

But it wasn't my place to show up uninvited, unwanted. And Will was still mad at me; we were barely talking. Movies never showed sisters of expectant fathers drinking that coffee. I'd get in the way. I wasn't supposed to be there. I was just the aunt.

I waited for Mama to tell me to go.

Of course, going meant I would have to see Will with this strange new family—Mrs. Elam flipping pages of a magazine, Mr. Elam shoving up his cuff to stare at his watch, Will bringing them cups of coffee, the baby, my brother being a father. It would all be real, finally and forever.

Aunt Aggy yelled, "Is that the phone?," and it felt like only a second passed before she yelled again: "Alice? Are you getting the phone?"

I picked up the receiver, listened to the dial tone buzz. Go, go, go, that voice echoed in my head. It was my own voice, not Mama's, urging me to go.

My own voice.

I looked around—same old kitchen in the same old house. Nothing looked different.

Then again, was it supposed to? Maybe once you stopped worrying that things like mothers and brothers and paintings and your whole life were supposed to be one certain way, that was when you could finally see how they really were.

"I'm going," I said, repeating the words though no one was in the kitchen to hear me. Didn't matter—the words were for me, the voice was mine. "I'm going!"

I called Joe, asked him to help me, to drive me to Mercy Hospital in Iowa City. A few minutes later, he pulled up and I ran out the door, calling to Aunt Aggy that I'd be back soon, hurrying beyond her shouted questions.

WE WERE most of the way there before Joe asked if I was hoping for a boy or a girl.

You were supposed to say it didn't matter, but I said, "Girl."

He was driving fast, like usual, and the tires hissed along the wet pavement. "Girls always want girls," he said. "Boys want boys."

My father wanted a girl named Alice. Wherever he was, I hoped somehow he knew he had that girl; that even if there were other daughters, I was the only Alice. I watched the wipers flick back and forth, pushing the drizzle across the windshield. I was tired of quiet, so I asked Joe how he got his name.

"Unimaginative Catholic parents," he said. "My older brothers got the good apostle names. It's not like they could name me Judas."

There were no other cars out, almost as if we were the only people alive, the only two people in Iowa who had somewhere to go. I said, "Don't you think they should name the baby after my mother?"

"Aren't they going to?"

I shook my head. "She should be remembered."

He started to say something, then pointed at the odometer. "It's flipping to eighty-thousand," he said, and we watched the nines turn over into zeroes, the seven into an eight. He asked, "What's your mom's name?"

"Annette."

"And what's her mother's name?"

"Rose."

"What was her mother's name?" he asked.

"Uh. Mary. Mary Louise." I had no idea. He was about to ask about her mother's name, but I said, "Enough. I get it." We were on the outskirts of Iowa City, passing the Purple Cow restaurant, which, of course, was closed. People went there for banana splits and sundaes; in the summer there'd be a long line snaking out the door. Now, just darkness.

"Look," he said. "It's just a name. A name is nothing."

That was the problem. It would be easy if it was only about the name.

Donutland came into view with its flashing neon sign looking sharp and bright against the dark. "Open 24 Hours," the sign flashed red, then "Good Coffee Too!" in yellow. All the inside lights were lit, making the small building look cozy, like someone's kitchen; I could almost breathe in the entwined smells of coffee, grease, and sugar as we passed. The world was filled with places like this, places that you drove by without enough time to stop. Maybe just knowing they were there was good enough.

"Doughnuts," I murmured, mostly to myself, but Joe heard and did a screechy U-turn into the parking lot. There was one other car, and Joe pulled in next to it. "Not now," I said, though the idea of showing up at the hospital was starting to make me nervous.

"What's wrong with now?" he said. "Sign says open twenty-four hours."

"The baby."

"It's not being born this exact second," he said, and we walked into Donutland, blinking at the bright light, letting the warm haze of twenty years' worth of grease and fried doughnuts envelop us. It was a small place, but everything felt exact: these countertops, white with flecks of faded silvery sparkles; these red stools, the kind with no back that spun around; the coffee machines here; the doughnut case this high, and this many shelves. It was the kind of place that looked best at night, especially if you were the only people in there, which, except for the counterman, we were.

"We could take doughnuts to the hospital," Joe said. He reached into his pocket and pulled out some crumpled bills. "Three bucks."

We stepped up to the counter, and the man in the white paper hat said, "Good morning." Maybe it was morning on a clock, but it still felt like night to me. His voice was gravelly, as if he'd been smoking since he was ten years old, but he was very patient as we took our time picking out doughnuts one by one, arguing the merits of maple walnut versus confetti versus powdered sugar. We were stuck on strawberry jelly versus raspberry when I apologized to the doughnut man for being slow.

"Take all the time you need," he said, and the longer he spoke, the more gravelly his voice got: "That door's open twenty-four hours, seven days a week."

"How many people buy doughnuts in the middle of the night?" I asked.

He nodded, as if he'd been asked that question before. "More than you'd think."

Joe and I finally settled on twelve and gave our change as a tip.

In the car, we split a chocolate-glazed doughnut, and I licked the stickiness off his fingers, and he licked the stickiness off mine because we had forgotten to grab napkins. "Who buys doughnuts in the middle of the night?" I asked.

"People like us," he said, starting the car.

I didn't know who that was exactly, but I was sure I would think of Joe the whole rest of my life whenever I ate a doughnut late at night. Like knowing my father picked my name. He wasn't just Bob Smith, he was Bob-Smith-who-wanted-a-girl-named-Alice: me. I could imagine him saying, "Alice," drawing out the "Al" and finishing up quickly. Maybe he didn't put me to bed at night or take me for ice cream at Dane's Dairy or teach me how to ride a bike, and maybe he'd never get a tie from me on Father's Day. But he was my father; I was his daughter.

The first red light we hit was the one at the bridge across the Iowa River. This wasn't the same way that Mama drove when we used to go together to Iowa City. The light turned green and we crossed the bridge, headed up the hill and through the dark, quiet downtown. The Iowa State Bank clock flashed 2:47. No one else was around to see it, just the two of us speeding past. I thought of that question about the tree falling in the forest—does it make noise if no one was there to hear it? Was it really 2:47 if no one looked at a watch?

We followed the "H" signs to Mercy Hospital on Market Street, and Joe parked the car. Neither of us got out. This was a big deal, going into a hospital together, waiting for a baby to be born. Almost as if we were adults.

"How long to have a baby, anyways?" I asked, fiddling with the seat-belt buckle, opening it, closing it.

"As long as it takes," he said.

"It's just that Annette would always be her name," I said. "Nothing is ever 'always.'" I thought about Joe graduating in a few months, driving off to Canada or somewhere else. Never seeing him again. Knowing that could be overwhelming. Or. I pushed aside the seat-belt buckle and grabbed his hand, squeezed hard enough to notice the bones in his fingers.

A moment later I was kissing him, and I pulled his body close up against mine, feeling the heat off him, his breath a tickle in my ear, warm and moist against my face, my lips, my neck. There was no "always," and maybe there never had been and never would be—"The only thing that's certain is death and taxes," Aunt Aggy liked to say. Mama was gone, dead, and no matter what I knew or found out, I'd never know why, never truly understand why. And yet the world was busy, kept moving, with kisses and babies and weddings and canvases covered with green paint and doughnut shops that stayed open twenty-four hours just so you could get a dozen doughnuts in the middle of the night if that was what you wanted. All the things people did every single day, all across the world, without thinking, as if their actions were nothing extraordinary, all those things still happened.

Because what could be better than this single, simple night with doughnuts in the backseat, Joe kissing me, Will's baby coming, spring almost here, a year gone, but a million more ahead?

I pushed Joe away, jumped out of the car, spun and hopped, twirled until I was dizzy. "Hurry!" I said, laughing. "The baby!" I ran around the car and pulled open his door, grabbed his arm and tugged. "Let's go see the baby!" I couldn't stop laughing—it was like that first breath of air you suck in when you come up from the deep end of the pool.

He laughed, told me I was crazy, then let me drag him out of the car. Hand in hand we ran across the street to the well-lit entrance of Mercy Hospital. Inside, everything was white and very quiet; I tried to control my face and be serious, but laughter kept bubbling up, about to erupt any second. A guard dozed in a chair in a lounge, a TV set flickering blue on the wall above him. There were all sorts of signs and directories, a rack of brochures, tables stacked with forms: information everywhere. I breathed in the smell of strong antiseptic; damp streaks zigzagged the hallway floor as if someone had recently mopped.

"The doughnuts," Joe said.

"We'll get them later," I said, and we hurried until we found a desk where a nurse with cinnamon-colored hair sat flipping papers in an open file folder. Her name badge said "Frederica Krouth, RN," and next to it she had pinned a giant butterfly with big orange and yellow rhinestones. It was so ugly that it was beautiful, and for one second I wanted it for myself. "Where are the babies?" I asked, trying not to stare at the butterfly.

"Excuse me?"

"Her brother's having a baby," Joe said, stepping up to the counter.

"Maternity is on the third floor," she said, "take those elevators to—" but I was already running, Joe behind me, still holding my hand. Our footsteps tumbled through the corridor, and Joe had caught my mood, laughing and swinging my arm.

I pushed the elevator button six or seven times, until the doors slid open. Inside, I leaned into Joe's arms and kissed him again and again, pressing him up against the back elevator wall. He laughed, said, "Crazy girl," like it was a compliment.

"I'm so incredibly happy." Maybe this mood wouldn't last long— another second or half second—it certainly wouldn't last forever. But right now, NOW, I was happy, and I kissed Joe again as the elevator dinged at the third floor.

It wasn't hard to find the maternity waiting room, where, I couldn't believe it, Will was pushing through a silver double doorway, bright light spilling out from behind him, and Joe and I watched Mr. and Mrs. Elam leap up from the fake leather couches as Will announced, "A girl!" Everyone was hugging and crying and talking at once, and Joe and I lumped ourselves into their hugs, fitting right in. No one asked how or when we'd gotten there, as if we had been right there alongside them the whole time.

As we untangled ourselves, Mr. and Mrs. Elam shot a bunch of questions at Will—*How is Paula? How big is the baby? Name? How long? How many pounds? Name? What color hair? Name?* I squeezed Joe's hand, and Will looked past the Elams, saw me, gave a half smile and nod as if he had expected me. "Got my wish, Baby Sister. It's Mama's birthday."

I felt a rush of happy sadness—or sad happiness—like water spilling from a faucet. But I corrected him: "Her birthday's on Thursday. The twenty-third."

"Today," Will said. "Wednesday. The twenty-second. Now."

"Does the baby have a name yet?" Mrs. Elam asked again.

I couldn't breathe. I had been thinking the twenty-third. Thursday. I had checked the calendar on the refrigerator, and the twenty-third was definitely Thursday. Was her birthday the twenty-second?

Mr. Elam said, "Who does she look like?"

"When can we see her?" Mrs. Elam asked. "What's her name?"

All this time I'd been thinking Thursday when it was now.

"Today, Alice," Will said softly. "It's okay." He looked tired; his whole body sagged.

"Today," I said. "Happy birthday . . . little baby."

"Summer," Will said. "Paula still wants Summer."

"Happy birthday, Summer." The name sounded right, and Mr. and Mrs. Elam repeated, "Summer," several times, starting out questioning, with eyebrows up high, then turning firmer, softer, lingering over each letter, each sound, the way you say the name of someone you love.

Will edged closer to me, away from the Elams. "Mama's here," he whispered. "I feel her with us."

"Always," I said. "Always, always," and I hugged my brother.

WHEN JOE and I passed the Iowa State Bank clock coming back, it flashed 5:32. The clearing sky was gray with streaks of orangey pink. There was a stillness in the air, a day eager to begin.

I was exhausted, yawning big gulpy yawns every few minutes. Will was asleep in the backseat, using the empty doughnut box as a pillow. Joe was driving fast. He didn't seem tired at all.

Joe said, "That baby was tiny."

I nodded. "Those little fingers." We'd only been allowed to look at her through the glass, sleeping in a crib. Mr. and Mrs. Elam were chattering away, saying she looked like Paula, and didn't someone named Bonnie have that same bushy hair when she was born, and gently arguing about whether they should make phone calls now or wait until people were awake. Then they went off to see Paula (we weren't allowed), and in the silence, I stared at Summer. How amazing to think she had a whole life ahead of her. I could tell her a million things—about the world and people and the sad stuff that happens, how every life comes down to unanswered questions, that "why" is a word that never goes away—but even with all that to say, there was nothing I could really tell her because the only way to really know all that was to find out for yourself.

There were a few cars and a couple of trucks in the Donutland parking lot; the car ahead of us put on its blinker and turned in, parking in the same spot where we had parked. I said, "It's good to know where we can always get doughnuts," and I watched the flashing neon in the side mirror slowly disappear behind me. "I mean, in the middle of the night and everything. If we really needed a doughnut." It was silly: Why would someone need a doughnut?

But Joe seemed to understand what I was saying. "It's always there," he said.

Mama's favorite doughnuts were glazed. Her second favorite were the kind with chocolate icing on top. Once she ate seven doughnuts for breakfast, one more than Will. They were having a contest, and the loser had to clean the garage. Will complained that she had knocked off the sprinkles so that shouldn't count as eating the entire doughnut—I remembered all that, but I had forgotten the day of her birthday.

Joe said, "You can go to sleep if you're tired."

I leaned up against his shoulder, said, "My mother would've been thirty-seven today." It was just a day. But it was and it wasn't.

"Want to go by the cemetery?" he asked.

"Maybe later." The cemetery. That night. I sat up straight. We had never talked about what had happened there. I wasn't sure exactly what needed to be said—or what saying anything would accomplish—but I was tired of keeping quiet, afraid of watching silences grow into that huge, unmovable thing constantly in front of me. I glanced in the backseat to make sure Will was asleep, pushed my fingers through my hair, took a deep breath and let it gust out. Then I spoke, the words a tumbling rush, "Do you still think about that night last summer?" I turned away from him, looked out the window, watched telephone poles zip by, so fast my eyes could barely keep up.

He didn't speak right away. When he did, he was cautious, as if feeling out each word before saying it: "I know I was sort of a jerk. I mean, there I was, friends with your brother, plus your mom had died, so I shouldn't have—"

"I'm not mad," I said. "Or sorry. Or anything like that." I looked over at him; half the collar of his jeans jacket was folded in. I wanted to pull it out.

"Then what?" His voice was soft like darkness, like someone who was listening, someone who really wanted to hear what you would say next.

But some things were hard to say—which must be why people chose silence, not understanding that silence turned out to be harder in the end. I said, "Sometimes that night seems so long ago, almost like it happened to another person." I waited, but he didn't say anything. His jaw seemed to tighten, but maybe that was my imagination. I reached over and pulled his collar to make it right. Then I went on: "I want you to always remember. So that if I call you up in fifty years and say, 'Do you remember that night?,' you'll know what I mean, and I won't have to explain one single thing. It just seems like it might be really lonely if . . . if I were the only one who remembered something important like that, the only one to know it happened."

He set one hand on mine, said, "You know I'll never forget you."

He meant it, he probably actually did; but suddenly it seemed as though what I wanted was so utterly impossible, that time just had its way of relentlessly moving on and taking things with it, no matter how hard you wanted to hold on to them. So much had happened this year: Trying to see it all at once would be like trying to see every sparkle on the whole big ocean.

I closed my eyes, repeated, "My mother would've been thirty-seven today." With my eyes closed, the noises of the road seemed more distinct, more particular to this one minute: the rush of the wind, Will's foot knocking against some papers in the backseat, the quick clunk of a pothole in the pavement. "I always got her birthday confused," I said.

"It's okay," Joe said.

Tears pushed up, out under my eyelids. They felt hot, and I let them come, feeling them scrape my skin.

"Really," he said. "It's okay."

"That's why I'm crying," I said. "That this is what happens. That this is how it is."

"I know," he said. "And that's what's okay. You'll see."

AT HOME, Aunt Aggy halfheartedly fussed at me for racing out of the house in the middle of the night. Mostly she hugged Will, hugged me, and made us tell her everything about Summer. ("What a darling name!" she exclaimed.) Then she brought her new painting into the kitchen: "Presenting, *The Precious Gift,*" she announced with a flourish. There had to be at least five tubes' worth of green paint thickly swirled on the canvas, almost like the finger painting you did in kindergarten. Will and Joe mumbled a few words—"so green"—then escaped to the living room to avoid saying more.

"What do you think?" She turned the chair it was propped on so I'd have a better view.

What could I say? I squinted, tilted my neck sideways like people in movies did at art galleries. "Like Will said, it's really green. And, um, unique." I stared harder at the glistening green surface, until my eyes lost focus and the swirls practically reached out to me—a smeary, hands-on mess; or an intricate pattern of over-over-under-in; or a drowning wave of green; or glimmers of meaning perpetually beyond reach—and I blinked and said, "The way every life is mysterious and unique. But sort of hopeful. No straight lines, just a swirling mass of color." I stopped. Were those things really in that simple green square?

She picked up the canvas, held it at arm's length, stared hard at it for a few moments. "I'm retitling this *The Unattainable Mystery.*" Then she ran upstairs to get dressed, almost tripping over her robe.

Joe turned down my offer of breakfast, probably because he'd already eaten five doughnuts, and went home to get some sleep before school. Will stumbled off to bed, so I was alone in the kitchen. I dropped bread in the toaster and stared inside, watching the coils glow orange-red. The refrigerator was humming, and outside a squirrel chattered from high up in the apple tree. Aunt Aggy clomped back and forth upstairs. I imagined Will asleep, Paula asleep, Summer asleep, each in their separate rooms for now, the sounds of their separate breaths, not yet a family exactly but connected forever nevertheless.

My toast popped up, and I pulled out the slices, dropped them on a plate, scraped butter across each of them, rummaged around the refrigerator for strawberry jelly. All I could find was grape, Will's favorite, and grape sounded just fine.

I cut my toast in neat diagonals, the way Mama served toast, "the only way that makes sense," she always said, even though, really, what was the difference? But she would send it back when we were eating at the White Front Café downtown. Eventually they knew that about her and automatically cut her toast and her tuna sandwiches in diagonals.

I blinked—more tears—and looked up, trying to get them to spill down the side of my face instead of dropping onto the table, and there was the kitchen clock, still stuck at 10:35.

It was just one stupid little thing, but I stood up and opened the junk drawer by the stove where we shoved bits of string, twist ties, scissors, tape, picture nails, the fly swatter, and anything else that fit. There had to be a battery in there somewhere, and there was. I dragged over a chair, stood on it, and pulled the clock off the nail in the wall. It was an ugly clock, a big disk the color of watery orange juice with thick, white tabs like hyphens sticking out from the circle where numbers would be on a normal clock. The hands were thick and white, too, and the hour hand was almost as long as the minute hand, so sometimes it was confusing to tell what time it was. The clock looked like a gear, like something grinding away day after day, something you might not stop to notice.

Why had Mama bought such an ugly clock? On the other hand, the bare wall without it looked empty and all wrong, as if something important were missing.

I popped out the old battery, leaned down to set it on the counter, pushed in the new one. I twirled the clock's minute hand with one finger, until it reached all the way around to 7:15, which was the last time I'd heard announced on the radio, and just like that, it was fixed. Maybe we'd be a little slow, but at least the clock was running. I stared at the minute hand, watching it move in its infinitesimal way, letting my toast get cold.

I knew Mama would never leave me. And I knew I would never hear her voice again.

THE SPEED OF SOUND

WHEN I told Mrs. Lane that I had heard my mother's voice talking to me for almost a year after she died, she didn't say anything right away. We were in the greenhouse, and she had been explaining to me that she liked to train her cucumber plants to grow upward, tying them to a trellis, to make more room in the garden. Plus it was easier to see the cucumbers hanging in your face, "instead of in that mess of vines underfoot."

The cat was sprawled on his back on the floor, framed in a big square of sunlight. The light was so strong his black fur glowed mahogany.

I'd decided I had to tell someone about Mama's voice, though I didn't expect it would be Mrs. Lane. But I heard myself saying the words, plain and simple, as if I was stating a fact, the way you would say, *It's sunny this afternoon*. Instead it was: "I heard my mother's voice talking to me for a year after she died." I blinked, almost as if someone had suddenly and quickly flashed a light directly into my eyes. I liked the feeling of having spoken those words out loud finally, the relief. Was what I'd said that much stranger than telling somebody you trained cucumber vines to grow upward?

Mrs. Lane set down the peat pot with the cucumber seedling she had been holding. She brushed one tiny leaf with the underside of her thumb.

I said, "I wanted someone else to know besides me."

Outside, the janitor, Mr. Liebbe, was riding on a big lawn mower, cutting the grass. He wore a red bandanna bandit style across the lower half of his face. A pleasant, distant buzzing seeped into the greenhouse. I watched him drive all the way across the school lawn, then come back.

Mrs. Lane picked up a watering can, sloshed the water around. She said, "The speed of light is constant—186,282 miles per second. But sound travels faster in water than in air. It's not constant." Then she pinged the metal of the can with her finger and thumb, added, "Sound travels even faster through iron and steel."

I waited. I had learned in the past few weeks that she almost always had a point. She liked to say she talked only when things were worth saying.

The cat's hind leg twitched rapidly. Mrs. Lane had told me last week that she was certain animals had dreams and nightmares. Maybe that was why now, all of a sudden, I was telling her about Mama.

She continued: "For example, sound traveling a mile through air will take five seconds. But traveling the same distance, sound will only take one second underwater and one-third of a second in steel."

Mrs. Lane loved facts. She knew a million of them—she could have won any quiz show if she didn't think TV was a big waste of time. It was like she had memorized the *Encyclopedia Britannica* word for word.

The cat's leg stopped twitching.

"So who's to say that a sound—perhaps a voice—couldn't manage to find a way to travel at its own individual speed through memory and longing and grief and hope? Who's to say? We both know the world is a strange and full place." Mrs. Lane kept staring straight ahead, through the glass greenhouse wall.

I followed her gaze. There was so much to see.

ACKNOWLEDGMENTS

Several people read this manuscript in its early stages and offered comments: Kate Blackwell, Kathleen Currie, Steve Ello, Rachel Hall, C. M. Mayo, Ann McLaughlin, and Mary Kay Zuravleff. I am grateful for their insight and unwavering support throughout the writing process.

Three books were particularly useful to me in the researching and writing of this novel: *Motherless Daughters: The Legacy of Loss* by Hope Edelman; *Night Falls Fast: Understanding Suicide* by Kay Redfield James; and *Waking Up Alive: The Descent, The Suicide Attempt, and the Return to Life* by Richard A. Heckler, Ph.D.

Special thanks to Gail Hochman, Jennifer Pooley, and Nikola Scott for their enthusiasm, careful attention, and tireless efforts on my behalf.